A WOMAN MADE FOR PLEASURE

Chase reached up and lightly caressed her cheek as he tucked a stray lock of dark hair behind her ear. He noticed her soft, pink lips had parted slightly. They were standing so close now, it would be effortless to satisfy this insane attraction and kiss her. One kiss and his curiosity would be vanquished and this charm she was weaving over him would disappear.

"In regard to this absurd promise you three made, what"—he stroked her cheek again—"is your particular exception allowing *you* to marry?"

Millie stared at him, unable to move under his gaze. The strength and gentleness in his eyes unsettled her, and she automatically clutched his shirt for balance. The action reminded her of just how small and light she was compared to him.

Her heart pounded in her chest. His touch was arousing unfamiliar and very feminine desires. She was both surprised and bothered to discover how much she liked it . . .

Books by Michele Sinclair

THE HIGHLANDER'S BRIDE

TO WED A HIGHLANDER

DESIRING THE HIGHLANDER

THE CHRISTMAS KNIGHT

TEMPTING THE HIGHLANDER

A WOMAN MADE FOR PLEASURE

HIGHLAND HUNGER
(with Hannah Howell and Jackie Ivie)

Published by Kensington Publishing Corporation

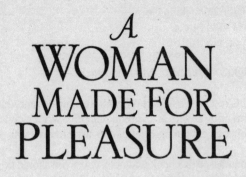

A WOMAN MADE FOR PLEASURE

MICHELE SINCLAIR

ZEBRA BOOKS
KENSINGTON PUBLISHING CORP.
http://www.kensingtonbooks.com

ZEBRA BOOKS are published by

Kensington Publishing Corp.
119 West 40th Street
New York, NY 10018

All Kensington titles, imprints, and distributed lines are available at special quantity discounts for bulk purchases for sales promotion, premiums, fund-raising, educational, or institutional use.

Special book excerpts or customized printings can also be created to fit specific needs. For details, write or phone the office of the Kensington Special Sales Manager: Attn. Special Sales Department. Kensington Publishing Corp., 119 West 40th Street, New York, NY 10018. Phone: 1-800-221-2647.

Zebra and the Z logo Reg. U.S. Pat. & TM Off.

ISBN-13: 978-1-4201-2649-5
ISBN-10: 1-4201-2649-0

First Printing: August 2012

10 9 8 7 6 5 4 3 2 1

Printed in the United States of America

To my wonderful mother—
the only one who would recognize all the
precious tidbits hidden within.

Introduction

I have endeavored to be as historically accurate as possible when writing this book. All main characters are fictional as are the two groups—the Rebuilders and the Expansionists. The story line involving these two groups is also fictional. All other historical trivia from battles, places, activities, and persons are based on the people, places, and times of the Regency period.

Prologue

Dorset, England, 1808

Millie narrowed her eyes slightly as they darted back and forth between the two most important people in her life. She gazed at the restless figure sitting across from her on the worn blanket before shifting to the hesitant one leaning against a nearby tree. Their reaction to a simple suggestion was baffling. Both should be leaping at the opportunity. Millie blinked with clear frustration. Her eyes were a strange shade of lavender, the large purple depths often mistaken for blue in dim light. But no one ever mistook them to be conciliatory. And Millie was certainly not going to surrender now.

Being what she considered an exceptionally mature twelve-year-old, Millie Aldon knew there were very few absolute truths in life. The first she discovered at age six, soon after her mother's death: A true friend was one of the rarest things in the world. And she had two. At eight, Millie had decided the male species had no idea how to have fun, and by the time she turned ten, she realized a boy's capacity for dullness only worsened with age. But the latest truth she had stumbled upon only last night, while spying on the various guests invited to the Wentworths' country estate.

Her original intention was to see if parties became more interesting as the night progressed, and from what she could tell, they did not. However, the night was not a total waste of time and planning. Overhearing one simple comment had made it more than worthwhile. Marriage, for a wealthy noblewoman, was not a requirement, but a *choice*.

"It would work!" Millie stressed again, throwing the loose strands of her long dark hair behind her shoulder.

"No one is keeping you from swearing off marriage, Millie," came a quiet reply.

Millie pursed her lips and huffed. "But we must *all* agree; otherwise, why do it? The pact is not just to protect us from a life of boring rules and pointless parties, but it's to keep us together! If we don't *all* make the pledge . . . well, why bother?" Millie challenged, throwing her hands up in the air for emphasis.

A young, willowy blond girl with curls bounding all around her face turned away from her view of the sea, walked over, and daintily sat down on the woolen blanket. Aimee glanced at Millie and took her time before responding, even though she knew how the exaggerated pause would excite her impatient friend to even higher levels. Millie loved drama, and considering all the accidents she had ever been in, one could easily believe that drama loved Millie in return. And while Millie had a point, Aimee was not about to sacrifice her dreams of an ideal future.

Picking a field flower, Aimee twirled it between her finger and thumb. "I have decided to join your pledge, Millie, but only if I can have one exception—Reece Hamilton." She jutted her chin defiantly and awaited her friend's expected explosion.

"Lord, Aimee, Reece Hamilton!" Millie cried, flailing back onto the blanket. Aimee retorted with silence. Sitting back up, Millie licked her lips and tried another tactic. "Reece Hamilton's interests are solely ships and the sea. You would need to have a hull and sails before he would notice you. Besides, he's old."

"He is not!" Aimee bristled, crossing her arms. She arched her eyebrows and said knowingly, "I think our age difference is just perfect. When I am old enough to wed, he will be ready to marry and have a family. Go ahead and roll your eyes, Millie, but I am quite serious."

"Really, Aimee?" chimed in Jennelle, the redhead of the trio. "And all this time I thought it was your brother, Charles, who was the serious one."

Aimee refused to yield. "I am indeed serious, Jennelle. And I will join the pact only if I can marry Reece Hamilton when he asks me." Although Reece was ten years older, Aimee had been positive since the age of six that they were destined for each other. He was smart, handsome, and from a good family. But most of all, he was the only boy she knew who was always going to be taller than she was. How she wished she could be small and petite like Millie, or perfectly shaped like Jennelle, but she was destined to be tall and slender like her mother.

Millie wrinkled her nose and adjusted herself so that she was sitting on her knees. "I don't know why you would want to marry your brother's best friend. He and Charlie have both interfered enough over the years with our adventures. Reece is too tall, and he's too big. And I highly doubt he would let you play with us anymore."

"One more word, Millie Aldon, and I swear I will get up and leave," Aimee warned. Her clover-green eyes flashed with anger. Aimee was as sweet as her beauty portrayed her to be, but she was far from a wilting flower and could stand up to her friends when riled.

"No, you won't," Jennelle countered calmly. With no mother and her father consumed with his research, Jennelle had matured faster than her years. "Since we are staying with you this summer, Aimee, we will simply get up and follow you. And, Millie, stop provoking her. You know she has been in love with him for years."

Aimee's blond curls started bobbing. "I have, I really have. Reece is so wonderful and handsome. If I cannot have him, I would want no other."

Millie inhaled exaggeratedly. "Hmm, if you absolutely insist, then . . . fine. Since the chance of Mr. Reece Hamilton asking for your hand in marriage is highly unlikely, I suppose we can allow that one exception," Millie reasoned.

Always full of energy and curiosity, Millie longed for excitement and was continually persuading her friends to participate in her unusual plots to seek and have fun. And from her point of view, the possibilities of losing her friendships and freedom were unacceptable results that too often accompanied wedding vows. Pledging her life to a man was the one promise she would never make. "So, let us swear an oath that none of us will ever agree to marry, unless the interfering . . ." Millie gulped as she caught Aimee's evil glare and quickly added, "and *handsome* Reece Hamilton asks Aimee to marry him."

She outstretched her hand. Aimee grasped it to seal the pledge, but Jennelle refrained. "I, too, would like to make an exception."

Millie stood up, frowning in exasperation. "Jennelle! Do not tell me you are in love as well? How could you!"

Jennelle leaned back and waved her hands, unperturbed by Millie's dramatics. "Oh no, I have not fallen in love, nor do I expect to. However, I would like to reserve the right to marry if an exception comes along," she said in her typical logical voice. Jennelle, like her father, had a passion for reading, especially history. As a result, she tended to be pragmatic and often quoted the lessons she had learned from her studies.

"Well, you have to be more specific than that!" Millie

stated, stomping her foot in frustration. "What good is a no-marriage pact if you can so easily get out of it?"

"Millie, calm down. You become so excitable over nothing," Jennelle coaxed, and moved to sit in the sun. The bright afternoon light captured the fiery red highlights of her hair. Aimee's mother called it rich auburn and constantly remarked how strange it was that the redhead of the group exhibited the most composure and self-control.

"And you are so *rational*," Millie retorted, trying to re-pin her hair so that it stayed out of her face.

Jennelle rolled her eyes. "My exception will be for someone who loves adventures as we do, is willing to take risks, *and* he must be a strong philosopher who enjoys reading, contemplation, and, on occasion, a good debate."

Millie brightened. The likelihood of Jennelle meeting and falling in love with such a person was even less likely than Reece swooning over Aimee's female charms. "A most excellent exception! That combination of traits surely does not exist within a single soul in all of England!"

"Do I not have those traits?" Jennelle asked, raising her voice slightly. "I believe I have accompanied you on many risky ventures, Millie Aldon."

Millie was instantly contrite. In truth, Jennelle was quite the adventurer. She was often willing to try new, unfamiliar things when Aimee refused. "Of course you do. Those traits and more! I just meant that it was doubtful the combination you want exists in a *boy*," Millie clarified. "So, for our pact . . ." She stretched out her hand to start again.

"But what about you?" Aimee interrupted. "Do you not want an exception? The pact isn't fair unless we all have exceptions. Is that not so, Jennelle?"

Jennelle nodded in agreement. "She is right, Millie. For our pledge to be equal, we must all have one, and only one, means of breaking our promise."

Millie started pacing, considering the facts carefully. As

usual, it was difficult to argue with Jennelle's logic. Millie suddenly stopped and knelt down by her friends.

"Fine. This is my exception. I promise never, ever to marry unless I find a man who allows me to hunt, ride astride, climb trees, *and* explore caves. He must not ever be dull, have an aversion to following rules, and possess as strong a passion as I have for adventures," Millie finished, smiling confidently.

"Lord, with that list you are surely safe from any and all men," Jennelle commented. Millie's grin grew, hearing the assessment. Jennelle shrugged her shoulders and continued. "But it does work as an exception. I am content. Aimee? Are you satisfied?"

"Oh yes. This is the best pact ever. Isn't it, Millie?" Aimee asked, smiling.

Millie enthusiastically agreed. "The very best. It will ensure our friendship will last forever. What better pledge could there be?"

"Oh, but, Millie, our pledge is ever so much more than that. We are promising to marry only for love," sighed Aimee. A romantic at heart, Aimee sought and usually found love everywhere. Her paintings, songs, and stories all reflected the affection she felt around her.

Jennelle gathered her knees up under her chin. She understood Aimee's reason for pledging, but it was not love that motivated Jennelle to make the lifelong promise. "I think it is a pledge of protection. Yes, with the way we have stated our exceptions, if we ever do marry, it will be to someone who is our true friend. And, believe me, I have seen how horrid it can be to marry someone you dislike and who dislikes you," Jennelle commented, remembering the numerous fights between Uncle Harry and Aunt Ethel. As a young child, she had often asked her father if her mama ever hollered at him. Every time, he replied that he had married his best friend, and best friends protected each other, and never sought to hurt the other.

Millie was not too sure she agreed with Jennelle or Aimee, but she didn't care. This pact was one of lifelong friendship. No boy could ever understand or respect each other's passions as she and her friends did.

"I believe we are now of accord," Jennelle announced. "All we have to do now is to find something that binds our pledge."

"Excellent idea!" Millie exclaimed.

Aimee's eyes grew wide with shock at Jennelle's declaration. She then glanced at Millie and realized her friend enthusiastically supported the idea. "Oh, not blood. Please, Millie, not blood," Aimee cried.

"I'm not partial to blood, either," Millie said absently, thinking on what they could use to bind their promise. "Besides, we have nothing with which to cut ourselves."

"And," interjected Jennelle, "Mother Wentworth would lock us up forever if she found out."

"I believe she would understand," asserted Millie in defense of Lady Chaselton. "She is a great supporter of our adventures."

Millie's and Aimee's mothers had been childhood playmates whose strong friendship continued into adulthood. When Millie was six, her mother had suddenly taken ill and passed away, and Cecilia Wentworth took it upon herself to help look after her best friend's daughter. That same summer, during a weekend country party, Aimee and Millie met Jennelle, who had also lost her mother. Seeing the inseparable bond grow between the three girls, Cecilia decided to nurture their friendship, foster their love for adventure, and, when possible, act as the mother Millie and Jennelle longed for. Soon they began calling her "Mother" Wentworth and often sought her counsel.

Every summer, Millie and Jennelle visited Aimee at the

Wentworth country estate in Dorset. For three months, they explored and pursued adventure wherever they could find it. They considered themselves enterprising, while most adults—especially Aimee's older brother, Charles—considered them reckless. Mother Wentworth creatively supported their efforts, calling them the clever "Daring Three," which was often shortened by family and close friends to just the "Three."

Millie clapped her hands together. "I know! Lavender! We can burn it in the fireplace this evening. Lots of cultures burn items to seal a promise. Is that not correct, Jennelle?" Millie asked rhetorically.

"Well, yes. That is true. Not often, though. And I have never read about any culture that used lavender, Millie. Usually it is a flag, or some symbol, and, of course, blood. But a flower?" Jennelle wondered.

"Sure. Why not?" Millie asked pointedly.

Jennelle shrugged her shoulders, conceding to the idea. It was better than blood.

"Lavender, Millie? Do we have any?" Aimee asked.

"We do! Remember? I put some in the cave we found. I'll go get it," Millie said as she prepared to run and search for the hidden dried flowers. Aimee grabbed Millie's skirt just in time to keep her from disappearing. When Millie was on a mission, she could run faster than anyone.

"Not the caves, Millie. Don't you remember last time? I promised Mother never to return there without Papa or Charles."

"Last time I didn't know how to properly climb down the cliff to the opening. Now I do. I assure you I will be perfectly safe. Or do you doubt my climbing skills?"

Aimee shook her head. Any other comment would have incited a quick response from Millie to prove her abilities. Aimee tried another tactic. "I just don't want you to go. We don't need the lavender."

Millie placed her small hands on her hips, believing the gesture made her petite stature more imposing. "Of course, we do. Jennelle was right. We need something to bind our pledge." And with that last comment, Millie dashed off to the seaside cliffs. Aimee glared at her redheaded friend.

"What?" Jennelle demanded defensively. "How was I supposed to know she would go crazy and chase after lavender in the caves?"

"I think we should go and get my brother, Charles."

Jennelle bit her bottom lip. "Millie will get mad."

"Let her. She's our best friend, and it is our duty to see to her safety," Aimee maintained as she started walking toward the stables. At this time of day, it was the most likely place to find Reece and Charles.

Jennelle folded the blanket and ran to catch up to her friend. "Well, let's just make Charles promise not to let her know it was us who tattled on her. She would never forgive us. She doesn't like him."

I'm in trouble now, Millie reflected, seeing the water rise almost a third of the way up the cave's opening. "I should have realized how late it was," she mumbled out loud, admonishing herself. She glanced at the water level again, knowing she was trapped until the sea retreated. Midway down the side of the Wentworth cliffs, the mouth of the dark cave became enveloped at high tide. Luckily, once inside, one could ascend an immediate and very steep, long, winding bank that kept the majority of the cave from getting wet.

Millie paced back and forth, trying to come up with options. She would be safe and dry if she remained where she was for the next six hours. Unfortunately, that solution would also mean Mother Wentworth would know of her latest adventure in the caves. She really did not want to worry her, or her friends, who would definitely panic and reveal all when she didn't return.

The only other option was to strip and swim. She eyed the cold, lapping sea water inching its way in. Maybe, if she was very careful, she could tie her dress, the lavender, and her shoes together and hold them high above the water to prevent them from getting wet as she swam to shore.

Millie started peeling off her stockings, trying to think of ways she could sneak back to her room without being seen. She was just stripping off her second stocking, when a cough echoed from behind, making her jump.

"Oww!" Millie hollered as she stepped on a rock.

"Whatever are you doing now?" asked Charles Wentworth, Viscount Erndale and heir to the Marquess of Chaselton, as well as many other titles. As the first and only son, he already retained the title of viscount.

"Charlie Wentworth! What are you doing here? Are you spying on me?"

Charles looked at the small, ragamuffin form standing in her bare feet. "Spying on you? Believe me, Mildred Aldon, I have better things to do than rescue a twelve-year-old child. Whatever are you doing taking your clothes off?"

Millie stopped herself from stomping her foot. Aimee's brother always had a way of discovering her latest scrape and extracting her from it in a most humiliating manner. "I am no child. And if you must know, I was preparing for a swim."

"A swim? Are you stupid? Do you realize how cold the water is? Or how strong the currents are?"

Millie gave him her most menacing glare. "Charlie Wentworth, I'll have you know I am an excellent swimmer. And don't call me stupid again or I swear I . . . I . . . I will hurt you. Don't forget that I know how to fight men of your enormous size!" For as long as Millie could remember, Charles Wentworth towered above her. He was also the most tiresome person of her acquaintance, continually quoting her rules and telling her things not to do.

"You? Hurt me?" Charles started laughing. "I would like to see you try. I think you are forgetting who taught whom, twig."

Millie considered her mode of attack, but decided against executing it. The last time she had tried to retaliate against Charlie, he had put her over his knee and swatted her in the most mortifying fashion. It was at that moment Millie began to invent and practice new ways of defense beyond those few tactics Charlie had taught her last year.

"Come on, Mildred," Charles said mockingly as he walked farther into the cave.

Millie glowered at the brute who dared to use her real name. He looked a lot like his father—dark haired, chiseled features, and tall. Suddenly Millie realized he was leaving her.

"Come on, where?" Then Millie looked back at the lapping water and wondered how he got into the cave without getting wet. He answered her with silence and disappeared around the corner. Millie threw on her stockings and shoes as fast as she could.

"Charlie! Wait!"

"I have asked you repeatedly to call me Lord Charles or Lord Erndale, *Mildred*," he replied, knowing how much she detested her birth name.

"Fine, but then you must call me *Lady* Millie," she said, out of breath running to catch up to him.

"Lady! The day I call you Lady is—"

"—is the same day I stop calling you Charlie." Suddenly Millie stopped, turned, and ran toward the cave's entrance, yelling, "I have to get the lavender!"

When she returned with the flowers, most of her dark hair had fallen out of its pins. "You are a mess," sighed Charles and resumed his walk into the dark bowels of the cave.

Millie straightened her shoulders and calmly smoothed back her long hair. "I may be a mess, but at least it comes from having adventures. I bet you have never had a day in your life where you didn't follow the rules," Millie snapped as she ran to keep up with his long strides. "Charlie, please slow down."

He looked back at the spitfire. Of the Daring Three, Charles admired her the most. He loved her zest for life, courage, and steadfast loyalty, but he would never let her know. "Hurry up, twig. Mother needs to put weight on you."

"Twig!" Millie huffed. She thoroughly despised him sometimes. Only bits of daylight peeking in from the random cracks and gopher holes allowed her to see his mocking stance. "Everything looks undersized to a giant of your height. You are ridiculously ill-proportioned. If I were as big as you, I would become a hermit, I would. No wonder you don't have any adventures. You're too big to have them!" she declared as she marched ahead of him, not knowing their destination.

He stopped and watched her for a moment before reaching up to climb through a shadowed hole. He was out and sitting on the grassy banks waiting when he heard her yelp in surprise. "Charlie? Where are you? If you believe you can scare me, think again!"

He reached his hand down into the hole and heard her scream. As he hauled her up, Millie shot daggers at him with threatening eyes. He grinned in return.

Charles laughed all the way back to the stables. Little Mildred Aldon was certainly entertaining. She had always been a tiny firecracker. When she first entered their lives, his mother had made him promise to look after her. And he soon knew why.

The girl was always finding new ways to entertain herself as well as his sister and their redheaded friend. She was ingenious and frightening with her creativity. He could not count how many times he had saved her from certain injury.

And did Millie ever thank him? No. Sometimes he would get apologies or looks of gratitude from the others, but never from her.

She would just explain how she was in absolute control of the situation and had a perfectly good reason for doing, escaping, climbing, or riding whatever he had interrupted. But best of all, she would then try to stare him down. Those purple eyes of hers could be hauntingly clear or dangerously dark when angered. He felt sorry for the men in her future who had to look into those eyes and tell her no.

He shook his head and felt somewhat sad for Millie. In just a few years, she would have to give up her adventuring ways. Daughters of earls were required to carry themselves with a certain deportment, especially if they wanted to marry. So many times, he had looked at the young Lady Mildred Aldon and envied her open and carefree ways. Her dogmatic ability to seek and conquer anything her heart desired.

At almost two and twenty, Charles knew he was unnaturally pragmatic for his age. People called him staid and pedantic, and it was true. He had been born and bred a marquess, and it seemed to him that the weight of his responsibilities—to his title, family, and father—were always pressing on him.

Soon, Millie would also discover the burdens of adulthood. But unlike him, he was sure that his little Millie would go kicking and screaming all the way.

Chapter 1

Spain, February 1816

"Chase," said a deep, familiar voice from the makeshift doorway. "There's someone coming. About fifteen minutes out. Does anyone know you are here?"

A powerfully built man with strong, athletic features was sitting behind a desk reviewing maps and communiqués. His chocolate brown hair was a mass of untidy long locks, and his golden eyes, despite their warm color, appeared cold and devoid of emotion. "Yes, a few. But no one knows of your presence. Let's keep it that way."

"Aye. And the traitor?"

Golden eyes glanced up and found the blue gaze of one of the few people Chase trusted. "I now have proof of his existence. Besides me, only you are aware of it." He looked back down at one of the maps depicting the Americas' coastline. Scattered beside the pen-and-ink diagram were the communiqués between General Sir Pakenham and a nameless murderer.

Chase stood and stared at the proof his father had sent him to find almost eight years ago. Proof that someone was more interested in conquest and power than in the lives of his countrymen. Someone who was willing to smear the names of good men in order to attain such power. Chase looked up and stared his friend directly in the eye. "That's why I sent for you. No one is to know I have left here until I am already in London. For that, you are the only man I trust, Reece."

Acknowledgment entered the shrewd, sapphire-colored eyes. "I have already loaded everything on board the *Sea Emerald*. Only what is here, remains."

Chase nodded and began stacking the documents on the table.

Reece moved to help but decided against the idea. His friend had always been driven. But when his father died, Chase had emotionally shut down and had become determined to finish his father's one last request. "What are you going to do without the name of the traitor?" Reece asked.

"Find it. My father sent me to locate the proof, and I now have it. I think this . . . this turncoat had much to do with the Peninsular War, but now I have proof of his motives and duplicitous intentions between our government and the Americas." Chase stabbed a stack of papers with his finger. "There is no longer any doubt someone was trying to stop the impending treaty between America and England. This"— he picked up a letter—"outlines plans to send General Pakenham, stripped of talented men, to attack New Orleans. Here"—Chase grabbed another hastily scribed document— "is the general's reply warning his superiors that their directed plan of attack was 'unimaginative' and 'deadly.' And these are the very proof I need to tie it all together," Chase added, pointing to a third set of documents. "I cannot believe Vandeleur had not even looked at these manuscripts before handing them to me."

The documents under Chase's fist confirmed that Pakenham was tricked into attacking New Orleans. Upon direct orders, he took his force ashore and ran into a defensive line of militia, Indians, black troops, and even pirates, hastily put together by General Andrew Jackson. Pakenham led seventy-five hundred men into an ambush of cannon and musket fire.

By the time the English soldiers had reached the American lines, the deaths of their commanders had thrown them into confusion. While trying to establish order, Pakenham was mortally wounded. Not realizing the English forces were on the brink of victory, a retreat was ordered.

Chase understood war was sometimes a necessary evil, but the Battle of New Orleans was an unwarranted, useless, preordained English tragedy. One nameless man had purposefully arranged those pointless deaths. And Chase knew the traitor would try again. Of that, he was sure. For despite heavy English losses, peace had been made with the colonies and the Treaty of Ghent had been signed on Christmas Eve.

"I met Ned Pakenham," Reece said respectfully. "He commanded the Third Division until the capture of Madrid. I was there in 1813, when he was given command of the Sixth Division at the Battle of the Pyrenees. He was a good man and an able commander."

"I want this traitor, Reece. I want him, and I will have him," said Chase forcefully, the depth of his desire evident. "But I am not going to sacrifice the names of good men while seeking the devil."

Reece nodded in agreement. The good men Chase was referring to were called the Rebuilders, a select group of noblemen with idealistic beliefs and purposes. Chase's father had been a member, and now, by default, so was his son. A few years ago, an inner faction began to grow and started calling themselves Expansionists. Their views of government, while not as peaceful, were not disloyal. If Chase were to reveal his proof and proclaim a member to be a traitor, without a name, all those affiliated with either group—Rebuilders or Expansionists—would be tagged as possible turncoats. Guilt by association could ruin a man's reputation, a necessary asset in a country ruled by Tories and an extravagant, vain prince regent.

Reece looked out the slightly cracked open door. "The rider is almost here. Looks to be a delivery boy from one of the larger battalions. I'll wait for you on the *Sea Emerald*. We'll leave as soon as you are on board."

Chase nodded as his friend silently disappeared through the back door. He sat back down behind the crude desk and hid the communiqués underneath a copy of the Second Treaty of Paris's terms and conditions for ending the Peninsular War.

The door opened and a uniformed man entered. "Captain?"

Chase grunted and pretended to be in deep thought over the papers. It was a common ploy to quickly establish levels of importance. Common, but effective. Chase finally asked, in a gruff voice, "What do you want?"

"Sir, name is Marshel. I am aide-de-camp to Colonel Vandeleur."

Chase looked at the ADC and quickly assessed the young man. "How long have you been with Vandeleur?"

"Close to seven months, sir. I was part of the Sixteenth Dragoons before Colonel Vandeleur took over for Lord Uxbridge last summer."

The young man was not as green as he looked. He had made it through Waterloo. "Light cav, I take it," Chase deduced. A critical function of light cavalry regiments was to monitor communications between enemy encampments. Only the good survived.

"Yes, sir."

Chase leaned back. The chair squeaked. "What do you need of me?"

"Not a thing, sir. I was just told to pass on this bag to the cap'n who could be found in Sofina's House of Pleasure near Bilbao." The young man glanced around at the crumbling structure. It had been a long time since the place had provided a man pleasure.

Chase saw the man observing his surroundings and took the bag. "You can go now. I have nothing to pass on. But tell your colonel of my appreciation for this." Chase knew what the bag contained. Letters from home. It had been some time since he had been in a location to receive any word from his mother and his sister, Aimee.

The man nodded, exited the building, and rode back toward Pamplona.

Chase leaned back on the small bunk as the waves rolled the *Sea Emerald* back and forth. An easiness fell on him he hadn't experienced for some time. Very few had known where he was located in Spain, and only a handful knew his identity. Vandeleur was one of those few. He knew it was safe for the ADC to make contact. Chase trusted Vandeleur, but a signed peace treaty could not instantly remove habits of caution and vigilance that had saved his life multiple times.

Chase opened up the bag and discovered several letters. Two were personal. He instantly recognized the handwriting on one. It was from his mother. He lit a lamp and proceeded to break the seal.

Letters from home were his rarest and most cherished treasures. After his father had passed away, only his mother's stories and amusing updates seemed to register with him emotionally. Tales of his sister and her two friends would bring him back to simpler times, peaceful ones in which he was unaware of the cruelty and duplicitous nature of men.

He unfolded the page and was surprised to see how short it was. He glanced at the contents. As usual, his mother never mentioned anyone's identity. Sometimes she would refer to the Daring Three, a private label his mother had given to his sister and her wild friends, but that was as close as she came to disclosing a name.

Chase wondered if Millie was still his favorite twig, causing chaos wherever she went. He suspected time and experience had changed her as it had certainly changed him.

> *Son,*
>
> *Your sister will be having her first Season in London this year along with the other members of the Daring Three. My earnest wish is for you to return, escort your sister and her friends, and find someone in the process with whom to settle down and live a happy, safe life.*
>
> *I have asked little of you since you have entered into manhood, understanding that your father asked much. However, he has been dead now for over two years, and the wars between England and France are over. It is time you returned home.*
>
> *Please send me a prompt response so I can plan accordingly.*
>
> *Your Mother*
>
> *P.S. Notice how I did not once mention your appalling lack of writing ability these past few years?*

Chase found himself grinning. His mother always had a way of breaking through his detached self, even when she was a country away. Possessing his father's naturally stoic personality, Chase realized how lucky his father had been to find his mother. He wondered if it was possible that he, too, would find a loyal and spirited woman who could love a self-controlled, serious man like himself.

He took a deep breath and exhaled, discarding the idea. It would not be fair to shackle anyone, especially a woman full of life, to the man he was now. Oh, he would marry someday; he had to, for the sake of his title. But when he did, it would be to someone who needed no emotional support. The arrangement would be simple. She would look beautiful and bear him a son, and he would drench her in Wentworth money. He would not care that she was shallow, and she wouldn't care that he was haunted.

He broke the seal on the second letter. As he read the contents, an icy rage reawakened deep within him. One he had long thought to have under control.

The Most Honorable, The Marquess of Chaselton

My Lord Marquess,
I am sorry I never had the opportunity to make your acquaintance. It is unfortunate that I now must introduce myself through such ineffectual means.
As a close friend of your father's, I am aware that you know about the organization to which he belonged and our current squabble over its direction. What you may not know is that your father, like myself, was one of five men working against the Expansionist movement. For protection, none of us knew all five members, a decision both wise and ill-fated.
When your father died, I was suspicious of the unusual circumstances but could not prove them otherwise. There was no motive. I now have been made aware of evidence to the contrary, and I regretfully inform you that your father, my friend, was murdered. With grave disappointment, I cannot say by whom.
Such tidings are not ones that should be scribed, but the situation has made it necessary. And so I write to the two men whose names have been entrusted to me of our small heroic group. You, in your father's stead, and to

*Viscount Darlouney, requesting that we meet as soon
as it is possible.*

*I understand the grave risk I am taking in
communicating to you by these means. It is my
fervent hope this finds you soon. Hasten to London,
and I will explain all upon your arrival. Be careful
of those whom you might meet. Trust no one.*

Eischel

Chase reread Lord Eischel's last words and it stirred
emotions he had long thought to have conquered—anger,
hurt, and guilt that he had not yet been able to fulfill his
father's last request. Only the knowledge that he would not
stop until he succeeded enabled Chase to suppress the intense feelings. And now, another—a more pressing, more
important, more necessary—entreaty had been issued from
his father. *Avenge me.*

After carefully refolding and hiding Eischel's letter, Chase
collected the one from his mother and went on deck to find
Reece. His friend had made the sea his home and looked
most comfortable with the ocean wind at his back.

Reece raised a single eyebrow as Chase neared. "So? Still
to London?"

"It seems, good friend, my titular duties have caught up
with me," Chase replied, handing him his mother's directive.

Reece quickly surveyed the item and grinned. "Your
mother, the vibrant Lady Chaselton, has spoken," Reece
replied, turning the wheel. "To London we go. Better you
than I, old friend."

Chase gave Reece a friendly elbow to the ribs and tucked
the letter inside his jacket. "A true friend would join me."

"Tempting, but I have a quick errand to run before I can
hang up my patriotic duties. Believe it or not, it is for Sir
Edward."

Chase's eyebrows rose in surprise. "Sir Edward? You mean *our* Sir Edward?"

"The one and only."

Chase joined Reece's gaze at the horizon. It was beginning to darken, and the late-afternoon sky was hazy with coral colors. "I have not heard from him in years. I believed him to be retired from the war department and making merry in Town."

"So did I, until I received his request," Reece replied quietly, reflectively.

Eight years ago, Sir Edward had been the man Chase's father had turned to when he needed to get both his son and Reece into key positions within the war department. Sir Edward had personally overseen Chase's and Reece's training, teaching them how to observe others without being seen, how to blend in to a foreign culture. He cultivated Reece's natural strategic thinking and used his love for the sea to help cripple the enemies' naval movements. But with Chase, Sir Edward recognized what he himself was—a born spy. He taught Chase how to build upon his already poised personality and how to remain indifferent—if only outwardly—to the events around him.

Chase owed his life many times to Sir Edward and his lessons.

Chapter 2

Millie awoke abruptly, feeling both frightened and on edge. She instinctively reached for the chain necklace on the night table and slipped it over her head. She glanced down at the gold and amethyst amulet and fingered the strange disk that now served as a pendant. Millie closed her eyes and took several deep breaths as memories of the late Lord Chaselton flooded her mind, calming her thoughts. It was nice to think of him as another guardian angel.

Nightmares did not interrupt her sleep often, but when they did, they were intense and disturbing. One of her last and clearest memories of her mother was being consoled after such a dream. After her death, Millie would stare at a small, handheld portrait of her mother, until the unsettling feelings subsided.

During one of her summer visits to the Wentworths', the portrait had been ruined, the victim of a tree branch, a broken window, and a nasty thunderstorm. That next day, Aimee's father Lord Chaselton had surprised them each with gifts. Millie's was an amulet. One night, after a particularly haunting dream, she had awoke and finding it next to her, clutched it in her palm, hoping it would provide some comfort. And it had worked. All the love and peace she sought from the face of her mother, that strange piece of jewelry was somehow also able to bestow during that visit. Seeing the item when rummaging through the attic in preparations for Town, Millie immediately donned it, hoping it would provide her luck if not fortitude to withstand the weeks ahead.

Millie winced when she heard her stomach growl. She lay still for several minutes, listening to the gurgling evidence of her earlier attempt to force the impossible. Knowing she would not be able to go back to sleep until having eaten, she slipped out from the covers. Quietly sneaking down the dark, unlit hall, her toe crunched against an unseen piece of furniture. Millie muffled a cry of pain and hopped to Aimee's door and cracked it open. Seeing moonlight pour in through the bedroom window, she heaved a sigh of relief and made her way across the room.

"Aimee? Are you awake?" Millie whispered, hoping for company while she raided the kitchen.

"No, and neither am I," came a muffled response from under a pillow covering Jennelle's head. Soon after Aimee's mother arrived at the Wentworth London manor, better known as Hembree Grove, she declared all the bedrooms to be in need of immediate maintenance. Jennelle's room was the first slated for transformation and received a fresh coat of paint and preparations for new wallpaper the following afternoon. Until the fumes from the newly enhanced walls diminished, Jennelle agreed to sleep in the spare bed located in Aimee's room.

"Whatever do you want, Millie?" Aimee asked, yawning. She stretched and sat up, causing waves of gold to tumble all around her.

"I was only wondering if you might be interested in . . . some nourishment," Millie murmured weakly. She had been famished for what seemed to be hours.

"Millie! I just *knew* this was going to happen," Aimee grunted, falling back against her pillow. "I warned you, and you didn't listen. You would not be starving right now if you had partaken of dinner. Your fast was a mockery, and everyone knew it."

"I was not fasting per se, Aimee. I was just vexed. And I still am. It is not fair, I tell you," Millie said reluctantly as she dramatically slumped onto a nearby velvet settee.

"Well, I think it is irrational for you to be the one fasting over Jennelle's shortened Season with us. If anyone should be starving in protest, it is she."

"I'm not starving," came a voice from under a pillow.

Millie huffed. "That is only because of your good nature, Jennelle. It was up to me to protest your leaving, and so I did. Besides, a monthlong Season is unreasonable."

"And this coming from the one who didn't believe in having a Season in the first place," the still muffled voice replied.

Millie shrugged, undisturbed by Jennelle's retort. "I just believe that if you are going to do something, do it right. The Season lasts from now until June. That's just over three months. It's practically a crime, Jennelle, that you are allowed to experience only half of it. Aimee, you, too, should have been fasting with me to persuade Lord Gent to change his mind."

"Would not have worked. My father would still have left, never having noticed." Jennelle's father, Lord Gent, was an avid researcher and had traveled to Town to purchase several books on medieval England. Disliking staying in London for any length of time at all, he had dined with his daughter at Hembree Grove, made polite but quick conversation, and then left. Lady Chaselton invited him to stay at least one night, but he had been adamant about starting his journey home immediately. Soon after he was assured Jennelle had settled in well with the Wentworths, her father had left for his country estate.

Aimee sat upright and looked her friend directly in the eye. "Millie, I truly love your dramatic soul, but do you not think you are being even slightly ridiculous? I mean, Lord Gent did allow her to stay for six weeks."

"But with only one new dress. It is dreadful," Millie replied, refusing to succumb to Aimee's censure.

"What need do I have for new gowns? I have no intention of capturing anyone's notice," Jennelle replied. She lifted her pillow and looked directly at Millie. "And I *thought* neither did you."

Aimee nodded her head and joined Jennelle's line of questioning. "Indeed, was it not you, Millie, who convinced us to delay our coming-out these past two years?"

Millie stood up and waved her hands, downplaying Aimee's question. "Oh, I still have no intention of agreeing to any type of commitment—especially with the dandies and fribble we're likely to encounter. And if I could have delayed this demand of my father's, Aimee, I would have. But now that our coming-out is a fait accompli, I have decided that it need not all be dreadful. Imagine the adventures we could have here and nowhere else." Millie began spinning about the room with her arms held out to her sides.

Those who assumed Millie Aldon's personality corresponded with her physical characteristics—petite, ladylike, and soft-spoken—usually found themselves either befuddled and confused, or enjoying lively conversation upon meeting her. According to Mother Wentworth, the Daring Three would soon redefine what Society considered diamonds of the first water.

Millie was the smallest of them all, and the most spirited. Yet despite her propensity for unorthodox activities, she possessed her mother's natural elegance and a charming wit that ensnared most of those around her.

Tall, slender, with blond hair and snapping emerald eyes, Aimee fit every Society mother's mold of ideal marriage material. And though a self-admitted bluestocking, Jennelle's flawless skin, shapely figure, and intelligent blue eyes would enable her to select from many eligible men.

Millie stopped twirling and looked beseechingly at her friend. "Jennelle, think of the societies that are here, many of which include people who love to learn and read as much as you do. Aimee! The museums, the art, the paintings!"

Jennelle sat up abruptly and signaled Aimee. "Reflect on our friend's sudden change in disposition toward Town, and I give you a chilling thought. She is *up* to something." Jennelle pointed a finger at Millie, who deliberately ignored her. "Yes, our clever friend is definitely up to something. Millie, what are you planning?"

Aimee looked perplexed. "Jennelle? What do you mean?"

"I mean, Aimee, that Millie is suspiciously correct in her assertions. *You* have things of interest here in Town. Even *I* am looking forward to visiting a multitude of places. But Millie? Tell me, Aimee. What does London offer a noblewoman who loves to ride, hunt, and generally cause trouble?"

Understanding suddenly crept into Aimee's face as the blood rushed out. "Oh no. You are right. . . . Millie! What *are* you planning?"

Millie spread her hands. "Me? You two are half asleep and spouting nonsense. I'm going downstairs before I vanish into nothingness due to hunger." She could feel the eyes of her friends on her back as she escaped through the door before they could probe further.

"There must be *something* edible here, though Lord knows how I am going to find it. May you experience a thousand hunger-filled days, Lord Gent," Millie mumbled to herself as she tiptoed around the kitchen.

"Oww!" Millie yelped and immediately strangled several sordid curses as she tried not to wake the house. "Bloody hell," she moaned, trying to ignore the pain radiating from her foot. "What fool put a stool in the middle of the floor?"

"I believe the last time we saw each other, you were hopping about precisely in the same manner. Including the bare feet," Chase reflected from the shadows.

Startled, Millie whirled around, searching for the speaker. "Who is there? Explain yourself."

She took a step forward and her long, dark brown hair shimmered in the moonlight. Chase lowered his gaze to skim appreciatively down the graceful line of her slender frame. He was not prepared for the petite but curvaceous beauty standing before him.

Little Mildred Aldon had grown up.

Her facial features had been replaced with those of a woman, delicate and feminine. Long lashes framed the unforgettable eyes that revealed both her curiosity and fear. Her lower lip was slightly fuller than her upper, and Chase found himself wondering if they were as soft and inviting as they looked.

"Charlie? Is . . . is that you?" Millie asked, hugging herself as she approached the large man looming in the shadows. She had been twelve years old the summer she had said good-bye to Aimee's brother, but his presence was unlike any other. Despite the years, she instinctively knew the voice belonged to the new Marquess of Chaselton, Charles Wentworth.

Though loath to admit it aloud, he had been one of her life anchors as a child. After her mother died, Millie had felt out of control and alone. Aimee, Jennelle, Mother Wentworth, and to a large degree even Charlie, had provided her a familial refuge that gave her a sense of belonging. She had not realized how much Charlie had contributed to that feeling until he had left.

Millie moved and Chase sucked in his breath. She had slanted her head to one side and unfolded her crossed arms.

The innocent act revealed the diaphanous condition of her linen shift. The tempting outline of her uptilted breasts, her shapely hips, and slender waist served as a reminder that his favorite childhood annoyance had grown up into a striking woman. Twig was reminding parts of his body that he had not been with a woman in some time.

"Why aren't you wearing any clothes?" Chase bellowed, mentally trying to envision her as a little girl with scabbed knees. It wasn't working.

"It *is* you, Charlie!" Millie exclaimed in a shocked whisper. "Heavens, keep your voice down. I cannot believe it. I have not seen you since I was . . . what was I, twelve? And already you are raising your voice and lecturing me. Good Lord, don't you know people are attempting to sleep at this hour? You should be ashamed of yourself."

Chase stood dumbfounded for a moment, feeling as if the last eight years had just disappeared. He was suddenly Charlie again and little Mildred Aldon of the thoroughly exasperating Three was lecturing him when it was she who was in the wrong. He shook his head and returned to the present, determined not to be deterred by her again.

His eyes narrowed in a futile attempt at admonishment. "I should be ashamed of myself? I am not the one who is traipsing about the kitchen half-exposed for anyone to see."

Millie thought his comment fairly nonsensical as she felt more covered in her nightdress than she did in some of her ball gowns.

Unaware of the transparent state of her dress, Millie put her hands on her hips and jutted her chin. Chase would have laughed at her old technique of trying to appear imposing, except the gesture had thrust her bosoms more fully into view. Instead, he found himself trying unsuccessfully to suppress unexpected and unwanted visions of her as she lectured him.

"Charlie Wentworth, you will behave like a gentleman

even if it has slipped your notice that I am no longer a child. You will remember your status and speak to me as a gentleman speaks to a lady." Then, remembering she had not expected to encounter any company, she pursed her lips and added, "Regardless of my state of dress."

Feeling ridiculous, Chase stood speechless as he tried not to gape at the soft swells of her breasts. Her body may have matured, but the fire and energy of her youth remained. Chase wasn't sure why, but he was glad Mildred Aldon retained the spirit he had once so admired. Not that she ever knew of his approval or was going to know of it now.

Puzzled by his silence, Millie moved the stool out of her way and took a step closer. Then suddenly it occurred to her that he must have thought she was right. It was a silent agreement, of course, but when Charlie believed her to be wrong, he was quick to let her know. At least, he *used* to be quick to let her know.

No longer half-hidden in the shadows, the moonlight illuminated Millie's face and accentuated the purple hue of her eyes. Chase took a deep breath as he watched her face brighten. Something had crossed her mind that pleased her immensely. The effect was mesmerizing. Millie would have to stop smiling or he would have to leave—and quick. He was already having a hard enough time reconciling this very attractive woman with his memories of a little girl who found trouble wherever she could.

"Oh, forgive my outburst, Charlie. It is just that I am surprised to see you . . . here . . . in London. We did not think you could attend this Season. Mother Wentworth wrote to you but never received a return response." Quiet filled the room, and she still could not make out his expression in the shadows. Millie took another step closer and unconsciously rested her hand on his sleeve. "Regardless, I know Aimee will be very glad that you have returned. She has missed you enormously."

He blinked, but the vision before him remained the same. Millie's heart-shaped face was definitely no longer that of a child. Her finely etched cheekbones perfectly framed her large eyes. He drank in the deep, dusty-lavender pools sparkling with delight. Chase coughed to mask his ever-increasing uneasiness. "Of course I came. My place is to oversee Aimee's first Season and ensure she makes a good match."

Millie's eyes laughed. "Oh, well, we all will be delighted with your company while in Town, but you need not have feared about any undeserving gentlemen attaching themselves to Aimee. That is my responsibility." She twirled back several steps and started tracing the kitchen table's edge with her finger.

Chase was barely able to keep the shock from invading his expression. "Your responsibility?" he asked with a hint of annoyance before inhaling deeply. *Some things will never change*, he told himself. Millie still had a way of twisting words that could make even the most reasonable man's head spin.

Millie's eyebrows rose, excited to know she still could agitate the unflappable Charles Wentworth. "Indeed, you understand me correctly. It is *my* responsibility. Just as it is Jennelle's."

Chase closed his eyes for a few moments, trying to decide whether he truly wanted to pursue this line of questioning. Curiosity forced him. "Do you actually believe you and Jennelle will be determining whom my sister will marry?"

Millie moved to place her hands across a tall, empty vase on the table. She then rested her chin on her entwined fingers. "Oh, heavens, no. We are here just to be of assistance."

"And exactly what is the nature of the assistance you intend to provide my sister?"

Millie gave a slight, elegant shrug with one shoulder, letting him know she was intentionally being coy. "I expect it to be similar to the kind she has offered me. And Jennelle, too, of course." Millie sighed. She had forgotten how much annoying him amused her.

Oh, of course! Chase sarcastically repeated to himself as he strode over to stand next to her. His eyes narrowed as he searched her face. She was deliberately being vague. Twig might have physically grown up, but her quick, impish mind had not softened. Despite her new figure, Mildred Aldon was still the most baffling, unpredictable female he had ever known.

Millie licked her lips, wishing she hadn't provoked him. He was no longer hidden in the shadows, and the man standing before her was not Charlie. Charlie Wentworth had been young when he entered the war. He had never been prone to laughing or smiling, but a hardness that had not been there before now outlined his aristocratic features. The years had changed him.

His tense stance stretched his snug trousers, highlighting his muscular thighs. His waistcoat had been discarded as well as his cravat and she could see his muscles rippling under the thin layer of his linen shirt. Amber-and-gold eyes stared down at her with an intense look that assaulted her senses. He exuded masculinity, and she could feel her pulse begin to race. Emotions churned inside her—ones she had never felt before. She looked down, unable to accept the idea it was Charlie Wentworth awakening her to such feelings.

"Enough, Mildred. Explain your meaning," Chase ordered as he reached down and trapped her chin in his rough fingers. The action compelled her to look at him. He silently swore to himself as her long lashes fluttered open, revealing the beauty they hid. He had always known those violet eyes would get a man into trouble someday. He had just never dreamed it would be him. Chase let go of her but could not bring himself to back away.

Millie considered continuing her elusiveness, but his golden gaze dominated the air between them. She had never feared Charlie. And while even now she was not physically afraid, Charles Wentworth had assumed a commanding presence that was unnerving her very core. She swallowed heavily. "We have no intentions of marrying . . . my lord."

"And . . ." Chase prodded.

Millie took a step back, rallying. "And nothing. That is all. Aimee, Jennelle, and I made a pledge never to make any life-long commitments that would require us to live by some absurd archaic rules. And in case a gentleman does not recall the meaning of the word *no*, we will be there to remind him."

Chase swore. He didn't know why he was surprised. "So if I understand this declaration correctly, *none of you plan to marry?*"

Millie cleared her throat delicately and looked him directly in the eye. "For clarity's sake, I shall repeat myself. No, we do not. Not this Season, not ever."

Chase gave her a speculative, shrewd glance. "Never marry? Under *any* circumstances?"

Millie shot him a scathing look. "No, not exactly. We can marry, but only if certain conditions are met." She shrugged her shoulders and turned to walk away. "And the chances of any man being able to meet them are closer to impossible than improbable."

Chase leaned back against the table's edge. *You may still know how to easily provoke me, Mildred Aldon, but I know what inflames your ire as well*, he thought triumphantly to himself. "It baffles me why you three insist upon entering into these idiotic, foolish pledges that none of you have a prayer of upholding. Do you not think it is time for you to refrain from childish promises and act like the lady you earlier claimed to be?" he challenged, knowing how she would respond.

Millie spun around. Her eyes flashed with anger. "I don't give a brass farthing for your opinion! Talk about immaturity! It seems that eight years have done very little to change your overbearing disposition. Only *Charlie* Wentworth would resort to such taunts."

Chase turned a dull red. "I am Charlie! I mean Charles. Hell, woman, these days most people call me Chase." It took him several seconds to regain his self-control. Mildred was doing it again. She could change the direction of a conversation faster than anyone. He took a deep breath and countered her jeer. "But in your case, I think *my lord* will do."

Ignoring the snide directive, Millie inquired, "Chase? For Chaselton? I think I like it. Suits you."

Millie's moods had always been fluid, quickly adapting to whatever emotion she was presently experiencing. Suddenly inquisitive, her eyes had warmed considerably. She cocked her head and looked up at him, scrunching her nose. It was completely endearing. On any other woman, it would have appeared ludicrous, but Chase felt as if he were under a spell. A spell he had best figure out how to break—and quickly.

He was about to end the chaotic conversation when he spied the gold medallion on her chest. "What is this?"

Millie looked down as he grasped her pendant. "What is what? Oh, my amulet. Your father gave it to me to wear when"—she paused, refusing to admit to Charlie that she could be frightened by a silly nightmare—"I want to remember him."

Mystified, Chase continued fondling the item in his hand. It was a three-dimensional rendition of the Rebuilders' crest. "My father requested you wear this necklace?" he asked incredulously.

Millie suddenly felt uneasy and retrieved the medallion from his grasp. "No, it was my idea to wear the ornament as a necklace," Millie answered. She then tried her best to dismiss him with a smile. "I pray you excuse me, Chase. I think I will return to my room and wait until morning to address my appetite. Good night."

A grown-up Mildred Aldon calling him Chase was disturbing. Although he had often requested—no, demanded—that she stop referring to him as Charlie, never before had she used any other name. He leaned over and seized her hand to keep her from leaving. Her skin was like touching the finest silk. Her tomboy days had done nothing to prepare him for tonight. "Oh, but I do mind, Mildred. I'm still curious concerning something you mentioned earlier."

Millie blinked in an effort to calm her nerves. The fierce planes of his face were not those one normally associated with a highborn, pampered aristocrat. His expression held no softness anywhere, and yet it was inexplicably alluring. She blinked again. He was just Charlie, she told herself, not some Greek god. She forced herself to appear relaxed. "One more question. That is all. I am exceedingly tired."

Chase reached up and lightly caressed her cheek as he tucked a stray lock of dark hair behind her ear. He noticed her soft, pink lips had parted slightly. They were standing so close now, it would be effortless to satisfy this insane attraction and kiss her. One kiss and his curiosity would be vanquished and this charm she was weaving over him would disappear.

"In regard to this absurd promise you three made, what"—he stroked her cheek again—"is your particular exception allowing *you* to marry?"

Millie stared at him, unable to move under his gaze. A golden brown, his eyes reminded her of firelight. The strength and gentleness in his fingers unsettled her, and she automatically clutched his shirt for balance. The action reminded her of just how small and light she was compared to him.

Her heart pounded in her chest. His touch was arousing unfamiliar and very feminine desires. She was both surprised and bothered to discover how much she liked it. Reacting on instinct, Millie rose on the balls of her feet to kiss him, and suddenly she realized where she was—in the kitchen, without a robe, in her bare feet, practically jumping into the arms of her best friend's brother. "Bloody hell," she mouthed and then fled to the staircase.

Chase watched her retreat, not understanding whether he felt relieved or frustrated. He wished Reece were in London and not on the *Sea Emerald*. He needed fortitude, and his mother's plea to play escort this Season was going to strip all the strength from him if Millie looked half as good in sunlight.

Chapter 3

The next morning after the excitement of Chase's return died down, Aimee's mother handed the Daring Three cards with names and addresses inscribed on them. Cecilia Wentworth was what each of them desired to be—elegant, beautiful, and most of all venturous.

"There, now. I wish I could go with you today, but I suspect you will have a much more enjoyable time on your own. Moreover, I have much to do in Town, and I want to be surprised with what you decide and select."

Cecilia sipped her tea, viewing the young women over the cup's brim. She secretly wondered how Society was going to respond to her Three. She and Millie's mother had been kindred spirits and sought excitement and thrills wherever they could find them. The year they were introduced into Society was quite famous with some of their exploits. Cecilia understood that encouraging the Three's love of adventure could limit their chances of making a good match, but she also knew that being true to oneself was the only pathway to lasting happiness. "Now, you may, of course, go to any modiste you prefer. The names on those cards are only suggestions. Jennelle, I specifically recommended Mrs. Brinson because I understand she is an excellent seamstress, very talented in remaking gowns into the newer fashions."

Aimee looked up quizzically. "Thank you, Mother, but I had thought we would be using your modiste, Madame Rosson."

"Hmm, I presumed as much. Your attempts to permanently evade your coming-out has left you completely ignorant of the basics all ladies of Society should know. Just being wealthy and wellborn will not get you entry into the *haut ton*. Besides having beauty and wit, you also have to be fashionable, which right now you three are certainly not. Your gowns are for country affairs, and that just will not do while you are in Town."

A quiet scoff came from the end of the table. Lady Cecilia Chaselton eyed Millie, who was still staring at the name on her card. "Whether you like it or not, Mildred, your father wants you to have a true Season. He wants you to experience a coming-out in all its glory. And perhaps, just perhaps, you will meet someone who will appreciate you for who you are. And, if remotely intelligent, he will find a way to sweep you off your feet as Lord Chaselton did me so many years ago." She paused for effect. "I know your mother would feel the same," she added with quiet emphasis.

Cecilia turned to her daughter. They shared many features, most noticeably curly blond hair and willowy height, but Aimee's snapping green eyes were identical to her father's. "Aimee, my modiste would certainly love to have more of my business, and you may go there if you wish. But you will leave with a dress for an older dowager of the *ton*, not as an eligible woman just entering into Society. Trust me when I say that going throughout Town ill-dressed is not an adventure that any of you seek."

Cecilia sipped her last bit of tea, stood up, and smiled. "Do as you like. Be sure to take Elda Mae along, and enjoy yourselves. Remember, I enjoy the wild, daring spirits inside each of you. We just need to find a way to balance that with your soft, feminine beauty. Have a good day. We'll discuss it all over dinner this evening." And then she was gone.

Jennelle watched with wide blue eyes as the woman she most admired in the world left the room. "Slay me. Your mother is truly something."

Aimee smiled with pride. "Yes, she is." She tapped her card on the table. "Now, I wonder why she suggested we each go to a different modiste."

Later that morning, they discovered the answer when their landau neared the address printed on Aimee's card. "I believe, Lady Aimee, your mother discovered this modiste last year." The statement came from Elda Mae, a stoutly graying woman whom all three girls had known for years. She had been Millie's nursemaid and now functioned as an additional lady's maid to each of them whenever they were together. Because of her unique and long-standing relationship with the Three, Elda Mae felt at ease going back and forth from reverence to reprimand and could often be found lurking behind doors, eavesdropping on her charges' conversations. The Daring Three loved her immensely, and she them.

Aimee lowered her head and peered at the name on the card one more time. "Yes, you are right, Elda Mae." She looked around as the driver brought the landau to a stop. Her modiste was located in the fashionable side of Town, where most of the quality seamstresses were found. "This is it. Madame Beatrice Summers. I am surprised Mother did not suggest someone French. I thought they were the rage in designers."

Millie rolled her eyes. "Personally, I am glad we are not going to any French modistes."

Jennelle assessed her dark-haired friend. "That is only

because you have heard it was fashionable. You, if anything, Millie, are reluctant to conform. I swear you live to be rebellious."

Millie shrugged unapologetically. "Perhaps, but I am still glad we are not going to someone French." Millie knew Jennelle had spoken correctly; however, Millie did not care. She often based her opinions on the illogical and refused to change her position.

Ignoring them both, Aimee changed the topic. "Let us go in. It looks soft and fairy-tale-like inside," Aimee said, standing in the open carriage as the footman unlocked the side door.

"It looks . . . pastel," Millie murmured disapprovingly as they entered the establishment. Millie knew the lighter colors, which favored her fair-haired friend, had never suited her. "I am now not only understanding, but filled with undying gratitude to your mother for sending us to different modistes."

Jennelle gazed at all the pinks, pale yellows, and faint blues and nodded in agreement. "I must admit I am in complete agreement with Millie. I am sending quiet thoughts of appreciation to your mother right now." She pointed at one frilly, lacy gown heavily drenched in pink and yellow bows. "Can you imagine me in something like that?"

"Unfortunately, yes," Millie answered, "and you look completely horrid."

"Oh my," Aimee added, seeing the item being referenced. "Those are my colors, and even I would look ghastly in that concoction."

Elda Mae nodded in agreement. "Milady, if you want my opinion, no intelligent gent would want a silly chit who thinks bows make her attractive to a man. Only a woodenhead would be wanting a woman in that eyesore. Mark my words. If you marry a woodenhead, you're doomed to have woodenheaded offspring."

All three were about to explode into laughter as a plump, middle-aged woman with tousled brown hair and kind hazel eyes stepped out from back. "Can I help you?"

Aimee smiled, swallowing her mirth. "Please, we are looking for a Madame Beatrice Summers."

The woman tried to tuck away some of the loose strands of hair. "I am Madame Summers."

"Wonderful," Millie said, grabbing Aimee's hand and prodding her forward. "Lady Aimee Wentworth would like to be fitted for some new ball gowns, visiting and afternoon dresses, and so forth. We," Millie added, pointing at Jennelle and then herself, "are just here to help, if possible." She looked at the modiste kindly, but made sure Madame Summers realized there was only one client there today. Beatrice nodded in understanding. She knew her wares primarily suited the fair.

"Of course. If you could just wait one moment while I finish with my current clients, then all of you can come back while I take measurements and discuss styles, needs, and so forth."

"Thank you," Aimee offered as the modiste dipped behind the curtain.

As they wandered around the shop eyeing different items, Millie spied one extremely tasteless accessory. "Bloody hell, would someone actually pay money to wear that? In public?"

Furrowing her brows, Aimee censured, "Millie, please!"

"Oh, I forgot," Millie said, wincing. "I promise to be more careful where my phrasing is concerned, but you must look at this, and then you will understand."

Aimee came over and her eyes widened in surprise. "Oh my Lord . . ." she softly exclaimed. Aimee's mild blasphemy immediately caught Jennelle's attention. Many things could get Millie excited, but to get Aimee to agree—it must in fact be something.

"What has you both so fascinated? Let me see. Millie . . ."

Jennelle's voice suddenly dwindled when she saw the item. "Oh my!" she murmured, raising her fingertips to her lips. "Why, that's a . . . that's a . . . and it's here." She raised her eyes to Aimee. "What would your mother say?"

Millie answered for her. "Nothing. She would have no idea of its meaning. The only reason we know that is the symbol of two people uh . . . you know . . . well, you know . . . is because you read it in a book and showed us one day."

"Why would a ladies' shop in London have a pagan South Seas symbol of lust on a gold brooch?" Jennelle wondered aloud, fascinated at seeing the symbol somewhere besides a picture in a book.

Millie turned away and sank down onto a nearby pink velvet settee. "Obvious. Some pirate must have sold it to someone, and they sold it again, never explaining its true origins and meaning. I bet that item was on a pirate's bandanna while he was murdering souls for their gold."

"Millie, you can be so melodramatic. Besides, this is a reproduction. Madame Summers is probably selling several of them every day," Jennelle commented, still staring at the item.

Aimee glanced down at the brooch once more before shaking her head and moving on. "Do you think we should tell Madame Summers its meaning?"

"Good Lord, no," Jennelle said abruptly, snapping her head up. "She would wonder how we would know. After our explanation, she would silently assume we conjured it out of some warped, country-girl amusement. Then she would tell anyone and everyone about our shocking behavior once we had left. Oh, the rumors."

They continued discussing the ramifications of such a revelation when two young women, followed by their maid, came from the back room, laughing and speaking excitedly and ignoring everyone around them. "Did you hear the

Marquess of Chaselton is back in Town?" a young, russet-haired woman asked the other.

"Yes, I am always informed of the most important news. He is so devilishly rich and passably good-looking. I hear he has finally returned to England in search of a bride. Now that he has inherited the title, he has to produce an heir." The proud woman had yellow hair to match her lacy day gown. Her eyes were large and black and her cheeks were fair, with just a touch of rouge. Based upon appearance only, she was a striking woman. Tall, statuesque, and lovely by all the conventional rules.

Millie, however, found the woman's voice excruciatingly grating.

"I hear he is called Chase by his friends," remarked her average-looking friend.

"Hmm, yes, I believe it is time to once again become London's *dernier cri*. The *ton* has been waiting patiently for me to choose my husband. And for that man's riches, I shall forgo applying my wiles to fill my bed and use them to fill my more long-term financial needs." The blonde pulled on her gloves, preparing to leave the establishment.

"Are you sure? You could have anyone you choose, Selena! Remember last year?"

"Yes, I do remember, and this Season, I am going to finally say yes. I, Selena Hall, am officially back on the marriage mart, and I fully intend to become the next Lady Chaselton." The two women left, barely aware of the four women they had passed when leaving.

Shuffled into the back room, the Daring Three had held their tongues while they picked colors, habits, cloaks, and gowns Aimee needed for the Season. Only when they were seated alone, with the landau's top up and secured, did Aimee and Jennelle explode. Millie sat in furious silence.

"Well, I never," Jennelle huffed. Adopted by the group as a little girl, she felt Charles to be her brother every bit as much as he was Aimee's.

"Can you believe that woman's effrontery? I have never before heard such arrogant presumptuousness from a person." Aimee was incensed.

Elda Mae was just as outraged. "Milady, your brother would see right through such schemes."

"I should hope so," Aimee said firmly.

"I understand Charles must marry someone," Jennelle ventured as she tried to secure a defiant lock of her auburn hair, "but I hope that vixen does not become your brother's wife. Having her as family would be quite awful."

Aimee tightened her hands into fists. "My brother wouldn't consider such a woman for even a moment."

"Do not be too sure," Jennelle countered. "He just may. I have read about women who set their caps for noblemen such as your brother. While we have witnessed her true nature, those creatures tend to have an unusual ability to hide their ugliest features when their prey is around."

"Hmm, and she was beautiful," Aimee said aloud, pondering Jennelle's words. She reclined against the cushions and crossed her arms.

Elda Mae pursed her lips and shook her head. "Maybe some would think that harridan was beautiful, but I stake my life that she has false hair as well as false bosoms, to go with her false personality, if you get my meaning."

Jennelle nodded. "Indeed, there was much to her that was insincere, Elda Mae. But there was something else about her that made me uneasy."

Millie spoke for the first time. "It was her eyes."

"Yes," Aimee said and turned to look at her friend. "It *was* her eyes. They . . . squinted so."

Millie suddenly sat up, accidentally knocking Elda Mae's

bonnet askew. "Oh, I am sorry, Elda Mae. But hell and the devil confound it, I have just had a *delicious* idea!"

"Oh no . . ." Jennelle's wariness sprang to life as soon as she saw the look in Millie's eyes.

Millie rapped the carriage roof and gave the driver the name and address of the modiste on her card. She then turned back and beamed at her friends. "We are going to have an adventure!"

Aimee was excited. "Fantastic!" she exclaimed, clapping her hands together.

Jennelle looked at Aimee as if she had just lost her mind. "Fantastic? Are you encouraging Millie's lunacy now?"

Aimee patted her friend's knee. "Do not fear, Jennelle. This time I am a completely willing participant in Millie's plan. And so are you. So, Millie, how are we going to save my brother? That is the focus of the adventure this time, is it not?"

Millie eagerly leaned forward. "It most certainly is. Now we know why we were destined to have a Season this year. We are here to save Charlie from a miserable marriage!"

Jennelle rolled her eyes. "I agree with the spirit of your plan, Millie, but can we keep the excitement to a minimum?"

Millie beamed a mischievous grin across the small compartment. "Against my nature, Jen, you know that. It would be as if I asked you never to read a book again." She turned to the other passenger. "Elda Mae . . . not a word. Promise?"

"Of course, Lady Mildred," the older woman replied as she made the sign of the cross on her breast.

"Not even to Aimee's mother," Millie added, knowing the workings of her companion's mind.

The carriage stopped, and seconds later the footman knocked on the door. All four stepped down from the carriage and looked around. Millie reviewed the card, and the address was indeed correct. Jennelle leaned over. "Are we supposed to be in the residential side of Town?"

Millie showed her the card. "I assume so. Mother Wentworth can be quite unconventional if she feels in the mood to do so."

Aimee nodded. "I think this is one of those times. My mother does have a sense of humor."

Millie went up to a massive red weathered door and knocked. Soon a lanky youth opened it and stuck his head out. "Eh, state your business an' be quick, I's got a pile of work waitin' on me," boomed a young voice with a strong cockney accent.

Aimee came forward and smiled at the long-limbed boy. "Hello. We are looking for a Madame Sasha. Does she live here?"

"She does," he said and then looked at each of them, clearly assessing their dress. "Hmm, youse obviously gots some blunt. Come in, but be quick. She as cross as crabs today, I tell ya. I gots to get back to the kitchen before the cook gets peltered up and goes into high fidgets. He's in high dudgeon today and likely to give me snuff just for openin' the door." The skinny boy opened the door wider and moved out of their way so they could enter. "Who should I say is callin'? Youse don't look like the widgeons the cook told me you'd be."

Jennelle's eyes popped open at the slang reference to an unintelligent female.

Aimee stepped forward and smiled. Its effect was instantaneous. "Thank you so much. Please let Madame Sasha know that we are here for her modiste services."

"Take yourselves into the study. I'll tell the madame 'bout your visit. Take care and don't touch the china. The missus is quite partic'lar that none o' her things gets broken. Never would believe the rake-down I gots just by nicking one o' dem things." He nodded and left. A few seconds later, they heard him yelling to someone at the back stairs.

All three looked at one another and then broke into laughter. "I wonder who he thinks we are."

"I do not know, but he was not fazed at all by our presence."

"Maybe even a little annoyed." And they all laughed again, made their way to the study to sit down and wait.

Several minutes passed by before the wooden study doors opened. A short older woman with graying brown hair and a portly figure walked in authoritatively. "May I help you?" Her English was heavily accented with a Russian flavor.

Millie stood up. "Are you Madame Sasha?"

The woman eyed Millie carefully. "I am. And you are?"

"Lady Millie Aldon." She cocked her head slightly and stared at the older woman. By the simple authority of her stance, it was clear she was no modiste. What was Lady Chaselton thinking? "Please let me introduce Lady Aimee Wentworth and Lady Jennelle Gent."

The Russian woman continued to stand just inside the study doors. "Hmm. Seems I am in the presence of high company, but I am unclear as to why. I am sure we have never met."

Aimee stood up and joined Millie. "My deepest apologies, madam. My mother suggested we visit, but I think there has been some misunderstanding. We were supposed to meet a modiste or seamstress. We are very sorry to have bothered you."

Madame Sasha raised her jeweled, wrinkled hand and dismissed the apology with a simple wave. She stared at Aimee for several seconds before asking, "Who is your mother?"

Aimee blinked. "Lady Chaselton."

"Would her given name be Cecilia?" The woman smiled as if recalling a fond memory involving Aimee's mother.

Aimee glanced at Jennelle and Millie, whose eyes were as large as hers. It was hard to imagine, but Madame Sasha and her mother knew each other, and based on the facial expression they were seeing on the woman's face—quite well. Aimee turned back to Madame Sasha and replied, "It is."

The woman's dark eyes gave them each a piercing look and then she hollered quite unexpectedly, "Evette! Come! Fetch my bag and tell Henry he needs to bring tea. My blend." Then, as if she had never bellowed a word, she turned back toward the group, composed as ever.

She looked directly at Aimee. "So, you are Cecilia's daughter. Hmm. You look like her—except in the eyes. But Cecilia is not faint of heart. Are you as timid as you appear and act?"

Aimee was taken aback, but Millie was incensed. "Aimee is no such thing. She has a venturous spirit, as we all do." Then, with more bite, she added, "She is simply the most polite of us."

Raising a single eyebrow, Madame Sasha replied, "I can see that you do not possess that fault."

Jennelle, who had remained sitting during this exchange, was perplexed. When was being polite considered a negative quality? "Madame Sasha. We are not in the wrong location, are we? You *are* the person Lady Chaselton suggested we meet. So, I assume that you know why we are here."

The portly woman turned and looked at the redhead with an unwavering gaze. "Yes. The dark, petite beauty here needs a wardrobe." The doors opened, and a young girl came in with tea.

Millie was able to keep her mouth closed, but her eyes were gaping. She swallowed. Jennelle reached up and encouraged her to sit down.

Millie plopped down beside her and leaned over to whisper, "Jennelle, I do not know what to make of this woman. Do you?"

"Not sure. Yet, it is clear she does know Aimee's mother by the way she reacted when she heard the name Lady Chaselton." The servant approached, and they both reached up to take the tea offered to them. Jennelle took a sip. "Mmm. This is excellent."

Sasha raised an eyebrow and responded, "Thank you. It is a unique blend I came across while in Russia. You," she said, pointing at Millie, "come here and let me take a look at you."

Millie set her cup down and went over to join Madame Sasha as if the Russian had control over her. When the woman clasped her waist, Millie managed to ask, "Who exactly are you?"

"I am Madame Sasha. I met her mother"—Sasha pointed with her chin to Aimee—"several years ago. She helped me out of an . . . hmm, unusual situation. Quite a woman, your mother is. Most willing to elicit exciting activity."

Millie was not daunted. "That does not explain why she directed us to you. Especially for our coming-out wardrobe."

"Let us just say that for certain friends, I am willing to extend my design services. No doubt, Cecilia sent you my way because of your coloring and your height. Most of the modistes around here are set up for clients such as Cecilia's daughter. The *ton* tends to be partial to tall, slender blondes. You, on the other hand, are dark-haired and quite short."

"I am petite," Millie countered with some bite.

Unfazed, Madame Sasha replied, "Yes, but not dumpy. You have a long neck and your bosom is ample but not enough to be considered large." Aimee and Jennelle looked at each other, wide-eyed as they listened to the woman continue.

"You have a natural grace to you and seem to have a commanding presence despite your size. Your dark hair and the unusual color of your eyes create a remarkable contrast. And even with your obvious athletic ways, you have managed to keep your skin from the sun." She took another sip of tea. "Yes, there is much we can do here. Is there some young man's attention you intend to capture this Season? For once

I am finished, you will be able to secure any gentleman of your choosing."

Millie bit her bottom lip and caved in to the compulsion. "Are you serious? Is it truly possible that a dress can make me look tall?"

"Hmm, maybe not tall, but I can make all the other women wish they were short." She offered a conspiratorial smile to the group. "Now, Evette, my bag."

For the next two hours, Millie was prodded, measured, poked, and stabbed, but did not mind at all. Madame Sasha turned out to be an adventurer, or at least had been one in her youth. She related story after story of her life before she had come to England. Tales of Russian nobility, interactions with the German Hessians, and late-night romantic escapades in Paris. The only tale Madame Sasha would not disclose was how Aimee's mother had aided her in becoming a London seamstress with a very particular clientele.

When they left, Millie had no idea exactly what creations to expect, only that they would start arriving within a few days. "Well, that was an experience."

"Indeed," replied Aimee. "A most delightful one. I wonder how my mother and she met. Madame Sasha seemed most determined not to say, despite Millie's clever forays into her past."

"Jennelle, it is time for you to enjoy the pain of a visit to the modiste," Millie said, stretching her back to ease her aching muscles.

Jennelle followed them into the carriage. "I do not suppose I can encourage any of you to delay this until tomorrow."

Millie shook her head. "Certainly not after what I just endured, and I hate such tedious activity. No, it is only fair you suffer as we have."

"Millie's right. And the sooner we leave, the faster it will be done and over with. Address, please, Jennelle." Aimee leaned over to procure Jennelle's card from her hand and gave it to the footman.

What seemed to be just minutes later, the carriage stopped again in front of another town house. Millie hopped onto the cobblestones in front of a small but much older home.

"Seems your mother has another friend she has helped during a pinch," Millie murmured aloud as her friends joined her.

Aimee agreed excitedly. "I wonder what type of gem this modiste is. What's the name, Jennelle? It might give us a clue."

"Hmm. Melinda Brinson. There is no title."

Millie raised her skirts and ascended the cracked stone staircase. She clicked an old brass knocker several times. "I hear the crying of a small child. Are you positive we are at the correct address?"

The question was still lingering in the air when a pretty woman in her twenties opened the door. Tendrils of strawberry-gold hair were loose from her braid, and she appeared to be quite harried. "Yes, may I help you?"

Aimee stepped up. "We were sent to meet a woman. Are you by chance Mrs. Melinda Brinson?"

"Yes, I'm Melinda Brinson." Crying erupted again from the back of the townhome. "My apologies, can you come inside for a moment? I need to see what happened."

The foursome entered as the young woman disappeared down a dark, narrow hallway. "Let us wait in here," Jennelle suggested, pointing to a makeshift sitting room just beyond the front door.

Moments later, Melinda appeared again, holding a small child with drying tears on his cheeks. "Again, my apologies. I was not expecting company today. May I help you?"

Millie took charge and went over to pick up the baby. "Come here, little one."

Meanwhile, Aimee tried to offer some clarification. "Do you

know my mother, Cecilia Wentworth?" she asked, deciding to use the name Madame Sasha had recognized.

Melinda smoothed back her hair as her brows came together, indicating sincere thought. "No, milady, I am afraid I do not. Should I?"

Jennelle let an "oh my" escape before she could stop herself.

Aimee smiled apologetically. "I think there has been a mistake. We were here in search of a seamstress. My friend requires a few gowns to be remade for some upcoming events. If you do not know Lady Chaselton, then somehow there has been a misunderstanding."

"Oh, but I know her son, the Marquess of Chaselton." The woman smiled in relief now that she was able to place the party and their purpose. "And I *am* a seamstress. I know that I do not have a shop, but I promise you I am talented as a dressmaker. Do you have the gowns with you?"

Jennelle looked confounded. "No no. My apologies. I did not bring the gowns themselves with me this afternoon. Of course, I *will* bring them. Today I was expecting to discuss only what you could and could not do."

Millie was bouncing the baby on her knee, cooing to the child, hoping it disguised her shock. It was the second time that day her composure had been unexpectedly and thoroughly rattled. The first blow came in the modiste's shop when that dreadful woman spoke as if Charlie was an easy mark and catch. The idea of Aimee's brother searching for someone to marry had not occurred to her.

This second blow was almost worse than the first. Mrs. Brinson was not only affable, but uncommonly pretty with red-gold hair and a figure that all women aspired to have. If she had money or a title, she would have the attention of the *ton*. But Mrs. Brinson had neither and still somehow, Charlie had met this affable woman and mysteriously decided to assist her.

Millie continued to bounce the babe, refusing to admit that a little bit of envy was at the root of her frustration. She was not accustomed to the sensation and did not like the feeling. She forced herself to shake it off and re-engage in the ongoing conversation.

Melinda nodded enthusiastically. "That would be more than enough. The gowns in those styles had yards of extra material. The current Grecian look uses a fraction of the cloth, and I would be able to completely change the appearance of the original gown. Please give me a chance, and I will prove my value."

"No need. I trust you and look forward to your creations. You seem to be blessed with a most enviable artistic eye." Jennelle smiled at the pleasant woman. "I will have my gowns delivered to you tomorrow. Design, change, renew as you will. I have complete faith in your abilities. It has been a real pleasure meeting you, Mrs. Brinson."

The four women exchanged a few more pleasantries and then left. Upon request, the driver had lowered the top of the landau for their return trip to Hembree Grove. Aimee leaned back against the plush burgundy cushions, enjoying the sensation of the light breeze, and said, "I cannot believe it."

Jennelle fell for her conversational hook. "Believe what?"

"Millie's maternal instincts. Yes, I believe out of the three of us, she is the most family oriented."

Millie glowered at her friend. She was still feeling restless not knowing the details of Charlie's relationship with the beautiful seamstress. "Bite your tongue, Aimee. I am nothing of the kind."

"No, Millie. I think Aimee has assessed the situation correctly. I have never seen you with children until today. You are a natural," Jennelle countered.

"I never knew you had it in you, milady. But I expects Lady Aimee here has the right of it," Elda Mae added in a singsong voice.

"Just because I can be kind does not mean that I have an aptitude for such domestic activity. I was merely being polite," Millie stated, clearly agitated.

"I'll drop the subject, then," sighed Aimee as she leaned over to view the passing buildings absentmindedly.

Millie nodded. "Excellent idea. So, when do you want to discuss how we intend to disrupt one very arrogant woman's plans?"

Jennelle sighed and smoothed out her skirts. "Let us do it after dinner. I'm exhausted. All of this primping and such wears on one," she said, hoping for some time to read a book she had found about one of England's most influential royals—Queen Emma, the fair Maid of Normandy.

"I agree," Aimee sighed. "What a day. If things continue to be this exciting, I just might like London."

Millie sat back watching the Bond Street beaus strut around doling out their rolls of flimsies as if money grew on trees. Aimee was correct. London was becoming more than what she bargained for. She had anticipated adventures, but never one that involved her heart.

Chapter 4

"I told you why, Charles," Cecilia Wentworth stated resolutely.

For the past three nights, Chase had been tormented with rousing dreams of Millie. Dreams in which Millie came to him dressed in a thin, clinging silver gown. She would stare at him with luminous violet eyes, smile, and then urge him to join her in some grand adventure. Her spirit, spontaneity, and passion would cause his body to come ablaze with a physical need for her that he could not explain or defend. And without going into these details, he was finding it difficult to convince his mother that Millie must leave.

Chase realized it was customary for Millie and Jennelle to stay with his sister and mother in Dorset during the summer. As a young man, he considered it a nuisance, but now it was dangerous. Millie was not just causing arousing images in his dreams at night, but also when he encountered her during the day. He could no longer deny that he physically wanted her, but he was unwilling to accept that he also longed for her in other ways. She was *little Mildred Aldon,* for God's sake. She was like a younger sister. But each time he had seen her this past week, either near or at a distance, she felt less and less as such. Either she or he needed to move out of Hembree Grove. Soon.

Chase ran his fingers through his hair and glanced at his mother warily. "I think it best that Millie stay with her father while in Town."

Cecilia Wentworth looked briefly across the study at her son, then reached for her tea and continued reading a letter that had arrived earlier. "I know, dear. You have stated your feelings quite clearly already."

"To no avail, I might add."

"Hmm. This new tea blend that Millie coaxed from Sasha is truly delicious."

Chase clenched his jaw. "Mother, as the new lord . . ."

Cecilia interrupted her son and gave him a pointed stare. "So, Lord Chaselton, before you issue an unwise command, will you explain why it is *only* Millie whom you have requested to leave?"

Chase was momentarily stunned, realizing his blunder and the fact that his mother had caught it. "Of course I meant Jennelle as well."

"I see," Cecilia replied and then slowly lowered her letter. "Yes, well, that would be somewhat difficult, if not impossible. Jennelle's father went back to the country to study some odd piece of literature, and Lord Aldon is forever at Tattersalls, busily preparing for the upcoming Derby." She took another sip of tea, snapped the pages of her letter, and began reading anew. Just before Chase could counter her argument, she casually added, "Lord Aldon has an excellent chance at winning the upcoming race. I saw his horse—a lovely little stepper—and he has procured quite the top sawyer for a jockey."

Chase recognized the not-so-casual change in the conversation's direction, and his frustration mounted. He knew his mother had won, but he was still unwilling to admit defeat. "And, pray tell, how did you come to learn of all this?"

"Charles, dear, to be successful in London, one has to be kept informed of the latest *on-dit*. Do not think I attend teas and play cards for sheer entertainment. Believe me, I have other methods to alleviate my boredom. That is why I will stress again how important it is for the Three to remain together—here at Hembree Grove."

"Fine, then. Have them stay, but damn it all, it is most inconvenient."

Cecilia Wentworth put down her cup and looked directly at her son. "I do not care if you curse in my presence, son. I am not offended by such nonsense as one's choice of words. However, it *is* important you escort them, and it *is* important the Three have each other this Season. As a member of the male side of our species, I would think it would be clear how much you may be needed to weed out any incompatible suitors."

Chase clasped his hands behind his back and began pacing. "Ha! They don't plan on having any suitors at all! They fully intend to become spinsters."

Cecilia folded her letter and placed it back into its envelope. "So you have said before."

"And you do not seem to be concerned at all with their latest nonsensical plan."

Cecilia began humming, quite low and almost imperceptible. It was something she did when her late husband would arouse her ire and she wanted to do the same in return. "I'm not entirely sure I think it is nonsense."

He stopped and stared incredulously at the beautiful but definitely batty woman pretending to be his mother. "Surely you don't want them to remain unwed!"

Cecilia Wentworth carefully put down her cup and stood. Her stance was both regal and firm. "I *hope* they find someone who will understand and treasure them as they are. I hope they are fortunate enough to find a man who makes them as happy as your father made me."

Cecilia had accepted her son's explanation for his unexpected arrival in Town, but both knew something besides escorting his sister and her friends for their first Season had prompted his early return. Charles's visits had been scarce these past eight years. His involvement in the Peninsular War had forced his stays at home to be few and far between. But neither he nor his father would explain the necessity of his continued absence. Every time Charles had returned home, he and his father would spend hours discussing and strategizing the war. They both denied it, but she knew them too well to be persuaded otherwise. She had worried, but she never interfered in their plans.

Cecilia eyed her son thoughtfully. "Charles, what is troubling you?"

Chase stiffened defensively. "Nothing. I just don't want my sister to become a spinster." Chase strode over to his desk and pretended to be interested in some papers. His demeanor was calm and composed. Many would have said he was relaxed or even bored. Only a few people who knew him very well could have sensed his tension, and his mother was one of them.

"What nonsense. Have you taken a good look at the Three since you have returned? Not one of them has a chance of fulfilling that promise. Tonight you will understand exactly why it is they need each other, how important their pledge is, and the low probability of it lasting." She walked over and laid a hand on her son's rigid arm.

"Charles, I know you are here for your own reasons, but please, look out for them. They need someone they can trust. Millie, especially. She loves adventure, but she needs a safe, strong port in the storm to which to return. Of the three, she seems to be the most restless these days. Millie appears strong, but believe me when I say that she is the most vulnerable."

Millie, vulnerable. The idea was both absurd and plausible at the same time. Unfortunately, the concept of being restless was also all too familiar.

He looked up and saw his mother's golden eyes beseeching him. "I promise," he murmured.

Lady Cecilia had been watching her son mentally work through whatever real issues he was having with Millie. Relief filled her when he promised to be the Three's escort. "Thank you," she said, giving his arm a last squeeze before letting go. "Now, I will go and see what is taking those girls so long. We need to leave for Lady Bassel's within the half hour."

Tonight was going just as expected, Jennelle thought. Admirers flocked, and then they quickly scampered away. Just as Mother Wentworth predicted, gentlemen gathered by her side singing songs of loveliness and enchantment, but just as quickly, they disappeared. If she kept mute, the men adored her. However, when she tried to shift the conversation to anything meaningful or interesting, the empty-headed fops quickly vanished, whispering words that would infuriate most ladies.

Jennelle was neither ashamed nor embarrassed at being called a bluestocking. In fact, she took pride in it. She wished more ladies were interested in books, learning, and scholarly pursuits. She often longed to have been born just a few decades earlier. Then she could have joined the real Blue Stockings Society and met with like-minded ladies who actually gathered to discuss literature and other matters, not sit about frivolously bandying shallow words.

In the past few hours, Jennelle had made more mindless small talk, labeled more women as gabbers, blabbers, and bleaters, and choked back more insulting words than she had thought possible in a lifetime. After tonight, she would dread

any and all Society events. Thank the Lord, she had to stay
here and endure this torture for only six weeks.

Tonight has been absolutely dreadful, thought Aimee. It
was just as her friends thought it would be. *Millie, you should
have found a way to delay our Season for at least one more
year*, she mentally admonished her friend. Surrounded by
vain men, dancing with wishful suitors, and making pointless
conversation, Aimee wondered how any intelligent woman
could find these events pleasurable.

Aimee knew she appeared to be the model young lady—
affable, sociable, intelligent, and beautiful. In reality, she
wanted only Reece. Last Christmas, she finally got the man
to admit that he had feelings for her. That was all she needed
to keep her faith constant. Although he told her to find
someone else, that he was not right for her, her heart had not
wavered. For the next few weeks, Aimee would act as was expected of a young, titled, wealthy, unmarried lady coming out
for her first Season. She would attend these social events, but
only to please her mother.

Boring, boring, boring. Millie spoke the mantra to herself
repeatedly. Tonight was incredibly monotonous, tedious, and
worst of all—dull. Every conversation centered around one
of two topics: upcoming social events or the current crush
and its participants. Each time a gentleman asked her what
she thought of someone else's gown, she had to fight the urge
to break out into fits of laughter. Where was the quick wit of
London's dandies that she had heard so much about?

Tonight is unquestionably successful, thought Lady
Chaselton. Her daughters were the epitome of beauty, grace,

and poise. They were surrounded by admirers from the moment of their arrival and had handled them expertly. Despite the farce of charm they displayed, Cecilia knew they were suffering and miserable.

It did not matter. Later in life they would understand, just as she had discovered, that true adventure lay ahead of them if they could find the right man to share it with. Most likely, those men were here. It did not matter that the majority of gentlemen who attended these events were vain coxcombs, foolish dandies, or elaborate popinjays. She had known only a few nonesuches, like her late Charles, who were unequalled titled peers. The Three's fierce devotion to one another would enable them to quickly weed out those without promise and force them into accepting the ones who did.

Tonight could not have gone any better, thought Chase as he stood by an alcove, watching the crowd. He had been successful in spreading his message. Soon he would meet with Eischel and relay his unexpected discovery. Until then, he could concentrate on his familial duties. As it was, he knew his mother was going to give him an earful for ignoring his chaperoning responsibilities so quickly.

As soon as they arrived, he had spotted his first opportunity to begin finding the man who had murdered his father. Unfortunately, that meant abandoning his mother, his sister, and her friends before they even had a chance to remove their cloaks. He knew his behavior was odd and uncharacteristically rude, but it could not have been helped. Time was of the essence. Now that his message had been delivered, he could make up for his earlier neglect.

Chase hid his surprise as he watched Sir Edward begin a seemingly aimless stroll toward him. Having been a student of Sir Edward's, Chase knew he never did anything without purpose. It was clear the man wanted to speak with him, but it was also obvious that Sir Edward didn't want anyone else to realize his intentions.

Edward was an average man in both size and girth, with only one noteworthy feature—that he looked much younger than he was. Born to a somewhat successful merchant, Edward Lutton joined England's war department at an early age. His pleasant but forgettable looks, as well as his ability to pick up languages, quickly enabled him to become the perfect spy.

After years of working in the field for his country, Edward was knighted and took on the position of training others to follow in his footsteps. Two of his finest products were Reece Hamilton and Charles Wentworth. At first, Edward was reluctant to train a nobleman born to such a prominent title. But Lord Chaselton convinced him to meet his son and his friend and to tutor them personally. Edward eventually agreed. Their collaboration during the war had saved countless lives.

Edward paused next to Chase as if he had just recognized him. "Lord Chaselton?"

Chase inwardly smiled, but no emotion registered on his face. "Sir Edward."

"So that is you. It has been some time. Didn't know you were back in London."

"Just recently."

Edward licked his lips and nodded. "Sorry to learn of your father. He was a good man."

"Yes, he was."

"Heard they call you Chase now." Edward smiled. "Beats Erndale," he added, referring to the title Chase used before his father had passed.

"It does seem easier to remember," Chase said as he downed the last of his ratafia. He took fortification where he could find it. Unfortunately, that meant enduring Lady Bassel's favorite potent red wine.

"Aye, that it does. So what brings you into Town? Haven't seen you in some time."

So this is the reason for the visit, Chase concluded. *Edward is curious as to whether I am here for war or familial business.*

Chase lifted one shoulder in an elegant shrug. "I've come to escort my sister during her first Season."

"Escort, eh?" his tutor said in disbelief. Edward glanced around the crowd, feigning a search for Aimee. "Ah, there she is. Your sister is quite the looker. Takes after your mother, I see. I do not envy you this Season. No doubt you will be quite busy shooing away the unworthy suitors."

"I expect so. She seems to have already spoken to several gentlemen."

"Has she? Do you think she will get a response?"

Chase raised a single eyebrow at his old mentor. Edward had effortlessly launched into double talk, referring to Aimee instead of asking outright about Chase's earlier activities. Chase decided to play along, curious as to Edward's intentions.

"She seems to believe so. The men she spoke with appeared to be interested in what she had to say," Chase answered, referring to his own discussions.

Edward coughed and bobbed his head. "Well, good for her. But tell her not to be too eager. Nothing good comes of it. If she is, in truth, here for her family, that's fine. But otherwise, she's waited a long time to come to Town. You might want to warn her that others might find her first actions odd. One does not rush into London and meet privately with so many men so quickly without a purpose."

Chase heard the warning. His old friend, though retired for several years, had obviously not given up his long-perfected habit of being aware of all that was around him. "I will be sure to tell her," Chase replied without emotion.

"Good. Now I have to find the dark-haired beauty who struck my fancy earlier this evening."

Chase's eyes widened in surprise. "Really, Edward. Which widow are you chasing after, this year?"

"Don't know exactly. Appears to be a maiden, but she certainly is older than most of the green chits who stroll through here each year. But if she is pure, she is unlike any maiden I have ever seen. Quite bewitching."

Chase raised an eyebrow. "She must be. I thought you avoided the messy entanglements that tended to accompany unwedded ladies."

"Usually I do—probably still do, but her eyes charmed me as if I were a snake emerging from a wicker basket. Take care, Chaselton. Perhaps I will see you later this Season."

"Possibly," Chase replied as he watched his mentor and friend blend in with the crowd and emerge again as one of many admirers surrounding a female of the Season.

As he was about to scan for his three charges, one of the men surrounding Edward's current interest moved, and Chase glimpsed the woman attracting so much attention. Millie. Suddenly, Edward's words came back to him—*dark hair, bewitching eyes.*

Chase had taken precautions before they left to minimize his time with Millie. He had waited outside until all the women had shuffled into the Wentworth carriage. When they arrived, he had disappeared into the crowd before she had removed her cloak. Now, seeing her for the first time in her ball gown, he realized he had been either extremely wise or enormously foolish in staying away.

She looked like an ethereal sprite visiting from heaven. Her orchid-colored gown slithered down her trim frame, giving her figure the illusion of height while accentuating her delicate features. The gown's slightly longer train was simple and unembellished, only adding to Millie's natural, regal beauty. The neckline was trimmed in stiffened white and silver lace, framing her neck as it scooped from one small puffed sleeve to the other. Two strands of pearls matching the ones in her hair completed the look. Chase stared transfixed at the woman he used to call *twig*.

As the crowd continued to swell around her, he felt unbearably possessive, as if he alone had the right to be in her company. Trying to craft a reason to remove every admirer from her presence, he suddenly saw the group disperse. It was as if by the mere wave of her hand, every man happily decided to give her space. He seized the opportunity and walked to her side.

"I'm impressed . . . Mildred." He had not intended to use her hated name, but tacked it on at the last moment. Just seeing her, so beautiful and composed, bothered him— enormously. It would be impossible to pretend any longer that she was still little Mildred Aldon. The feeling left him desperately and futilely seeking any means of gaining the upper hand.

Millie bristled. "Why, if it isn't Charlie Wentworth. You have been quite the busy man this evening," she said, looking at the crowd, never visually acknowledging his presence.

He smiled at her rejoinder. "I thought you were going to start calling me Chase. Though *my lord* sounds quite nice, coming from your lips."

"If I were greeted by the gentlemanly Lord Chaselton, I might be inclined. But, alas, I seem to be in the presence of someone who is acting similar to a mocking young man whom I once knew by the name of Charlie."

One eyebrow rose in admiration. "You have managed to preserve your quick wit, sprite. It can still easily cut a man in half."

Millie gave in and looked at him, exaggerating his height by raking her eyes up and down his tall frame. "Unfortunately, my wit has never had the ability to reduce your sense of self."

Chase could not keep himself from grinning. "Glad I was able to hide it from you."

"Bah. You never hid anything from me. You were always annoyed with me, and you certainly let me know."

Chase shrugged noncommittally. "You would be, too, if you constantly had to interrupt more important activities to chase down a mischievous little girl bent on hurting or killing herself." He stepped in a little closer and whispered, "Maybe you secretly liked it when I saved you."

Millie's stomach fluttered. She squeezed her eyes shut for a moment and got her nerves back under control. "Such abysmal attempts will not work."

"What won't?" he choked, realizing he was too close. It was hard enough to match wits with Millie, but being so near, her scent filled his head, claiming his senses. Suddenly he was in his dreams again, agonizing to know the taste and feel of her lying naked beneath him.

Millie eyed him warily and turned back to watch the crowd. "This little stratagem you are trying to apply. It will not work anymore. You used to intimidate me or provoke me by twisting my words around. I'm older now and recognize those types of ploys used by gentlemen."

Chase was instantly surprised and jealous at the same time. Unaccustomed to the sensation, he did not like the feeling. Who were these men trying different methods to manipulate Millie? He never believed himself to be a possessive man, and tried once again to convince himself that the stirring within him was only a brotherly need to protect her.

Millie interrupted his racing thoughts. "Be honest with me, Charlie. Enough of the superficial banter. You mysteriously disappear as soon as we arrive, to meet with several odd gentlemen, and now you come over here seemingly to pick a fight. What is really on your mind?" Millie wondered if Chase would admit his real purpose for being in London, for it was definitely not to escort her and her friends.

Chase watched her with unfathomable eyes. "Again, I am impressed, sprite."

Millie gave him a placating smile and returned her gaze to the dancing couples. "Sprite, now, is it? Whatever happened to twig?"

"That nickname definitely no longer suits you. I don't believe you realize how lovely you look this evening. Something of a mixture of youth, innocence, and regal beauty. It is as if an angel came down from heaven and transformed you into one of their own." Leaning down, he whispered into her ear, "But your angel forgot to replace your impish grin. Bedevilment still rides there."

Millie brushed the comment aside. "Such flattery, Charlie. I know not whether to swoon at your words or retaliate." As soon as she voiced the two choices, Millie deftly and quickly—so that none saw—elbowed Chase in the ribs with painful precision.

Grimacing in genuine distress, he replied, "I noticed you chose the latter."

Facing him now, she looked up at him and very innocently commented, "Oh, my deepest apologies. Did I hurt you?"

"You tried."

His denial caused Millie's eyes to snap with frustration. "It was a natural response to insincere adulation. I assure you that if you spoke similarly to any woman of gumption, she would have reacted in a like manner."

Chase's eyes locked with hers. "Trust me when I say this, Millie. You are unlike any woman I have ever met or will likely meet in the future. You are one of a kind. An original. And you *are* stunningly beautiful tonight."

Her breath caught in her throat. He was telling her the truth. Chase thought her pretty. She had never wanted to be pretty before, but now that she heard the words, she suddenly wanted very much for him to consider her beautiful.

Studying the intricate folds in his cravat, she cleared her

throat and tried to return the compliment. "Well, uh, thank you, Charlie. You look very fine, too."

In truth, he looked amazing. So amazing she continually returned her vision to the crowd to prevent her from stammering. He was dressed in a black, perfectly tailored jacket that, with his white waistcoat and cravat, emphasized his muscular build. His black trousers were tight fitting and revealed the sleek, powerful contours of his legs. And each time her gaze connected with his, he seemed able to see right to her very soul, leaving her completely naked and vulnerable.

Chase sent her a speculative, sidelong glance and wondered what she was thinking at that very moment. "So are you going to tell me how you did it?"

Still thinking about how solid and large his body was, how completely masculine he appeared, she was caught off guard by his question. "Did what?"

Chase moved his arm in front of them, indicating the lack of company. "How you so easily cleared the drooling crowd of men surrounding you earlier."

Her eyebrows rose. So Chase had been watching her. "Hmm, when I was younger I would have offered a lot to know how to do something the great omnipresent Charlie Wentworth did not."

Chase gave her an irritated look. "Mildred, what are you talking about? What is all this babble about omnipresence?"

Millie shrugged. "Oh, nothing, really. When I was young, I used to think that you had the ability to be anywhere and everywhere."

"That's nonsense," Chase responded.

"I agree, but I could never figure out how you always seemed to know when I was doing something that you thought I oughtn't."

"Simple. I followed you." Watching her eyes narrow, he probed again. "So? What is your secret?"

Millie sharply shook her head, releasing a couple of locks of hair so that they framed her face in a most appealing way. "No, I do not believe I will reveal my methods of dispersal. It is an enjoyable sensation, knowing how to do something you do not. It is an infuriatingly uncommon event, and I would like time to bask in the feeling."

Chase dropped his voice to a quiet, private whisper. "You could teach me a number of things, Millie."

The change in his voice made her insides race with sensual excitement. She had to regain control of the conversation and her emotions. If she continued to allow him to flatter and tease her, she would be completely flustered. And to be flustered around this new, very male Charlie was dangerous and unwise. She had to turn the tables on him—now, and fast.

"I spoke with your friend Sir Edward this evening. He's one of the few gentlemen whose conversation I thoroughly enjoyed."

Alarm shot through Chase. He caught her wrist and deftly maneuvered her to a more secluded area in the room. "What do you mean, *you conversed with him*? I thought he had just met you when you sent all your admirers scurrying."

She rubbed her wrist, resentment darkening her eyes. "Hmm, no. We met and danced earlier. He was telling me how he used to be a spy. Is it true?"

His insides clenched, wondering just what game Edward was playing. "I think it would be wise if you avoided Edward in the future."

"Why? You were talking with him. Besides, I like him."

"You should. He's a likable man and a good one. But he is also much older than he looks and is used to playing in a field that uh . . . well, requires no commitment in order for a gentleman to be entertained."

Millie flashed him a blindingly bright smile. "Yes, I surmised as much. Regardless, I think Sir Edward and I could be friends. Besides, he now owes me a favor."

Millie was doing it again. She had total control of the conversation, making him batty with the double talk. She could give Sir Edward lessons. "Friends? A favor?"

Millie twirled around the private alcove, feeling free to be herself for the first time that evening. "Indeed. I might have let it slip that if it was a beautiful and *available* woman's attention he sought, Mrs. Wollsen would be amenable. She's lovely, intelligent, and searching for a new partner." She stopped twirling and chuckled to herself. "Remind me to inquire if he *embraced* my suggestion."

Shock filled Chase's expression. "Mildred Aldon, what in all that is holy is going through your mind? *Ladies* do *not* suggest paramours to men they barely know!" Sensing her imminent retort, he added, "Not to any man—ever!"

She placed her hands on her hips and tried for a cool, amused tone. "Excuse me? Should I call him back and declare that I have had second thoughts and would love to entertain the idea of him as a suitor?" Watching Chase stumble about for a quick reply, but finding none, Millie snorted, "That is what I thought."

Chase's mouth tightened. "How did you even know of Mrs. Wollsen's particular inclinations?"

Her chin came up proudly. "I didn't. At least not until I met her a few hours ago, and then her intentions became quite obvious. Upon introductions, I sensed a bit of friction from her, but once I conveyed that neither Aimee, nor Jennelle, nor I intended to encourage *any* man's attention . . . we got along splendidly. I do hope we can become good friends. She was quite intelligent and capable of stimulating conversation." Millie paused and gazed wistfully around the room. "Something that seems to be lacking in most of the ladies of the *ton* wandering about tonight. Jennelle must be going mad."

Chase's head was spinning. "I'm going to regret this, but

I must ask. How did you *convey* your intentions? Did you tell Mrs. Wollsen of your marriage plans, or lack of them?"

Millie wrinkled her nose, and once again Chase found it strangely appealing. "Of course not. Your mother would be horrified and extremely ashamed if any of us verbalized our promise in public. I used . . . a type of . . . woman's language."

Chase rubbed the back of his neck. "You could try a saint, Mildred. Explain. And do not attempt to tell me that you can read and send thoughts."

She crossed her arms and looked at the tall, frustrated figure in front of her. "Sometimes, Charlie, you propose the strangest ideas. Suffice it to say—and you will just have to take my word for it—that women have other ways of speaking to each other beyond that of speech."

"Millie . . ."

"No, seriously, Charlie. I'm being earnest. A man and a woman could meet another couple on the street and exchange greetings and walk away. The men would have thought from the conversation that their companions knew each other and were friends. However, in reality, both women told each other quite the opposite. I don't know a better way to explain it. There are just some things women can best say without using any words. And *that* is how Mrs. Wollsen knew I was no threat."

Chase nearly choked on her response. "Bloody hell. Come with me," Chase said, bridling his inner thoughts.

As he grabbed her wrist again, she managed to utter, "Where are we going?"

He stopped abruptly and faced her. "I am either going to throttle you, kiss you into submission, or dance with you. Given we are at a ball, and what my mother's reaction would be to the second suggestion, that leaves dancing. Believe me, if all things were equal, dancing would not be my preference."

Seconds later Millie was whisked into a waltz, gracefully

performing one spin after another. Despite their difference in size, she and Chase moved remarkably well together, as if their sense of timing and balance had been tuned only for each other.

Millie wanted to ask which of the remaining suggestions had been his preference but was afraid he would reply with throttling. So she remained silent and enjoyed the first pleasant dance she had experienced all evening. She had never waltzed with Chase before, and now that she had several other dances to relate it to, she knew there was no comparison.

Chase thought he handled the rest of the evening superbly, all things considered. He danced with his sister and Jennelle and again with Millie. And all three were out of character. Instead of the daring, outspoken women he knew them to be, they held themselves as refined ladies with impeccable manners, graceful in all ways, including conversation. No one would guess their true natures. He was about to suggest they leave for the next event, when he was suddenly accosted by a beautiful woman in a pale blue dress with her hair dressed in ringlets.

"Oh no," Aimee whispered.

The tone in her voice caught Millie's attention. "What?"

"That Selena woman has Charles trapped." Aimee, Jennelle, and Millie had been surprisingly successful in their covert plans to keep the shrew away from Chase, but the woman was relentless.

Damn her lack of height. Desperately, Millie sought some way of looking over the multitude and seeing what her tall friend witnessed so easily.

Jennelle gasped as she saw Millie climb onto the edge of a potted plant. "Millie! Get down from there!"

Millie ignored her friend's plea as she spied Chase walking arm in arm with the yellow-haired vixen who called herself a debutante. He was smiling, and as he disappeared outside, Millie witnessed him laughing. Actually *laughing*. Forgetting where she was, Millie stomped her foot, missing the edge of the pot. Instantly, her slipper was soaked in mud.

"Bloody hell."

"What? What happened?" Then Jennelle saw Millie's face. "What did you do?"

"Help me down from here. Aimee, you might want to go locate your mother. It appears we will be leaving shortly."

Aimee looked relieved. "Thank you, Millie, for coming up with a reason for us to depart." Aimee kissed her friend's cheek and rushed off to find her mother.

Jennelle was not so easily mollified. "Though I echo Aimee's sentiments about leaving, what actually happened?"

Millie lifted up the hem of her dress and showed the grimy results of her impulsive behavior. "Do you think anyone noticed?"

Jennelle exhaled, shaking her head. "No, most likely not. Even standing on that pot you barely were above normal height."

Millie grimaced. "I hate the feel of mud between my toes."

"You? The queen of all things adventurous?"

Millie shot Jennelle a scathing look. "Stop it. That was no adventure. That was just a dismal display of clumsiness. Whatever is Charles thinking?"

"Charles?"

"I mean Charlie."

"You said Charles."

"Same person. What's the difference? *You* call him Charles."

Jennelle smiled as if she had some secret that others would dearly love to know. "Oh, it is just that I do not recall ever hearing you refer to Charles by any name other than Charlie. But as you said, completely insignificant," she finished mischievously.

Millie was about to clarify Jennelle's obvious attempt

to read into something that was not there, when Cecilia Wentworth arrived.

"Oh dear." Cecilia looked at the pot that had done the deed and sighed in understanding. "Well, I suppose one must improvise when one needs to observe a man."

Not wanting to explain who the man was or why, Millie remained silent. Jennelle and Aimee protectively gathered around Millie to hide the bottom of her dress as they moved toward the front door. They said their good-byes and made their way to the Wentworth carriage.

No one saw the man in the shadows silently watching them. He quashed his rage. He would have other chances, he reminded himself. Plenty of opportunities. He was, after all, a man of means, money, and title.

Once inside the private rolling sanctuary, Cecilia sighed and removed her gloves. "Well, we departed a little earlier than I planned. No doubt, most believe we are on our way to the next crush of the evening, and therefore we will receive no undue notice. You were all a smash hit, and I am proud of each of you."

Millie envisioned a supple, tall viper attaching its hooks into Chase. "It appears our entire party was successful. Some so much they are still being entertained and are unaware of our departure."

Cecilia waved her hand, dismissing Millie's telling comment. "Do not overly think on such matters. I sent a message to Charles letting him know we were leaving early and that I would send the carriage back around for him."

"Oh no," Aimee whispered. She looked at Jennelle and Millie. Each of them silently worried that Selena would try to fulfill her promise.

Cecilia Wentworth watched as the looks of fear filled her daughters' faces. "Don't let Charles concern you girls so. He will see through Selena Hall. She is more transparent than she believes."

Aimee turned to her mother. "You know about Selena?"

Cecilia scoffed. "Well, not until tonight. But it became obvious that Charles was this year's catch after seeing her try to corner him all night. She looked too pleased with herself when she finally did. That seemed to happen near the time you had your accident, Millie. Did you happen to see them?"

Millie tried to sound indifferent. "I believe he was laughing as he escorted her out into Lady Bassel's garden."

Cecilia smiled to herself. Charles and Millie would make an excellent couple. That afternoon, her son had been so adamant about Millie leaving—not Jennelle, just Millie. Now, Millie's very strong reaction to Selena's flirtation had Cecilia convinced it would be her adopted daughter, not Selena Hall, who would become the next Lady Chaselton.

Cecilia would have to be careful and ensure the proper distance was maintained. On the other hand, with these two stubborn, independent creatures, a certain degree of proximity was critical to success. And if two people ever needed each other, it was Charles and Millie. He would be her anchor, her steady rock. She would be his salvation, bringing life into all the dark crevices he never let anyone see. Even as a child, Millie was the one person who could unsettle her all-too-composed son.

"Oh, isn't that nice. It is so good to hear that Charles is laughing again," Cecilia commented blithely.

Millie clasped her hands together and looked out the carriage window. The arrogant man deserved that she-devil, she thought and then instantly retracted the words.

Cecilia continued. "So aside from Charles and the dreadful Selena, what did you think of the evening?"

All three sat in silence, unable to think of a response. They didn't want to spin tales, but how could they relate how very dull it had been?

Looking at her charges, Cecilia wished Millie's mother were here. She would be able to make them understand. "Come now. I know that it was ghastly, but what delightful tidbits did you discover? Please tell me you observed something in the few hours we were there."

Blinking several times, Aimee ventured, "Mother, are you saying that you knew we were not enjoying ourselves?"

Cecilia sat back and chuckled. "Of course, I knew! Believe me, when Millie's mother and I went to our first ball, we were just as miserable. But we learned to make our own fun. To do that, we first had to discover who the players were," she said with a wink.

Millie sat back and grinned. "Lady Bassel wears a wig."

Aimee shot up, looking at her with wide eyes. "She does not! Does she?"

Jennelle piped in. "She does. I saw her repositioning it in the powder room when she didn't think anyone was watching."

"Sir Gant wears a girdle," Aimee added, not to be bested.

Millie bristled. "I know. I felt it when he asked me to dance with him. Doesn't he realize that a lady would notice?"

Cecilia smiled and stated, "Probably believes that you think he is strong and athletic." She relaxed against the cushions, listening to her prodigies relate all they had heard and seen. She was pleased they could so easily spot the people who possessed sincerity and those who played others false. Yes, tonight had gone exceedingly well.

Chapter 5

The next morning Millie decided to forgo joining the others in the dining room. She had been awake for most of the night and her patience to endure the chatty conversations that often accompanied the morning meal was limited. Unlike her nocturnal self, all of the Wentworths—Aimee, Charles, and their mother—were morning people with the strange ability to rise before nine o'clock. And though awake, without the fortitude of sleep Millie did not think she could answer any of the questions that were likely to arise—such as the status of her dancing slippers.

After what seemed to be an interminable amount of time, her stomach refused to let her wait any longer. Millie opened the doors to the dining room, hoping the morning crowd had left to continue their conversations in the salon. But as soon as she entered, her hopes of sneaking quickly in and out died.

"Millie, glad you have finally arrived, my dear," Cecilia Wentworth said as she rose to greet her. "It seems you were a complete success last night. Already you have received three invitations from gentlemen callers."

Cecilia subtly observed Chase's demeanor abruptly change from partial awareness of the conversation to keen interest. The mention of Aimee's and Jennelle's callers had not had the same effect. Cecilia smiled to herself, feeling quite contented. Chase was definitely interested in Millie—more than he realized.

Hearing how the Daring Three had already created a stir among the *ton* did not come as a surprise to Chase. All three had been completely captivating. Jennelle's auburn hair and shapeliness had fascinated the men—that is, until she revealed her intelligence or their lack of it. His sister, the classic Society beauty, also delighted those who had met her. Yet it was Millie, with her stunning dark hair and petite features, who had stood out in last night's crowd. She had conducted herself impeccably, comporting herself as the daughter of an earl seeking to be a duchess. She had laughed and smiled and appeared to all to be having a lovely time. After a single encounter, men were entranced by her charm.

Before the Season was over, Millie would be surrounded by would-be suitors desperate to enjoy even one kiss. He knew. He was already one of them. And Chase wasn't sure he liked the idea.

"I'm already dreadfully bored," Aimee mumbled, looking warily around the much smaller party, which included both dancing and a musical interlude by a woman who could not sing. The three of them huddled close to one another, each afraid that at any moment some large, uncoordinated man would grab them for another dance.

"Bored? I would sincerely love to be just bored. I cannot express the pain I am suffering even at this very moment. My toes have been trampled mercilessly," Millie moaned as she kicked off a slipper and reached down to rub her aching feet. "I told you we should have attended the theater again."

"Millie, good Lord!" Jennelle hissed. "What if someone should see you?"

Millie rolled her eyes and continued her massage. "Hopefully they would realize that I absolutely do *not* want to dance again. Besides, no one can see me with the two of you standing there."

Jennelle crossed her arms. "This is ridiculous. We have been in Town less than two weeks, and the only respite we seem to have found is in complaining. We need to find something besides these silly parties to amuse ourselves."

"Exactly! We need a new adventure," Millie exhorted as she quickly stood. The plan to keep Selena Hall away from Charlie had been somewhat successful, but not completely. Not only did it entail attending one boring function after another, it required constant vigilance. Unless the Three were willing to entertain the idea of causing bodily injury, Miss Hall was going to find ways to force herself into his company.

Jennelle began pacing as she tapped her finger against her lips. "Well, there are Society meetings."

"And I understand there are some very interesting museums," Aimee piped in.

Millie couldn't believe what she was hearing. "Museums? Society meetings? Do I know either of you? We need excitement, *adventure*."

Jennelle elbowed Aimee and whispered in her most medieval brogue, "Beware what cometh next. The sorceress plots even now and shall lead us unto temptation."

Undaunted, Millie continued. "We could always dress in costume and venture toward Vauxhall Gardens."

Aimee gasped. "Mother would kill you—and us."

Millie ignored her friend's warning. "There is also Astley's Royal Amphitheatre. I read a circular telling of circus events such as horseback riding, clowns, and acrobats. Oh, how I have always wanted to see acrobats."

Having been subjected to the repercussions of similar conversations, Jennelle grabbed Millie's arm. "Millie, it just is not done. Well-bred ladies do not attend such events. Especially unmarried ones, as we three are."

"Jennelle, when did you become such a priss? What do you care if someone thinks me boisterous and unladylike? I am no more playing at deception than any one of us is. You know you would rather be reading a book than pursuing a man. And you, Aimee, you pine away for Reece, all the while pretending to be available and interested."

"Enough," Aimee said forcefully. "Everyone is right. These parties *are* boring. We all want adventure, yet we all know we cannot pursue the things that inspire us. Jennelle, I know how frustrating it has been, speaking with those who are ignorant and have no interest in expanding their minds. And as for me, I do want Reece, but, for Mother's sake, I am trying to at least appear flexible. And despite tonight's mumblings, you have been wonderful, Millie. The *on-dit* is that you are quite the original, but if anyone got a whiff of how original, we would all be doomed."

Millie frowned, and after a brief moment nodded her head. "Perhaps you are right. There must be some acceptable adventures around us. We just need to find out where."

Aimee and Jennelle exchanged looks. Millie's acquiescence had come a little too easily. They would have to keep their eyes open and ensure she did not get herself—and them—into trouble.

But despite their fears regarding Millie's growing restlessness, the remainder of the party continued as it began—eventless. At least for them.

All evening, Selena Hall had contrived ways to be near to, speak to, or literally hang upon, Chase. Millie could not understand why the woman and her scheming ways bothered her, but they did. So much so that even during the carriage ride home, she could not focus on the conversation.

Sitting across from her, Chase was also pensive and quiet. Millie wondered if his silence stemmed from the absence of

Miss Hall's company. With each encounter, the time he spent with her grew.

"Did you see Mr. Gerthing, Jennelle?" Aimee asked, completely shocked by what had happened.

"Of course I saw. Everyone did. Including Mrs. Gerthing . . . finally. It was awful."

The buzz inside the Wentworth carriage was filled with awe and shock. Only Millie and Chase remained silent as the others discussed the one notable event of the night.

"I heard someone say Mr. Gerthing has been acting in this lewd manner for years."

"And Mrs. Gerthing only noticed tonight?" Jennelle shook her red head in disbelief.

Aimee shrugged her shoulders. "Appears so."

"I don't believe it. We were there only a few hours, and all of us noticed it. Mrs. Gerthing may be a dull-witted woman, but she is not blind," Jennelle replied, skeptical that anyone could be so imperceptive.

"Some women only see what they want to," Cecilia offered.

Jennelle countered, "How can you miss seeing your husband squeeze women's derrieres all evening? And I cannot believe that rumors of his appalling behavior have never met her ears."

"I'm just glad he did not attempt such a move on me," sighed Aimee, shaking her head.

"I, also, am thankful to have escaped. But a strange little part of me wished he had attempted his uncivilized stunt on our Millie, though," Jennelle mused aloud.

Aimee nodded. "It certainly would have spiced up the evening."

The sensation of possession and protectiveness suddenly surged through Chase, causing him to respond before he considered how his abrupt reaction would be perceived. "He didn't touch you, did he?" His voice was low, demanding, and the question was directed toward Millie.

Jennelle noticed the swift change in Chase's body and tone and silently wondered at its meaning. Aimee, however, was oblivious to her brother's sudden reaction. "Hah, I only wish."

Confused, Chase asked, "Why would you want someone to mistreat Millie?"

His sister smiled as if she knew some great secret. "Not just someone—Mr. Gerthing. And the reason is that he wouldn't have gotten away with it as he did with all the others. Probably the worst thing that is going to happen to the man is that he finds himself sleeping in the parlor for the next fortnight. If Mr. Gerthing attempted such a stunt on our Millie, he would never be able to paw a woman again."

"I see," Chase replied skeptically.

Jennelle carefully regarded his doubting expression. "I doubt that you do. Millie?"

Millie turned to look at her friend. "Yes?" she replied, speaking for the first time since leaving the party.

"What would you have done if Mr. Gerthing had tried any of his revolting antics on you?"

Millie narrowed her eyes. Jennelle's question had mysterious and duplicitous undertones. "I am not altogether positive how I would have responded."

Jennelle took a quick sidelong glance at Chase and decided to press the issue. "Yes, you do. How much of the toad would you have damaged? His hand? His arm? How about his smug face? I would have loved to see that pompous expression wiped off it by one of your fancy moves."

Millie rolled her eyes. "My, look who is being dramatic now." She took a deep breath and exhaled. Jennelle was about to ask again when Millie put a hand up to stop her. "Enough. Yes, I most likely would have disabled his hand. And depending on what he did and where, his injury would have been permanent. Satisfied?" she asked, not expecting a reply. Feeling strangely uncomfortable discussing her skills in front of Chase, Millie moved the carriage window's thick brocade curtain aside, hoping to find something outside to focus on.

Chase regarded her for several seconds as she stared out the small window. She had meant every word. Millie truly believed she could inflict harm on a much larger and stronger man. And while the concept seemed ludicrous, he knew it to be otherwise. "I have no doubt that you could."

Chase's low, serious tone compelled Millie to glance at him, and she was instantly seized by his heated gaze. The others in the carriage disappeared and she became aware of only Chase and the mysterious pull growing between them. It frightened her, but she could not look away. Then Aimee leaned forward, cutting off their intense gaze. Millie felt herself yanked out of their private realm and was back in the carriage. She immediately resumed her study of the passing buildings and fought to steady her racing pulse.

Aimee lightly tapped Chase on the knee. "You would be amazed at what she can do, Charles. Millie is quite the expert in defense. She has taken on and defeated every stable lad we have ever had. She is so good they run and hide anytime she comes near."

Chase sat back and contemplated the delicate-looking woman who had just been declared quite dangerous. "Is that so?"

Millie dropped the brocade, sat back, and quietly stared at him. Chase knew Aimee spoke truthfully. And he knew why.

As an adult, Millie was considered petite, but that was only after she had had two summers of highly welcomed growth spurts. Before those blessed years, she had been constantly teased and harassed by bigger and older children. That was, until Charlie came along one day and witnessed such an occasion. Outraged, he secretly worked with her one summer, teaching her ways to protect herself that did not require girth, but speed and accuracy. No longer believing herself helpless and vulnerable due to her small size, Millie had begun to seek adventures wherever she could find them.

The carriage rolled to a stop, and the footman hopped down to open the door. Chase and Millie were the last two to emerge. Before she could join the others, Chase reached out for Millie's gloved hand. Her pulse was beating at an accelerated pace, and his lower body tightened in response. "So you continued practicing?" he whispered for her ears alone.

She looked directly at him with gentle eyes full of gratitude. "That summer you gave me the greatest gift anyone has ever given me. You gave me the ability to be me." Millie held his gaze for several more seconds before turning to follow her friends inside.

Chase watched her disappear, still mesmerized from their silent exchange. Millie was evoking feelings he had never expected to experience upon his return to London. He had come back for one purpose. To complete his father's mission.

Eischel had either failed to receive word he had arrived or was unable to meet. Neither boded well. Chase had only one other option: to continue with his original plans. But one misstep and the traitor would end Chase's life. The possibility of becoming sidetracked was unacceptable.

It was also unavoidable. How could it not be, when the one woman who had reawakened his sexual desires slept just down the hall?

"Millie, would you care to concentrate? If not, I am going to find a whist partner who can exhibit more intelligence than that of a pea."

Jennelle was beyond a little frustrated. The last few card parties had offered only inane games based solely on chance. She hated faro and believed only the most mentally challenged could enjoy betting on what card would next appear from the bottom of a deck. Tonight was the first party featuring her favorite game of strategy. And Millie was ruining it.

"What was the leading suit?" Millie asked. Hearing several people grumble "hearts," she laid down a trumping card. It was the first trick she had won in the last quarter of an hour.

Normally, Millie enjoyed playing whist, especially with a ruthless partner. Jennelle, an outwardly passive person who typically liked to watch and examine others, transformed into an aggressive opponent during a competitive card game. Both she and Millie were usually a formidable duo, able to gather an alarming number of tricks. But tonight, Millie had not been able to concentrate and lost more than one hand she should have won.

As usual, Chase had escorted them to the evening's event and disappeared shortly after. Millie wondered if anyone else suspected he was using his chaperoning duties as a mask for a hidden agenda. She considered broaching the idea with Aimee and Jennelle, but knew their response would be one of skepticism. Especially after tonight.

Once again, Selena Hall had seen her prey and pounced accordingly. And again, Chase seemed to welcome her company. Neither of them chose to play cards; instead they walked about, laughing and talking in hushed tones as if they were becoming best friends. The scene was nauseating.

Unable to focus, Millie asked Aimee to take her place. Desperate to find any type of distraction, she rose too quickly and bumped into something wide and very solid.

Millie turned and looked fixedly at a handsome man with elegantly chiseled features. His sandy brown hair was cut fashionably short, with trimmed sideburns. He was of average height, but he carried himself in a way that made him appear much taller. His smile was charming, and he moved effortlessly.

Dressed in a snug but well-fitting maroon coat, a matching

waistcoat, and tan breeches, he looked impressive and alluring. Then Millie saw his cravat. Unlike the simpler, shorter version Chase preferred, this dark-blond gentleman wore a pink cravat folded in a most complicated way. Encircling the outside of his collar, the neckcloth became absurdly large before being intricately knotted and turned down. Rather than fashionable, Millie thought it made him look pretentious and artificial.

He bowed with practiced flair and spoke. "Do not concern yourself overmuch about your cards, my lady."

Millie looked up, confused, and curtsied automatically. "I apologize for my running into you, sir. However, I am unclear as to why I should be worried over my cards."

"Whist, my dear. A very difficult game to master. You should not feel distressed regarding your performance."

Millie stared flabbergasted at the irritating fop while trying to keep her temper under control and her jaw from becoming slack. The pompous man actually called her *my dear* before he insulted her. He might look like a dandy, but he was a complete oaf. "I think, sir, that it is your turn to apologize to me. Such endearments usually are *bestowed* upon one, and only then when agreements are in place. If you would excuse me."

The man's eyes narrowed in burgeoning anger. He was being dismissed. Women attached themselves to him. They did not dismiss him. He forced warmth into his voice. "My deepest apologies, my lady. I assure you, I meant no offense."

The tone of his apology was like warm honey, but Millie noticed it did not reach his eyes. "Yes, well, thank you for your kind words, but I must . . ."

Determined not to miss another chance, he interrupted. "I am Lord Marston. I have wanted for some time now to make your acquaintance." Leaning in closer, he deftly captured her hand and bent down to kiss it. Slowly he rose and whispered, "Are these parties not dreadfully boring? I believe you may be one of a handful of women who could recognize the sheer monotony of the Season."

Ensnared by words of a kindred spirit, Millie ignored her instincts to leave. "My lord, you have uttered the very words of my soul."

Marston smiled, and the ice shards in his eyes began to melt. He exhaled. The wait had been worth it. Assuming the blond Wentworth chit would eagerly accept his attentions, he had moved in too quickly. The woman was nothing like her appearance and quickly drove him to scurry away. But he was no fool. No, this time he had hidden, listened, and learned about his new target. He considered himself fortunate. While the blond wench might have been a more direct line to his goal, the brunette was much more his type.

Mere minutes ago, he had unwittingly insulted her and almost missed his chance. Now that he had her interest and attention, it was imperative he kept it. "I was afraid this Season would resemble the rest. Exceedingly dull, and therefore, for me, exceedingly short."

His voice was low and intense. Millie was both intrigued and cautious. "If you find them so dull, my lord, then why do you attend?"

"Ah, but it is not all dreary and monotonous. There are a few times in which London is the most exciting of places to be."

"Are you seriously in earnest? I find it difficult to understand how you can characterize any of these events as exciting," Millie said, her spirits suddenly deflating.

"Maybe not the events themselves, but I assure you, London can stimulate the soul. Why, this Saturday for instance. Vauxhall Gardens is having the most marvelous masquerade party."

The mention of London's notorious entertainment venue recaptured Millie's interest. "Vauxhall Gardens? Have you been there?"

Inwardly laughing at her naïveté, Marston answered, "Why, of course! How could one ever visit London and not go to Vauxhall? Only old dowagers, tabbies, and easily offended maidens avoid the Gardens. Do not tell me you have not yet attended? I had thought you, with your wit and zest for fun, had at least visited the stimulating venue."

Millie absentmindedly rapped her fan against her palm. "Oh, I am going. As soon as there is a break in these endless social events."

"Ah, then it is only a scheduling problem that prevents you from enjoying one of Town's more entertaining settings. That is easily remedied, and I encourage you to do so at once. I mean, Vauxhall's is done by simply everyone. Or at least by those with any spirit. I cannot imagine attending only tea parties, these horrid little gatherings, and crushes every other night, without having some element of fun."

"I wholeheartedly agree with you. I am beginning to understand why many young women accept offers so early in the Season. I half believe it is to avoid having to endure any more card parties."

"You are quite refreshing, lady . . . ?"

"Oh, my apologies. I'm Lady Aldon."

"Ever a pleasure. I wish we could have met earlier. I tried at Bassel's when you so deftly shooed all of us would-be admirers away. I am so glad my continued efforts are now being rewarded."

"Admirers? Efforts? Are you implying, Lord Marston, that you are a would-be suitor?"

"Quick intelligence as well as beautiful. A dangerous combination for men like myself."

"You did not answer the question."

"Based on my observations from afar, I seriously doubt my suit would be accepted. However, I can and would like to be your friend. Perhaps we could be secret adventure partners?"

Ignoring every instinct she had about him, Millie fought to suppress her desire for illicit excitement. "I am a well-bred lady, my lord. Women do not entertain secret partners, nor do we plot escapades of adventure."

Millie remembered Mother Wentworth's words: *We learned to make our own fun. To do that, we first had to discover who the players were. . . .*

Millie wondered, *Could Lord Marston be one of those people? And how does one make one's own fun?*

Marston heard Millie's halfhearted refusal but was not offended. He could see by the sparkle in her eye that while she did not know it, she was firmly ensnared in his web. He would ease away now, only to spring upon her later. Before the Season was half over, he would have what he wanted. It was his destiny.

"I cannot *believe* I let you talk me into this, Millie." Jennelle's voice was laced with skepticism and repressed excitement.

"She didn't *talk* us into doing anything. It was more like threatened," Aimee corrected.

"Blast it! Shush! If I had known either of you were going to be so unusually whiny, I never would have requested your company."

Millie situated her mask and got out of the unmarked carriage, leaving her dark cloak within. Aimee and Jennelle followed suit.

Supposedly needing a reprieve from the constant nights of balls, parties, and theaters, the Three had convinced Mother Wentworth that they could miss this night's scheduled events. After hearing the doors close and the carriage leave with Mother Wentworth and Chase safely inside, Millie had run to one of her trunks and opened it. Aimee and Jennelle were rendered speechless as Millie pulled out three elaborate gowns of different eras.

"Why, Millie . . . are those . . . I haven't seen those since . . ." Jennelle had mumbled, unable to hide her shock.

"Oh, my cursed teeth! You didn't bring those!" Aimee hissed.

Millie had smiled and nodded. "Oh yes, I did. Jennelle, here. This black one, I believe, is yours. The gold can be for none other than our blond seductress. And me? Why, I shall be the virginal maiden in white!"

Aimee and Jennelle had robotically collected their gowns and stared for a moment, hesitating before Millie chided them. "Oh, please. You cannot tell me that you are anything but just as eager to wear these gorgeous ensembles as I am." Seeing their unconvinced expressions, Millie had let go an exasperated sigh and pressed again. "Lord love you both, but we *are* going to Vauxhall Gardens. We will be wearing masks. No one will know our identities."

Aimee had watched as Millie reached into the trunk once more. She knew Millie would venture to the famous resort alone rather than miss this opportunity for fun. And though Aimee feared encouraging her daring friend's adventurous ways, she did want to see the Gardens. And this could be her one chance. "No one will know our identities? How can you promise such a thing? Anyone we run into will know us in an instant."

Millie had thrown three sparkly items onto the bed and then reached down into the trunk to pull up an assortment of wigs. "Not if you are wearing these!"

Looking at the elaborate masks lying beside her and the fanciful items in Millie's hands, Aimee had realized Millie's plan just might work. "Where in the saints did you get these?"

Millie had grinned mischievously. "From Madame Sasha."

"You told Madame Sasha!" Aimee exclaimed.

"Calm yourself, Aimee. It was not *I* who raised the subject of Vauxhall. It was Madame Sasha. I was telling her about all the gowns we had discovered in your attic. She asked if I brought any of them to London, and, well, I could not lie to her. She would have known. I suppose she surmised the possibility of our venturing to the Gardens. Anyway, she handed these to me with a promise not to ask where she and your mother procured them and then used them. Now, here, let me help you with the back."

Two hours later, Millie sauntered into Vauxhall with a confidence Jennelle had always envied, especially in situations like this.

Aimee took a few deep breaths, telling herself it genuinely was quite exciting. Vauxhall was *the* pleasure garden of the Thames, offering an assortment of entertainments. She looked at Millie and mentally garnered her poise. After all, Millie was completely unrecognizable, just as Jennelle was.

The summer before they had turned eighteen had been a bittersweet one. Searching the attic during a rainy afternoon, they had found a trunk of old, elaborate silk dresses. Jennelle had immediately recognized them as French theater dresses that were highly fashionable—and highly recognizable—as "working women" wares.

The gowns were daring, fun, and beautiful. Unconcerned with their meaning, they had often donned the garments. One afternoon, the Three were playacting when Aimee's father found them. Lord Chaselton had never before yelled or cursed at the girls, but he had more than made up for it that day. It was the last time they had even touched a stitch on the bold clothing.

Later that night, he had invited them into his office and had given them each unique presents. Aimee and Jennelle maintained the gifts were symbols of Lord Chaselton's remorse for being so harsh. Millie would have agreed if it had not been for the terrible dream she had had the night before, and his private explanation that he hoped the item would give her some comfort.

Then the next week his heart failed, and all three gifts were left in the attic, with everything else they held precious. Until Millie found them as she was packing to leave for London. She fingered the pendant she had been wearing almost every night. It felt good to hold his memory close. No longer did the loss feel so intense, and Millie suspected he was out there somewhere, quite pleased with his Daring Three.

"Relax, J," Millie instructed, using their secret childhood designation. "Come this way. The path is fairly well lit and I can hear music. If we are lucky we are not too late for the fireworks show."

"Did you say fireworks?" Jennelle asked with sudden interest.

"I did," Millie replied with a knowing smile. Her friend was finally mentally—and not just physically—committed to their outing. Several years ago, Jennelle had read a couple of articles on fireworks and convinced the Three to create some themselves. Explosions had happened, but not quite in the sky. Afterward, Aimee's father banished any and all fireworks on his premises. The Daring Three's entreaties to try again had fallen on deaf ears. And though their mishap terminated any further personal experiments, it had not ended Jennelle's interest in the lively diversion.

Jennelle righted her shoulders and waved her hand. "Then let us not dally, M. Lead on!"

In the shadows, a man with wavy, dark blond hair watched as the three women ventured farther into the Gardens. He decided to remain hidden and wait.

He prided himself on the forethought to hide and follow them after they had emerged from their home earlier. If he had not, it was doubtful he would have recognized any of them behind their masks and their bold garments. Definitely old-fashioned, but at the same time, very appropriate for tonight's hedonistic theme at Vauxhall.

He had hired a hackney to follow their unmarked carriage, and then stealthily entered the Gardens, waiting for the right time to approach. Soon Mildred Aldon would be alone. Until then he would be patient. It would be an hour or so until the fireworks, and the comments from the scholarly redhead made it clear that none of them would leave before they had seen the display.

"Lady Aldon, we meet again."

Millie's pulse began to race. She whirled around to see a man emerge from the shadows wearing a common dandy's outfit and a plain mask. Lord Marston obviously intended to be recognized. What was disturbing was that he knew her identity as well. She thought that nearly impossible.

Millie rallied herself and responded. "Pardon, my lord? I think you have me confused with someone else. I do not believe I know a Lady Alstan."

Marston smiled at her intentional mispronunciation. "Ah, well, then my apologies, madam. However, I must say you look delectable this evening . . . my lovely nameless one."

His comments and tone of voice were unnerving, and Millie wished she had not left Jennelle's and Aimee's side to get a better view of the tightrope walkers. "You are forgiven. Now I must get back to my friends, my lord."

Marston's blond eyebrows shot up as he moved to block her way. "Leaving so soon? One would think you were running to find the arms of another . . . say, the Marquess of Chaselton."

Millie fought to avoid revealing any visible proof of her

heavily beating heart. "The Marquess of Chaselton . . . why would you think I was going to meet with him?"

The lips below the scant mask smiled into a disingenuous smirk. "Only that many women this Season seem to be drawn to the man. For instance, the lady I had originally believed you to be—Lady Aldon—is extremely interested in the marquess."

Again flustered, Millie opened and then closed her mouth, searching for something to say. But even when she found her voice, she found it difficult to speak. "I think you misinterpret Lord Chaselton's . . . relationships. I, for one, have long been in acquaintance with the lord. But I can promise you that I am not *drawn* toward him. Rather the opposite, as we often find ourselves taking the opposing sides of an issue."

"How a gentleman would ever consider differing with a woman of your startling beauty is a great mystery."

Millie tightened the grasp on her fan. "I mean every word. Lord Chaselton and I usually bicker regarding my inclinations. He is not one for any type of sport that provides for levity or amusement." As soon as the words escaped her lips, she rebuked herself. Lord Marston could no longer have any doubt with whom he was speaking.

Marston leaned in closer and lowered his voice. "My lady, if you desire companionship during these, um, inclinations, I would be delighted to take on the duties of a friend who encourages and supports your enthusiasms, rather than hinders them."

Marston's quick and abrupt interest made Millie uncomfortable. However, she was even more intrigued to understand the true cause of his curiosity and decided to stay. "Have you ever considered that you lavish your charm on a person rather profusely? Especially on someone you have never met?"

Marston smiled at Millie's attempt to continue her facade. "I must confess, the possibility seems rather improbable.

Most women desire men to impart a constant barrage of compliments about them. You, however, are unquestionably not most women. A lapse in my judgment that shall not happen again."

His unsettling voice and close presence made Millie remember her initial impression of Lord Marston. She had been incredibly naïve. Marston had lured her here, for this very evening. She had fallen for his light banter and inducements for adventure, like a fool. The man had specific motives for introducing himself and drawing her to Vauxhall. Millie wanted to know why.

"You suppose a great deal, my lord. Our encounter tonight was a bizarre happenstance. I doubt there will be another time when we shall meet again," she said deprecatingly. Millie hoped he understood that she was aware of his games, and was not going to naïvely participate in them any longer.

Millie saw his jaw clench. Marston moved in closer and spoke softly. "I shall not need another time, my lady. I only need tonight. You see, you have . . ."

Suddenly Millie's arm was yanked by a very strong grip. "Excuse me, but this lady came with me."

The very tall man began hauling her away, and Marston, doing nothing to stop him, quickly retreated without a word. At that moment true fear engulfed her and as she was about to retaliate, Millie found herself without her mask, looking up at a very angry Charles Wentworth. He had brought his face within inches of hers so that she had no trouble seeing just how blazingly furious he was.

Chase knew only sheer luck had enabled him to save her this evening. Learning the Daring Three had elected to avoid the night's events, Chase had disentangled himself from the Octopus—his new endearment for Selena Hall— and returned home to work on some communiqués and try again to locate Lord Eischel. He was surprised to be interrupted by a footman who asked if he still wanted the unmarked chaise to be made ready, or if he would prefer to use the Wentworth carriage.

Chase had been about to dismiss both vehicles when he sensed a Mildred Aldon plan brewing and lay in wait to see what and where the Three were going. After one look at their outfits, he knew their destination: Vauxhall. Nowhere else in London could masked women dress as though they were extremely high-class French demimondes.

He had quickly located his own mask, donned his jacket, and rushed to prevent his sister and her friends from getting caught in their latest foolish adventure. He arrived later than he had anticipated, and the crowd was growing. If he had not seen their dresses, they would have been impossible to find, let alone discern their identities. He hated to admit it, but their outfits were rather ingenious and their masks very concealing.

"You little fool," he hissed.

"Chase! How did you know we were here?"

"I saw you leave Hembree Grove. Of all the half-brained, rash things you have tried, Mildred Aldon, this has to be the most reckless. Do you know what would happen if someone actually *recognized* you dressed like that?"

Millie barely suppressed a scathing retort about that being impossible when she remembered someone *had* recognized her—Lord Marston. Millie pursed her lips and decided it was not the ideal time to impart that piece of information. "We were just preparing to leave. Jennelle wanted to see the fireworks."

"Don't try that with me, Mildred." His gravel-toned voice brooked no disobedience.

Millie swallowed. He had used her given name, and she should be bristling with indignation. Instead, powerful emotions threatened to take over. Their mysterious connection had again flared to life, and suddenly Millie was intensely aware of him as a man. His lean, solid body, the strength of his hands, his masculine scent—all contributed to the unfamiliar feminine urges being aroused under his golden gaze.

Millie slanted him a defiant glance and reminded herself how much she hated his male arrogance. "I would appreciate it if you would stop using my full name," Millie admonished and started to back away, puzzled as to why she all of a sudden found his arrogance to be appealing.

Chase clamped a hand over her wrist, eliminating any further retreat. "Right now, I'll call you whatever I damn well please. In fact, I'm half inclined to place you over my knee."

Millie managed a polite smile as cold anger flared to life. "Try it, Charlie Wentworth, and you'll regret it. My fighting abilities have significantly improved since you stopped your instructions. And if you continue to provoke me, I'll be inclined to give you a lesson," she warned, struggling to keep her voice low.

"Your threats affect me less today than when you were a child, Mildred. And if you think you can palm off Jennelle as the cause and instigator for tonight's foray into potential disaster, think again. And after seeing you alone with a man, cozying up to him, do not think you can persuade me that you were preparing to leave!"

Millie gave him her most wintry smile. "My, that's quite a lot of thinking you have me doing when I have only a *half a brain*."

"And I am not sure even that half is working, with what I just witnessed."

Millie's eyes popped open in defense. "And just what did you just witness? Some man cornered me and asked me a few questions. It is not as if he accosted me, swung me into a dark path, ripped off my mask, and started berating me. Now, if a man did something like *that*, I could understand why you would be upset if I did nothing about it."

Chase took a deep breath and raked his fingers through his hair. "You could try a saint."

"You practically are one, with all of your holier-than-thou attitudes, opinions, and most of all . . ."

Millie did not have a chance to complete her sentence when Chase manhandled her again without warning. Suddenly she was pressed tight against his chest, his mouth capturing hers in a searing kiss that made her body yield in submission. Only temporarily stunned, Millie was about to fight back when she heard nearby voices talking . . . about her.

"Come along, darling. This man is experiencing the pleasures of his lady's lips. I want to experience yours."

Millie felt relief when the overly sultry voice faded away as the couple rounded a hedge farther down the path. Then alarm shot through her. Chase was not ending the kiss.

At first, Chase had pulled her into an embrace to protect her. Crushing her lips with his own, he had not expected nor wanted her to respond. The kiss was hard and commanding, in retribution for all the trouble she had caused him. But when her lips trembled, and he felt the shiver of fear that went through her entire body as the couple went by, a surge of desire swept over him.

The kiss changed from one of retribution to one of passion. Somewhere in his mind, Chase knew he should stop. But he could not summon the will to ease her away. Not yet. Cradling her face in his hands, he deepened the embrace, kissing her slowly, thoroughly, knowing no man had ever kissed her this way before. Never had the touch of soft lips so quickly and fully aroused him.

He brushed his lips lightly, persuasively, across hers, encouraging her mouth to open. The moment her lips parted, his tongue surged inside in an act of possession that excited her more than any daring escapade she could have conjured.

Millie moaned softly as her hands clung to his shoulders as a whirlpool of deep, feminine curiosity started swirling within her. Her throat constricted with desire. She felt alive in a way she never had before, and she wanted more—needed more. This was an adventure her body demanded she not end too soon.

Feeling her arms steal slowly up around his neck, a sense of triumph washed through Chase. His dream lover was real, and she wanted him with a passion that equaled his own. Heightened desire shuddered through Chase, and his already aroused body tightened even more with fierce, compelling need.

Never had he wanted a woman as much as he wanted Millie. She was a firebrand, a constant whirl of energy, a blinding beam of light in his otherwise orderly world.

And then he remembered.

His world was a dark, dangerous place, and every day it became only more perilous as he learned about the men that his father had called friends. The honest passion he was finding with Millie was everything he had ever dreamed of having, but he could not do this. Not now. Maybe not ever.

A cool breeze floated across her lips as Chase ended the ardent, stirring embrace. Millie's heart was racing; her senses were muddled. Uncertain how to handle the strange new sensuality Chase had ignited within her, she clung to him for both comfort and support. Burying her head against his chest, she held her breath.

Chase had kissed her. Really kissed her. Until tonight, the small pecks she had been given by young men attempting to attract her interest were all she had ever experienced. The idea that a man could create such powerful feelings seemed ludicrous until now. She had never dreamed of kissing anyone so . . . intimately. She certainly never thought she would like it.

But she did.

Millie was aware that over the past few years she had blossomed into an attractive woman who could interest the opposite sex. However, not once had a man interested her. Until now. Until Chase. Charlie made her feel like a disruptive schoolchild in need of reprimanding, but Chase . . . he made her feel something entirely different. In his arms, she not only looked like a woman, but felt like one.

Entrapped by its implications and the lingering sensation of their kiss, Millie had not heard Chase ask her repeatedly for the location of Jennelle and Aimee. "What?" Millie asked as Chase lightly shook her a second time. He returned her mask. "Oh, thank you," she replied, absently sliding the white beaded cover back over her face. "Aimee and Jennelle went to see the fireworks. I had heard there were acrobats and left to find them."

The white of her mask only accentuated the deep violet of her eyes. Chase forced his inflamed desire back under some semblance of control. He needed to get the Daring Three home and avoid being alone with Mildred Aldon.

Before she could argue or respond, he seized her hand in his just as explosions could be heard across the main garden. "Good. The exhibition just started. They should still be there. Let us go," he muttered, heading toward the crowd of fireworks spectators.

Lying on her bed rethinking the night's events, Millie heard a light tapping at her door. She sat straight up in her bed and whispered, "Yes?" Jennelle tiptoed in.

Millie tried hard not to show her disappointment. She knew it would not be Chase, but when she heard the knock, her heart had stopped for one moment, hoping to see him step through her door.

Jennelle, misunderstanding the sadness on her face, tried to mollify her friend. "Millie, I just came in to thank you. I do not care a fig if Charles did find us at Vauxhall. I had a marvelous time, and I owe it all to you. So don't be too offended by his lecture. He was only trying to protect us. You are not terribly upset, are you?"

Millie shook her head. "No. Although it has been awhile, I am still rather impervious to Charlie's sermons."

"Well, take care, get some sleep, and know that Aimee and I had a wonderful time—just as you promised."

Millie watched her friend leave, and lay back down. Not a minute had passed before she heard a second light tap. This time she was not surprised when Aimee entered.

"Millie, are you awake? I just wanted to reassure myself that you were not too distressed regarding your promise to never enter Vauxhall again."

"No, not too terribly. Especially now that I have been there."

Aimee smiled and hugged herself. "Oh, it was exciting, though, wasn't it? I'm so glad we went. What an adventure— just like you said. Although someday I hope to understand exactly what it is about our dresses that agitates every man in my family so. I mean, they cover and display no more or less than our ball gowns. Oh well. Good night. I'll see you tomorrow, and again, do not fret over Charles. He has always been overprotective. I guess he always will be," sighed Aimee.

Millie heard a soft click as the door closed moments later. The dim hall light glowed through the crack under the door. She waited for a long time to hear a third knock. A knock she knew in her heart would never come. Should never come.

It never did.

Much later, Chase entered Hembree Grove. After ensuring the Three were safely and discreetly inside the manor, he had decided to take a walk and clear his mind.

Tonight's embrace had been a mistake. A large one. An inevitable one.

Ever since he had seen her stumbling around in the dark, he knew kissing Millie was predestined. He had not expected, however, for Millie to be just as aware of what had been building between them. Even worse, the kiss had been for her what it had not been for him—a one-time event. A means to end this insane attraction. A reminder that she was little Mildred Aldon, a child more inclined to climb trees than turn a man's desire. *It was supposed to end her nightly invasions into his dreams*.

Tonight's embrace, however, had done nothing of the sort. Millie had been warm and willing, innocent but ever so pleasing. She had responded to his need with similar hunger and passion. Even now, he could taste her on his tongue, hot and intoxicating.

In the carriage ride home, he had forced himself to compartmentalize his feelings, a natural ability he had perfected during the war. His face betrayed no emotion—not anger, nor disappointment, nor displeasure. Chase knew Aimee believed him to be furious with her behavior. Jennelle had probably known him long enough to realize he was not as indifferent to their adventure as he appeared. And based upon Millie's silent response to his lecture, he assumed she was unaware of the mental battle he was waging. But when she had exited the carriage, he was surprised to learn he had been wrong.

"Chase," Millie had whispered when Aimee and Jennelle were no longer within hearing, "don't overanalyze what happened between us. You are angry with yourself when there is no need. I do not know why, but it was destined to happen. You wanted it, and in truth, so did I. Let it end at that. Thank you for seeing us home. Good night."

He stood transfixed, watching the small version of a French demimonde in maiden white enter his home with the bearing of a duchess. She had not been fooled by his lecture or cold demeanor. He knew of no one, including his mother, who could have known what was truly on his mind. Not even Reece could discern his thoughts when he intentionally hid them. How had Millie?

When the door closed behind her, he had turned and begun walking aimlessly through the side streets of Mayfair. Tonight's encounter had done nothing to satisfy the aching hunger in his loins. Instead of relief, his desire for the bewitching brunette had only grown. He would not be content until he possessed her. And when it came to Millie, possession meant marriage. A commitment he was unwilling to consider—for now.

Chase headed for his study with no more clarity than when he had left. Turning toward the darkened hallway, he saw a shadowed figure sitting on a velvet bench opposite the main staircase. Upon seeing him, the figure rose and moved to confront him. It was Millie's maid and self-imposed protector of the Three, Elda Mae.

"Your lordship, I cannot tell you how your arrival eases my heart."

Chase raised an eyebrow. Elda Mae was always one to speak her mind, but rarely was she complimentary, and for the past few weeks she had been avoiding him. "Thank you for staying up for me, Elda Mae, but I am home now."

"Like I'd stay up for your lordship. Me girls, I know what they did—no, I didn't know about it prior to their going out and about—but I knew Mildred brought those dresses. When I checked on the three of them this evening and realized they were gone, along with them gowns, it was clear to me they were up to no good. I was afraid for them. But when I saw them return with sunken faces, I knew you had found them and ensured they got back home no worse for wear. My lord, I doubt you will get any apologies from the Three for ruining their fun, but I thank you."

"Yes, well, Elda Mae . . ."

"Oh, and I promised Alfred to let you know that you had a visitor this evening. I'm sure the gentleman is no longer here, but he might have left something for you in the library.

That was where he was waiting. Well, good night, your lordship. And again, I thank you for rescuing me girls." Elda Mae turned and disappeared down the narrow unlit hall that joined the servants' quarters.

Chase sighed and headed toward the library. When he entered, he was startled to see the visitor had not left.

A tall, lanky man dressed in tailored, though not expensive, navy breeches and a matching coat, stood as Chase entered. Chase eyed his impassive, time-etched face, and determined the man to be the unexcitable sort, able to remain calm and composed for hours regardless of the circumstances.

"Lord Chaselton?"

Chase closed the door. "I am. And you are . . . ?"

The man bowed quickly. "Name is Sanders, my lord. My late employer directed me to give this to you and in person."

Chase raised his eyebrows. Whoever his employer was, this man certainly followed directions. The hour was half past four in the morning.

Chase turned to look at the sealed note. It was addressed to him, and though obviously written with an unsteady hand, the script was familiar. Tension instantly flooded Chase's veins, and he forced himself to appear relaxed as he opened and read the contents.

The Most Honorable, The Marquess of Chaselton

My Lord Marquess,
 As you might have surmised by my mysterious absence, I have retreated into hiding to escape an unavoidable fate. It seems my efforts were for naught and an ungentlemanly death awaits me. I only recently learned of your arrival and your quiet search for my whereabouts. And in my last hours, I hope to right our missed opportunity by relaying confidential information using the only means available to me—this note and my

man of affairs. I have trusted Mr. Sanders for nearly two decades. He is a gentleman of impeccable honor.

As stated previously, I am now assured your father had not fallen to his death, but was murdered. I last wrote to you after discovering a letter mistakenly placed in my late wife's belongings. It was from your father. He had proof identifying the traitor and urgently needed to meet with his two contacts, one of whom was I. Regrettably, the meeting never took place.

Since writing to you, I have also tried to contact Viscount Darlouney, the second of my contacts. He has not responded and since disappeared. I no longer maintain hope he lives. If correct, then when I die, only two of the five of us will remain. You are the only son amongst us, so the duty of seeing the dastardly traitor exposed falls to you if we fail.

When Darlouney and I last met, I witnessed Lord Brumby leaving by way of the back door, believing himself unseen. While not absolute in my belief, I suspect he is Darlouney's second contact. Find him, for if I am correct, Lord Brumby is the only one who knows the fifth man in the group seeking to find the turncoat who betrayed not only us, but thousands of brave young Englishmen who were intentionally sent to their deaths.

Avenge them. Avenge us. Avenge your father. I fully expect that as the Marquess of Chaselton and as the son of my late friend, you will ensure that we have not died in vain.

And whatever you do, tell no one—trust no one.

Eischel

So Lord Eischel had feared for his life. A fear not unfounded, as he was now dead. That explained why in the past two weeks Chase could not find him.

Slowly depositing Eischel's letter on a nearby desk, Chase assessed Sanders once again. "How did your employer die?"

"Of consumption, I was told," Sanders replied without hesitation.

"How long had Eischel had consumption?" Chase asked, knowing those suffering with the disease experienced a long, painful death.

"As far as I am aware, less than two months." Sanders's voice had little inflection.

Chase eyed the man. "Two months? That's all?"

"Aye, my lord."

Chase sat down behind the desk and propped his index fingers together, forming a steeple. "Odd, for consumption."

"If you say so, my lord."

Chase eyed the man carefully and estimated that while he was assessing Sanders, Sanders was likewise appraising him. "Your employer wrote that I was to trust you."

For the first time, Sanders appeared uncomfortable. "I wish I could have done more."

"Did Lord Eischel have something besides this missive for me?"

"No, my lord. His final request was that I personally deliver his message to you without delay, regardless of the time of day or night. That is all." For several moments, Sanders stared at the patterned rug on the floor before he looked Chase directly in the eye and replied in a vengeful tone, "There are the letters Lord Eischel received from your father. Some of them quite long."

"Letters?" Chase demanded. "There was more than one?"

"Indeed. Several just before Lord Chaselton—your father—passed away. In his last weeks, Lord Eischel pored over them again and again. He suspected they contained a clue, but he could find nothing of import, just news of government. Maybe you can . . ."

Chase leaned forward, interrupting. "Did you bring them with you?"

"Indeed, my lord," Sanders replied, reaching into the breast pocket of his coat to bring out a stack of missives.

Taking the outstretched documents, Chase silently wondered why his father had written only to Eischel and not to him as well. He took a deep breath and escorted Sanders to the library door. "Your account was a heavy burden, Mr. Sanders. Consider it lifted. I thank you for your service. Do you have another position?"

Sanders nodded once. "Before his demise, Lord Eischel was kind enough to ensure I had employment."

"If you would wait, I will call for my carriage and have my man take you home."

Sanders shook his head decisively. "I would prefer you did not. I took great pains to keep secret my coming here this evening, and though the hour is late, I have no wish to advertise my brief association with your lordship. And, in fact, if it is not too much a burden, I hope to leave by the servants' entrance."

Chase nodded in understanding and led the man to a side door leading outside.

Sanders descended halfway down the small brick staircase and stopped. He turned and bowed his head for a final time. "Good night, my lord, and may you obtain what you seek."

"Rest assured, Mr. Sanders, there shall be meaning in their deaths."

Sanders nodded and proceeded to squeeze by a hedge and enter Queen Street. In two blocks, he would be at the Regent Quadrant with ample hired hackneys from which to choose. Chase stood for several moments in the dark, watching the tall, purposeful figure disappear from view. Chase doubted he would ever see or hear from the man again.

Closing the door, Chase turned and headed toward his

study. The fire in the hearth had died a few hours ago and the normally warm and inviting room was cold and dark. It fit his mood.

He sat down and began to sketch the relationships of the five men, beginning with his father's name.

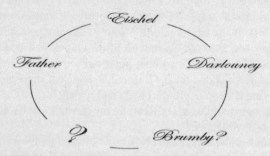

Eischel

Father   *Darlouney*

?   *Brumby?*

If Eischel was correct, then Brumby would know the identity of his father's second contact. And if his father had intended on telling Eischel, then surely he would have told his other contact—or at least he had tried. Chase put down the quill and tapped the stack of letters. His father was not adverse to writing, but neither could Chase remember him being so prolific.

He sat back and opened the first letter, ignoring the twisting of his insides. The handwriting was definitely his father's, and though the lengthy message had been sent to Eischel, it had been meant for him. Chase immediately recognized the cipher he and his father had developed in his youth.

Over the next hour, he decoded the letters. The details were scant and they did not mention a name. His father must have feared someone else discovering and deciphering the code. Instead of a name, he wrote about three markers. One marker that would be overlooked by most would lead to others. Only with all three markers could someone find the proof and present it to the House of Lords. Without them,

Chase could do nothing. If Chase brought any of what he knew to the House of Lords and they discovered the extent of their being manipulated, blood would be sought immediately. Without a target on which to focus their anger, many of the legislators would not discriminate in favor of caution and justice.

Chase leaned back behind the distinctive writing table that had been his father's and lightly stroked the inlay on its surface. The dark patterned wood formed the Chaselton crest. He depressed two inlay pieces simultaneously, and a secret drawer was freed.

Chase placed the letters and his sketch in the hidden drawer and closed it. He leaned back in the well-worn chair and considered his next move. He had no doubt that the marker "overlooked by most" was the amulet his father had given Millie. The idea of her continuing to wear the item filled him with unease, and he dreaded the barrage of questions that were likely to ensue when he demanded she give him her necklace.

He was considering just how to deflect her inquiries when an idea struck him. Maybe he could delay that argument for a little while longer. Millie had been wearing the amulet for nearly every event, and anyone who had recognized the crest most likely had already seen it. Like he, they must have thought it nothing more than a trinket given to her by his father. An assumption that might prove to be useful.

He did not like the idea of using Millie unwittingly, but letting her continue to wear the item might be the most effective way to achieve his goals. And if the amulet ever did pose a danger, just how he decided to make it disappear could be key to protecting her and his family.

Meanwhile, he needed to learn just how the marker led to the other two. And for that, he had to find Lord Brumby. But before anything, he needed to leave Hembree Grove and his mother's and the Three's ever-observant eyes.

Chapter 6

Millie froze. Her mind and body went completely numb as she clutched the drapes in her motionless fingers. It had been nearly four days since Chase had moved out of Hembree Grove, and she had no doubt his abrupt decision to relocate was prompted by their kiss. When she had first learned of his absence, a strange feeling of relief flooded through her. Since discovering his impromptu arrival in London, silent fears and uncertainties about her future—ones she held deep within her—had reawakened. Never before had her childhood promise felt so burdensome. Now it nearly choked her with its weight.

The first day after Chase left, and even during the first event that she had attended with only Mother Wentworth as an escort, Millie had felt free and confident. But she could not escape the disquieting memories of their embrace. One moment she was in anguish wondering how she compared with his undoubtedly numerous other conquests. Then she would remind herself of her desire to be unattached, free, and beholden to no one.

Millie had been completely truthful when she had told Chase their kiss was inevitable. And now that it had occurred, her curiosity should have been assuaged, and the strange pull between them should have vanished as mysteriously as it had appeared. Yet with each day that passed, it became harder and harder to disillusion herself. She began to wonder just what she wanted of him, of herself, of the future.

Aimee and Jennelle had not said anything, but they were aware of Millie's mood swings and had tried to transfer her energies elsewhere. Earlier that morning they had once again pleaded with her to attend one of Jennelle's many afternoon Society meetings. And once again Millie had declined, choosing to be alone with her thoughts.

Standing immobile by the front window, Millie suddenly wished she had accepted. The one person she had not expected to see was standing outside Hembree Grove. Chase. He was casually pretending to address a man whom she knew was not his driver.

Gradually, a sense of unexplainable loss filled Millie. She did not want to know if their single stormy embrace had satisfied his curiosity. She did not want to know he desired her no more.

Millie let the heavy, tasseled material fall from her fingertips and reminded herself she wanted no man. And even if she did, it certainly would not be Charlie Wentworth. Turning, she headed toward the back entrance, deciding to pass the rest of the afternoon in the stables. Hopefully by then Charlie would have come and gone, never knowing she was there.

She kicked open the large hinged door and inhaled the smell of fresh hay and horses. Millie missed the country and looked forward to returning home, abandoning Town life and all its restrictions set by the *haut ton's* most shallow and vane.

A shadow moved and skirted out the side door. She rolled her eyes as the stableboy's comrade quickly followed. Both obviously feared she was there to practice her self-defense moves. Picking up a brush, she ventured toward a huge black horse prancing with excitement in the far stall.

"Shhh, Hercules," Millie whispered as she drew him out to the center of the stable. She began stroking the muscled neck of the monstrous animal. "I've been neglecting you, haven't I, boy? Are you going mad here in Town? Was it terribly cruel of me to insist on your coming?" she asked, laughing as the dark head nudged her shoulder.

The unusually large Friesian had been a gift from her father for her sixteenth birthday—one he had not realized he was purchasing. After weeks of hearing Millie's incessant pleas, he had acquiesced and allowed her to pick her own horse from a neighbor's stock. When she had come home with the huge black animal, he had threatened to fire the stable master and then forbade her to ride the thing that threatened his only child. After a tremendous amount of coaxing and sustained confirmation of the horse's docile nature, Lord Aldon finally consented to her keeping and then riding the beloved horse. Hercules and Millie had been inseparable ever since.

When her father decided she was to have a Season, Millie again pleaded with him to change his mind. Realizing her entreaties were falling on deaf ears, she agreed to stop fighting the inevitable if she could stay with Aimee in London *and* if she could bring Hercules. Her father quickly agreed, with the sole purpose of reestablishing peace in his household. While he disapproved of the horse—especially in London—the compromise allowed him to stay in the countryside. He did not relish the idea of dealing with the *ton*. Ever since his cherished wife had died, Lord Aldon preferred to live a quiet life away from pressuring widows. Millie's mother had been the love of his life, and he would never want another. Since her death, he ventured into London only to visit Richard Tattersall or for Derby-related activities.

Millie heard the door open behind her and turned, expecting to see one of the footmen or stable lads ordered back to their chores. She was about to ask if they would take Hercules out for some exercise when she realized who was entering the stables. Chase.

Sucking in a quivering breath, Millie tried once again to persuade herself that her fascination with Charlie Wentworth was foolish and unwanted. She tried to muster some displeasure at having to face him, despite her intention to do otherwise, but she could find none. The man was undeniably alluring. Seeing him alone, Millie thought her racing heart would never beat normally again. She knew she was staring at him, but could not bring herself to stop.

Chase's light camel-colored breeches and beautifully polished black Hessians outlined the strong, muscular lines of his calves and thighs. He wore a striped tan-and-gold waistcoat underneath his dark brown frock coat. The immaculately tailored clothes emphasized the natural elegance of his powerful, large frame. He looked every bit the marquess. A nobleman, born and bred to his title.

Chase entered the stables and looked around for the groom. He had just received an unexpected visit and decided to go for a ride while he grappled with his warring thoughts. He needed to make a decision—soon. It was difficult not to give in to the old habit and tell his mentor everything and ask for advice. But he decided, at least for now, to heed Eischel's wisdom and *trust no one, tell no one*.

Closing the stable doors, Chase caught Millie studying him, and his mouth curved faintly. He thought everyone had departed Hembree Grove for the day, and was suddenly glad to be wrong. Then Chase saw the black, muscled monster hovering over Millie. Alarm and fear flooded his veins, resulting in an uncharacteristic roar. "What in bloody hell are you doing?" He instantly regretted his reaction as the horse shifted, clearly agitated by the unexpected sound.

Instantly, Millie felt all her trepidation about encountering Chase dissipate. In its place, her temper flared. "Excuse me?"

"Millie, carefully walk away and come over here," Chase replied with quiet, even emphasis.

Millie's brows drew together in confusion. Chase was obviously afraid for her. Hercules nudged her hand for a treat. As the prized small sugar cube was nibbled out of her hand, Millie realized the impetus of Chase's bizarre behavior. Having been away for so many years, he did not know about Hercules.

In retaliation for Chase's abrupt and dictatorial behavior, Millie rubbed the large animal's neck and nuzzled the black nose before turning with an impish smile. "Chase, meet Hercules. He's my horse."

Chase's eyes narrowed in unmistakable disapproval. "Does your father know you have that beast?"

Millie nodded, continuing her loving ministrations. "He bought him for me. And he is no beast. Hercules is my friend."

Chase watched in astonishment as Millie gave comfort to the large animal. It was enormous and powerful, and its sheer size had to make him difficult to control. Terrifying thoughts of Millie being injured or even killed beneath its hooves flooded his mind. He could not believe Lord Aldon would ever allow his only child near such a potential killer. "I do not believe you."

Millie raised her chin defiantly and gave him a pointed and unswerving stare. "I assure you he did."

Chase growled through compressed lips. "And I assure you I know your father, and I know you. You tricked him into purchasing that oversized beast, and afterward you consistently plagued the man until he yielded to your whimsical demands."

Millie shrugged noncommittally. "Perhaps. But if you got to know Hercules, *as my father did*, you would see he really is quite gentle."

"Hmph," was Chase's only reply. His initial fear for her

safety slowly evaporated as he witnessed the animal's and Millie's interaction. Chase looked around to pinpoint who was charged with helping her, when he realized they were alone. "Where is everyone?"

Millie glanced around, trying to see for whom Chase was searching. It was rare someone remained in the stables when she visited Hercules. "I am here," she replied with a shrug of her shoulders and recommenced her grooming.

Chase stared at Millie, not comprehending the sarcastic tone in her voice. He watched her body move provocatively as she brushed the horse's coat, left to right. His gaze skimmed hungrily down the graceful line of her spine as it swayed side to side. With each stroke, he felt his body respond. He had hoped that by keeping his distance his craving for her would lessen, but as his gaze dropped from the creamy skin of her exposed neck to her shoulders, and lower, his ever-present hunger for her flared to life. He felt himself visibly harden and immediately shifted his stance.

Vauxhall Gardens had only enhanced his need for her. Since his foolish attempt to satisfy his carnal desires, his dreams had become more disturbing. Every night, a fantasy-Millie would invade his unconscious, and with each visit, her demeanor became more seductive. She would entice him to play with her, chase her; and when he did, she would disappear, leaving him wanting. And the few times he had caught his phantom enchantress, he had immediately awakened, robbed of pleasure and hard with desire.

He shook his head and once again tried to remind himself she was Mildred Aldon, his little sister's best friend. She was a child.

But even as the hollow words flowed through his mind, he knew them to be wrong. The female tending the enormous horse was no child. Millie was small, but she was definitely a mature, well-developed woman. And each time he encountered her, his desire for her grew stronger.

Chase took a deep breath and remembered what Aimee had said about Millie and the stable hands. She used them as sparring partners. And based on their absence, it appeared, unwilling partners.

"So Aimee was not exaggerating. The stable grooms are afraid of you."

Millie shrugged her shoulders again and rocked gracefully back on her heels as she continued brushing the muscular animal with graceful, fluid strokes.

Chase knew he should leave. Being with Millie was a self-inflicted torture, but one he was tempted to endure for a few precious moments. And right now, he welcomed any excuse to extend his time alone with her. "Seems you lack willing partners. Would you like one now?"

Millie whirled to face him. Her face glowed with the idea. "Oh, please tell me your proposal is in earnest. Are you seriously offering to spar with me? I have not been able to practice in several months. Nobody will even consider being my partner unless I provide them some type of financial inducement."

Shocked by her genuine excitement, Chase replied, "Well then, I am ready. . . ."

Millie beamed him an eager smile filled with delight, and exclaimed, "How incredibly exciting! Oh, Chase, this is positively the most exhilarating opportunity I have had since we arrived in London. I just need to change into a pair of breeches I brought along with me. I will be back in a quick moment."

Chase reached out and lightly grabbed her arm as she started to flee past him. "Breeches?"

Millie's brows furrowed. "You cannot expect me to spar in my day dress." Her comment sounded more like a question than a statement of fact.

Chase met her eyes and nodded brusquely. "Absolutely. What are the chances you will be wearing breeches if attacked? Do you spar to improve your skills or to belittle untrained stableboys?"

Neither thought had ever occurred to Millie. She had always worn male attire when practicing new defense moves. She had no idea how effective she would be in a dress but was eager to discover the answer. "You present an excellent argument. At least let me change into an older house dress. I promise to be quick." Her last words were barely spoken before Millie rushed out the doors to the main house.

Chase watched her leave and smiled, his mood significantly improved. The similar change in Millie's disposition had been undeniable. When he walked in and caught her staring at him, she had seemed bereft and in an odd way defeated. He knew life in London was constraining for someone like Millie, especially after experiencing the excitement of Vauxhall. She liked adventure, to be outdoors and active. Jennelle and his sister could occupy themselves with their more sedentary hobbies, but if Millie was anything close to the young girl he once knew, she would continue to seek pleasure in less safe and approved outlets.

A quarter of an hour later, Millie reentered the stable sporting a challenging smile. Her dark eyebrows slanted into a frown as she saw Chase spreading a significant amount of Hercules's straw on the floor. "Whatever are you doing?"

Chase momentarily stopped and weighed her with a puzzled expression. "Do you not normally spread something on the ground to cushion your falls?"

Millie crossed her arms in front of her. "I do not fall."

His mouth twitched with amusement. "You will today," Chase replied with an unmistakable chuckle to his voice.

His smirk irritated her. He still believed her to be the same helpless little girl he had saved so many years ago. Well, he was going to find out different, she thought as she lunged after him.

Chase easily sidestepped her assault and laughed at her

effort. The combination of failure and embarrassment goaded her into a follow-on move that landed her flat on her back, pinned, and looking up into golden eyes sparkling with laughter.

"Now, are you not pleased that I thought of the hay?" Seeing the hot, furious tears welling in her eyes, he realized her pride was seriously bruised. "Millie, never let emotion rule your actions. It makes you vulnerable and forecasts your intentions."

Millie choked back her humiliation and stared into amber eyes that captured hers, taking in her every move. Her embarrassment quickly dissolved, and mounting desire filled its void. Conscious of his hard thighs holding her down, Millie fought the unwelcome desire to be kissed by him one more time.

Several silent moments passed before Millie spoke, her voice trembling. "I'll have to remember that."

Chase released her reluctantly and fought to retain control. Their proximity disturbed him more than he had anticipated. Regardless, he could not force himself to prematurely end their time together. "Well, then, since I highly doubt you go around Town haphazardly attacking gentlemen, let us practice a more real-life situation. I would like to see how you would react if someone came after you."

His crisp voice was distant and detached, a complete turnabout from the smoldering looks he had just been sending. *Get control of yourself*, Millie silently chided herself. *He obviously couldn't give a fig over what happened. Focus.*

For the next half hour, Chase worked with Millie. He was surprised to discover she was much more skilled than he originally imagined. While at any time he could render her helpless, he recognized that many of his sex—including those noblemen who thought they knew something about combat—would be on the ground if they challenged her. She had expanded the few techniques he had shown her and reinvented them so that her small size was now a benefit rather than a disadvantage.

He was impressed.

Millie was frustrated.

She knew she was not entirely unskilled, but Chase was certainly making her feel that way. She had ended up on the ground countless times, and he had yet to lose his footing even once. At first, she had blamed her dress, but she soon realized the result would have been the same even if she had been wearing breeches.

Preparing for his next move, Millie decided to see if Chase's rules applied to him. What did he say? *Never let emotion rule your actions*. Just as he approached her, she spoke up. "I saw you with Sir Edward earlier. I guess I should have believed him when he told me he was once a spy."

All Chase was able to get out was half a *What?* before he found himself on the dirt floor, looking up.

Millie continued to straddle him as she gazed down, her dusty-purple eyes sparkling with satisfaction at her accomplishment. She didn't care what happened for the rest of the day; she would be in a good mood.

Something akin to alarm flickered briefly in Chase's eyes. Millie saw him suppress it almost at once, but it had been too late. Realization dawned on her. She was not supposed to have seen that meeting. Nobody was supposed to have seen it. "No one saw anything of any import, Chase. I assure you. Sir Edward's disguise was most excellent."

Chase lay motionless for several seconds, quietly digesting her words. He thought of denying her conclusions, but knew the effort would be futile.

His silence flustered Millie. "Honestly, Chase. Even I did not realize it was Sir Edward until he took a deep breath and nodded his head at that odd angle. I saw him do the same thing at Bassel's when you were speaking together then. Trust me when I say it genuinely did look as if you were giving instructions to your driver. It did not appear that you were meeting with anyone, let alone Sir Edward."

Under a dark brown curtain of her tousled hair, their eyes locked, and Millie felt an overwhelming warmth again flow through her veins. Her heart began to pound. If she didn't know better, she would think she was falling in love with the man.

Chase looked into her tumultuous gaze, gave a low, frustrated groan, and flipped her over, easily reversing their positions. He framed her face with his hands while pinning her to the floor with his hips. His breath fanned her cheek. "Forget what you saw, Millie. Do not tell anyone—not even Aimee or Jennelle. It's important."

Her heart skipped two beats and then went into frantic overdrive. She couldn't speak. Her only response to his request was a quick nod before he lowered his head and invaded the soft, vulnerable warmth behind her lips.

For days, Chase had been dreaming of this. He felt her shiver in his arms, but Millie did not pull away. Instead, her fingers clenched his shoulders, evidence of her own sense of need and urgency.

He uttered a low growl as his tongue caressed, hungrily tasting the sweetness of her mouth. Her response was intoxicating. She was soft and welcoming and Chase felt his control almost shattered by her eagerness. She was so receptive to his touch. He immediately craved more.

Chase raised his head and stared down into darkening lavender pools swimming with passion. Marveling at her beauty, he felt her stir beneath him. The movement sent a surge of burning fire through his loins. The sweltering heat arcing between them was almost palpable. Chase knew he should stop, but when the flowery scent of Millie's skin invaded his senses, he dismissed all reason and recaptured her mouth. Deepening the embrace, Chase plunged inside, drinking in her adventurous spirit in hopes it would dispel his demons and make him feel like a whole man, not the emotionless creature he had been for so long.

The gleam in Chase's eyes before he had recommenced his kiss had been ravenous. Millie clutched at him, overwhelmed with innocent desire, unable to rationalize what was happening. She knew she should do something to stop his passionate assault, but she could not muster the will to push him away. Ever since she had seen him again, she had wanted Chase to kiss her, totally and completely. And now that she was in his arms, the last thing she wanted to do was leave. Never had any adventure made her feel this alive, this complete.

Chase slowly released her lips and began to trail kisses down her cheek and neck. "Charles, I don't understand what is happening to me." Her voice was distant music.

Chase trapped her head gently between his hands. Millie stared up at him through her lashes. "Millie. Know that I would never hurt you. Just be with me." And then he bent his head and trapped her lips with a slow, inviting passion that took her breath away.

The hot, sweet, sensual embrace went on and on, suffusing his body with an aching need for more. The searing kiss took on a new excitement as his mouth explored the skin around her nape. His hands were roving along her spine, cursing the thin cloth blocking her skin from his touch. Chase heard himself moan and knew he was on the brink of no return.

Millie quivered with pleasure and instinctively arched her back, pressing her breasts into his chest. Her pulse raced. Warmth welled up inside of her in places she never knew existed. It was mingled with a sense of need so acute it made her tremble.

Gathering her in his arms, Chase returned his mouth to hers. Their lips moved hungrily against each other. His thumbs traced the lines of her cheekbones.

Chase could feel his raging hunger for Millie begin to roar past the last of his defenses. A great shudder of need wracked him. He had to stop before he could no longer find the ability to resist.

Slowly, he raised his head and peered into her passion-filled eyes. He stared down at her tempting lips, and every muscle in his body tensed. It took all of his will to not bend down and plunge into her mouth again. He wanted her. Badly.

Chase buried his head against her neck and breathed in her scent, wanting to just lie there and not worry about anything else. Instead, scraping up the last crumbs of his honor, he rose to his feet and offered her his hand. "Come, let us go back to the main house." His voice was gruff.

Unable to speak, Millie nodded and headed toward the manor, sensing Chase behind her.

They entered through the back door, both trying to decipher, emotionally and logically, what had just happened. Their encounter at Vauxhall Gardens could be easily explained by heightened emotions, anger, and fear of discovery. It had been passionate and wild. But what had transpired between them today had been something much more—a driving need to possess and completely consume the other.

Standing alone with Chase in the hall by the rear stairs, Millie had never been so acutely conscious of a man's presence before in her life. There was danger in Chase's masculine power, she realized. Danger that, when it came too near, she was powerless to resist.

Deep into her internal monologue, Millie was not aware of Elda Mae speaking to her.

"My lady? Did you hear me?"

Startled, feeling as if she had just been caught, Millie swung around, wide-eyed. "What? Uh, no, my apologies, Elda Mae. What were you saying?"

"I said that a Lord Marston has just arrived and is waiting for you in the drawing room. He said you were expecting him."

Millie's eyes grew large, and her lips parted in surprise. "I . . . Oh my, I completely forgot I agreed to meet with him. Please ask him to wait, and say that I will be down to visit soon. I must change my dress before I meet with him."

Elda Mae eyed the straw clinging all over her charge's old, worn day gown. It was obvious Millie was unaware of her state or that hay was poking through what remained of her coiffure. Then Elda Mae's gaze narrowed on Chase, who was leaning on his right fist against a narrow hall table. His knuckles were white with tension. She glanced back at Millie and replied, "I expect a change of gowns would be in order, my lady. I'll send one of the maids up to fix your hair."

Chase ignored the scathing look Elda Mae issued him as she departed to deliver Millie's message. Millie took a step toward the staircase and Chase moved to block her path. He was furious. He forced himself to speak slowly and deliberately on the off chance that he had misunderstood.

"You agreed to meet Lord Marston?"

Millie frowned, hearing the disapproval in his voice. "Yes, I did. He sent a note this morning asking if he could visit, and I replied that he could."

Knowing she had rejected countless other requests, Chase's expression was ominous, his golden eyes flashing with fury. "Do this often? Kiss one man before entertaining another?"

Millie flinched at the harsh coldness of his tone. She took a firm grip on her resolve. She had to stay relaxed and rational if she was to have any chance at calming Chase down.

"Do not be ridiculous. I assure you, *nothing* could persuade me to be interested in that man."

Chase's face hardened. "I think not. You agreed to meet with him. And the other night at cards, you didn't retreat from his advances as you were doing with the others. I saw you."

Millie felt her anger take over. How dare he? She raised her chin, her violet eyes flashing with outrage. "Oh, really? Was this the same night Selena Hall decided to drape herself all over you? I certainly did not see you disentangling yourself from her tentacles. Your reaction was quite the opposite, if I remember."

Chase blinked. Her expression was both mocking and defiant as she confronted him. He listened to her words, but what was much more telling was the sound of her voice. Millie was jealous. And the idea that Mildred Aldon had been as aware of him as he had been of her, assuaged his envy-driven anger. "Millie, that was different. I am not interested in Selena."

Millie was not mollified. "I must say that it certainly did not appear that way. *However*, I can claim the same lack of interest toward Lord Marston. I have my own reasons for meeting with him, and now, Charlie, if you will excuse me, I must leave and change into something suitable."

Millie quickly sidestepped his blockade and headed up the back stairs. She was halfway up the steps when Chase realized she had reverted to calling him Charlie again. It was not intentional. She probably was not even aware she had said it. In fact, her combative demeanor toward him strongly resembled her attitude when they were younger. Suddenly Chase wanted to hear his name on her lips. The one she had used outside in the stables. The one she had uttered when she was aware only of him.

Near the top of the stairs, Millie suddenly felt strong fingers grasp her arm. "Charlie, whatever are you do—"

Chase cut her question off, pulling her into a deep, bone-rattling embrace. He held her head between his hands, urging her to her tiptoes. He was kissing her long and soft and deep, delving possessively into her mouth, capturing her tongue, and drawing it into his own. The kiss was intense, mind numbing, and brief. She was noticeably shaking when he finally released her.

"What is my name?" he growled in her ear, supporting her limp frame in his arms.

He delved his hands into Millie's hair and pulled her head back. She looked at him, her eyes sparkling like large amethysts. Chase felt his whole body tighten. "What is my name?" he asked again, his voice husky with need.

It took several seconds for his words to penetrate her drugged state. "Charles," she murmured and then rested her forehead against his chest.

"Never forget it," he whispered, holding her close.

Though still reeling from the kiss, his arrogant command rankled as her head slowly cleared. Millie pushed back and squared her shoulders, faking indignation. "What were you trying to prove?" she asked, trying to sound displeased.

An unmistakable smile mixed with satisfaction and possession tipped the corners of Chase's mouth. Her attempt at an icy stare did nothing to diminish his pleasure at hearing his name. She had called him Charles. "Just reminding you of who I am, love. Go greet your pompous guest, but *he* had better remember who *I* am."

Millie did not move. Chase was acting too self-satisfied. "And just who are you, *my lord*?"

Chase drew her close again. "Who I have always been. Your protector," he said, leaning down to brush his mouth possessively across hers. Releasing her lips, he turned and descended the staircase, exiting out the back door. For several moments, Millie futilely tried to digest what had just happened. Giving up, she again headed toward her room to prepare for her treacherous guest, Lord Marston.

Chase watched from across the hall as Millie glided gracefully into the drawing room to meet Marston. She had prepared herself quickly, but the results were remarkable. Donned in a simple dove-colored half dress with white Vandyke trim on the puffed sleeves and along the short train, she looked incredibly alluring and untouchable at the same time. Her dark hair was swept up high in a simple knot, intentionally allowing several soft curls to escape.

Even from his semi-concealed vantage point, Chase could see Lord Marston's favorable appraisal as he greeted her, kissed her hands, and smiled quite charmingly, before the door was closed. Unfamiliar emotions—intense and dark— raced through Chase's veins, along with a powerful need to protect. He despised Marston. He was vain, shallow, unfaithful, and one of the most dishonorable noblemen Chase had ever known.

Chase had fully intended to go riding when he left Millie on the rear stairs, but when he came back in to retrieve his gloves, he had spied her descending the main staircase. Ignoring his internal counsel, he surreptitiously followed her to the drawing room. Deep down, he knew Millie had no tendre for Marston. No, she had been truthful earlier. Her interest in the handsome blackguard spawned from very different reasons than that of lust. Reasons unknown to him.

Witnessing Marston's physically demonstrative greeting, Chase decided to put his riding plans on hold. He convinced himself he needed to know why Millie had agreed to the social call, but more importantly, he wanted to ensure she did not fall into one of Marston's scandalous traps. He cracked open the door and covertly positioned himself to listen and discover her plans.

Millie's voice was warm and inviting. "Lord Marston, I cannot tell you how surprised I was this morning to receive your request for a visit."

"My lady, I hope not unpleasantly surprised. I believe I expressed a desire to liven your stay here in London."

Marston's veiled suggestion of continued companionship made Chase's insides knot.

"Oh? And how would you enhance someone's holiday while in Town?" Millie's tenor was that of a perfect hostess asking an innocent and commonplace question.

"May I suggest a ride tomorrow?"

Millie scrunched up her nose. The excursion was exactly what she desired, but after what happened in the stables, she wanted to ride only with Chase—not this slick nobleman oozing charm. It was obvious Marston wanted to be in her good graces for a reason, but what could it be?

Marston misinterpreted her unenthusiastic facial expression. "My lady—Millie—you do not have to be afraid. I have the perfect mare for you. She is very small, like you, and extremely gentle."

Millie could not help her reaction as her eyebrows shot up in complete horror. She swallowed and moved to sit down in an isolated chair that prevented him from sitting next to her. "And I suppose you are going to assure me this mare has no capacity for speed."

Marston moved to sit on a light-blue velvet settee across from her. He leaned forward and placed his elbows on his knees. "You have my absolute promise of her submissive nature. I do not think the little animal could even trot faster than I could run. There now, does that reassure you?"

Millie held her breath and stared with hooded eyes for several moments at the man who was obviously well practiced in deceitfulness. Again, he insulted her by underestimating her nature and her abilities. First at cards and now at riding.

The thought of being on a small, pathetically slow animal was worse than not riding at all. Despite her desire to get outdoors and discover Marston's true purpose in seeking her out, Millie found it easy to decline. "While tempting, my lord, I am afraid I must refuse your offer. In spite of your assurances to the contrary, I just cannot see me on top of a *small* horse."

Relief flooded through Chase. When Millie had not turned Marston down immediately, he wondered if she was going to accept. Since her arrival in Town, she had been unable to persuade a chaperone to join her in the permissible things she loved to do, such as ride. If Millie was not provided an acceptable means of entertainment soon, she would seek adventures where Chase feared he could not protect her.

Chase refocused his attention on the conversation, realizing Marston was not deterred by her refusal.

"I understand, and do not trouble yourself regarding your fear of riding. I spoke to Lady Alstar earlier this week, and I understand that you have accepted her invitation to Saturday's ball."

Marston's demeanor and tone had changed. In a heartbeat, he went from an affable man relying on his charm and dashing good looks to one significantly more aggressive. He was taking control of the conversation. Millie recognized the change but had no idea how to stop him. "Well, uh, yes . . ." She stood and moved toward the window in hopes to put some distance between them.

As if realizing her intentions, Marston immediately rose and followed her. "Lady Millie, if I cannot persuade you to ride with me, I must insist you allow me to escort you to Alstar's ball this Saturday."

He stood very close, using his height to intimidate her. It was an obvious maneuver employed by men who were either extremely insecure or closet tyrants. In the past, when gentlemen callers performed such ploys, she quickly denounced their behavior, which normally resulted in the offender's humiliation. But with Marston, Millie instinctively knew it would not be wise to summarily cut off the man's heavy-handed approach. He was different. Marston didn't want *her* per se, but something she could give him. And he would continue his insistent pursuit until he had what he wanted. She was both fearful and curious to know what it was.

"Lord Marston . . ."

"Call me Neville, Millie."

It was a command, not a request. And he had used her given name again without permission. Everything she knew about noblemen was based on the principle that they behaved as gentlemen, especially in the presence of higher-bred ladies. Marston might be of noble birth, but he was no gentleman, and Millie had not a clue how to regain control of the conversation and situation.

Unable to see Marston's looming stance, Chase had continued to let the conversation play out, although he could hear the apprehension growing in Millie's voice. But when he heard Marston's latest demand, a fierce wave of protection took over, and he stepped into the room.

"Lady Mildred, my mother wanted me to remind you that I will be escorting you to Alstar's this Saturday. She expects all of us to attend and travel together. Please coordinate the exact time of our departure with her."

There was no room for misinterpretation. Chase was going to escort Millie Saturday—not Marston. Chase knew his timing was obvious but did not care. And looking at the relief in Millie's eyes, he was positive she did not care, either. The only one who did mind was standing near the window, livid at the intrusion and disruption of his plans.

Marston watched as the dark-haired vixen and Chaselton exchanged looks. He had been right about Lady Mildred Aldon. The interruption at Vauxhall Gardens had been no accident. Chaselton was definitely more interested in the beauty than he let on. Marston had been dithering as to whether Chase's interest was strong enough to be used to his advantage, but now he knew for sure. Marston opened his stance, to be less confrontational. He needed to present himself as someone harmless.

Millie watched Chase stride into the room, his power and authority permeating the room. His amber eyes captured hers. Millie could feel the heat rise in her cheeks at his look of cool possessiveness. Her lips curved into a tentative smile conveying her gratitude.

"Certainly, my lord. I will meet with your mother this afternoon to discuss, uh, the details," Millie replied, using the opportunity to distance herself from Marston's overbearing company. Now standing next to Chase, she felt much less the ensnared animal in a well-laid trap. She gestured toward Marston, who stood scowling in the corner. "Let me introduce . . ."

Marston interrupted her. "Chaselton and I are old acquaintances."

Chase locked eyes with the man. Untold words were spoken during the seconds they exchanged stares. "Marston."

"It appears you have the privilege of escorting this charming woman to Saturday's main event. I hope I have the pleasure of such duties in the future."

Over my dead body, thought Chase. "It may prove to be difficult. It has taken me eight years to acquire the chance. I doubt I will be willing to relinquish the privilege so very soon." *If ever*, Chase thought.

"I see," said Marston. "Well, Lady Aldon, let me detain you no further this afternoon. Although I do hope Lord Chaselton will not monopolize all your attentions this weekend. I meant what I said earlier in regard to providing you the freedom to pursue your, um, 'inclinations.'" Marston then quickly waved his hand in a flowery motion as he bowed and then pushed through the drawing room doors.

Millie took several retreating steps as she saw golden flames of anger flicker in Chase's eyes.

"Care to explain Marston's last comment? In fact, do you care to explain *any* of what he just said?" Chase asked sharply.

Millie's jaw tensed and her lavender eyes flashed in response to his challenge. "No, I would not." She straightened her shoulders and headed toward the back doors to leave the room.

In four steps, Chase caught Millie by the shoulders, whirling her around to face him. "I suggest you change your mind."

Millie struggled for composure. Adrenaline pumped through her veins, causing her to tremble violently. His cold eyes sniped at her, and Millie's instinct was to flee. But she knew the only way she was going to escape was to tell Chase the truth—or at least some of it. "Earlier, before today, Lord Marston and I discussed the absence of excitement in London life. He offered to alleviate my boredom. He . . ." Millie paused to lick her lips and gather fortitude. "He was the one who mentioned Vauxhall Gardens. Today he offered to take me riding. And do not pretend you are unaware of what I am referring to—I know you were listening. Bloody hell, Lord Marston knew you were listening, the way you barged in here."

Understanding her motives, Chase's voice warmed a few degrees. His amber eyes softened as they drank in her proud, delicate face. "I know, but Marston excels at trapping women in difficult situations, one of which he was well on his way to entangling you into. Or had you intended to go to Alstar's ball with him?" Chase asked, knowing the answer.

Millie bristled at the idea. "Of course I had no intention of letting him escort me. I was just trying to summon a way of refusing his offer without raising his ire."

A swift shadow of possession took over Chase's expression. "What do you care if his ire was raised? What are you up to, Mildred Aldon?" he asked roughly.

Millie shrugged and twisted her hands unconsciously. "I do not know exactly. But I think Lord Marston has some ulterior motive driving him toward me, and I want to know what that is."

Standing so close to her, Chase's dissipating anger was being replaced with a renewed desire to pull her back into his arms. There was no mysterious reason behind Marston's motives. Lust. And Chase found the idea of another man besides himself craving *his* ethereal beauty intolerable. If he found it near impossible to quash the rush of sexual need her presence stirred in him, he had no doubt that Marston did as well. He decided to take measures to ensure the man kept his distance from Millie.

Chase reached out and wound a loose lock of her hair in his hand. "Maybe the fact that you are an incredibly beautiful woman is his reason."

"Perhaps," Millie answered, his comment not truly registering. But she knew that was not it. No, women did not motivate Lord Marston; power did.

Chase looked at her slender white neck and fought his desire to lean down and taste its softness. He needed to leave. If he stayed, he was going to find himself compromising her in a way he would kill any other man for doing.

He clenched both fists. How could this particular woman affect him so? He had known many ladies, both beautiful and desirable, but never had he had to fight to maintain his self-control around them.

But Mildred Aldon was complex.

Her determination and spirit both captivated and frustrated him. She was beautiful, graceful, and charming. She could play the role of the model duchess to perfection.

But he knew the real Millie.

The one who was infuriatingly stubborn, crafty, and willing to use devious means to achieve whatever goal she set for herself. He also knew her heart. The unswerving loyalty and infinite love she had for her friends. And for the past three weeks, he had repeatedly wondered what it would be like to have all that devotion and passion directed at him.

He shook his head to clear his mind, reminding himself for the umpteenth time that now was not the time for anyone to enter his life in a permanent way—especially not Mildred Aldon.

Millie would not be satisfied to live a life separate from his. She would demand a partnership in every sense of the word. Unlike most females, who preferred to have their husbands completely removed from their daily activities, Mildred would want to be involved in the kinds of decisions other women avoided. And on a subconscious level, Chase knew that was why his attraction to her was so much stronger than what he had felt for any other woman.

They had an instant connection, for reasons that could not and need not be explained. Remembering how passionately she had responded when he'd taken her into his arms, he knew that she wanted him as well.

Even now as she looked at him, her violet-blue eyes were luminous with desire. He was almost afraid to breathe knowing her elusive, womanly scent would arouse him even further.

Chase raked his hands through his hair and grappled with his honor. He wanted her more than ever. Millie was a woman he could trust with his heart and soul. She could fill the cold void he had lived with for so long. Her energy and spirit and warmth were what he had longed for, and now that he had found them, he was forced to push all of them aside.

He took a deep breath to clear his mind. His life was too dangerous to manage an independent wife with unlimited curiosity and opinions of her own. Millie and he would have to wait.

"I have to go. I will see you Saturday."

And then he was gone, leaving Millie mystified. Twice this afternoon she had been with men whose moods altered in the blink of an eye.

"And they say women are unpredictable," she muttered to herself.

Chapter 7

Alstar's ball was the last stop on Saturday night's tour of "must attend" Mayfair parties. "Unbelievable how this pushy crowd of ruffles will be touted as a successful crush," Millie murmured to herself as she stared at the throngs of people pretending to enjoy each other's company. Anyone who was anyone had arrived at Alstar's unusually early rather than risk being missed and losing their standing in Society. Mother Wentworth, as usual, had sensed the *haut ton's* delicate mood and had timed the Three's arrival perfectly. And though they would have liked to deny it, Millie, Aimee, and Jennelle were quite the attraction.

All three of them looked exquisite in their newest creations. Millie had met with Madame Sasha the day before and had no idea what to expect based on her fitting. When the unusual creation was delivered in the morning, the three of them had been awed.

"Millie, your modiste is a rare find. If Madame Sasha ever would allow us to make her name public, she would be swarmed with new clients. Look at this—she even made you a special chemise," Aimee said, staring at the undergarment the color of black pearls.

Though secretly agreeing with her friend's assessment,

Millie reminded herself of the torture she'd had to endure to get the luscious garment that now lay on her bed. "Ha! Your modiste never makes you stand still for hours, only to poke, prod, and curse at you in Russian."

Surprise lit Aimee's face. "Do you honestly think she is cursing?"

Millie's mouth curved with envy. "Yes, I do. I wish I could curse in a language no one understood. Then I could say whatever I felt like in any company."

"It would be a convenient skill," Jennelle murmured, fondling the soft silver folds.

"I do not care what you say, Millie. This gown is worth whatever torture you went through," Aimee said wistfully.

While the dress still maintained the preferred Empire look, it was wispy, soft, and utterly feminine. The gown's underlayer was made of a very light-colored dusty blue-gray silk. Over it was a watered gauze material. Pleated along the bustline and sleeves, the delicate fabric formed distinct vertical ridges cleverly tucked into a wide, silver-embroidered trim with sporadically placed gemstones. Fixed to the back was a slightly darker shade of delicate, diaphanous tulle. Both the tulle and the gauze fell straight to the floor with a slight train that sparkled with clear jewels. Madame Sasha had included a headband trimmed in the same silver pattern as the dress, with similar, but smaller, gemstones.

By the time Millie had dressed, no additional adornment was needed. The gown emphasized her light skin, dark hair, and unusual eyes. Unfortunately, the striking combination made it much more difficult for Millie to remain unnoticed. As soon as she arrived at each event, she found herself constantly inventing excuses to extricate herself from the company of unwanted admirers.

Even Jennelle could no longer shoo the men away with her odd discussions of other countries and cultures. Her new fondness for Society meetings had introduced her to several unattached gentlemen who found it difficult to meet women who understood their passions. Thankfully, though, these passions were mostly reserved for their topics, not for her.

Aimee and Millie were glad Jennelle had finally found people in Society whose fascination for odd trivia matched her own. However, Jennelle's merriment meant they had to rely on each another for rescues from men who were just a little too persistent.

Chase escorted the Three just as he promised, but quickly mingled with the crowd after they arrived, at which point Millie's torture commenced. She was surrounded by men who appeared charming enough, but every time she compared them to Chase, they seemed more like boys and less like men.

Chase was a man unlike any other. He moved effortlessly through the mayhem with self-confidence unmatched by any gentleman in the room. Even at a distance, his presence was both compelling and so very disturbing. He exuded strength and masculinity, and every woman was aware of his appeal.

His dark coat was perfectly tailored and cut to subtly accentuate his large frame. He had chosen an unadorned white silk waistcoat rather than one with the heavily embroidered design most of the noblemen fancied.

She also preferred the simple configuration of his snowy white neckcloth. Too many of London's dandies wore their collars so high they covered their ears. Many actually weaved in whalebone stiffeners to hold the heavily starched cloth away from their necks. As a result, they could no longer turn their heads but had to rotate their entire bodies, making them appear absurd and foolish.

The ends of Chase's cravat were brought forward and tied in a single, simple large knot. Rather than choking on layers of fabric in hopes of following some silly rule of fashion, Chase confined his cravat to circling his neck only once. Instead of hiding his stubborn and arrogant facial features, the shorter collar accentuated them.

Though Millie hated to admit it, even to herself, Chase had been at the forefront of her mind all evening. She constantly found herself glancing around searching for him. And each time she located his whereabouts, she wished she had not. For in those rare moments when Selena Hall was not clutching his arm, she was hovering nearby. Only Chase's reserved, rugged face kept Millie sane. Not once did she witness any sign of pleasure soften the granitelike rigidity of his appearance. And while his detachment was keeping Millie from making a fool of herself, she knew Chase was unusually skilled at compartmentalizing and hiding his feelings. Selena was undeniably stunning tonight. It would take an exceptional man to be in her company and not be affected by her beauty—and Miss Hall knew it.

When the Three had first spied Selena making a grand entrance, Aimee had caught Millie's look of disgust. "Be mindful of others, Millie. One would think you were jealous right now."

Millie's mouth twisted wryly. "Do not try to fool me, Aimee Wentworth. I know you detest Miss Hall clinging to your brother as much as I do."

Jennelle had laughed. "Aimee might detest it, but I doubt whether anyone could match the antipathy you hold toward the woman. What is the matter with you? I thought Charles was most unpopular in your eyes, since Vauxhall. I was under the impression that you were pleased with his decision to live elsewhere."

"I was . . . am. Despite his enjoyment at seeing me miserable, I cannot understand why he would pretend to take pleasure in *her* company."

Jennelle's eyebrows shot up. "Are you so sure he is pretending?"

Millie had bit her bottom lip, realizing her folly. "Mother

Wentworth believes he is, so he must be. Regardless of his interference in our affairs, I do not wish him to be permanently attached to a manipulative temptress. Even an intelligent man can get caught in the clutches of a scheming vixen."

They had stood silently and watched the gorgeous woman slither among the crowd. Aesthetically speaking, Selena was beyond compare in her rose and gold gown that perfectly highlighted her pink lips and the rouge in her cheeks.

Her low-cut dress was stunning and heavily ornate. Selena was one of only a select few who could wear fashion's elaborate gowns without drowning in their flashy trimmings. The dress was a golden silk, heavily embroidered with copper flowers. A long, rose velvet train flowed behind her, requiring others to watch their step lest they tread on the expensive fabric. In addition to the dress, Selena wore large pearl earrings, which matched the set around her neck. Her hair was piled high on her head in layers of intricate yellow curls, all encased in a formidable feathered tiara matching the embroidery of her gown.

Jennelle had let out a low, barely audible whistle. "Quite dramatic, especially for an unmarried woman trying to appear chaste."

"Indeed," Millie had replied under her breath.

The rest of the evening Millie continued her covert surveillance of Selena Hall as she danced, conversed, and laughed appropriately with the numerous faceless men vying for her attention.

Tonight was the first time Chase had seen Millie since that heart-racing afternoon. After saving her from Lord Marston's untoward plans, Chase had decided to stay completely away from Hembree Grove and focus on contacting Brumby.

While his desire for Millie had not lessened, Chase believed he had regained enough of his self-control to be a true chaperone to her this evening. But when Chase saw her descend the staircase on the way to the carriage, he knew he had been wrong.

She had appeared petite and delicate, not at all like the passionate woman he had embraced only days before. As she moved gracefully down each step, the soft folds of the under-layer of her gown had clung to her curves, revealing slender, straight legs and a narrow waist. He smothered a groan as she walked toward him to curtsy. When she rose and tipped her head back, exposing the milky skin, he almost ordered her back upstairs to prevent any other man from appreciating her beauty.

Only after they arrived at the ball did he realize that Millie was not wearing the amulet and was secretly relieved. He reminded himself that all who would recognize the item had done so already, but no one would miss it tonight. Millie was perfection and had no need of additional jewelry.

Putting distance between them, Chase tried to focus on his mission. But the sight of other men ogling Millie when she was unaware made him continually look for her and ensure himself of her well-being.

Spying a well-known lecherous lord trying to steal an unauthorized caress, Chase moved swiftly to Millie's rescue. As he approached, Chase issued the man a scathing look that sent him scampering away. Reaching her side, Chase expected to see warmth, eagerness, or possibly anticipation shimmering in her eyes. Instead, Millie's expression revealed annoyance—with him. He decided to take a light, playful approach.

"I see you are studying people again."

Millie tilted her head in a nod to acknowledge his presence but refused to look in his direction. "It is a common pastime, I assure you. It is amazing the things you notice if you are observant enough. For example, I noticed after a certain conversation you brightened a bit. Though I found it to be a tad odd that you appeared to be happier in the company of a graying, rather plump gentleman than in the arms of the alluring Miss Selena Hall. Either you are an unprofessed actor or you are up to something, Charlie." Her voice was clipped, more than she intended for it to be. Yet, after hours of quashing fits of rising jealousy, it was also to be expected.

Chase's dark eyebrows slanted into an almost imperceptible frown. He could have sworn he had been discreet and inconspicuous when he had met Lord Brumby. In fact, he knew he had been. He had consciously kept his face impassive and his stance relaxed the moment Brumby confirmed that he was indeed Darlouney's second contact.

Chase calculated the impact of Millie's unnerving and dangerous ability to discern his reactions to supposedly casual meetings. After her detection of Sir Edward in disguise, he should have anticipated Millie would recognize and comprehend which of his meetings involved ulterior motives, and which did not.

Millie had been correct. While not ideal, his long-awaited conversation with Lord Brumby had gone well. And while Brumby did not feel comfortable speaking tonight, he had promised to meet the next morning. Gathering together the remaining members of the secret group and analyzing what they knew, Chase hoped they would soon be able to discern the traitor's identity and bring him to justice. Then he could concentrate on more pleasing aspects of his homecoming. Before long, he might even be able to plan his future and consider the idea of a life with a spunky female who looked devastatingly attractive when she had a mind to.

Misinterpreting Chase's prolonged silence as apprehension, Millie fought to remain calm as he lingered beside her. "Charlie, do be at ease. I am quite positive I am the only one who noticed your conversation to be something more than a mere greeting. However, if you are looking for someone to never notice a thing beyond her own self-important world, I believe your simpering Miss Hall would be an ideal candidate."

So, Millie was jealous—and feisty. Both moods Chase knew and liked well. "Why, my impish sprite, your beauty can hide your true nature from others, but not from me."

"Meaning?" Millie inquired, her scowl matching her crisp tones.

Despite the brittleness in Millie's voice warning him to retreat, Chase decided to tell her the truth. "Meaning, you are magnificent tonight, Millie. I do not believe I have ever seen anyone lovelier. But I know you, and while the world might be seeing a paragon of virtue and a shining example of grace and manners, I know you are a fraud."

She whirled around to face him, glaring at him with burning, reproachful eyes. "A fraud?" she hissed. "How dare you, Charlie Wentworth! How dare *you* call *me* a fraud after all your covert meetings this evening."

Chase briefly skimmed the crowd around them to confirm no one had overheard her. "Calm down. You are attracting attention."

Millie's dark lavender eyes were blazing with fury. Drawn in by their threatening beauty, Chase had to suppress an impulse to pull her toward him and kiss her into submission. "I only meant I know you would rather be anywhere than here right now." Holding her gaze so she would see his sincerity, he added, "As would I."

Millie had felt the sexual pull between them since Chase had moved to her side, but not until he whispered those three words did she realize he had also been suffering. She swallowed and tried to direct the conversation to something neutral and safe. "I wish I did enjoy these parties and small, meaningless conversations—for your mother's sake as well as my father's. They so want us to be a success this Season."

"Trust me, you are." Knowing key members of Society had been observing the male vultures circle round Millie,

Jennelle, and his sister, Chase was positive that, after tonight, the *ton* would spread the word about London's three newest diamonds of the first water. Selena's continual snide comments about Jennelle and Millie were all the proof he needed that the Daring Three were encroaching upon what Miss Hall considered her private territory.

Millie unconsciously studied Chase's square jaw. Her lips ached for his touch and longed to be crushed beneath his own. Her growing desire for him was becoming near impossible to resist.

Millie took a firm grip on her nerves. "Appears that you, too, are a success. Miss Hall cannot seem to find any place to put her hands except on you. How in the world is she coping with your absence?"

Trapped by his unpleasant decision, Chase could not deny Millie's observations. He had his own reasons for encouraging the clingy woman, and they were not ones he wished to explain. He longed for a smooth, simple defense justifying his actions, something that would pacify Millie. But in her current mood that idea was implausible—at least with people watching. "She flocks to my title, not to me."

Not remotely mollified, Millie retorted, "There is more to you than your title, and trust me—she knows it."

Chase couldn't help himself and smiled. The sound of jealousy had never before been even remotely appealing, but now—coming from Millie—it was like music. He wanted to hear more. "Care to expound?"

Realizing she had been caught by her own admission, Millie tried to make light of the remark. "You are an extremely handsome man, Charlie. Unfortunately, I have known you too long to be deceived by your good looks. You are much too perverse and tall to be truly attractive."

"Tall?"

"Indeed. You try to frighten and pressure one with your height. You enjoy your ability to hover when you argue a

point." Her violet eyes reflected the light from the chande-
liers, making them more difficult to read. "Do you not notice
how even now I must crane my head to speak with you?"

Her attempt at levity backfired. Instead of humor, hot, intense, sexual desire blazed in his eyes. Chase reached out to
catch her chin between his thumb and forefinger, holding her
still so that she could not break from his dangerously compelling eyes. "It does not seem to work with you."

Her pulse raced as Millie felt the electricity of his touch.
"That is because you cannot intimidate me. You said you
know me; well, I know you," she barely whispered.

Chase's heart was pounding so loudly he thought the
whole room could hear. Touching her soft skin seemed to
prevent his ability to breathe. He let go and asked, "And who
am I, precisely?"

He was no longer holding her, but she could not tear her
eyes from his piercing gaze. "Somebody haunted, like me. I
just choose to react differently to my ghosts."

Her words pierced him. Gone was Millie's false confidence, her flippancy, her jealousy. Before him stood his soul
mate, and suddenly he needed to be alone with her.

But just as he was going to guide her away from the ever-
increasing mass of attendees, Neville Marston parked himself at Millie's elbow.

"Excuse me, Lady Aldon. May I ask you for a turn on the
floor?" His invitation was spoken loud enough to ensure
several people overheard.

Millie had no desire to dance with Marston. Yet staying
with Chase also made her feel uneasy. Their conversation had
resurrected memories of her childhood promises, including
one particular one.

Realizing Millie had to accept or risk generating tomorrow's gossip, Chase didn't interfere as he watched Marston
guide her away from his side. The *haut ton* loved an original,
but they also loved to find any opportunity to find fault with

women who attracted too many men. Turning down Marston, regardless of the reason, would have made Millie a target for the *ton's* oftentimes temperamental jealousy.

Chase felt his insides boil as he watched Marston smoothly waltz across the dance floor, guiding Millie, holding her hand, fondling her waist. Undoubtedly the man had been waiting for the one dance that allowed him constant contact with a partner, before making his request. Watching the two swirl around, gliding forward and backward to the steady rhythm, Chase realized he was not alone watching the couple.

Marston was undeniably good-looking, and Millie was a petite and graceful beauty. The pair of them was striking and attracted the notice of many a gossip-maker in the room. Despite Millie's flattery, Chase knew he was not what Society defined as handsome. Unlike Marston's golden wavy locks, his hair was dark, thick, and straight. Rather than trying to force it into the shorter, fashionable styles, he chose to let it grow long, pulling it back into a loose ponytail.

Long ago, Chase had accepted the fact that his naturally stoic expression and dark features held no attraction for the fairer sex. Only his money appealed to beautiful women such as Selena. It was that way with every female, except Millie. Millie knew everything about him—his personality, his impassive nature, his thoughts on reckless adventure, his preference for rules. But when she was in his arms, he knew Millie wanted to be nowhere else. And it was not because of his title or his money.

Mildred Aldon was his destiny. His alone.

Chase's hawklike features glowered as he watched Lord Marston become more and more insistent on handling Millie. Marston's embrace smacked of possessiveness. Chase's scowl intensified. Only Millie's reputation kept him from pounding the triumphant look off the vile man's face.

"Your keeper seems to take his role seriously," Marston remarked, observing Chase's unswerving glare.

Millie smiled casually, trying to downplay Chase's fierce expression. "He is protective of all three of us—Aimee, Jennelle, and me."

Marston leaned down and whispered into her ear. "I can be protective, too. You are by far the most sensational woman here this evening. Your dress is mesmerizing. I could stare at you all night."

And you have been, thought Millie as she twisted again. She was constantly adjusting her position so his hands stayed where they belonged.

Marston pulled her into another long twirl, exaggerating the dance's spins and turns. It was another piece of evidence of his need to control and push people around. Millie suspected he was much more dangerous than she first realized.

"Seems you have been reprieved."

Feeling Marston's hot breath against her cheek, Millie fought her instinct to flinch. "I am afraid I do not understand your meaning."

"Your protector. It appears there is another who needs his attention more than you."

Millie swiveled toward Chase's last location just in time to see him disappear out of the room with Selena Hall.

Marston smiled to himself. Chaselton's timing could not have been better. Realizing Millie was focused on the disappearing couple, Marston cleverly spun her into a twirl and held her tightly to him as the dance ended, forcing her to partner with him for the following quadrille.

Only after the music had started did Millie realize her folly. Too upset to handle Marston on her own, Millie quickly scanned the room for either Aimee or Jennelle. She spotted them, made the signal, and sent secret looks of gratitude after they replied with a quick nod of their heads. At the dance's end, they swiftly came over and extricated her from Marston's grasp. Fortunately he seemed unperturbed by their interference.

As the Three walked away, Jennelle commented, "Lord Marston seems very interested in you, Millie. The other night at cards, and now tonight. I believe he would have danced another with you if he thought you would agree."

Millie frowned as Jennelle's words sank in. "Yes, well, he can remain interested, but from a distance."

Aimee looked at her friend, hearing the seriousness behind Millie's words. Jennelle, though, was openly puzzled. "He appears to be well dressed and quite witty. Definitely elegant. There are much worse with whom you could be forced to spend time."

Millie stopped, turned, and gripped Jennelle's hand. "He is elegant in appearance only, I assure you. Believe me when I say he is dangerous."

Jennelle was not convinced. "Are you sure you are not looking for something?"

"What would I be looking for?"

Jennelle gave her a quizzical look. "Why, excitement, of course. I know it has been difficult for you since our arrival in London. Believe me, both Aimee and I agree Society can be fairly confining, but let us not be hasty and label what is probably a very decent man as 'dangerous' just to pacify our whims."

Millie's voice was full of warning when she spoke. "Jennelle, listen to me when I say this. He is dangerous. You have never spoken with him. You have never danced with him. You have never been cornered in his evil wordplay. The man is no gentleman."

Aimee coughed. "I did. Or at least I spoke with him at Lady Bassel's," Aimee explained, sipping her punch and watching Marston.

Eyes wide with surprise at the news, Jennelle prompted, "And?"

"And, well, Jennelle—Millie is right. Lord Marston is . . .

there is something . . . false about him. He makes me nervous."

Millie nodded, relieved to find an ally in her assessment. "We should stay away from him."

Jennelle's brows creased with concern. "That may be difficult. He is at all the events we attend, and he is definitely interested in you, Millie."

Millie bit her bottom lip. "Hmm, but there is something very odd about his interest. It is as if he has a plan and I am part of it," she murmured aloud as she covertly watched Marston meet with the gentleman Chase had cornered earlier. The plump man was the nervous sort with sweaty palms he continually wiped on his clothes when he thought no one was looking. As she watched through lowered eyelashes, Millie could see the gentleman's anxiety rise as Marston's interrogation grew more animated.

Millie was not alone in her observations. Chase had also been watching from a discreet distance. And knowing Millie's innate talent for noticing the obscure, he had been watching her as well. And what he saw sent bolts of fear coursing through him. For what Millie had witnessed was enough to get her killed.

An hour after they arrived home, Millie tiptoed into Aimee's room and paused just inside the doorway. "Aimee?"

"Good grief, Millie," came a muffled moan from the bed across the room. "I realize you are something of a night owl, but I, however, am not," added the semiconscious girl.

Millie grinned. "Aha, you speak and therefore you are awake. Stay that way while I go fetch Jennelle."

Once all three of them were settled on Aimee's bed, Millie began. "I am fairly certain Lord Marston is planning something, and not for the good. I think we should discover the exact nature of his intentions."

Jennelle moaned and fell back against the large goose-down pillows. "Millie, not that again."

Not to be deterred, Millie continued. "Jennelle, the fop specifically set out to charm Aimee and then myself. I assure you, even the most ardent of admirers would be put off by my coldness by now. Are you not the least bit curious as to why he is so keen on our small party?"

Millie had promised Chase she wouldn't tell anyone—even her best friends—about her observations. But lying in her bed earlier, she could not ignore the fact that both Chase and Marston had had confidential meetings with a seriously nervous man. If she could determine Marston's plan, she could relay the information to Chase. Now she just needed to persuade her friends to help her with this bizarre pursuit without breaking her promise.

"I thought you said Lord Marston was dangerous?" Aimee inquired, obviously puzzled by Millie's quest.

Leaning back on the bedpost, Millie nodded. "He is. He is also controlling, calculating, and scheming."

Jennelle rolled over and crossed her arms behind her head. "Are you completely sure of your opinion, Millie? Could it not be that you are looking for any means of adventure? Is this not a manifestation of your constant need for excitement and danger?"

Millie's jaw clenched defensively. "I agree I have an inner compulsion toward such things, Jennelle. But this is not one of those times."

Jennelle shrugged, caving in to a large yawn. "I think he just genuinely likes you. I mean, he may be somewhat aggressive, but he appears to be quite charming."

"From a distance, I assure you. I cannot explain the reasons to persuade you, Jennelle, but I can promise you he is not interested in me, but something related to me. I earnestly believe this man is up to something, and it is important we find out what it is."

"Why?"

Jennelle's question was simple and without malice. It deserved an answer. Unfortunately, Millie had none. The truth was out of the question. But before Millie could come up with a plausible explanation, Aimee did it for her. "I think Millie is right, Jennelle."

"You do?" Jennelle looked around the room. "Am I still dreaming?"

"No, and it is time you realized the difference between Millie's search for entertainment and when she is seriously concerned." The demure side of Aimee's nature completely disappeared. Being so tall, she constantly worked at being delicate in other ways, such as with her manners and voice inflections. But when she wanted to, she could command someone's attention.

"I did not want to say something, because I thought, as you, Jennelle, that Lord Marston was most likely a nice, affable man who, for some peculiar reason, made me feel uncomfortable. But after tonight, and listening to Millie now, I realize she may very well be correct—Lord Marston *is* up to something, and unfortunately, he needs at least one of us for his plans."

Jennelle's disposition immediately changed from casual to intensely interested. "What? Why? How do you know?"

Aimee bit her bottom lip. "I do not know what or why, but I don't think Millie was his original target. Millie, do you remember when Lord Marston first tried to engage you?"

"Umm, near the end of Bassel's ball, if I remember correctly. Right before I saw your brother. I do not think I realized it until just now, but Lord Marston was the real reason I dismissed the crowd around me. I felt . . . hounded."

Aimee crossed her arms and nodded her head. "Then it fits."

With eyebrows furrowed, Jennelle raised her hand. "Wait a minute. How did you do that, Millie? Get everyone to leave you alone, I mean, without it turning into a scandal?"

Millie threw her hands up in the air and smiled mischievously. "Simple. I pretended to be a green girl unused to the crush. I told them I was overwhelmed with the excitement and the attention I was receiving. And if I were to entertain calls from anyone the next day, I simply needed some space away from their admiration."

"And that worked?" Aimee asked incredulously.

"But I thought you refused to receive any callers following Lady Bassel's."

Millie smiled. "Indeed, your memory is not faulty—I refused every request, just as did both you and Jennelle. I guess I was still a little overwhelmed. . . ." Millie put her hand against her forehead and pretended to swoon. She only wished she had continued her original philosophy and turned down Lord Marston's request to call upon her.

Aimee swatted Millie's knee. "Please keep your mind focused on the main purpose of the conversation, Millie. This is important. Anyway, very early in that same evening, Lord Marston was paying *me* a great deal of attention. Immediately I felt uncomfortable, but no matter what I did, he followed me, trying to engage me in conversation."

Completely riveted, Jennelle leaned in. "What did you do?"

Aimee looked at Jennelle, then at Millie, and then back again at Jennelle. "The only idea I could muster without your assistance was a . . . a 'Derrick Burchenal,'" she said, wincing in preparation for their forthcoming reaction.

"You did not!" Millie and Jennelle exclaimed at the same time.

Jennelle was the first to recover. "It is a wonder that anyone has said two words to you since that dreadful night. Just to think of you doing it again makes my ears ache with horrid audible memory."

Several years ago, after attending their first dance as young ladies, Derrick Burchenal, a short, fairly nice but persistent son of a local gentleman, decided he had fallen in love with Aimee. Nothing any of the Three did could persuade Derrick to leave her alone. Everywhere they went, he would show up. Exasperated, Aimee decided to play along and pretend to be likewise interested. However, she made some quick—and ghastly—adjustments to her personality. They were so awful that one night Jennelle and Millie had almost demanded she end the charade—no friendship could endure the offensive sounds. Fortunately, that same evening, Derrick decided he, too, was no longer smitten with the blond beauty.

"But you see, that just proves my point," Aimee stated matter-of-factly.

Remembering how awful Aimee could sound when she tried, Millie nodded. "You are right. Word *should* have spread everywhere about your nasally voice and how it could peel the paper off walls. To what degree did you apply your charms?"

Rolling her eyes, Aimee replied, "You would not believe how horrible I was. I was even clingy. But it worked, and Lord Marston has left me alone ever since. But it seems quite coincidental that in the same evening he decided to set his sights on you, Millie, especially knowing you are friends with me."

Unaffected by the innocuous insult, Millie agreed. "Yes, our friendship alone would have kept any normal, halfway intelligent man away from anything that could put him near a 'Derrick Burchenal.' I will say it again. Lord Marston is up to something, and we need to find out what it is."

Jennelle stood up and began pacing. "Wait a minute, here. Let us all agree that Lord Marston's admiration and intentions are not sincere. And your efforts at persuasion are slowly convincing me he is most disagreeable, but is it wise to get involved with a man you consider dangerous? Why can we not just avoid him?"

"You answered your question earlier. He attends practically every event my mother accepts," Aimee answered.

Millie shook her head. "There is an altogether different reason why, Jennelle. Because I am certain we have something he wants. Even if we were to avoid him, he would not avoid us. We are in a disappearing position of power. Lord Marston currently believes he can achieve his mysterious goal by courting me and gaining my trust. Without a doubt, the conceited man is trying very hard to quickly develop a rapport with me, continually asking me to ride, escort me to parties . . ."

Jennelle stopped pacing and interrupted. "He asked you to ride with him?"

Millie hugged her knees to her chest. "Yes. It was a few days ago when you and Aimee went to one of your Society meetings regarding the Orient or something. He came by to visit, and I made the mistake of accepting his call. It was the most uncomfortable discussion I have ever had in my life. He seemed determined to make me feel . . . vulnerable."

"My God," Aimee whispered. "Whatever you do, do *not* be alone with him again."

"What if that is the only way to discover what he is truly after?" Millie countered.

Aimee reached out and squeezed Millie's hand. "No, that is going too far. I do not know what drives you to take such chances, but not this time. Promise us you will not *ever* meet him alone."

Aimee's words rang coldly in Millie's head. Slipping off the bed, she walked to the door and turned. Seeing the fear in her friends' faces, Millie reluctantly agreed. "But that does not mean I am going to stop looking for opportunities to discover what he is doing."

Millie opened the door and quietly returned to her room. Crawling back under the covers, she thought again on

Aimee's comment and its similarity to one Chase had made at the ball. What drove her to take chances? What compelled her to chase the formidable, to seek danger and then to conquer it?

It was a question Chase had often asked when they were young as he was saving her from some new perilous activity she was undertaking. As a child, she had often retorted "Because it was fun" or "I wanted to." Now, when asked what drove her, she had no answer. She just knew she could not fall into the trap of becoming like everyone else.

Chapter 8

Chase glanced at the time and then released his watch fob to dangle back into place on his waistcoat. He had two more errands to complete before his appointment with Millie. He wondered again at the wisdom of requesting a private meeting and again reminded himself of its importance. His ability to sleep at night had already been compromised, and after the disappointing news he had received yesterday morning, he had no choice. They had to meet.

Chase longed for a life of order and clarity. He preferred living by rules, but at the age of twenty-one, when he had learned of the Rebuilders—and his inherited membership—his life had turned upside down.

Although he had been forced by circumstances into the war, Chase discovered that his natural inclination to remain composed regardless of the situation made him very good at his duties. His success was in large part due to his ability to assert control over both himself and others. As the protégé of the famed Sir Edward, Chase quickly harnessed the skills it took to be a strong soldier, an excellent spy, and a cunning strategist.

Lord Brumby and he had met as planned, but Brumby's willingness to share information had disappeared. The man had been extremely susceptible to the tactics Chase had employed at Alstar's ball. Unfortunately, Brumby's weak spine also made him vulnerable to other forms of persuasion. Forms that had convinced the foolish lord to break his promise to Chase and suddenly "forget" the identity of his second contact of the secretive group that opposed the Expansionist movement. This left the name of the fifth member unknown. Chase received small consolation from knowing who was behind Brumby's sudden resistance—Lord Neville Marston.

After watching the heated exchange between the two men Saturday night, Chase had no doubt Marston was behind Brumby's sudden memory loss. And though the nature of Marston's involvement was unclear, it did give Chase new avenues to pursue. Brumby would be made to see reason as soon as Chase discovered how Marston had pressured him into silence. Marston was clever, but far too pompous and undisciplined to be the traitor. More likely, Lord Marston was just an unsuspecting puppet and following him would be fruitless. While his drive for power made the lord an easy target to manipulate, it also made him far too untrustworthy. The traitor knew of and used Marston, but it was highly unlikely Marston knew of the traitor.

Meanwhile, Chase had an even larger hurdle to overcome: convincing Millie to do the impossible—and on blind trust.

Mildred Aldon had been both the bane of his childhood as well his most secret pleasure. Chasing after her enabled him to climb trees, explore caves, and generally act young under the acceptable guise of "watching out for Millie." Only one time had his best friend, Reece, been foolish enough to ask him if he actually encouraged Millie to be boisterous so that he, too, could have fun. Reece never teased him again about his odd bond with the little hellion.

Never had Chase dreamed their connection would evolve

from youthful diversion to heart-pounding passion. But it had. Saturday night when he saw Millie in Marston's arms, a cold possessiveness had swept through him. It had been as if he instinctively knew someone was trying to steal something very valuable of his.

After rescuing Millie the day of Marston's inauspicious visit, Chase had been convinced of her indifference to the man's charms. But Chase had also been so desperate to leave the drawing room before disgracing himself and giving in to his baser desires, he had not realized her interest in the lord was more than just casual. Even at Alstar's, after Marston had forced her to dance, Chase had assumed she would disentangle herself quickly and avoid him for the rest of the evening. But not Millie. After extricating herself, she had covertly followed Marston's every move. She had been cleverly discreet, and her actions had not gained any notice, but her curiosity about the man was undeniable.

"I may not understand the reasons behind your interest in Marston now, Millie, my dear, but I will. And Lord help you when I do," Chase muttered to himself as he stepped down from the carriage to enter his tailor's shop.

Millie was perplexed by Chase's missive. It was brief, vague, and a bit abrasive.

> *We must discuss Saturday night. Prepare Hercules for riding. Be ready at five o'clock this afternoon.*
>
> *Chaselton*

Saturday night? Millie wondered as she paced back and forth in the empty library. They had barely spoken to each other at Alstar's ball, and when they had, it had been more confrontational than pleasant. And now, two days later, Chase wanted—no, *demanded*—to meet with her.

The request to go riding could indicate their conversation needed to be in private, but that could easily be achieved without leaving Hembree Grove. Maybe Chase needed to curry favor. He knew of her love for riding and her lack of willing chaperones. It would be an excellent way to make her more amenable to suggestions. And Chase was forever eager to offer those.

Millie had been relieved when Aimee decided to join Jennelle in her visit to Melinda Brinson's. Mrs. Brinson was an excellent seamstress, and for the price of one original creation, she had converted four of Jennelle's older gowns into new fashion statements. Millie had intended to spend the time rethinking every conversation she'd had with Lord Marston. Yet shortly after Jennelle and Aimee departed, Chase's note had arrived.

Millie tapped the folded paper against her chin. What had happened Saturday night that prompted a private conversation? Miss Selena Hall? No, she had draped herself on him, but that was nothing unusual. Sir Edward? Chase could want to discuss him, but it seemed unlikely.

Pausing to look out the window, Millie considered all the reasons why Chase might want to speak with her. "Only one thing remains. He wants me to stay away from Marston," she whispered to herself.

Despite his demands to the contrary, Millie fully intended to continue her plan to pursue Lord Marston. Chase had made it clear he disliked the idea of the handsome lord dancing with her, but he had not said a word or made a single move to intervene when Marston had stepped in and deftly swept her into a waltz, and the quadrille after that. Instead, he had chosen to spend time with Selena.

The memories of Saturday evening bubbled in her mind again. The more Millie mulled over Chase's written commands, the more offended she became. *Come five o'clock,*

Charlie Wentworth, Millie thought, *I will be ready to discuss Saturday night, but I doubt you will be.*

Chase silently led Millie through a remote area of Hyde Park, avoiding Rotten Row, the Grand Strut, and any other populated path or area. She had not spoken a single word since he had arrived exactly at five o'clock, and his words had been limited to "Good, you are ready."

The ride was a far cry from any romantic afternoon jaunt in the park. Chase had been paying more attention to random passersby than to her. Where the park is usually a place to see and be seen, they were riding in remote areas, avoiding any and all people. Millie wondered if it was as intentional as it appeared. She soon received her answer.

They were entering a deserted section of the park, thick with trees and several unusually high hedges. Chase stopped beside one and dismounted. After helping Millie down from Hercules, he turned and paced to one particularly thick hedge, staring. All of a sudden, he stopped, grabbed his reins, and disappeared with his horse through the eight-foot brush.

Millie's breath caught in her throat. "Chase?" she called out quietly. Receiving no answer, she moved closer to the thick brush and asked in a somewhat louder and more perturbed voice, "Chase? Where did you go?"

Suddenly he reappeared in front of her again. "Follow me. Bring Hercules," he ordered in hushed tones.

"Chase, wait. Where are we going?"

Chase's look was one of barely disguised impatience. "Come and see."

Millie took a stubborn stance and crossed her arms in front of her. "You demand my attendance on today's jaunt and then practically ignore me. And now you think to order me into a . . . a *bush* with nary an explanation. I think not, Charlie Wentworth."

Chase fought the instinct to roll his eyes. She was back to calling him Charlie. And all because he had said very little since they had left Hembree Grove. She was not the first female to admonish him about his aloof nature.

He had been in his midtwenties and was supposedly home for a short respite from the war, when a very intent and aspiring marchioness-to-be had continually tried to engage him in conversation or some type of activity. He had apathetically obliged, not because he wanted to, but to maintain the country party facade that masked the meetings taking place among him, his father, and other key Rebuilder members. The young woman, after a few weekends of fruitless pursuit, decided to seek titled men far more complimentary and engaging than Chase. And though Chase had cared nothing for her, her parting words had remained with him throughout the years. "As a wealthy future marquess, there can be no doubt of your ability to find a wife when you deem yourself to be ready. However, if by that time you still hold no value in charming the fairer sex, prepare yourself. For you *will* have a wife, but you *will not* find the happiness all men seek."

While her comment was memorable, he had not cared if she spoke true or not. Now, surprisingly, he did.

"Where are you taking me?" Millie demanded again, pointing at the mysterious greenery from which he had reappeared.

He took a step closer. "A place where we can talk privately."

Millie retreated a step. "Why could we not have met in the study and just closed the doors?"

Chase stopped his advance and frowned. "Elda Mae."

"Oh . . . Elda Mae," Millie repeated, her voice dwindling as she realized Chase was correct. The older woman, while devoutly loyal, was also very protective and extremely prone to eavesdropping.

Chase grabbed Hercules's bridle and then Millie's gloved

hand. Seconds later she found herself in a large enclosed garden about the size of Hembree Grove's library. Surrounding her were a series of neglected, very tall, dense hedges in the shape of a warped rectangle. No entrances or exits could be seen. While trees were ample outside the strange enclosure, none grew inside. Nor were there any flowers. The natural greenery would require very little maintenance. The only man-made items in the private garden were four very old cement benches set in the shape of a square in the middle of the clearing.

Stunned, Millie haphazardly brushed the stray sprigs that had caught on her dress upon their entrance into the hidden sanctuary. Unpinning her light-blue ruched bonnet, she removed it and took in the setting. "What . . . Where are we?"

"As I said, a place where I know we can meet privately and without interruption," Chase replied, plucking the remaining loose leaves caught along her shoulders. The action felt natural and gave him a surprising amount of pleasure.

Oblivious of Chase's ministrations, Millie walked a few steps forward and waved her hand. "Yes, well, um, this is definitely private."

Chase let go of Hercules and the horse joined his to graze in the far corner of the garden. "Come, relax for a moment."

Millie turned and sat down on one of the cool benches, still marveling at how they and their horses had got in without leaving any signs of entry.

"Um, Chase, just how did we get in?"

Chase looked bemused. "You were with me."

Millie shot him a frustrated look. "Yes, but it does not seem possible. With the exception of a few fallen leaves, the hedge looks undisturbed, and with Hercules . . . well . . . how did we get in?"

"Many years ago, when the bushes of this garden were much smaller, there was a clear entry point. Initially, this place was used by gentlemen trying to romance their intendeds, but over the years the hedges grew and it became less and less popular to ride so far from the Strut. The public avoided, and then eventually forgot, its existence."

"But not everyone," Millie countered.

Chase smiled. "No, not everyone. My father needed a place to meet with . . . certain nobles outside of Hembree Grove and servants' ears, and remembered this spot. The dense growth on either side of the entry had grown, masking the opening. One simply has to know where the entrance is and push the branches out of the way. And as long as this garden is not overused, it will remain hidden, providing an ideal meeting place when one needs privacy."

"Oh," was all that Millie could think to say. Suddenly she realized they were alone. *Really alone.* The thought made her heart race. Swallowing heavily, she tried to move the conversation to a topic she hoped would ease the pounding in her veins. "You wrote that you wanted to discuss Saturday night. I cannot imagine anything about this past weekend's activities that would require such lengths for privacy."

Chase recognized the conversation's shift and guessed at the reason. Millie was just as aware as he regarding the sparks flying between them and was attempting to divert their attention. He was unsure whether he welcomed her attempted diversion or was annoyed by it. "I wanted to discuss Marston."

Millie punched her legs with her kid-gloved fists. "I knew it."

"You did?" Chase asked, surprised by her anticipation of their discussion topic.

Millie searched his face. "What else could you want to discuss regarding Saturday's events?"

Actually, quite a lot, Chase thought. "Let us just start with Marston."

"Yes, let us. *You* start with Lord Marston, and *I* will begin with Miss Selena Hall."

"What about Miss Hall?"

"What about Lord Marston?" Millie countered.

Chase stared at Millie, his golden eyes gleaming with frustration. "Fine, Millie. I will answer your question. I want you to stay away from him. Trust me when I say Lord Marston is dishonorable and a scoundrel of immeasurable proportion. I do not want Aimee, Jennelle, or you having anything to do with him."

What had she expected? Concern for her, just for her, because of her? Hurt manifested itself into a sharp retort. "He is at the same events. I cannot refuse a dance without repercussions, Charlie. And his attentions are bound to be paid again Wednesday. We were just invited by Lady Castlereagh to Almack's. Your mother would be rather upset if we declined our guest vouchers, and I do not imagine she would find your lack of fondness for Lord Marston an acceptable excuse for our refusal."

As Chase listened to her cavalier remarks about his warning, fear ripped through him and a protective anger flared to life. He gripped her shoulders. "He is not for you, Millie. Do you understand? *He is not for you.*"

Millie shrugged him off, stood up, and looked down at him. "Oh, really? And since we are on the subject, just who is for you? Selena Hall? That woman set her sights for you early in the Season. And it seems to be working. Every time she calls, you fall in line, following her around like a lost puppy."

Chase rose to his feet and held her flashing eyes with his own. "Did I just hear you call me a *puppy*?"

His question caught her off guard. Chase might be many aggravating things—but a weak-willed puppy was not one of them. "That is not what I meant. I was just . . ."

Chase pulled her up against his chest. "Just what?" Before Millie could respond, he said, "Selena may be every noble's dream of a wife, but she means nothing to me. She is insincere and fairly one-dimensional."

He was holding her so close Millie could feel their breath mingling. Her pulse raced. "She is also self-absorbed and artificial," she said.

"You forgot shallow and unattractive."

Millie blinked at him. "You think Selena unattractive?"

"Very."

"Oh," Millie murmured, trying to weigh his words against what she had seen.

"And Marston?" Chase probed.

Millie's eyes had locked with his, and only thoughts of Chase remained. "Who?"

Chase gave her a slight squeeze. It worked.

"No . . . No, not at all," Millie responded. "The three of us were just talking last night about avoiding him and . . ."

Chase's mouth covered hers, silencing her words of explanation with lips so tender she could not form a coherent thought. Millie melted as his tongue entered, gently stroking the inside of her mouth. As before, she eagerly responded in kind, innocent of the uncontrollable storm she was creating. Tongues teased, tasted, and tantalized.

Chase slowed the kiss. As soon as Millie had denied any affection for Marston, his need to claim her as his own could not be contained. This time, though, he wanted to take his time and let her feel the endless longing inside him. She trembled under his lingering, compelling caresses. She wanted more, needed more, but didn't know what. All Millie knew was that she wanted Chase more than she had ever desired anything in her life. She clung to him as the heat in her veins turned into a blazing fire.

His hand curved around the back of her neck, savoring the silken feeling of her skin. Her scent, her response, her softness—it took all his concentration to suppress his need to lay her down and make love to her. He knew he should stop kissing her before their passion grew into something uncontrollable. It was too dangerous here. He was not afraid they would be seen. The danger lurked from knowing there would be no witnesses. His desire for her was exploding, and the knowledge he could take her now, and no one would be the wiser, was so very tempting.

Slowly he pulled away, but found himself drowning in her crystal-clear violet pools. They had the power to strip any man of reason.

When Millie felt his lips completely release hers, her chest was heaving with the effort it took to breathe. Millie knew she was losing her heart to Chase and that was the real reason why he could so easily rattle and provoke her into childlike retorts. She was falling in love and desperately didn't want to.

She had sworn never to marry, and of the Daring Three, she believed most strongly in her pledge. Or at least she had. Now, Millie wanted so very much to break it. Who would have thought a man's kiss could ruin such a well-intentioned promise?

"Maybe this wasn't such a good idea." Chase's voice was deep and affected, husky with desire.

Millie's quizzical look was filled with misunderstanding and hurt.

He tucked a loose wisp of hair back behind her ear. "I just meant that it is harder keeping my hands off you than I imagined it would be. I believed I could keep my passions under control. I refuse to force us into a quick marriage based on my compromising you, Millie."

Millie heard only a fraction of his words. They had centered on how easily Chase had expected to remain indifferent to her and how he didn't want her—at least not for a wife. While she had always known this, the words now spoken aloud had a ring of perpetual loneliness. Only pride kept her from crying.

Millie jutted her chin slightly, trying to appear poised and unaffected by his statement. She needed to leave before Chase saw through her ruse. "I think it is time I return to Hembree Grove. I have to prepare for the theater."

Chase walked over and grabbed the reins to their horses. He returned to Millie, extended Hercules's reins to her, and finally broached the topic that had prompted his request for their private meeting. "Millie, I have an important request of you, one I ask you not to take lightly."

The seriousness in his tone caught her attention, as did his implication that she tended to approach all serious things in a childlike manner. "My lord?" Millie prompted.

The simple phrase was laced with a little more venom than she had intended, but never once did Millie consider apologizing. She took Hercules's reins and stared pointedly at Chase, refusing to flinch when he stared back.

Millie's biting tone was not lost on Chase. Neither was the intentional slight she expressed through her sudden formality. Her eyes had darkened, which usually indicated her pride had been injured. If he had not witnessed, at least a dozen times in the past few weeks, Millie controlling her anger in much more pressing and justifiable circumstances, Chase would have deemed her reaction to be incredibly immature. No, just as she was affecting him, he, too, was affecting her. And while he fully intended, in the near future, to explore the reasons behind their strange behavior when in each other's company, right now Chase was more interested in gaining her promise to what should be a very simple request.

Chase took a deep breath and exhaled. "Millie, you have a rare talent for observing the details surrounding you. And while this is in many ways a useful talent, it is also an inconvenient one. In short, I need you to refrain from noticing things any normal young lady attending her first Season would not. To be even more clear, I want you to ignore me and anyone in contact with me, whether it is I or they who have initiated the conversation."

Stunned, Millie's mouth opened and closed several times before she could respond. "Pardon me, my lord. Did you just ask me to *stop watching people*?"

Chase could feel his jaw tighten. Millie had a way of twisting even the most straightforward of requests. "Indeed, that is *exactly* what I mean. Do not deny this habit of yours to alleviate boredom. You relish being aware of things that others are not so keen to observe."

Millie was tempted to smirk, but refrained. "You know me so well."

"I know you well enough to realize this may be a futile plea. But there is one man in particular I must request you to feign absolutely no knowledge of—Lord Brumby."

It took several seconds before Millie could recall to whom Chase was referring. Lord Brumby was the nervous man, the one with the sweaty palms. "Such a bizarre appeal, and, as you say, one that is against my nature. Before I agree, let us talk of *your* inclinations, Charlie Wentworth. You string words together smoothly, as a polished gentleman should, but I know you as well. You have not issued a request, but a demand. Can you at least tell me why?"

"Not particularly. Only that the reasons behind your pastimes and interests could be misconstrued and place you in considerable danger."

Millie at first believed him to be teasing. The idea seemed ludicrous. How could simply observing a short, balding man put her in any danger unless . . . *Oh my*, Millie thought as she tried to keep surprise and understanding from registering on her face. Brumby must be the man Chase and Sir Edward had been discussing. If anyone saw her watching the jittery lord, then it could impair Chase's ability to complete his mysterious mission. "I understand, Chase."

She had called him Chase. He was winning the battle, but knew better than to believe she had so quickly acquiesced to his request. "And?" Chase asked with deliberate emphasis, remembering her many verbal traps in which he had been caught.

When they were young, Millie would say she had understood a direction or command he gave, only to find out later that she had completely ignored it. When confronted, Millie would look directly into his eyes, display no remorse, and point out his folly—that she had never promised compliance, only an understanding of his desires.

The first time Millie successfully used this stratagem, Chase had been infuriated. Mostly because she had done it in front of his parents, who had laughed heartily at her witticism. He swore never to be caught again by her clever mind. Unfortunately, he had found himself in similar predicaments time and time again.

But he was no longer a naïve young man. Years at war had taught him the value of evaluating one's words and being patient until he was sure that he got the compliance he needed.

"And?" Chase asked again, a little more forcefully.

Millie inhaled deeply. After several silent seconds, she ended the battle she was waging against herself and shook her head. She did not like being trapped into pledging oaths, but her instincts told her Chase was not going to succumb to her tricks. "*And* I will not overtly watch the man. Goodness, Charlie, I doubt whether anyone but you has noticed my little ways of keeping myself sane at these endless events."

"I realize you have not been overt, Millie. You have actually been very clever about concealing your observations, but the men I am after are cruel and ruthless. They have committed unspeakable crimes and have no morals in their character to prevent them from doing so again. Especially if they judge you a danger by assuming you know something regarding Brumby, even though you do not. So I need your pledge, Millie, and we are not leaving without it."

She stared at him through lowered lashes. The stubborn, black-and-white, unyielding Charles Wentworth had returned. For so many years, she could see him only as the sole impediment to any fun she, Aimee, and Jennelle wanted to have. But now, hearing the sincerity and appeal in his voice and the residual passion in his eyes, Millie realized Charles, Charlie, and Chase were one and the same. And they always had been. And suddenly he meant more to her than any other man ever would. Somehow she was losing her heart to the one man who physically desired her—but not as a partner, and especially not as a wife.

Aimee had warned her that love was not something she could choose. That controlling one's heart was as impossible as controlling the direction of the wind. Only now did Millie understand. She was falling in love with Chase. It mattered not that he did not love her in return, but she would do whatever she could to keep him safe and put him at ease.

"I promise not to consciously watch or observe Lord Brumby and will take steps to avoid him when at the same events. Satisfied?" she asked quietly, trying halfheartedly to retain some morsels of her pride.

Chase studied her. He had expected Millie's final acquiescence to be full of defiance, but not of sorrow. Even the small sarcastic quip carried a tone of grief, as if by yielding to his demand she had lost something very precious in the process. He so wanted to know her thoughts and the reasons why she had relented. Even her unusual eyes held no clue. Soon he was going to let himself drown in those purple pools. But he could not allow himself to do so today.

Millie let out a deep sigh as they rode back to the more populated parts of the park. She was maneuvering Hercules to head toward Grosvenor Gate, when suddenly a familiar figure appeared on horseback.

"Lady Aldon, how nice to see you again so soon."

Millie stiffened. The words were friendly, but the voice was not. "Lord Marston, I believe you know the Marquess of Chaselton."

Marston's eyes narrowed as he took in the huge black animal underneath Millie. The woman had played him for a fool. Something no one ever did without consequence. "Indeed. I see your fear of horses has abated since my invitation to ride."

Millie's gaze grew shrewd. "Lord Marston, I do not recall ever saying that I was afraid of horses. However, I do remember being shocked into silence upon your assumption of my timidity. I saw no reason to correct your offensive misjudgment."

"I see," Marston replied, his voice low and ominous.

Chase, who had been quiet up until now, responded in a flat monotone. "See that you do, Marston." The quiet power of Chase's words was unmistakable.

Marston gave a perfunctory nod, turned his horse, and cantered away. Lady Aldon had led him on a merry little chase. He had intended to use her to get inside the Wentworth home, seduce her, and eventually discard her. But seeing her emerge from the less populated areas of the park with Chaselton, Lady Aldon could no longer be viewed as just a dear friend of the family. Chaselton's involvement and protection might make things more difficult, but in truth, it changed the plans only slightly.

Marston grimaced as he dug his heels into the sides of his mount. He would still get what he wanted from Chaselton *and* from Mildred Aldon—one way or another.

Chapter 9

Millie flipped over and disentangled herself from the twisted bedcovers. The moonlight pouring in told her morning had not yet arrived. Letting her arm flop against her forehead, she stared at the ceiling and wondered if she would ever have a good night's sleep again. Once more, she tried to convince herself that it was a good thing Chase did not want to marry her. Chase embodied an emotional trap from which she had vowed to be forever free. Yet at every event she attended, Millie could not stop herself from searching for him and wondering if he would ever again be present. She looked, but Chase was never there.

Her frustration was mounting, and Millie needed a way to relieve it. Rising out of bed, she lit a lamp, dressed, and found herself about to embark on the unthinkable. Four hours later, she heard the squeak of somebody entering her short-lived sanctuary.

"Millie?" Aimee asked as she opened the study door to find her friend at the desk, busily scribbling away. Aimee had just finished her morning meal and was passing the study on her way to awaken her normally last-to-rise friend when she heard the furious scratching of a pen. Aimee stood, shocked for a moment. Millie was not in bed, but writing. And from the stack of correspondence in front of her and the ink stains on her fingers, Millie had been awake for some time. "Heavens! Millie, look at your hands! Whatever are you doing?"

"Just answering all our requests for calls from the last few nights' events. Several more arrived early this morning." She stopped and pointed at a stack. "Those are yours. I am answering in the negative, by the way. So, if there are any that you want to accept, pull my response out. You will have to write the positive ones yourself."

Aimee retrieved two stacks as Jennelle wandered in and collapsed onto a gold velvet high-back chair. Aimee handed her a stack of responses.

Jennelle took them. "What are these?"

"Millie wrote them."

A single eyebrow rose in disbelief as Jennelle opened one and read it. "Millie, this is wonderful. You do have quite a knack for turning a man down without hurting his pride." Jennelle took in her voluminous stack and then glanced at Aimee's. "My goodness, Millie. This is a lot of work. It must have taken you hours to compose all of these."

Millie sighed without looking up. "We are going to have to find a different way of turning these gentlemen down. At first, the requests were manageable, but, Jennelle, you are getting quite popular. I believe you are now the current leader in visitation pleas. Who's the original now?"

Jennelle let out a low whistle as she thumbed through her pile, silently reading the names. "Who would have thought . . ."

Aimee put her stack back on the table. "I would have."

"So would I," Millie added, finishing the last response in her own stack of "thank you—but no" replies. "There. Finally, that is done."

Aimee looked at her friend more closely. "Frankly, Millie, this is most unlike you. How long have you been at this writing frenzy?"

"Since before the early meal."

"Why, that was hours ago! How are you able to appear so alert?"

"She is experiencing a chemical reaction induced by high anxiety," Jennelle answered as she pulled out one response, read the name, and smiled before replacing it. "I was reading on the subject in one of my travel journals. It seems the body has the ability to produce a chemical that stimulates the mind and keeps one awake. During the war, several studies were conducted on soldiers who, though lacking sufficient sleep, were able to remain alert in times of stress." She paused mischievously for effect. "So tell us, Millie. Are you stressed?"

Millie clenched her teeth and gripped the edge of the desk. "No, I am not stressed. I am just a little upset."

Jennelle released a small chuckle of disbelief and tucked her feet underneath her. "Millie, you have just composed over fifty regrets in a single sitting. Although I must admit you did a splendid job, it is most unlike you to volunteer for a chore you hate."

"Jennelle has a point. What has you so troubled?" Aimee inquired as she sat down on a dark settee.

Millie pursed her lips and then rolled her eyes, deciding to surrender now rather than submit to hours of hounding. "If you must know, I have been up most of the night thinking about Lord Marston. We have to develop some kind of plan that, without letting him know of our intentions, gives us the needed insight as to what he wants with us and how to stop him. Unfortunately, I produced not a single idea worth mentioning. Frustration led me here," Millie stated. Then, pointing at the stack of replies, she added, "And those are the direct result of my need to accomplish *something*."

Aimee scrunched her nose. "It is a shame Charles is no longer staying at Hembree Grove. He would have at least kept you company."

Jennelle hummed happily as she continued flipping

through the correspondence, reading the names of all the gentlemen who had requested her company. "Hmm, where could Charles vanish to in the middle of the Season?"

"Oh, he has been staying at Reece's town house in St. James's," Aimee replied casually. "Now, do not look at me like that. I only found out yesterday when I saw one of the footmen sneaking out a large trunk out of his room. The poor lad panicked when he saw me. So of course that made me only more curious."

Millie fought hard to appear disinterested.

Jennelle rose and placed her stack on the desk next to Aimee's. "And just what did you do to the unlucky footman to assuage your curiosity?"

Aimee shrugged her shoulders. "Perhaps I might have threatened to make him practice defense moves with Millie." An impish smile grew on her face. "Her reputation has quite a unique power of persuasion."

"Oooh, that is evil—and brilliant," Jennelle said, nodding in approval.

Millie rose from the desk chair and pulled the drapes back from the window to look out at the gardens below. The scene was very peaceful, but Millie felt surprisingly hollow inside. She had not seen Chase since he saw her home from Hyde Park—several days ago. Suddenly, despite her friends' company, she felt alone. Vulnerable.

Millie rubbed her arms and mentally rallied herself. It was silly to feel this way. It had been just four weeks since they had been reacquainted after an eight-year absence. Was it not better that he was no longer about? Would it not be torture to see him daily and know he would never be hers?

Aimee watched, slightly perplexed by the sadness in her friend's face and decided this time she would not take no as an answer. "Well, Jennelle and I want to propose something that is sure to lift your spirits. There is a special event we are attending this afternoon, and you will be coming with us."

Millie could not help it. A groan escaped her lips. She let the drapes fall from her fingertips and turned to refuse the offer when Aimee rose, waving her finger back and forth.

"Ah-ah-ah, before you speak, realize this. You *are* coming. Besides, you will love this particular event. And if you roll your eyes at me one more time, you will find them stuck in the back of your head when I give you a thump."

"Boo, boo, scary, scary," Millie said sarcastically.

"Seriously, Millie. You will love this one. I promise."

Millie walked back over to the desk, placing it between her and the unrelenting looks of two pairs of eyes. She sat down and crossed her arms. "Really? As much as I just *loved* Almack's?"

Aimee grimaced. "Honestly. How was I to know? It was supposed to be a great honor to be asked to attend the Assembly Rooms. It is terribly exclusive."

Jennelle shivered at the memory of being scrutinized and judged as if she were a horse at Tattersalls. "Well, I have to agree with Millie on the horror of Almack's. I still cannot believe people actually *pay* to attend a lousy dinner and a taxing all-night dance afterward."

Aimee turned and gave Jennelle a look that clearly conveyed her exasperation. "Well, it made Mother happy, and I expect we will have to attend at least one or two more times this Season."

Millie looked down at the stack of regrets. "Yes, unfortunately, being proclaimed 'worthy' by that bunch of doughty ladies has labeled us as aspiring debutantes. My poor, cramping fingers are the result."

"Hmm, at least you were not the focus of their attention," Aimee moaned daintily, as only she could.

Millie produced an exaggerated shrug. "Do not blame Jennelle and me that you are tall, blond, and beautiful. If 'the queens of London Society' could write a book on . . . what did they call it, Jennelle?"

"The social acceptability of young ladies," Jennelle said, exaggerating the formal tone of the oldest Almack patroness.

"Yes, well, Aimee's picture would be on the cover."

Aimee narrowed her eyes in mock protest. "Well, just be glad we were only invited as guests and are not members."

Millie snorted. "Believe me, and I do not jest, that has been added to my prayers at night."

Jennelle grimaced, realizing the depth of her friend's frustration. "You are in a mood, Millie. Come with us. The main speaker is a woman explorer who loves adventure. I am sure you will find it exciting."

Responding to Jennelle's support, Aimee asserted, "If you do not, then we will stay home with you. And keep in mind our history, Mildred Aldon. The 'queens of London Society' might not understand my stubborn nature, but you do. Understand now: either you go—or we stay."

Millie bit her bottom lip. It was clear Jennelle wanted to go, but it was even more evident Aimee was going to win this argument. And despite appearances, Aimee could be aggravatingly mulish when she had a mind to be. Sighing, Millie relented. "As long as I do not have to dance. If I have to perform one more elaborate, intricate cotillion for half an hour with a man who cannot tell his left foot from his right, I will surely scream."

"Warm up your lungs, then. You will not be dancing at today's Explorer Society meeting, but you will be this weekend at Lady Sefton's."

Aimee put up her hand when she saw Millie prepare her protest. "I know, I know. It will be Almack's all over again. But just think. There is an excellent chance Lord Marston will be there."

Millie tapped her lips with her index finger, her eyes sparkling with interest. "There is that." Surely by Saturday she could think of a way to discover the slick man's true intentions.

"Come on," Jennelle said, standing. "We cannot go as we are, and I need to stop at Mrs. Brinson's to collect my dress for tomorrow night's ball. If we do not leave soon, we will not arrive early enough to get a good seat."

Deciding to collect Jennelle's gown afterward, they headed directly to the meeting in hopes of arriving early. Within a block of the event, they realized that though they had arrived early, the hall was already quite crowded. They quickly headed in and were thankful to find three seats together near the back of the lecture hall.

"Is it usually this crowded?" Millie whispered, looking around, surprised by the number and different types of people attending the lecture. The speaker was drawing a strange gathering. Last time she had attended one of Jennelle's meetings, the audience was comprised only of people with strong scholarly and literary interests. Today's crowd was incredibly varied, ranging from Bond Street beaus, whose focus was solely on fashion, to cits from the business side of London, to more well-to-do merchants.

Jennelle shook her head. "No, it is not at all common. The crowd is especially large. But as Aimee and I told you, today's speaker is special. I expect a third of the onlookers are here to gawk, another third are here to discover if a new investment is at hand, and the other third are here because of their true and pure interest. I think once you find out who it is, you will find yourself in the third category, Millie. Do not be surprised when you hear me utter the words 'I told you so' upon our departure."

Despite her expectation otherwise, Millie found herself enjoying the event much more than she had supposed she would. She loved to watch people and fantasize about their thoughts and motivations. Chase was right, she thought. It would be an impossible task to completely refrain from her favorite pastime of studying people. Then she noticed two men crouched together, speaking softly but animatedly. They were upset about something.

Millie elbowed Aimee. "Aimee, look over there."

"Where?"

"Over there. Can you see those two gentlemen? One is in green with a striped waistcoat. Do you know who they are? Do they normally attend these things?"

Aimee shrugged. "I do not think so. Jennelle?"

Turning to see to whom Millie was referring, Jennelle took a good look. "They have not attended since we arrived in Town, but I think I recognize one of them."

"Maybe they are friends. What do you think they are discussing?" Aimee mused.

"I do not believe they are friends at all. I think they are arguing," Millie said in hushed tones, concentrating on the heated exchange.

Jennelle looked at her friends, who were openly staring at the argument across the room. "Can I be the voice of reason here? Why do you care whether those three men know one another or if they are friends or enemies?"

Millie whipped around. "There are three?"

Jennelle rolled her eyes and pointed. "Yes, Millie, look. Now you can see the third."

Millie craned her head, trying to see the third person, when she suddenly realized what she had done. The third man was Lord Brumby. She quickly turned away and tried to get her friends to do the same. "I believe you are right, Jennelle. It is rather silly. Forget I mentioned them," Millie murmured, glancing one last time at the men huddled together.

Millie was sure they were the same men she had seen Chase speaking with at the Bassel and Alstar parties. Surely none of them had any interest in the speakers or the discussions that were about to start. They must be here at this event for one reason only—to meet privately in a crowd. Something people did if they believed they were being followed.

Millie took several deep breaths and forced herself to avoid watching the clandestine meeting. Chase had no idea what her promise to him was costing her. Fortunately, she was saved as the main speaker moved behind the podium.

Minutes later, Millie found herself getting drawn in by the discussion. The speaker was a Miss Jeanne Labrosse. She was the first woman to ever fly solo in a hot air balloon, the first to have an all-female crew, and the first to use a parachute. To Millie, Miss Labrosse was the model of a truly adventurous woman.

Balloon exploration was the theme of the whole afternoon. Each speaker would build excitement by repeating the mantra, "Anyone can do it." They cited Madame Elisabeth Thible, a French opera singer who became the first woman to fly when she went up in a Montgolfier balloon. When they discussed the business advantages of ballooning, the cits suddenly became animated, asking questions about costs, speed, reliability, and the possibilities of using balloons for shipping.

While the meeting was not as exciting as an actual adventure, Millie did concede the topic was much more interesting than those at the *ton's* tea parties. Millie closed her eyes and began to daydream about what it would be like to be Madame Thible and fly high as a mountain, looking down at Gustav III, King of Sweden.

"Millie! Snap out of it," Aimee hissed.

Millie blinked. "What? Why?"

"Look at your three men," Aimee whispered harshly.

Millie pivoted to see what Aimee was talking about. By now so many people had stood up from their seats, she could not see a thing. She was torn between her promise to Chase and her desire to know what was going on. "I cannot see anything."

Not even looking at her, Jennelle whispered, "Then stand on a chair."

Millie's eyes turned into large violet saucers. Jennelle never advocated a deviation from decorum. She might acquiesce and abandon good behavior, but she never suggested it. Millie scrambled onto the chair she had been sitting in. Finally able to see over the heads in the room, she glimpsed the focus of everyone's interest. It was Lord Brumby, and he was yelling something unintelligible.

Millie strained to hear and froze when a shot rang out. She watched in horror as Brumby fell. His two earlier companions were nowhere in sight, and whoever the shooter was had vanished into the crowd.

Standing transfixed on the chair, Millie remembered Chase's words. *The men I am after are cruel and ruthless. They have committed unspeakable crimes and have no morals in their character to prevent them from doing so again.* Millie's stomach turned. Whatever Chase was doing with these men was more dangerous than she had assumed.

Millie stepped off the chair and sat down, oblivious to the madness going on around her. If she knew about the connection between Chase and Brumby, she was sure that others did. She had made a promise not to observe Brumby, but she had never pledged not to watch the other two. If they came anywhere near Chase, she was going to know.

"It will not take but a minute," Jennelle remarked as they approached her modiste's residence. Despite its being in a side of town not normally frequented by nobility, they had been to Melinda Brinson's several times. It was warm and inviting, and all three enjoyed playing with her baby son.

"Stop! Stop now!" Millie cried, getting the coachman's

attention. The closed carriage came to an immediate halt just before they were to turn onto Mrs. Brinson's street. They were in the Wentworth carriage today because Chase had taken the curricle with him several days ago, along with the post chaise used for distance traveling. And right now, the curricle was parked outside of Mrs. Brinson's small residence.

"What in the world?" Aimee asked under her breath, peeking out from behind the carriage curtains.

Millie was looking out the window also, sitting across from Aimee. Jennelle peeked over Millie's shoulders just in time to see a crying Melinda Brinson throw her arms around Chase as they were standing outside.

Jennelle gasped. "Why that's . . . that's . . ." she stammered.

"My brother," Aimee finished, her voice barely audible.

"Yes, but he's with . . . with . . ." The back of Jennelle's wrist pressed against her mouth, halting her attempt to state the obvious.

Millie had seen enough. Silently she released the curtains and sat back in the carriage seat, forcing herself to breathe.

Aimee closed her curtain and she and Jennelle leaned back in unison. "Why would my mother send you to Mrs. Brinson's? This cannot be a coincidence."

"It's not," Millie replied, fighting to keep her tone even and unaffected. "Not at all. Remember when we first arrived here, and we mentioned Lady Chaselton? We received blank stares until you mentioned your brother. It is obvious that Mrs. Brinson's name and your mother's instructions came from him."

Aimee checked the window again. "He's gone now."

Millie was about to rap on the roof to signal the coachman to continue, but Aimee stopped her. "Are we still going to get Jennelle's dress?"

"I do not think I want to any longer. At least not today,"

Jennelle said in soft, sympathetic tones. She had seen the blood drain out of Millie's face when she had witnessed the emotional embrace. Jennelle did not know the depth of the feelings Millie had for Charles Wentworth, but she knew they went beyond friendship. And for that to have happened, Charles must have encouraged her, repeatedly. The defensive walls around Millie's heart were too solid for any other explanation. "Let us go home. I am not in the mood for a new dress. In fact, I am not too sure I ever want to visit that place again."

Jennelle saw Millie's unshed tears as she stared out the window. As the carriage began making its way through the crowded streets, Millie silently thanked her friend for understanding and not inquiring about what was in her heart.

Chase left Melinda's and headed straight for White's. Upon his arrival in Town, Chase had decided to become a member at one of London's exclusive clubs for gentlemen. He had chosen White's. Established in the early seventeen hundreds, it was the oldest club in London, and it was one of the few that had set itself up with premises of its own. Those who regularly attended were categorized as simple men whose lives centered on gaming, gossip, and being fashionably dressed. It was perfect for a nobleman who wanted to be close enough to hear the gossip without actually having to participate in it.

Chase entered and looked around. It was early in the afternoon, but several members were loitering, listening for the latest *on-dit*. Chase spotted Sir Edward sitting in front of the bay window, leisurely partaking of some port. He took a seat nearby.

"Nice view."

Sir Edward turned around. "Hmm, yes," he replied, his tone and demeanor edgy. "Now that Brummell is quite financially ruined, this view has become available to all members—not just Brummell and his cronies."

Chase eyed his old mentor. "I believe he referred to them as dandies."

Edward shrugged. He had little use for Brummell and his short-lived dictates on fashion.

"The place is fairly active for it being so early," Chase remarked as he fixed his coattails.

Edward coughed. "Been a busy afternoon. Something happened and the pointless nobles are here to discover what, and then indulge in their foolish prattle."

Chase observed the excited hum in the room and agreed with his former mentor. "Must be fairly high-profile prattle today. Even the Beef Steak Society is present to discover the news," Chase remarked, indicating the presence of the society's leader, the Duke of Norfolk.

"Really? Charles Howard is here, and at this hour? Should he not be off gorging himself on red meat?" Edward asked, craning his head around the approaching servant to verify Norfolk's presence.

Chase took the pint of ale being offered and sampled the crisp flavor. He sat back, pretending to be relaxed and bored. "They meet tomorrow, and I doubt whether there is any gossip worthy enough to drag those men from their five o'clock steaks on a Saturday."

Edward nodded as he downed the last of his port. "So, if it was not interest in today's gossip, what brings you by?"

"Just came from Melinda Brinson's place," Chase replied, stretching his feet in front of him, feeling the heat emanate from the nearby hearth.

Relief flowed through Edward, evident in both his expression and demeanor. "In truth? How is Geoffrey's widow doing?"

"Better now. It was rough for a while, especially with the baby."

"Hmm, that was unfortunate. She was lucky you were there."

Chase's eyes grew hard with the memory. "I owed it to Geoffrey."

"He was a good man."

"Yes. Yes, he was," Chase replied so low he could barely be heard. He swirled the pint for several silent moments and then swallowed a large portion. The memory of his partner's death was difficult.

Geoffrey, Reece, and Chase had worked very closely together for several years. When Geoffrey met Melinda and decided to marry, Reece and Chase had surmounted many obstacles to be at the wedding. After inheriting a sizable amount of land, Geoffrey had decided to resign his commission and go home to a blushing bride. Chase remembered how he thought his friend had it all—wife, future, happiness, plans beyond the war. But right before his return, Geoffrey had received a tip on the location of a longtime target of the war department.

Chase had been with Reece on a separate assignment. Consequently, on his own initiative, Geoffrey undertook the reconnaissance by himself. It was a trap. His body was deposited in plain view with a clear message. *We know who you are.*

Afterward, Chase did what he could to help Geoffrey's wife. Things went well at first. She had the land, and she had friends. But when her brother-in-law accumulated considerable gambling debts, he demanded and eventually received Geoffrey's land. Melinda's friends quickly disappeared along with her assets. With no living relatives, and Chase and Reece away, Melinda found herself in London searching for a way to earn a living.

Shortly after arriving in Town, she met a kind lord who showered her with flattery and attention. He gave her shelter and, in return, she gave him love. But when Melinda discovered she was with child, she learned the true nature of her lover's character. Instead of support and an offer of marriage, she found herself abandoned. She and her son were barely living on the money she had left from her pawned jewelry when Chase had found her in one of the worst parts of Town.

He immediately set out to move her into an older, empty dower house that, while not in the fashionable part of Town, was safe and respectable. It had been difficult, knowing that if they were caught, both their reputations would be affected. When her lover abandoned her and the baby, Melinda allowed everyone to believe the baby was her late husband's. Chase agreed, knowing what the label of bastard could do to a child.

His visit this afternoon had been full of shocks. First, he had been surprised to find the young toddler large and mobile. His second shock was the child's demeanor toward him. The boy, obviously disappointed to see that the visitor was a large man and not the friend he was expecting, began crying very loudly for his "Miwee." But nothing could have stunned him more than when Melinda told him that "Miwee" was none other than Lady Mildred Aldon, who would entertain her son, oftentimes for several hours, whenever Melinda needed to focus on the needs of Lady Gent.

Knowing how garrulous the Three can be, Chase had feared what might have been said during their meetings, but Melinda had immediately assured him otherwise. She had avoided any topic of conversation that could have led to questions about her past or hint of her association with Chase. It helped that all three women had acted as if her situation was what most assumed—she was a widow and that the baby was her late husband's. Sympathetic to her situation, all three had been extraordinarily kind. Especially Millie, for with her quick wit and ways of persuasion, she had secured Melinda several new clients. As a result, she could now fully support herself and her son.

Oddly, Melinda's admission had enabled Chase to make one of his own. And there, outside on her doorstep, he had told her that he intended to have Millie for his bride. Never did he dream such news would bring tears of joy nor did he anticipate Melinda would congratulate him with a hug. Even now, he felt an odd sense of betrayal that he had allowed another woman to embrace him in such a manner.

"Chaselton!" said a familiar voice behind them. "Surprised you are here, my good man."

Chase turned and inwardly grimaced. The speaker was Lord Pomfrey, a large, round man who relished learning and spreading gossip.

Chase nodded and returned to his comfortable sitting position. "Surprised? Why? It is you, Pomfrey, who is the surprise. I thought you preferred Watier's . . . and their chef." Chase hoped his ungentlemanly comment would put the man off. He soon realized he was not going to be that fortunate as Pomfrey waddled around, placing himself in front of the hearth.

"Ah, great place, Watier's. Not your style, of course. Don't know if you would be allowed in with your preference for trousers and short neckties. We men who are concerned with our dress and appearance"—the stout man puffed his chest out in pride—"have our standards, you know."

Sir Edward coughed. "Ah, well, Watier's has selected well in letting you in."

Chase smiled at the disguised barb. Watier's might have great food, but its existence was going to be very short-lived if it continued to funnel noblemen's fortunes into blackguards' pockets.

Pomfrey, on the other hand, did not comprehend the gibe. "Yes, I know. Unfortunately for you, White's allows anyone in. Although today there seems to be a much higher quality of patronage than the norm. But I suppose that is quite understandable in light of what happened. But I must admit to my surprise, you being amongst us, Chaselton." He paused, as though dangling a juicy morsel no one could resist.

Chase looked up, creasing his brow. "Again you hint I should not be here. Where else would I be, Pomfrey?"

"Why, at home comforting your sister, or did you not know she was there?"

Chase said nothing. He was battling with himself whether to hear the man out or physically throw him from his presence. He looked at Pomfrey's girth and frowned at the seams struggling not to burst. Any unexpected movement would surely result in a vision that should remain behind tailored clothing. Chase decided to let the man have his say.

Pomfrey smacked his lips together several times. He loved gossip. "Rather a ghastly sight for a well-bred lady. Too bad about Brumby. I have been going from group to group, but no one has a clue who performed the foul deed. Can you imagine? Snuffing someone in the middle of a Society meeting with people surrounding you—and getting away with it. Absolutely amazing. Someone *must* have seen something. Well, cheerio. Give my regards to your family for me, Chaselton. I must be off."

Chase remained silent as he watched the heavy man recede into the crowd. His knuckles were white with fury. He had warned Brumby about the Expansionists, but his warnings had fallen on deaf ears. After a heated discussion, Brumby vowed no knowledge of the traitor—certainly not a name—and swore that he had never exchanged any letters with Chase's father. He insisted that he had received only the one brief request to meet, and he had burned that note years ago.

But when Chase inquired about the identity of the fifth man in their group hunting for the traitor, Brumby's nervous fidgets multiplied tenfold and he became immediately recalcitrant. He refused to capitulate to Chase's request, deeming it safer for Chase to forget everyone and everything regarding his father, including the traitor and the ill-fated group.

Chase had known that with time and appropriate pressure, Brumby would eventually break. The traitor must have known this as well. It left the foolish lord in a precarious position. Chase had encouraged Brumby to leave Town immediately, but he would not listen. Brumby thought if he kept visible, proving his silence, he would be spared. He had been wrong. Now only Chase remained between the Expansionists and their goal.

Chase forced his jaw to unclench. The killer he was after was not normally a daring man. There was a reason he shot Brumby in public, and a reason he chose the setting of that particular Society meeting. It was a message for him. The killer had just announced that Chase's family, and maybe even Millie, were potential targets if he did not stop his pursuit.

In silence, Sir Edward carefully watched his protégé war with his emotions. He nodded when he saw Chase rise.

"I must take my leave. Good day to you," Chase said, standing to pick up his gloves and hat.

Chase was going to have to accelerate his plan. Without the identity of the fifth man or the location of the other two markers, he would have to do the unthinkable. Put Millie in danger. At tomorrow night's ball, he would let it slip about the existence of the markers and how they were the key to exposing the traitor. In doing so, Millie's amulet would immediately become of high interest, and only at that point, could he protect her from the danger it put her in.

It would also give him the leverage needed to join the Expansionist cause. The traitor would force his pawns to agree to the admittance, for he would not chance Chase's having proof of his treacherous deeds. Chase just hoped it would give him the time needed to learn and expose the traitor's identity. For it would not be long before his own ignorance of the second and third markers was discovered.

Chapter 10

Millie could not understand why Jennelle was being so adamant. Normally, her conservative friend was incredibly casual about her dress, hair, and overall appearance. But tonight, Jennelle was demanding that all three of them look their best—especially Millie.

"Millie, I think it is time for the egg-white satin."

Aimee's eyes popped open. "But I thought you said it was indecent."

Jennelle waved her hand. "Only for a small gathering. It is perfect for tonight's ball."

Aimee was oblivious to Jennelle's hint. "But you . . ."

Jennelle grabbed her friend's arm and pulled her aside. "I *said* that a woman who wore such a gown was on a mission. And believe me, tonight Millie is one."

Mimicking Jennelle's hushed tones, Aimee asked, "What mission?"

But before Jennelle could answer, Millie came over, suspicious that her best friends were about to decide something contrary to her desires. "If this private discourse concerns me, I would like to be included."

"Of course it concerns you, and no, you cannot be included," Jennelle responded.

Millie crossed her arms and donned a look of inflexibility she had perfected long ago. As a child, it had worked like a charm, but as she grew older, her friends somehow learned how to discern when she was bluffing.

After a several second stare-down with Jennelle, Millie finally warned, "Tell me now. For I will leave neither of you alone until you do."

"Fine. Our discussion is then concluded," Jennelle retorted, surprising Millie by grabbing her shoulders and whirling her around. And with a gentle shove, Jennelle pushed her stubborn friend back toward the dressing table to finish preparing for the evening.

Working with their most talented lady's maid, Jennelle oversaw all aspects of Millie's hair, ensuring perfect placement of every pearl in the intricate mixture of dark curls and waves.

"Perfect. Now for the dress," Jennelle said, smiling at the outcome of her efforts. She rarely liked to apply her talents for styling hair, preferring instead to spend her time reading about far-off countries. Millie might have natural grace and wit, and Aimee the gift of beauty and song, but tonight, it would be Jennelle's eye for perfection that would end Charles's roving eye.

Aimee watched as the pale silk material settled around Millie's curves. The gown certainly did not follow the dictates of fashion. Looking at the creamy vision, Aimee remembered what Madame Sasha had said when they had asked her if it was too risqué. The modiste had been insulted and stated that only a person with dark hair, a little waist, and ample bosom could wear her creation. Worn by anyone else, they would appear like a *blyad*, whatever that meant.

As Millie turned around, Aimee uttered a low whistle. "Why, Millie, I hope Madame Sasha did not underestimate your bosom." Realizing she had spoken her thoughts aloud,

Aimee looked up and caught the stunned looks of her friends. Seconds later, they were all laughing so hard their sides hurt.

Millie wiped away the tears of laughter, thankful for the unexpected moment of mirth. All afternoon, she had been unusually compliant, allowing Jennelle and Aimee to dictate her hairstyle, her gown, and her jewelry. Yesterday's vision of Chase embracing Melinda Brinson still haunted her. Chase was no rakehell. Millie was sure of that. If he were involved with the woman, his heart was committed. He would never put his sister or his mother at risk of ridicule. And that realization made her quite depressed.

But when Millie turned to view herself in the looking glass, her spirits lifted. She saw a beautiful, composed lady who could meet anything life threw at her. She was the same girl who had decided long ago to remain unmarried. Chase might not understand that now, but tonight he would see what Melinda Brinson was costing him: Millie.

Jennelle could see the effect the dress and change in appearance had on her friend and was thankful. Most gowns had puffed sleeves that attached to a straight gown with a trimmed neckline. While Millie's ensemble had no train and no defined neckline per se, it was almost brazen the way it framed Millie's figure. Madame Sasha was right. Only someone with Millie's coloring and figure could pull off this look and still look pure.

The gown was an off-the-shoulder, egg-white-colored dream that gave her skin a porcelain effect. The silk was pleated all around, but instead of gathering underneath her bosom or at the back, it loosely hugged her petite figure at her waist before fanning out to the bottom. A small bit of lace trimmed the petite sleeves and the top of the gown. The hemline was straight and unruffled.

Jennelle had declared jewelry unnecessary. The only adornment Millie was to wear was her amethyst pendant, something Chase had hinted that she should wear that evening. Her hair was piled in soft curls with a single thick coil hanging over her shoulder, giving a look of innocence that countered the alluring essence of the gown. The final element was a sheer shawl, adorned with small pearls scattered over its surface, draped softly across her shoulders. Millie was the perfect combination of the forbidden yet tempting maiden.

Upon his mother's insistence, Chase had agreed to act as the Three's chaperone to Lady Sefton's. It allowed him to feign reluctance in attending the event while enabling him to execute his plan. If all went as planned, his sudden, unanticipated revelation would rattle his adversary, making him vulnerable.

At first, Chase thought arranging to meet the Three at the ball was exceptionally clever. He could execute his chaperone duties with just a few nods and hellos while keeping a safe, but observant distance from Millie. But when Chase saw her, he became instantly aware of every man in the room besides himself.

Possessiveness slammed through him as he watched men openly admire the one woman he considered his. He wished he had the power of ordering Millie to return home and dress into something less . . . imaginative. Objectively he realized her garment exposed nothing except her shoulders. But unlike her other gowns, it made the male mind wander with lascivious thoughts. The instant he saw her in it, he envisioned her naked in his arms. He was positive that every man between the ages of seventeen and ninety was envisioning her the same way, which only inflamed his state of anger.

Chase covertly watched as Millie worked the crowd. She was stunning. Mixed emotions stirred within him. Pride that she would soon be his. Satisfaction that he was the only man in the world who knew what passion lurked beneath those soft feminine tresses. A deep sense of possessiveness that grew stronger every time she was near. And an overwhelming sense of fear.

She was wearing the pendant. He was certain she would be after he blatantly mentioned it that morning when he stopped by to verify the timing of their departure. But seeing it on her, realizing what he was about to do, sent a shiver of apprehension through him—something he had never before experienced.

Chase wanted nothing more than to stand by her side the whole evening, not only to ensure himself of her well-being, but to convey to everyone present *she was his*. However, he knew any announcement—verbal or implied—about Lady Mildred Aldon becoming the next Marchioness of Chaselton would only put her in even more danger. If his enemies realized how deep his affection for her ran, Millie would become a target and be used as a means to control him. In order to protect those he loved, he would make the request to join the Expansionists and their cause.

Immediately following yesterday's Society meeting, Millie had wanted nothing more than to speak with Chase. She had almost suggested going directly back to Hembree Grove rather than stopping by to see Jennelle's seamstress. Now, after witnessing Chase embrace Melinda, she could not make up her mind whether or not she was glad to know the truth. Best to be informed, she told herself once more as she mingled with the crowd. But as soon as she saw Chase waiting for them, Millie knew ignorance would be better than the pain of knowing.

Chase would never marry Melinda Brinson. She had a son and was not of Society. But she was undeniably pretty, and tall, and fair: everything Millie was not. But if Chase really loved Melinda, he would need a wife who would care very little if he had a lover on the side. He would need Selena Hall.

Suddenly it made sense why Chase had been giving the woman so much attention.

Fighting tears, she silently walked by him and ascended the long staircase leading to the main ballroom. Immediately upon entering, she donned her "social" demeanor and avoided looking at or interacting with Chase in any way.

"Lady Aldon," a voice whispered into her ear. The accent was typical. Its tone, normal. However, there was something sinister about its inflection. It could only belong to one man.

Millie took a deep breath. She was about to risk all. By watching Lord Marston from afar, Millie had not discerned his motives or plans. Politeness had brought forth even less information. It was time to see what Marston might say when angered.

"Lord Marston," Millie replied with tediousness, refusing to turn around.

The insult was not lost. "You make it clear that I bore you, madam. And if you would risk looking at me directly, I am sure that I would see antipathy in those rare-colored depths."

Millie continued to stare straight ahead into the crowd. "Then you and I are both in good fortune. I will not have to endure looking at you to ensure I am understood, and you will be spared seeing the disdain I have for someone who pathetically attempts to manhandle those he believes are weaker."

Marston saw red. For one blistering instant, he nearly lost his temper and disclosed more than he intended. "I am a dangerous man, madam. One you should not cross."

Millie turned slowly; cold anger hissed to life. "You do not intimidate me, Lord Marston. You annoy me. It is not surprising that green and unwise girls fall so easily at your feet. No doubt, you cannot understand why I do not. However, I think you are just a little too perfect, a little too polished, and definitely too smooth. In summation, I do not think you to be honorable or trustworthy."

Marston's eyes narrowed to thin slits that fully reflected his tightly leashed anger before he carefully responded. "Until we meet again, my lady. I believe our next encounter will go more my way."

Millie's heart was racing. The moment of imminent confrontation had passed. Their quarrel had been laced with innuendo and threat. Suddenly she wished she could tell Chase what had just happened. Instead, she rubbed her arms vigorously and went up another set of stairs to find a place where she might regain her composure.

Emerging from the lady's powder room and feeling much more in control, Millie paused, looking down at the crowd from a small balcony. Instinctively looking for familiar faces, she spied the two men from the Society meeting who had argued with Brumby just before he had been killed. They spoke briefly and then exited to the garden. Without considering the repercussions, Millie dashed down the staircase and followed them.

After a few wrong turns, she spied them walking rapidly toward a part of the garden with multiple hedges and areas nestled away for private conversations. If she did not move quickly, she would lose them.

Millie rounded a series of rose bushes and glanced around. They were gone. Silently cursing her lack of height, she looked for something to stand upon to see over the tall greenery. Nothing but dark pebble paths and dense foliage were in the immediate vicinity. Conceding defeat, Millie began walking toward the noise and light of the party when she heard voices on the other side of a nearby hedge.

She paused to listen for a female voice. There was none. Just two men—arguing. It had to be them. She stood frozen on the other side, straining to overhear their conversation.

"Did you know what he was planning to do yesterday?" a dark, chilling voice demanded.

"I did not," the second man squeaked, asserting his innocence. "I cannot imagine what he was thinking, taking such an action."

"I agree, and I do not like it. Killing Brumby in public, that close to the girl, was just too risky."

"Maybe it worked. Tonight Chaselton let it slip that he does have the proof, or at least the items that will lead us to it. He says he only wants to join our cause."

"Hmm. An odd request that feels a little too convenient." Millie bit the inside of her cheek hearing the hardness in the man's tone.

"What if Brumby's death convinced him that it would be safer to join us?" the second man asked shakily.

"Possible."

Suddenly, a third voice entered the conversation. It was very deep, with a heavy accent that sounded foreign as if he were from another country. And yet there was something vaguely familiar about it. Part of her was sure she knew no one with that voice, but another part was just as sure she had heard it before.

"Chaselton is a problem," said the deep voice.

"I agree," spoke the deep baritone who doubted the convenient change of heart.

"Now, wait a minute," inserted the most nervous of the three men. "We could use Chaselton. He is no coward—you saw his war record. If there was ever a man we want on our side, it is him."

"I disagree. If there was ever a man we *do not* want alive and fighting us—it is him," added the cold man.

The deep, foreign voice ended the debate. "We are not going to take the chance. We will agree to meet with him, get what is mine, and then . . ." He took a finger and crossed his neck. Millie leaned in closer, trying to hear what was being said.

The jumpy man's level of anxiety increased. "But another death? Even as an accident, there have been just too many, too close together."

The deep voice sneered. "There is room for one more. Find your spine and prepare for Chaselton. He won't be easy. He will be ready for us, but it will not matter. We will confront him when he is alone."

"When?"

Millie instinctively leaned in closer. "Not until after we have the markers."

"It's true. They exist. We saw one tonight on Lady Aldon."

Millie's already motionless frame became even more rigid. *A marker was on her?* She thought of her gown, the pearls in her hair, and then she knew without a doubt what the man had meant. Her pendant. The one Charlie had mentioned only this morning. He had *wanted* her to wear it tonight. But why? Why would Charlie intentionally put in her in danger?

The accented voice hissed, regaining her attention, "We all saw it, you fool, but I need all three markers. Only then can we be assured that no one will be able to stand in the way of our success. We shall convene in a week's time. If by then our good marquess has not provided the other two markers, we shall find a way to locate them without his assistance. Next Saturday, we shall meet at one in the morning at the back entrance of . . ."

Before Millie could learn the exact location of the meeting, a man's hand encircled her mouth, muffling any scream that might erupt. He masterfully hauled her off with extreme speed.

Only temporarily shocked, Millie quickly recovered and began fighting her assailant by employing several of the moves she had invented when she was younger. They worked.

Now in a private alcove well away from the clandestine meeting she was spying on, Chase let go and grabbed his shin.

Millie spun around, ready to strike her attacker head-on.

"Bloody hell, woman. Where did you learn how to do that?" Chase snarled, surprised by the pain she had inflicted in such a short time.

Millie leaned closer. "Charlie? Is that you?"

"Yes, it's me!" he shot back. "My God, woman! What were you trying to do? Kill me?"

"As a matter of fact, yes! I was being attacked, and I was defending myself. If you were hurt in the process that was your own damn fault."

Chase's golden eyes bored into her lavender ones. "Well, I was not even close to being incapacitated by you. And if I truly was an attacker, I would be severely annoyed by now."

The hint at her inadequacy infuriated her. "If I am so *ineffective*, then why are you hopping around on one foot?"

Chase put his boot back down, determined not to display any more signs of the damage she had done. "You may find this amusing, Mildred, but, I assure you, I do not." In fact, for the past twenty minutes, his heart had been racing faster than he could ever recall. Fear had overtaken him when he had lost sight of her and it only doubled finding her at the hedge eavesdropping on the very men who would kill her if she were discovered.

Millie began pacing around Chase, exaggerating her ability to walk without pain. "Am I laughing? Has a chuckle escaped my lips? This may surprise you, Charlie, but I do not find being abducted and dragged into a dark corner of a garden remotely humorous."

Chase took a firm grip on his resolve. "I was not trying to abduct you. Damn it, I was protecting you, Millie!"

"How was I supposed to know that? When you come

behind a woman and drag her off to unknown parts, she will defend herself and fight back. I am sorry I hurt you, but you should have expected me to react. You are the one who trained me, after all."

Chase's expression hardened as he gazed at her unrepentant face. "I never taught you to do any of those wild moves you just executed. I would have remembered."

Millie shrugged indifferently. "They are old moves I created a long time ago. Honestly, I didn't even remember them until you grabbed me. I was actually quite frightened."

Chase inhaled. "Indeed. Well, that makes two of us. You have no idea how terrified I was seeing you so close to danger. Do you have any idea who you were listening to?"

Shock invaded Millie's features. She dropped her voice to a low whisper. "Then you know? You know what they were saying? You know about the meeting?"

The question rendered Chase speechless. His amber eyes were hard with fear and fury as he thought about just where and how he had found her. "Of course I know. This is what I *do*, Millie. I am a spy—and I'm damn good at it. So stop being so infuriatingly excitable."

Millie's jaw dropped. "If I am excitable, I have a very good reason to be. Those men are after you!"

Chase clutched Millie's shoulders, forcing her to listen. "They aren't *after me*, as you put it. They want me for something. There is a difference. One I can control. And I am not the one in danger—you are!" he hissed, pointing at her chest.

"Me?!" Millie exclaimed. Then, she realized what he was pointing at and recalled overhearing how it had some meaning. Her hand flew to the necklace, protecting it for she knew what he was going to say next.

"Your pendant. I need it."

Millie swallowed. "Why?"

Chase sighed and raked his hand through his hair.

"When we leave here, it is important that you spread the word that it is missing. That someone must have stolen it without your knowledge."

"Why?"

"So those who might have hurt you in an effort to get it will think that I have it and leave you alone—safe."

Millie clutched the pendant even tighter, her expression a mixture of confusion and tenacity to seek and receive answers. "But why would they think you stole it?"

"Because that is what I will make sure a few select people learn, Millie."

Millie shook her head and took a step back. Several questions were racing through her head, but she only managed to ask, "How?"

"The same way I have been communicating at these infernal balls—carefully." Chase could see his acerbic answer held no persuasion and he could feel his limited patience dwindling. "I don't have time for this, Millie. Those men killed a man just yesterday. Bloody hell, you witnessed it!"

She remembered the gruesome murder, but it paled in comparison to what she had seen afterward at Melinda's. Millie felt an empty, angry, cold knot tighten within her. "I know what I witnessed."

Hearing her cold rebuke, Chase's jaw tightened. "Well, you certainly don't act like it. You went home, refused to speak to anyone, and then spent all of today getting dressed for the evening in . . . in . . . that, making men think of . . . things they should not. Then I find you actually a few feet away from the very men I have been tracking and watching. You are bloody lucky I don't bend you over my knee and teach you a lesson."

"Do not lecture me, Charlie Wentworth," Millie said crisply, releasing the pendant to point her finger at his chest. It was an undignified action, but after his last threat, she felt no restraint from doing so. "Do not dare assume anything about what I did or how I felt about yesterday afternoon. And as for my dress, I will have you know I have received many compliments on it this evening. Even Lady Cowper said I was the woman all young ladies envied this Season."

Chase muttered darkly. His brown eyebrows came together in a straight line. "I'll bet. Your demeanor is above reproach. But that dress alone will make tonight's ball *the* event of the year. And for the next several Seasons, men will be flocking to Lady Sefton's in hopes of meeting other ladies who dare to wear such a gown."

His words stung, and Millie felt the urge to flee. "I'm going," she said in a broken, irascible whisper.

"Not with that pendant, you're not," he countered bracingly.

Millie thought to leave anyway, but she knew Chase well enough to realize he would track her down and drag her back.

Their eyes clashed in brief, savage conflict before Chase tugged her roughly to him. Her body was stiff and unyielding, but he felt her tremble.

Millie did not want to kiss Chase. During their prior embraces, she could allow herself to believe he really cared for her, wanted her, and only her. But now she knew the truth.

As she opened her mouth to protest, he smothered her words with his lips, moving them forcefully against hers. He used his tongue to still hers, kissing her hard and deliberately, letting her feel the frustration and temper she had aroused in him.

Millie tried to resist, but it occurred to her that this might be the last time she was ever going to be in his arms. A muffled cry erupted as Millie threw her arms around his neck, kissing him feverishly.

"My God, Millie, don't ever scare me like that again," Chase implored, his voice raspy with constrained emotion.

"Just kiss me, Chase. Make me believe you will never let me go," Millie murmured against his lips, the pleading in her voice unmistakable.

"I never will, love. I never will."

Though she knew the truth, Millie savored his words. Something deep inside her responded to the primal need of his touch. All she wanted was more. She tightened her arms around his neck and urged his mouth down to hers.

Chase groaned with irrepressible need. She was furious with him and still she responded with a passion that would drive the most composed man to the edge. "Millie, oh, Millie, I need you so much. You have no idea."

Hearing him whisper her name chilled her bones. She would never love a man again, like she loved Charles Wentworth.

Chase's growing desire for her was almost all-consuming. He had to stop now, but instead of listening to the inner voice in his head, he lifted her in his arms and walked over to a garden bench hidden in the shadows. Tonight he was going to show Millie another way to express her passionate side. For never in his life had it been more important than it was right now for Millie to become his.

Chase inhaled her scent, reveling in the mixture of perfume and feminine arousal. "You are so beautiful," he muttered, awed by the softness of her skin. Groaning, Chase bent his head and took her earlobe between his teeth. One hand tightened tenderly on the nape of her neck as the other skimmed the graceful line of her spine.

Unable to think clearly, Millie finally gave in to the sensations Chase was arousing. Everything was happening so fast. It was as if she were caught in a lightning storm—wild and exciting. Feeling secure and wanted, she again hugged his neck, resting her cheek against his.

Assured that she was not going to fight him, he eased her back and let himself drown in the love reflected in her eyes. So many years ago, he offered sympathy to the one foolish enough to get caught in their violet trap. Now he considered himself a lucky man.

Millie felt him stroke her cheek with his knuckles. There was so much meaning in the featherlight caress. The touch and his possessive gaze caused her body to respond with a feverish intensity she did not know she had. Her blood began to pound in her veins, and without conscious thought, she drew his lips to hers. Millie's tongue tentatively probed the warmth of his mouth before boldly inviting him to taste her.

Chase needed no further encouragement to deepen the kiss until she completely surrendered. Each time he held her, the crazed passion Millie ignited inside him grew. He wanted her more than he thought was possible to want a woman. He nipped playfully at her lower lip before moving to the nape of her neck and then to her shoulders. As his mouth moved across the softness of her skin, Chase decided her V-shaped décolletage did have at least one redeeming asset.

Millie sighed softly and closed her eyes as he eased a sleeve down her arm to expose her breast. His thumb slowly grazed across her nipple. It hardened to the tender touch. Entranced, she sank her nails into Chase's perfectly tailored jacket, glorying in the sensual torment he was creating. She didn't want the feeling to stop. Whatever he was doing to her, it was wonderful. "Bloody hell, I can barely breathe. Chase, I don't think I can take any more. Good Lord, anything this exciting must be wrong," she stammered, her voice soft and unsteady.

The notion that this woman who seethed with such vitality could be excited by him was incredibly seductive. Chase had never thought a man like himself could be enslaved by passion or instigate such a fervent need in another. "No, love. You and I together will never be wrong."

Chase cupped her cheek, his touch so tender she dared not to move, hoping the moment would last forever. Then he lowered his mouth and continued the onslaught his fingers had begun. The longer his lips caressed her, the less will she had. Feeling his warm tongue swirl and lave each bud, she instinctively arched herself against him, moaning softly.

Millie's trembles made him shudder with his own need. He wanted her badly. And with each sweet, soft sound she cried, he had to fight the fierce desire to throw her on the soft grass and bury himself in her. He could not even explain to himself what he felt. His need to be with her. The sense of intoxication when she responded to his caresses. She was made for him—just him. And only when he was with her was he whole.

Turning his attention to the other breast, his hand lowered, finding the hem of the pale silk barrier. Ever so slowly, knowing that he was about to touch a piece of heaven, he let his fingers drift up the warm softness of her inner thigh.

Stroking her smooth skin, he sensed the sultry heat emanating from between her legs. His hand slipped higher along the side of her thigh, gliding lightly over her silken hair covering the heart of her own fire. His fingers closed gently around the warm mound.

Millie gasped, trembled, and closed her eyes. Never in her life had she dreamed a man could make her feel so alive, so incredibly *female*. She knew there was more, and tonight she wanted it all. She clutched at him, lifting herself, straining for a more intimate touch.

Excited by her response, Chase gently tested her with one finger. She was wet and tight and so very hot.

Millie cried out softly as a deep tremor shook her. "Oh

my . . . I didn't know . . . my Lord, this feels so bloody good."

Assaulting all of her senses, he retook her parted, pink lips and kissed her mouth hungrily, thrusting his tongue deep, his control almost shattered by her innocently whispered words.

Slowly his finger started to move in a gentle rhythm. Millie sucked in her breath, her fingers biting into Chase's shoulders. She was ruining his jacket, but he didn't care. He was discovering what heaven was like.

Chase stroked her slowly, parting her with his fingers, opening her. A sweet, hot flame scorched through him. The sheer enjoyment of giving pleasure—not just receiving it— was incredible. He had been dreaming of touching Millie like this every night since he had first seen her in the kitchen moonlight. Now, being able to fulfill that dream was all-consuming. The intensity he felt for her made the memories of the women in his past fade away.

Millie was his lifeline. The one person who made him feel alive. She brightened his world, challenged him, and desired him. This gorgeous sprite made him realize just how lonely his life had been these past years.

Millie did not understand the raw sensations that were erupting violently all over her body. She had never dreamed of a man touching her there, intimately. And if she had, she would never have believed it could feel so—*right*.

Chase's fingers continued to move in her, drawing forth her wet heat, stroking the flames until she was half mad. Still his onslaught continued. His lips trailed the ridge of her jaw, down the column of her throat, caressing her sensitive flesh.

She shivered, and he groaned. Chase was so hard he hurt, and his imagination was going wild, thinking of all the ways they would share their passions once they were married.

Chase was kissing her again, softer this time, with so much tenderness it felt like her heart was swelling in her chest, nearly choking her. Suddenly, a delicious twisting sensation began exploding inside her.

Sensing her imminent release, Chase whispered, "Let go, my love. Let go to it," and then swallowed her cry of pleasure.

With a tiny muffled shriek of surprise, Millie shuddered in the throes of her first climax. The rapid rise and fall of her chest pressed her breasts against him, and he could feel the pulse in her neck pounding against his shoulder.

Chapter 11

They sat for several minutes holding each other, quiet with their own thoughts. Chase could still feel the softness of her skin and grew hard again.

Millie knew she should be ashamed of what had happened. That she should pull away from his embrace. But despite the awareness of what she had done and where she was, she could not. These last few moments were all she would have with him.

Finally, Chase released her. Silently he fixed her gown and straightened his own jacket. Millie wanted to speak but could not. Instead, she stood dumbfounded, staring at him with wide, deep violet eyes.

"You did nothing wrong, Millie. I promise. I promise I will make it all . . ."

"There is no need," she interrupted. Her voice was detached, as if she was trying to distance herself emotionally from what happened. She reached up and slipped the necklace over her head and handed it to him. "I will do as you ask and say that I lost it. But I have been gone for some time, and I really should be returning. If you do not mind, please wait here for a moment before following."

Chase grabbed her arm, stopping her retreat. "Millie, we need to talk."

Millie didn't want to continue the conversation. She did not want to hear why he was with Melinda, and why he was compelled to have her, too. She didn't blame Chase. If she had at anytime asked him to stop, he would have. But then she would not have been able to treasure the memory of what they had shared. She just wanted to leave without hearing Chase explain it all away.

Millie looked up briefly and closed her eyes. She needed to get away, quickly, before she broke down. "Yes, yes we do need to talk. But not now. I really must return to the party. Maybe later tonight . . . or tomorrow." Leaving Chase no chance to restrain her, Millie darted out and headed back toward the lights and noise of the ball.

She had not traveled far when another familiar voice stopped her cold.

"My, my, if it's not this Season's favorite little original. And here you are, returning by yourself from the dark corners of Lady Sefton's garden. Intending to keep the gossip about you alive, are you?"

Selena Hall reminded Millie of a colorful viper. Smooth, slick, and full of venom that could be launched with lightning speed. "And, pray tell, Miss Hall, whatever brings *you* to the dark corners of the garden—alone?"

Selena produced a frosty smile and lied, "Chaselton requested my presence, of course."

Millie casually fixed her gloves and kept her voice relaxed. "What an amazing change in his personality. For as long as I have known him, he has detested those who chase after him."

Selena's eyes narrowed and quickly reassessed the repartee she was having with this unexpected rival. Too many times she had witnessed the marquess and Mildred Aldon in deep discussion. This encounter was supposed to intimidate the petite creature and verify that Chaselton's interest in her did not go beyond that of designated chaperone. Never did

Selena dream this dark-haired beauty might be an actual threat—until now. It was time to let the little girl know she was playing with adults far more cunning and vicious than she. "Ahh, that's right. You're his baby sister's friend. No doubt your memories are somewhat distorted. You must have been a little girl when he left for the war. It is no wonder he disappeared so quickly after arriving tonight. I would escape to the garden, too, if I was forced to coddle the three of you week after week."

Millie saw the glint appear in Selena's eyes. She did not know why, but the viper had decided to exhibit her fangs. Millie chuckled softly and then sighed, realizing the appearance of boredom and indifference would be the most effective of retaliation strategies. "Ah, but at least I am still young enough to require a chaperone, *Miss* Hall. Please enlighten me. It has been how many Seasons since your coming-out? Must be several, since you seem to attend so many of these events without a guardian."

Selena's face was taut, as if she had been slapped. Millie smiled. While Selena had delivered the first shot, Millie's comment had been the first to hit its target.

Recovering quickly, Selena brushed imaginary dust off her shoulder in an attempt to mask her anger. "It is obvious you delayed your first Season by several years, and the idea of a chaperone for you and your friends is a mere formality. I doubt Society will still welcome your eccentricity next year. Interest in your unconventional appearance will soon fade. And, unlike myself, you will no longer be anyone of import—just simply another unmarried woman."

Millie calmly reached over and plucked a long blond hair from the shoulder Selena was just brushing. Millie twitched her fingers and let it fall to the ground. "Ahh, but I will be a *wealthy* and *titled* unmarried woman. And I believe you would agree, that does make all the difference. Now, if you will excuse me, I see my friend calling me. No doubt she needs some coddling. Good evening, *Miss* Hall."

Selena was seething. Never had anyone humiliated her so openly and defied her in such a caustic manner. She was just about to send a final scathing remark when Chase emerged. Ever the actress, Selena waved and smiled and then fluttered over to him. Grabbing his arm, she pecked his cheek. "There you are! I never thought we would find each other in this crush. What a delightful idea to tour Lady Sefton's gardens. Why don't we turn here and avoid the crowds for just a bit longer."

Maneuvering Chase to go in the direction she desired, Selena looked over her shoulder and was frustrated one last time. Mildred Aldon wasn't looking in her direction. In fact, the unanticipated adversary was laughing with her redheaded friend. *Well, cackle away, Lady Aldon, but it will be I who laughs loudest and last when I marry Chaselton and become* both *wealthy* and *titled.*

Millie was thankful when Jennelle appeared just as Selena ran off. Only once did Millie look to see who had saved her from further conversation with the toxic woman. Millie watched in silence as Chase deftly led Selena farther into the garden. She wanted to see no more and quickly turned away to greet her friend.

"Thank heavens! You have no idea what you saved me from," Millie said as Jennelle came close.

Jennelle tilted her head toward the retreating blonde. "I can imagine. You and she appeared to be having a somewhat heated dialogue. Quite surprising, as she has avoided any and all interaction with us."

Jennelle paused, and Millie fought her instinct to turn and see whom the focus of Jennelle's interest was. "Pray tell, are you intentionally driving me mad? Whatever are you looking at?"

Jennelle twitched her lips. "Millie, laugh. It will drive Selena insane. Trust me."

Not a second later, Millie's hand flew to her mouth as she erupted in elegant laughter. Jennelle joined, but hers was not false. She only wished Millie could have also witnessed Selena's frustration. But Jennelle saw more than Selena's expression; she also noticed Chase's. It was filled with suffering.

"May I stop now?" Millie asked behind her hand, hoping to end this phony display of mirth.

Startled, Jennelle replied, "Oh yes. You can stop. You would never believe how that bothered her. I must say it had the opposite effect on me. I found the charade quite entertaining."

Millie was about to reply when Aimee appeared by their sides. "Fiend seize it! I missed something, didn't I? No doubt something salacious and interesting."

Before Millie could deny it, Jennelle affirmed Aimee's statement. "It was Selena. She confronted Millie, but Millie had the last laugh—and I mean literally!"

Millie rolled her eyes. "We were just returning. And don't ask me what Jennelle meant," she ended, raising her hand. "Is your mother near?"

Aimee cocked her head with eyes full of confusion. "Yes, I just left her near the balcony doors speaking with Lord Pomfrey."

Millie bit back a sigh of relief. She could think of few men who enjoyed spreading gossip more than he did. One mention of her supposedly missing pendant within his hearing and all within the *ton* would know about it by morning. "I need to tell her about my pendant—it has gone missing."

All Three went to tell Cecilia the distressing news, who was quickly freed when Lord Pomfrey quickly scuttled away to share the latest gossip. Millie was relieved when Mother Wentworth declared the evening to be at an end.

As they were about to enter the carriage, Aimee touched

Millie's arm to gain her attention. "You no longer have to worry about Selena," she whispered. "I spoke with Charles, and he is not even remotely interested in the falsity of that woman. He just finds her easy to manipulate, and she keeps others away without any effort on his part. I told him he is a genius."

"Yes," Millie murmured, "quite clever." Those were the last words Millie spoke all the way home. She had much to consider. Melinda, the men in the garden, what had just happened between her and Chase, her feelings . . .

An hour later, Millie was still contemplating the undying images of Chase walking arm in arm with Selena back into the gardens, when she heard a knock on her door. It opened and Jennelle and Aimee stole into her room.

"See, Aimee? I was correct. I told you she would still be awake."

Aimee plopped down on the bed beside Millie. "Thought we would come to you first."

"First?" Millie asked, sitting up to watch as Jennelle sauntered over with a satisfied expression.

Jennelle shook her finger at Millie in mock conviction. "Do not deny it. You would have banged on our doors in an hour, right after you figured out whatever it is that has been bothering you."

Aimee nodded. "Yes, but then we would have been asleep. So, we are coming to you now. So speak up. What is on your mind?" Aimee asked, tucking her robe in around her.

"Nothing," Millie replied before collapsing against the pillows, resting an arm against her forehead. "At least I hope it is nothing. I just cannot figure out what to do regarding Chase . . . I mean Charlie."

Jennelle and Aimee did not say a word, but the fretfulness their friend was displaying over Chase was not missed.

"My brother can take care of himself."

Millie sat up again. "Yes, if he is paying attention and aware of the danger in front of him. But what if he doesn't know the danger exists?"

Jennelle and Aimee stared at each other quietly for several moments. Millie's propensity to look for excitement wherever she could caused them to momentarily pause before reacting to her words. They were more interested in Millie's quiet but emotional outburst—over a man.

Jennelle leaned over and whispered something into Aimee's ear. Aimee nodded. Millie gritted her teeth. "What are you whispering so *obviously* about me?"

Jennelle returned Millie's earlier "Nothing" and got up to feign a casual stroll.

Millie glared.

Jennelle met her eyes. "Lord, Millie. It was nothing worthy of such energy. I just asked if Aimee remembered what your exception to our most treasured vow was."

"And I do," Aimee quickly added. "I believe you pledged never, ever to marry unless you found a man who allows you to hunt, ride in breeches, have adventures, climb trees, and explore caves."

Jennelle smiled and continued. "Do not forget, he must not ever be dull, have an aversion to following rules, and possess as strong a passion as our Millie for adventures."

"My brother knows you can ride. He doesn't even mind you riding Hercules."

Jennelle leaned casually against the door frame. "I believe he even rode with her recently," she added with mocking innocence.

Aimee smiled at the reminder. "You know, you are right. He did."

Playing with the ties on her robe, Jennelle added, "I've noticed our Millie seems to be interested in anything that your brother offers to do with her."

Aimee bobbed her head in agreement, her smile very large. "Practically leaps at the chance. Very different from our youth."

Jennelle ran and jumped on the bed, landing beside Aimee. Millie was struck dumb with their quick exchange and hints.

Suddenly Aimee looked Millie directly in the eyes and asked, "Tell me, Mildred Aldon, have you ever kissed my brother?"

Millie stammered and retreated as far back as she could until she hit the headboard. "Your brother? Why would your brother ever want to kiss me?"

"Rubbish," Jennelle drawled. "I know you, Millie Elizabeth, and you are avoiding the question. We want to know. Did you ever kiss Charles Wentworth the Third?"

Millie bit her bottom lip. She could never lie to her best friends. Avoid answering, yes, but not lie. And there was no way they were going to leave without an answer.

"You can be quite the horse's arse, Jennelle. Do you know that? Fine. The answer is yes. Yes, we did kiss. Satisfied?"

Jennelle swung off the bed and twirled around the room with a look of deep satisfaction on her face. "I am, indeed. This particular thoroughbred's arse thanks you very much."

Suddenly Millie was being hugged by Aimee. "I knew it! I knew that *something* had occurred when Jennelle told me she had found you and Charles in the gardens. You kissed, and you liked it. I can tell."

Millie looked puzzled. "Aren't kisses always enjoyable?"

Aimee's eyebrows immediately furrowed as her hand lightly gripped her neck. "Oh no. I know you have managed to avoid the experience these past several years, but unfortunately, I have been kissed by men. It was completely awful."

Millie jumped up on the bed and softly yelled, "You've kissed men and I am just now finding out!"

Aimee wrinkled her nose. "Well, as I said, it was completely *awful.*" *And I now know just how wonderful and powerful a kiss can be*, Aimee silently added to herself, remembering her and Reece's Christmas encounter.

The look of satisfaction on Jennelle's face was replaced with repentance. "I, too, have been kissed."

Millie and Aimee turned around and stared. Jennelle gulped under their astonished expressions. "Well, it was not at all pleasant. It was wet, hard, and disgusting. I just wanted the kiss to end so I could erase it from my mind."

"That was exactly how it was with me," Aimee remarked as she turned back to Millie. "But it was not that way with you, was it?"

The question immediately sent Millie back in time. Tonight's kiss had been wonderful, and the memories of what she had shared with Chase still made her heart pound. Just the thought of it evoked the same powerful urges in her lower body. The kiss had been hard but sensual. Wet but intoxicating, and when his tongue had touched hers, sparks flew. She had only wanted more and more. Not less and less.

Millie closed her eyes and raised her hands to ward off her friends as she slowly sank back down to her knees. "I am not going to talk anymore on the subject. I have more important things on my mind."

Aimee began shaking her head in confusion. "Wait a minute. I thought you said you were worried about my brother. You cannot be worried about Mrs. Brinson, can you?"

Jennelle moved close. "Millie, I have been giving yesterday afternoon some serious thought, and I do truly believe that what we witnessed was not at all as it appeared. First of all, they were outside."

Aimee nodded her head in agreement. "That is true."

Jennelle began to pace alongside the bed. "Secondly, while familiar, their embrace did not resemble affection. Rather it was more like the type he has given me on occasion."

Millie sat back and crossed her arms. She was not sure she

entirely agreed with Jennelle's assessment but decided to listen to any theory that contradicted her own interpretation.

"And last, she was crying."

"I thought she was smiling," Aimee inserted.

"Yes, another strange fact. Her tears appeared to be ones of joy. I believe she was *thankful*."

Millie shook her head and waved her arms, dismissing their logic. "It is not that. It has nothing to do with yesterday." *At least it is not all about yesterday*, Millie added to herself.

"If that is not what is troubling you, then what is? What is agitating you so?" Aimee asked, puzzled.

"Something unpleasant happened tonight, and I have not quite figured it out."

Blond curls bounced as Aimee shook her head. "Uh-uh. Obscure statements like those will not be permitted. Is it Lord Marston? I saw him corner you early in the evening. He looked furious when he left. I thought we agreed to avoid him."

"We did," Jennelle piped up.

Frustrated, Millie responded, "The man is impossible to ignore. And I made it very clear I found his company most unpleasant. Still he promised to harass me in the future, vowing that our next encounter, and I quote, 'will go his way.'"

Aimee sighed. "Well, then I am glad he did not come over to chat during yesterday's Society meeting. Especially with what happened to poor Lord Brumby."

Millie sat up and looked directly at Aimee. "Excuse me? Did you say Lord Marston was at that meeting?"

"Strange, is it not? He never struck me as the type who would enjoy those types of speakers."

Millie took in a deep breath and slowly exhaled. "No, he would not. I am fairly positive lectures on hot air balloons, the West Indies, and the Far East do not interest that man. He has a very limited view of the world."

"He was probably there to meet someone. I saw him speaking to one of those men you pointed out," Aimee said casually as she leaned against the bedpost and stretched her long legs in front of her. "Why is this so interesting?"

Now sitting in a thinking pose, Millie wondered the same thing. Why would Marston be at a lecture on a topic that would hold no interest for him? And what did he have in common with . . . And then the answer became alarmingly clear to Millie.

The combination of Millie's silence and the look in her large, violet eyes worried Aimee. "Millie?"

Millie looked up and saw the concern in her friend's face. She forced her voice to sound light and untroubled. "It's nothing. I am just glad Lord Marston did not see us."

Jennelle shook her head. "But he did. He looked directly at you."

Millie gulped. This was not good. She needed to think. "Listen—thanks for the late-night visit. You know how I enjoy them, and I promise I will not wake you later. But I have a small headache and . . ."

"And nothing. Do not think you are going to shuffle us out of here as easily as last time," Jennelle interrupted. "The blood just drained out of your face. You should see how pale you are. What are you not telling us?"

"I made a promise—to a friend. They bade me to tell no one, not even you. And until I am able to speak with . . . them, I'm afraid I can tell you nothing more."

Jennelle reached out and clutched the sleeve of Millie's thin nightgown. "Millie, are you in danger?"

"I do not believe so, but I am afraid someone else is. If you will excuse me, I need to think of a way to warn them," Millie muttered, gesturing her friends out of her room.

As the door closed, Jennelle turned to Aimee. "Well, how do you like that? To think someone so little can be so effective at dismissing a person."

"Never underestimate Millie. It would be a mistake. I wonder why she thinks she has to protect Charles."

"Notice that, too? That *someone* asked her not say something, and *someone* is in trouble? How many people do you know who could make Millie swear to keep from disclosing all to us?" Jennelle asked rhetorically, making her way back to her room.

Aimee paused at her door and looked at Jennelle. "Yes, I wonder if Millie is just being Millie. Or is my brother genuinely in trouble?"

After everyone had left, Millie replayed the conversation she had overheard in the gardens again and again in her mind. Chase said he knew about the meeting and everything that was being said. But what if he was wrong?

Whomever she had overheard in the garden had decided not to risk believing in Chase's sincerity about "joining" their cause. "And why would they?" she asked herself aloud. "Who would believe Charlie would willingly join a bunch of murderers?"

Those men in the garden didn't.

Millie knew she had to warn Chase, and she had only tonight to do so. He had returned to stay at Hembree Grove the night of Brumby's death, but last time they kissed, Chase had left. After what they shared in the garden, she wagered he would leave again—and soon.

Millie rose and donned her robe. He was most likely at one of his clubs. The best and quickest way to warn him would be to leave a note in his study. If she waited until morning, she could miss him again and then it would be too late.

She quickly tied the loose ribbons on her robe and tiptoed down the staircase. Rounding the newel at the bottom of the stairs, she stopped short. The study door was ajar, and there was light and movement within. Chase was still here!

She debated whether to fling open the doors right then and tell him what she had heard, or risk the chance he might go to his chambers while she ran upstairs and dressed. The decision became moot when she heard a second voice.

It belonged to an older gentleman who sounded firm and businesslike. Millie moved closer to hear.

"Come now, Charles. Do you not think it is time you explained what you are doing?"

Chase sighed. "As I told you before: nothing. Just escorting my sister and her two friends during their first Season. I apologize if my activities are too mundane."

"Hmm. Seems like you are up to something more, my boy. You have been far too diligent in your chaperone duties. It must be a cover for more interesting activities than those of parties, theaters, and balls. I could help you, you know. If you would let me."

"It has been a long while since someone has called me 'boy.' Probably because it is has been a long time since I have been one." Millie heard the curt tone in Chase's voice and quietly moved closer to the door.

"Don't be that way, Charles. You are very much like your father, you know. He, too, was easily annoyed by someone's mere choice of words. Remember, he trusted me, probably more than anyone."

Millie heard a long pause and then drumming of fingers on a desk. She knew it was Chase. He always did that when contemplating a decision.

"You're right. I am doing double duty while in Town," Chase admitted. "Although this second duty—about which you have so much curiosity—is far less interesting than you have conjured it to be. My father left behind some items I do not consider to be of value; however, some other men do. They have made me an offer, which has generated my interest. And since I have no need for the trinkets, and after what

I have seen these past several years, I am considering joining their cause."

"Sounds like tricky business," the older man replied.

Millie wished she could see reactions as well as hear them, but she was not going to risk getting caught. Listening to Chase's conversation was giving her more insight than any other tactic she might have employed. No wonder Elda Mae eavesdropped on her so often.

"Tricky? No. It is rather straightforward. Once they pay me for the items, I will either join them or I will not."

"So very simple," the old man said softly without the confidence Chase had evoked. The man coughed. "What are your plans when this is over? England might be at peace, but there are plenty of . . ."

"No. You can rethink that idea. No more missions for me. I have served my time."

"Not denying that. Just didn't see you working the dandy scene."

"God forbid!" Millie heard papers plop down on the desk. "Actually, I was contemplating marriage."

Cold shock invaded Millie. She wanted to get up and run back to her room, but her legs wouldn't move. She stood frozen, listening as her heart broke in two.

"Really!" The older man sounded just as surprised as she was. "Never thought you were the type, honestly."

"I, too, never thought I would get married so soon. But with the title, it was inevitable."

Millie held her breath. Inevitable? Chase had made it very clear at Hyde Park that marrying her was not his choice. Then who could it be? Selena? Even Chase had admitted that she met all the requirements needed for nobleman's wife.

"Of course, I knew you would eventually do your duty, but I imagined that you would have delayed that responsibility until you could not put it off any longer." Millie caught herself silently nodding in agreement. "What changed your mind? Some pretty girl catch your eye?"

Millie strained to hear Chase's response. She wanted to hear every word.

Chase's voice was full of disdain. "There are always pretty girls in the Season. If all it took was some blue-blooded chit that looked nice in a dress, Reece and I would have found wives long ago. No. I was searching for something; I just didn't realize what it was until she pushed her way into my life."

Oh my God, it *was* Selena. Millie's back slid down against the wall until she was sitting on the floor. Selena was by far the pushiest woman she had ever witnessed. Unfortunately, she was also pretty and came from a somewhat prosperous, respectable family.

"Let me understand this correctly. *You*, the Marquess of Chaselton, the most unemotional of men, are in love."

Millie held her breath. She knew Chase did not love Selena. He might consider her appropriate for a wife for she would not care about a mistress if situated with jewels and a large enough allowance. But he did not love her.

Chase's voice changed. It rang with pride, possession, and affection. "Yes, I believe I am, and with the most extraordinary woman. Although the people closest to me will be surprised, she is good with children and I like myself more when I am around her. I have no doubt that she will be an impeccable marchioness."

"Has she agreed, then?"

"I was going to ask earlier this week, but decided to wait until I had put this other matter to rest."

Millie clutched her knees. It was not Selena. It was Melinda Brinson. Millie knew Chase had feelings for the seamstress; she had just not dreamed they were this strong.

"Hmm, so she loves you?"

"Don't sound so surprised. And while she has not uttered

the words aloud, she has expressed similar feelings. I do not think I have misread her."

No, Millie thought. *It's hard to misread someone hugging you so close you look like one person.* Jealousy raged through Millie's veins. Never had she envied anyone as much as she envied Melinda Brinson.

What was it about the pretty seamstress? Why did Chase feel the need to protect her? It was not as if Mrs. Brinson's son was his. If he were, Chase would have married her long ago. Maybe the older man was right. *Chase was in love.*

The visitor cleared his throat. "Well, I wish you the best. When are the banns going to be posted?"

"They will be read next week. I believe I should be able to wrap up this other matter by then."

"It would be a shame for England to lose you. Are you sure you want to marry and settle down?"

Settling down with the beautiful seamstress would hardly be boring, Millie thought, imagining Chase bouncing Melinda's son upon his knee.

"I am sure," Chase said resolutely. "I will soon introduce you to her. You will then understand the ease of my decision."

"Pretty, eh?"

"I am fairly confident you will think so. But it is not just her beauty. It's the way she handles herself and others—even me—which has me ensnared. She is the most beguiling creature I have ever known. And yesterday, I realized that I want her with me all the time, not just when I can sneak her away. I like her honesty and dedication to those she loves. If she accepts, I will be a lucky man."

"She will accept you. Every unmarried woman in England has vied for your attentions. There will be a lot of sad faces come next week."

Chase moved toward the study door, hinting he was ready to end their conversation. "Well, I must say, this was an unexpected visit. But I appreciate the call, despite the late hour. I must finish up here and then get some sleep. I have much to do before next Saturday."

"Well, good-bye, my friend."

Millie was barely able to move into the shadows before she saw Sir Edward leave the study and exit through the front door.

She felt like curling up in a ball and crying. Chase was in love and he was going to marry Melinda Brinson. He thought her beautiful, graceful, honest, and dedicated. The very words Millie would have used to describe the kind seamstress who had worked miracles with Jennelle's outdated gowns. She could not bring herself to hate the woman for loving Chase.

Millie huddled in the shadows, wiping away her tears. Her world had narrowed considerably. She felt she would be crushed with the weight of impending loneliness. She had been foolish not to acknowledge the true depth of her feelings before now. She loved him deeply. And had for some time.

As a child, she loved how he would argue with her but would acknowledge her ingenuity. He thought her clever, and most boys had thought her small, weak, and ill-mannered.

When they met again, Chase had changed into a powerful and alluring man who haunted her every thought. She relished each conversation—whether pleasant or confrontational. And she secretly yearned for each meeting to end with his touch. She had not realized it was all one-sided. Those few precious kisses were merely ways to entertain and control his sister's reckless friend. How could she be so foolish to think that it was anything more?

Millie took several deep breaths, trying to regain control of her emotions. She would not have had him anyway, she told herself. She promised long ago to avoid men like him. As Aimee and Jennelle had reminded her earlier, she wanted someone who was averse to following rules. Someone who possessed a strong passion for adventures. That certainly didn't describe Charles Wentworth III.

Then Millie remembered Chase's haunting, prideful elocution of his bride-to-be. *He liked himself more whenever she was around*. When he had spoken the words, she realized that was exactly how she felt around him. She was more comfortable with herself. Her petite stature was never an issue. She did not have to pretend to be polite or continually speak like a well-bred lady. He didn't even mind when she cursed in front of him. Chase knew and, in an odd way, accepted all of her eccentricities.

The only type of adventure Millie could recall Chase genuinely frowning upon was her love for cave exploration. She could have given that one up to keep the rest. The one man in the world with whom she could be herself—and she had lost him to someone she actually liked. Why couldn't it have been to the well-bred society priss? With Selena, Millie would have had no reservations about employing every scheme possible to prevent the marriage.

Millie was about to begin crying anew when the study door opened. Through tear-filled lashes, she watched Chase ascend the stairs with a candle, leaving the study in darkness. She remained where she was for some time. Only after she was sure he was in bed did she rise and proceed toward her room. She took off her robe and sat on the edge of the soft mattress, feeling completely dejected as she recalled their last conversation once more.

Chase had told her he knew about the meeting she had overheard. He said he knew what was going on and that he wasn't in danger. He was laying a trap for them. But what he did not seem to understand was that *they* were laying a trap for *him*. They suspected his dual purpose and were preparing to kill him.

Oh no. . . . Millie winced.

The note. She forgot the note. Even if Chase were pledging himself to another, she was going to save his life. It was not for her sake; it was for Aimee's. She lit a candle and quickly descended the stairs back to the study. When she rounded the newel, Chase suddenly appeared in the shadows.

He had returned to finish what he had been doing when Sir Edward had interrupted with his unexpected visit. Chase had just spent the last week making everyone believe he was staying at Reece's place in St. James's to escape the torment of chaperoning three young women. In truth, he had traveled to Dorset and spent the past four days searching his country estate for the other two markers. Despite having carefully searched every room, he could find no hint of what the items were, let alone where they could be. Even more disturbing was the slight pieces of evidence that others had been exploring through his childhood home in a similar manner, taking advantage of the minimal staff while his mother was in Town.

Rounding the darkened corner to search his late father's study, Chase was not prepared to see Millie once again, dressed in a thin linen chemise backlit from the candlelight. "What the devil?"

Millie reeled backward, feeling her heart instantly begin to pound. "Bloody hell, Chase. You startled me."

She straightened herself and continued into the study. When she turned, he was following her. He was still wearing his breeches, but his cravat and jacket were gone. His white linen shirt was loose, and he had released the ties around his neck so that a good portion of his chest hair was peeking through. Millie could not help but stare.

Her intense gaze instantly ignited every physical need Chase had spent the last several hours suppressing. "Bloody hell, yourself. What in the name of all that is holy are you wearing?"

"No need to raise your voice. You know perfectly well what I am wearing," Millie said, straightening her back in an automatic show of indifference to his sharp question.

Chase felt his usually well-controlled temper start to rear. "Where in damnation is your robe?"

"Honestly, you are beginning to curse more than I do. I wasn't thinking clearly when I left my room, but in truth, I had not expected to run into anyone while completing my errand."

Chase ran his fingers through his hair and roughly rubbed his scalp. The woman was going to drive him insane, he thought. Did she not know how sheer her chemise was? How it affected a man?

Each night he battled himself to keep from entering her room and taking what was his. He had already introduced more to her in the gardens than he had planned. Chase fully intended to be married when he made Millie completely his, but she was making it exceedingly difficult, standing there in her practically transparent chemise.

Chase felt himself grow hard, straining against his breeches. He could see the clear outline of her nude body beneath the seemingly sheer cloth. If she didn't return to her room now, he would not be able to keep himself from throwing her down and burying himself in the warm softness of her.

He blew the candle out.

Chase knew Millie was incensed. "What the . . . whatever are you thinking? I need this candle to finish my errand!"

He reached out and seized her free arm. "Come on. You are going to bed." Chase knew Millie did not understand. That she didn't realize how close he was to losing control and attacking her.

Millie wrenched her arm free, walked to his desk, and placed the smoking candle down. "I am not. I have something to do and I am going to do it," she murmured angrily, searching for pen and paper.

Chase swallowed, as unfulfilled need threatened to

consume him. The candle had been nothing compared to the moonlight highlighting her beautiful assets.

Her hair was loosely braided and her feet were bare. He reminded himself to breathe. He stood there for a moment just staring at the vision when he realized where she was—in his study, behind his desk.

Chase's emotions boomeranged between confusion and sexual aggravation. "What, pray tell, does your errand have to do with my study?"

Millie was concentrating on her task, and it took her a minute to understand his question. She put down the pen and lightly chuckled to herself. "Oh, I forgot. I must be more tired than I realized. I was going to write you a note."

Intensely aware of the sensual hunger in his loins, Chase responded harshly. "For the love of God. You were writing me a note? What kind of foolish . . ." Seeing the reflections of pain in her lavender gaze, Chase immediately regretted his tactlessness.

His harsh tone and words, mixed with the emotional shock of learning of his intention to marry, was the last straw. Tears sprang to her eyes. Millie blinked them back. The mockery in his voice was her undoing. Millie fought impending tears. The man had severely wounded her pride too many times in one day. He deserved whatever he got. She straightened her shoulders and proceeded to head out the door, dismissing him as she brushed by.

"Oh no, you don't." He reached out and pulled her toward him. He knew he had hurt her with his last comment. It wasn't his intention at all, but he was going crazy. She was so close, and her state of dress made her incredibly tempting. Worse, he was unable to do anything about it. Chase grabbed her shoulders and quickly realized it was a very unwise thing to do in his state of arousal.

"Tell me what is so important," he demanded softly.

Millie gulped. "Those men don't believe you really want to join them. They believe you are lying."

"Of course they do. But it doesn't matter. I have something they want," Chase said, stroking her cheek.

"And Marston. He was there when Lord Brumby died. I think he knows those men."

Chase gathered her face into his hands. "When will you begin to trust me? Believe in me?" He asked the question but never gave her a chance to respond. She was standing too close to him. She was too beautiful. Her scent too intoxicating. And her eyes. Her striking eyes, glittering with so much emotion he could no longer prevent the inevitable.

He closed his hand around the back of her head and brought her mouth to his. Her lips parted beneath his gently persuasive caress. The taste of her tears was on his tongue when he plunged into her mouth.

She clung to him and kissed him with a surge of exasperation and desperation. *Just one more kiss*, she promised herself. Millie knew she should have stopped him immediately, but it was too late to retreat even if she had wanted to do so. Her whole being was already committed.

Chase felt the initial resistance in her and sighed in satisfaction as her arms stole gently around his neck. Her soft breasts were crushed against his chest. Chase shuddered in response. His lips closed over hers warmly, again and again, working their magic while his hands, warm and possessive, cupped her breasts.

She shivered as he stroked each nub, making them come alive. "Chase, my God, what you do to me."

"Just let me touch you, sweetheart. I need to touch you like this. I can never get enough of you." And then his mouth was on her breast. He laved it with his tongue through her chemise, taking the nipple into his mouth and teasing it until she squirmed with want of him.

At first he did no more than gently hold the bloom between his lips, flicking his tongue over the sensitive flesh, but her impassioned response caused him to lose restraint. Pulling down the thin layer of fabric to expose her breasts, he began to suckle. The added stimulus was intense, and Millie writhed beneath him.

Chase knew he was on the brink of taking her then and there. "God, how I want you. More than you know. More than you understand. I must stop now, Millie."

Millie reached up and pulled his head down until their lips met once more. He drew her into his arms. They were strong and secure. He kissed her forehead, brushing his lips softly against her skin. And again, ended the kiss.

He pulled her arms from his neck and swallowed. Never had anything been so hard. "We must stop now, or I won't be able to stop at all."

Chase's words slowly sank in, and Millie realized what she had allowed him to do—and he was in love with someone else! He was cradling her in his arms but intended to marry another. She found it hard to reconcile in her mind that he was like so many other men—a cad at heart. Well, she was not going to let him have all the satisfaction this coming Saturday. No, her pride would not allow that. She righted her nightdress and stepped out of his arms.

"My apologies. Teach me to wander around without at least a robe on," Millie said, trying to sound indifferent.

Chase smiled and unknowingly licked his lips. "I doubt a robe would have prevented my kissing you."

Millie realized she had to get out of there now, before she completely broke down. "Well, we are going to have to stop these little tutoring sessions, aren't we? I just wanted to let you know that you will not be forced to chaperone me next Saturday to Lady Castlereagh's ball. A handsome gentleman asked if he could be my escort for the evening. I have decided to accept."

Despite the darkness of the room, Millie could see Chase's

expression turn dark and stone hard. The look of fury on his face was unmistakable.

Chase suddenly rounded on her, his eyes so cold they chilled her heated blood. "So, what was this? Training? Now that you have learned how to kiss and turn a man into a whimpering mess, you are going to try your luck with other gentlemen? Is this your game?"

Millie jerked her shoulders, turning her back on him as she blinked back the mist pooling in her eyes. She refused to give him the satisfaction of seeing her reduced to tears.

"Why is it that only men can test the waters without shame? And what have I been to you? A mere dalliance to pass the time with—but see? I am not offended. So go off, meet other women, kiss and marry whom you please. Your actions are none of my affair, and *my* actions are none of yours."

And suddenly Chase found himself staring at the closing door through which Millie had just disappeared. He had been wrong. Millie was not honest at all. She had just been using him.

He sank onto the settee and buried his face in his hands. He thought about her in his arms and knew the emotion and passion they shared was unique and real. She said that she was *going* to accept an invitation. Meaning she had not done so yet. It was as if she had made the decision as the words came out of her mouth.

He stood up. *No, something else was going on here*, Chase thought as he began to pace back and forth across the floor. He had known Mildred Aldon all her life, and she was a fiercely honest and loyal person despite that little act she had played tonight. Something had happened since the party this evening to spawn this little performance.

And despite Millie's promises to the contrary, he would discover what and who had caused it.

Chapter 12

Millie woke up with a start and sat straight up. Lord, what was she going to do now? She had told Chase she was going to be escorted by another man to next Saturday's ball. Hosted by Lady Castlereagh, one of the main patronesses at Almack's, those who were invited, attended. If they did not—especially if they were young women of marriageable age—they would be summarily blacklisted. So canceling without an impeccable excuse was not wise.

Millie had less than a week to find someone to accompany her. But how? Last week, her written responses had such a note of finality to them, she had no hope that any of the recipients would request to escort her to anything. Millie knew of only one person who could help her out of this scrape. It would be embarrassing, but nothing close to the humiliation she would endure if she arrived at Lady Castlereagh's with no one by her side.

Millie rang the bell cord beside her dressing table and waited impatiently for Elda Mae to arrive. As soon as Millie heard the light knock she opened the door and pulled the older woman in. "Elda Mae, is Mother Wentworth awake?"

"Lady Chaselton? Why, yes, yes, my lady, she is. She is preparing right now for . . ."

Millie didn't hear the rest of Elda Mae's comment as she raced out of her room. Tying the ribbons on her robe, Millie ran barefoot, down the hallway to Cecilia Wentworth's sitting room. She knocked, and at the first sound she opened the door and rushed in.

Cecilia Wentworth had just finished getting her hair in place when her adopted daughter darted into the room. "Why, Mildred! What on earth is the matter with you? You are acting half-crazed."

"Mother Wentworth, I am in desperate need of a favor."

Cecilia quickly assessed the chaotic brown hair and the dark, red-rimmed, luminous eyes. It was clear Millie had not slept for most of the night. Cecilia indicated to her maid to leave them for a moment.

"How can I help?" Cecilia asked and pointed to a nearby settee.

Millie bit her bottom lip and walked over to the light gray sofa. She picked up a matching velvet cushion and clutched it as she sat down, hoping the action would give her some courage. "I . . . I . . . need an escort for Lady Castlereagh's ball."

Cecilia's reaction was strangely relaxed and unconcerned. "That should be no problem, my dear. I am assuming only one escort is needed, or will Aimee and Jennelle require one as well?"

Completely shocked by the casual response, Millie stared wide-eyed as she shook her head back and forth.

Deciding to ignore Millie's obvious confusion, Cecilia continued. "Are you particular? Or will anyone do?"

Millie expected some resistance to her request, or at least a demand for an explanation. She had been prepared to fall to the ground and grovel. "I uh . . . um . . . no." Lady Chaselton raised a single brow. "I mean, yes. He needs to be"—Millie winced, remembering her words to Chase the previous night—"handsome."

"Well, of course he does, if your plan is going to work."

"Plan?" Millie choked. She was not aware she had a plan. She just knew she had to have an eligible man accompany her or die of mortification.

Cecilia eyed her protégé with sympathy. The girl was transparent, but obviously too tired to realize how much. She knew her son and Millie had fallen in love. She had seen them both fight it. Up until now, she had decided to refrain from interfering, but was it considered meddling if the assistance was requested?

"Never mind. I have the perfect man for you. And do not be concerned about inconveniencing him. For I know you will be able to help him a great deal as well."

Millie was completely thrown. Usually it was she who discombobulated others. "I . . . uh, how?"

Cecilia Wentworth swiveled around in her chair, back to her mirror. She dabbed lightly at her hair, pretending not to have heard Millie's stammered question. "Now, I think it would be best if you both met first. Can you meet tomorrow afternoon, say two o'clock? I think a ride through Hyde Park would be good. His name is Mr. Basil Eddington."

Millie was completely mystified. "Did you say Mr. Eddington?"

"Yes, a completely delightful young man I met at Lady Bradshaw's tea a couple of weeks ago. You two should get along splendidly." Cecilia turned and overtly scanned Millie as if assessing her for an assignment. "Mmm, yes. Definitely mutually advantageous. Now, if you will excuse me, dear. When you step out, can you ask Susan to come back in?"

Millie nodded blindly as she opened the door to let the maid finish with her interrupted task. Just as Millie was about to close the door, Cecilia called out, "Millie, dear!"

Millie turned back around, eyebrows pinched together. Cecilia gave her a look of sympathy. "Go get some sleep, daughter. I promise it will all work out."

Millie nodded her head and slowly wandered back to her

room. She entered and closed the door. It was rare for her to be rendered speechless, and Lady Chaselton excelled at the ability to make her so. Millie leaned against the door and stood staring at nothing.

She had an escort to Lady Castlereagh's. Her pride would be intact. If only she had the man she wanted, as well. Millie felt like crying again and crawled back into bed. Sleep came upon her quickly.

Chase paced the floor, waiting for his mother to descend the stairs for the morning meal. His mother had always been an early riser. She would be able to clarify the nightmare that had been plaguing him for the past several hours. He knew deep in his heart Millie did not have another escort. As soon as his mother verified this fact, he would be able to rest easy.

He paused by his study door and visualized Millie standing there last night. Her diaphanous chemise had clung to her gently curving breasts like liquid silver. Just the memory made him writhe with sensual need. He needed to be sure he was the only one. That there was no one else. Unfortunately, Chase knew there were several men ready to jump at the opportunity to escort her. Many had already tried, but the Daring Three had become very skilled at dissuading men. He never realized before how reassuring that was.

Chase did not know how it had happened, but he had fallen in love. He had seen so much pain, anger, and corruption, he had forgotten how to live, how to seek and derive pleasure from the world. With Millie, he would learn how to do so once again. He didn't know what life would be like married to Mildred Aldon, but he was sure it would not be boring. For the first time since he could remember, Chase looked forward to his future. He would find his father's killers, announce his marriage intentions, marry the feisty woman, and live happily ever after. It was supposed to be simple, and it would be once again, as soon as his mother verified that *he* would be Millie's escort next Saturday.

Cecilia Wentworth eyed her pacing son as she descended the staircase. She loved him a great deal and was pleased with his choice for a wife. Her son was a lot like his father. Composed, calm, and always levelheaded. She knew Millie and Charles would be good for each other, just as she and her husband had been a good match. Millie would bring Charles excitement and keep him from turning old early. He would be Millie's safe anchor in life's many storms, her trusted confidant, her biggest believer, and most of all, her hero. What Charles did not understand yet, and might not for many years, was that he needed to be a hero.

"Good morning, Charles. What keeps you at Hembree Grove? I thought you would have returned to St. James's by now," she said innocently as she reached the bottom of the stairs and headed toward the main dining room.

Chase quickly followed, suddenly unsure of how to proceed. "Mother."

Cecilia entered the dining room and went to take a seat. "Are you going to dine with me? What an unexpected and delightful surprise."

Chase had not intended to eat. He had wanted to ask one question, receive an answer, and leave before anyone else came down the stairs. While part of him wanted to speak with Millie and compel a confession out of her about Saturday, Chase knew he needed a few days to calm his sexual hunger before he saw her again. Soon, he told himself, soon he would wed Millie and these insane actions he was taking to keep his hands off of her would no longer be necessary.

"Mother, I just . . ."

She interrupted. "Do not concern yourself so. Sit down with me. No one will be up for some time."

Chase looked unconvinced, knowing Millie's penchant for appearing when least expected.

"I mean it, Charles. Sit. I just sent Mildred back to bed. Poor thing is so worn out over these parties, and I would like her to be fully rested when her suitor arrives tomorrow afternoon. Right now she is quite drained."

As she expected, this got a reaction. Chase found himself suddenly needing a seat, and slid into one across from his mother. "Did I hear you say . . . ?"

"Suitor. Do not act so surprised. After all, that is the reason she is here in London. To come out, find an eligible gentleman, and get married."

Chase felt as if the wind had just been knocked out of him. A sudden, horrible thought occurred to him. "Is this the same gentleman, by chance, escorting Millie to Lady Castlereagh's?"

Forcing herself not to smile, Cecilia inconspicuously appraised her son. "Why, I believe he is." She turned and accepted her usual breakfast fare—a piece of toast and hot tea.

Chase dropped his head into his hands. What was going on? Just last night Millie had been kissing him so earnestly, so completely, he knew he was the only one. How could she be so duplicitous?

Cecilia saw the emotions flicker on her son's face and knew what he was thinking. It was time to play matchmaker. Yes, Millie was going to have her escort. And yes, her son was going to be jealous—more so than he would think likely. But an out-of-control jealousy never led to anything productive, and that was exactly where Chase was headed.

"If you would excuse me, dear. If you intend to resume lodging at Reece's, will you still be able to escort Aimee and Jennelle Saturday to Lady Castlereagh's?"

Chase looked up and focused on his mother's words. "Yes, yes, I can escort you three to the event, but I might have to leave early."

"I should not think that a problem. I will ask Millie's escort if he can see us home. I must go meet with him this morning about tomorrow afternoon and Saturday." She rose, took one last sip of tea, and casually left the room.

Cecilia was in the front foyer, preparing to leave, when Chase rushed forward. "Mother, did I understand you correctly?"

Lady Chaselton adjusted the sleeves of her pelisse as it was a fairly chilly morning. "Yes, dear? I am sorry, but I have several stops this morning."

"I asked if I understood you correctly."

"I believe so. I did speak succinctly and your hearing has always been excellent," Cecilia said, buttoning her coat.

"Does Millie have an escort for this Saturday or not?"

"I suppose it depends on your point of view. She came in this morning asking if I knew of an available gentleman, and I agreed to help her. I am confident I can obtain one. Now I must go, love. See you Saturday."

He knew it! Millie *didn't* have an escort. Oh, she would have one Saturday. Millie would try to pass off the fool as the gentleman she had taunted him with, and he would let her . . . for a while. And when he was ready, he would cleverly disclose his knowledge that her escort for the evening had been arranged by his mother.

Chase stood elated as he watched the woman who had saved his sanity enter her favorite landau. Only after the small four-wheeled carriage disappeared around the corner did Chase realize his folly. He had forgotten to ask whom his mother had selected as an escort for Millie.

The next day Millie found herself having a surprisingly good time with Basil Eddington. Affable and witty, he was a complete change from most of the jack-a-dandies infesting the large crushes she had been attending. Of average height, he had wavy reddish-brown hair, cut fashionably short, and long sideburns. His warm smile and easy manner put Millie at ease immediately upon meeting him. She quickly agreed to an afternoon ride in his new curricle.

Basil glanced once more to his side, again surprised to find himself in the company of such an unusual beauty. He looked forward and picked up the reins. "Let us be off then. I assume you have been to Hyde Park?" Basil asked as he flicked the leather straps. The two grays leading the high-perched two-seater jerked into motion.

"Ah, yes. Yes, I have," Millie said, grabbing her bonnet and trying to figure out a way to tie it more securely so as not to lose it altogether.

"I apologize for the horses. They are a new team and are very spirited, especially after standing for so long. I promise they shall settle in in a moment," Basil said apologetically. "Lady Chaselton told me you, too, have a love for horses and would not be unduly put out." He tried to appear calm as he controlled the eager team. He was wearing gloves, but Millie guessed if she could actually see Basil's knuckles, they would be white.

"Uh, no, Mr. Eddington. The horses are just fine. I just wish I had known to put on a different bonnet," Millie responded, still attempting to secure her hat in the swift breeze. "There, nice and tight. You were saying something in regard to Hyde Park?"

Basil released a sigh. The team was starting to cooperate. Keeping a firm grip on the reins, he chanced another side glance. Lady Aldon was smiling. For the first time in weeks, he felt like smiling as well. "Seeing that you live in Mayfair, you have undoubtedly been to the fashionable location numerous times."

Not numerous, Millie thought. *Just once, and once was enough.*

The grays continued easing up on the reins and their pace slowed to a more genteel rate. Basil took the opportunity to regard his fortuitous companion more thoroughly. He had been intrigued yesterday when Lady Chaselton had suggested that a ride with Lady Mildred Aldon could solve all of his problems.

Lady Chaselton had come to his place of work in the City, very unusual for one of quality. Typically, men of affairs visited him, not the nobles themselves. Immediately, though, he realized the wealthy dowager was nothing typical. And although she did not give voice to his trouble, she seemed completely aware of its nature. She seemed undaunted by the fact that he was man of trade, a trait that, despite his wealth, was upsetting to many in the *ton*.

Most men would have been compelled out of curiosity to meet Lady Mildred Aldon before agreeing to escort her, but desperation had prompted Basil's agreement.

So far, his estimation of the petite, dark-haired lady was quite high. Lady Millie was surprisingly clever, and Basil quickly found himself fascinated and charmed by her. Her mannerisms and grace of movement indicated she was a lady of high birth, but her tolerance for many things Society believed improper was delightfully welcoming. Basil decided to test his theory.

"I am not sure whether Lady Chaselton relayed to you my background, but you should know that I am a cit."

Although Millie had been in London for only four weeks, she was familiar with the term for merchants and middle-class residents of the City and disliked the negative connotation associated with it.

Millie pursed her lips. She didn't know how to take his comment. "Are you always so self-deprecating, Mr. Eddington? If you are soliciting a companion for such depressing talk, I am afraid you are wasting our time."

Basil could not help himself and laughed aloud. "Not I, my lady. Not I. I am proud of being a merchant. It is others who often find fault with a man who earns his blunt. And when such a man is successful, as I have been fortunate enough to be, they resent it all the more."

Millie exhaled a telling sigh. "I wonder if Society will ever realize how much its rules of inclusion and exclusion only hurt itself," she said, unconsciously waving her hand to accentuate her point.

"I believe one day it will, Lady Aldon. Unfortunately, however, that day has not arrived."

Millie caught the change in his voice. The undertones of anger had been unmistakable, but just as she was about to probe, the horses turned onto a very crowded street.

"Mr. Eddington, may I ask where we are and where we are going?"

"Do not tell me you have limited your shopping tours to only those around Bond Street? Lady Millie! I have known you for only a short while, but you have misled me to believe you were of the adventurous sort."

Millie laughed. "Why, I can promise you, Mr. Eddington, that shopping in Mayfair can be something of an adventure. However, I must admit I avoid Bond Street activity with one exception. Hookham's."

"Hookham's Lending?"

"The very one. My friend cannot go three days without visiting a library to study its vast selection of books, and that particular place attracts a diverse group of people."

"And are you not also taken with books?"

"To a degree, though I fancy the newer ones. My friend, however, looks for rare old books detailing England's past," Millie clarified. She paused and then added, "Mostly, I go with her to watch."

"Watch?"

"People," Millie answered, wondering if he would think her odd.

Basil surprised her. "Ah, an excellent pastime I enjoy myself, Lady Aldon. Cannot tell you how many successful deals I have entered into—and failed ones I chose to walk away from—simply by being observant." He smiled at Millie and refocused his attention on the horses, which were becoming distressed with all the activity on the street.

A few minutes later, the curricle turned off Piccadilly and into Bath Gate, its occupants unaware of the eyes that had spied the couple's jovial conversation.

"Ah, this is much better, is it not?"

Millie smiled at Basil, enjoying the new scenery. "Better than what? The clatter of the street back there or the Grand Strut of Hyde Park?"

Basil smiled. "Now, Piccadilly Street represents blokes like me. It's named for a tailor who owned a shop selling pickadils."

"Pickadils! Why, those have not been in fashion for . . . oh my, at least two hundred years!"

"It seems your friend is not the only one who knows her history."

"Not exactly. Jennelle really is the expert. She can be completely consumed by a subject for weeks, often relaying odd bits of information. For unknown and bizarre reasons, some tidbits stick." Millie watched as Basil masterfully handled the horses. Though she felt no attraction to him, she was extremely comfortable in his company. Their easy repartee reminded her of conversations between a brother and sister; more specifically, Aimee and Charles. "How does that busy street represent a gentleman such as yourself?"

"Ah, well, the pickadil merchant was fortunate to be wise in business and soon became very wealthy. So much so, he was immortalized by a street, a now very pivotal street in west London." His reply had not exactly answered her question, but it did convey that he enjoyed the idea of a main thoroughfare named after a successful merchant, running through the heart of the *haut ton's* residential neighborhood.

Refusing to release even one hand on the reins, Basil used

his chin and pointed at their surroundings. "How do you like Green Park? Or do you miss Society's promenade of gawkers?" Basil asked with a strong hint of enmity. No longer was he containing his dislike for Society and the nobles who belonged to it.

"I like Green Park well enough," Millie agreed thoughtfully. "But I must say that I miss the affable gentleman with whom I left Hembree Grove. Can you tell me where he went, Mr. Eddington? Or would you just like to disclose why I have earned the brunt of your sudden hostility?"

Basil brought the horses to a stop and looked ahead at the meadows. "My deepest apologies, my lady. My only excuse is that you are looking at a wounded man, and your very nature pains me with memories."

"My nature?" Millie asked incredulously. "I readily admit I am often difficult, but I doubt I have the ability to create wounds."

"Do you by chance know Miss Lilith Moreland?" Basil asked bleakly.

Millie thought for a second before the name registered with a face. "Yes, I believe so. Tall, fair, dark eyes? If I remember correctly, she is one of the few ladies I have met in Society possessing wit. However, I have not seen her for some while. I believe the last time I saw her in passing was at Sadler's Wells Theater. Why? Are you acquainted with Miss Moreland?"

Basil sighed. "Not acquainted. In love. And the reason you have not seen her lately in Society is that she is avoiding me."

"You? Why would she wish to avoid you?"

"Because Lily is afraid of being in love and marrying a merchant."

"But I thought her father was in trade," Millie half asked, half stated.

"No. Lily's *grandfather* was in trade. He made a good deal

of money in spices. Since then, the Morelands have lived not extravagantly, but well."

"Oh. So Mr. Moreland is not titled, but he likes to act and think of himself as such."

"Bluntly stated, but correct," Basil replied. Realizing he had been unconsciously twisting the reins in his hands, he let go of the straps and smoothed them out, hoping she had not detected his emotional state.

Millie had noticed but chose not to say anything. She understood what it was like to be both angered and hurt by love. "What does Miss Moreland think?"

"It is difficult to know. One moment Lily and I were in love and all seemed perfect. Then I met Lily's father and suddenly her interest in me waned."

Millie's brows came together. "That is odd. I assume she knew of your position when you first met?"

Nodding, Basil asked, "My lady, can you help me? I know it is an odd request, but Lady Chaselton seemed to think you would be in a position to solve my heartache. At first, I thought she meant to lure my attentions away from Miss Moreland. But after meeting you, I believe Lady Chaselton thinks you might be able to discover what happened."

Without hesitation, Millie made up her mind. She knew exactly how to help Basil. She also hoped the lighthearted adventure would focus her mind and energies on something other than Chase and his upcoming marriage announcement. "Mr. Eddington, it will be a grand and glorious day when fathers realize it is better to have an agreeable gentleman like you, who can support their daughters in a way befitting them, than a penniless man with the title of lord. Until then, you have me. Now, I must make some preparations. We will need to meet again in two days' time. Have you been invited to Lady Castlereagh's ball this coming Saturday?"

"Two days?" Basil asked, more to himself. He mentally reviewed his schedule. "I will make myself available for our next meeting; however, obtaining an invitation to a ball hosted by *the* Almack's patroness may be more difficult."

Millie bit her bottom lip in deep thought. "Hmm, it may take a little more finessing than normal to obtain you an invitation, but it should not be insurmountable. Yet, it would be better if you could get one on your own merit."

"I will do what I can, Lady Millie." Basil picked up the reins, suddenly feeling a spark of hope about his future. "Would you enjoy taking a ride around Green Park before we return? Unlike its famous northern neighbor, it has no lakes nor any statues or fountains. Yet its wooded meadows are some of the loveliest you will see in Town."

"Yes, I would enjoy it very much, and do not frown so, Mr. Eddington. If what you relayed to me is true, then you and Miss Moreland will be back together before this week's end."

"Thank you, Elda Mae. You may go now," Millie said quietly as she sat in front of her dressing table, staring at her reflection. The figure in the mirror seemed drained of emotion, a mere shell of the woman that used to stare back with strength and purpose.

Elda Mae nodded at her longtime charge, saddened to see her in pain. Just as her old but nimble fingertips touched the doorknob, she turned around. "My lady, I've known you since you were a halfling. I know who you are, the good and the bad. And believe me when I tell you that whoever has broken your heart does not deserve you. My three girls are the best in England, and any man that doesn't recognize that fact upon meeting you is muttonheaded for sure."

Millie turned and looked at Elda Mae with tears brimming in her eyes. A few days ago she had hidden her sorrow, but after meeting Basil Eddington and then Lily Moreland the following afternoon, Millie realized she could no longer suppress the truth. Basil and Lily were both depressed at being separated, and they loved each other very much. They had hope. Something Millie wished for, but did not have. "Thank you and good night, Elda Mae," Millie said as she wiped the falling tears from her cheeks.

Distressed to see the most fearsome of the Three crying, Elda Mae ran over for a final hug and whispered, "There now, my lady. Broken hearts mend. Give it time, and I promise you, yours will as well."

Millie patted the old woman's hand, not trusting herself to say another word, and turned back to look into the mirror. Hearing the door click, Millie dried her tears again and began brushing her hair in long, steady strokes. Aimee and Jennelle were due to arrive back at Hembree Grove in a few hours, and it would be impossible to avoid their inquisition.

She sighed, laid down the brush, and rose to disrobe. But before Millie could pull the strings loose from her wrapper, she collapsed on her bed crying. It had been four nights since she had learned of Chase's intentions to announce his banns. Four nights of no sleep.

Millie abruptly awoke, sweat pouring off of her. She should have expected to experience a nightmare in her exhausted state. They always claimed her when she was most vulnerable. She leaned over and reached for the portrait of her mother on the nightstand, but hesitated at the last moment. Without analyzing her reasons, she got out of bed and went to where she hung the amulet along with her other jewelry.

Finding it missing, she remembered that Chase had it and she wanted it back more than ever. It was a piece of Wentworth jewelry, the only piece she was ever likely to own. All other gold and gems would go to Chase's new wife.

But the pendant was hers. And when it was back in her

possession, she intended to wear it every day to remind
Charlie of her unique bond with his father.

Something his new love would never have or understand.

"Millie?" came a quiet voice from the other side of the
door. The question slowly penetrated Millie's sleep-fogged
mind. "Are you awake?"

"Yes," Millie moaned, loud enough to be heard. "I am
now," she muttered and buried her head under a pillow.

"It's two o'clock in the afternoon. Jennelle and I were
wondering if you are well."

Millie jerked upright. She was never the first of the Three
to rise, but two o'clock! What had happened? And then the
memories came crashing back. Basil, Lily, Chase . . . Melinda.

Slowly Millie's door squeaked open and her two friends
entered. Millie shook herself and realized she still was wearing her robe from last night. Jennelle eyed the crumpled material with an arched eyebrow and moved to sit down on a
nearby settee beside Aimee. Millie watched suspiciously as
they both shifted nervously. Their worried gazes were leveled
directly at her.

"What is wrong with you two?" Millie demanded. "You
are both walking around as if I were an escapee from
Bedlam."

Jennelle let out a deep sigh of relief. "Well, you must
admit you are acting like one."

Millie felt her jaw slacken and then retorted, "I admit no
such thing."

Jennelle stood up with uncharacteristic animation. "Mildred Aldon! You refused to go out yesterday to play cards—
which was understandable—but last night! Last night was the
theater, and it was a damn good play you missed."

Jennelle's outburst shocked both of her friends. Aimee

was the first to recover. "You have to admit, Millie, your behavior is odd. You oversleep. You go riding with a stranger to Green Park. You . . ."

Millie threw her hand up. "Wait . . . how did you know about that?"

Aimee walked over to the bed and very mischievously trailed a finger along the edge of Millie's bed frame. "Charles. He came charging in right after he saw you, demanding Mother give him an explanation. He was yelling so loudly it was impossible not to hear."

"That and Aimee's ear was pressed to the door," Jennelle said, coughing into her hand.

"That is beside the point. I knew *you* were involved when Charles came in spitting fire." Aimee paused, pointing her finger at Millie. "No one can flap my unflappable brother like you. What were you doing, riding down Piccadilly in a man's lap?"

"Where did you get the idea I was sitting in Mr. Eddington's lap?"

Jennelle produced three apples from her apron pockets and threw one to Millie. "From Charles, of course. And who is Mr. Eddington?" she asked, offering an apple to Aimee.

Aimee took the apple and added,"Is he really a madman unable to control a pair of horses?"

Jennelle leaned in and grinned. "Mostly we want to know just what you are up to now."

Closing her eyes, Millie shook her head and reminded herself that having best friends was a good thing, not a torment. "He is a friend of Mother Wentworth's. The team was new and spirited and he actually handled them exceedingly well. And as for what I am up to—a favor."

Aimee paused just before she was about to clamp her teeth down on the red apple. "A favor? What favor? Why were we not told?"

"Mr. Eddington is in love with Lily Moreland, and after

calling on her yesterday afternoon I have concluded that she is very much in love with him." Millie took a bite of the apple, enjoying herself for the first time in days. "Thanks for this, by the way."

Jennelle shrugged and leaned against the sturdy bedpost. "Thought you might be starving, and you are not leaving here until Aimee and I are satisfied. So, if Mr. Eddington loves Miss Moreland, and she feels the same about him, where's the difficulty? Where does this 'favor' come in?"

Millie took a deep breath. "Well, to explain I have to go back to last Saturday night."

"The night you dismissed us," Jennelle said.

"I never dismissed you. . . ."

"Yes, you did," Aimee scoffed.

"I believe I explained that I had to warn a friend about something. What I neglected to tell you was that it was your brother, Aimee . . . and that he is getting married."

"Married? You are getting married?" Aimee asked, practically falling off her chair. "And you didn't tell us?"

Seeing the unhappiness swimming in Millie's eyes, Jennelle realized the truth. "You went down to warn Charles and somehow discovered he was getting married . . . to someone else."

Millie swallowed heavily and continued. "Yes, uh . . . well, back to your original question about Mr. Eddington and Miss Moreland. When I went down to write a note warning your brother, I overheard his announcement and . . . he caught me. I was so shocked by his declaration of love, I blurted out some crazy comment about having an escort to Lady Castle-reagh's ball."

Aimee's eyes popped open. "And you went to Mother for help." She clicked her tongue several times, her mind whirling as she visualized the resulting sequence of events. "Knowing Mother, she gave you someone who needed your assistance as well . . . hence, the favor you spoke of."

Jennelle moved to sit on the bed beside Millie. "So it looks as if we have three problems to solve. One easy, one moderately difficult, and one dangerously complex. Let's start with the easy one. What is your plan to get Miss Moreland and Mr. Eddington together? That is the favor, is it not?"

Seeing Millie nod, Aimee grimaced and joined them on the bed. "That might be more difficult than you think, Jennelle. At the last party, I overheard Lily's father refer to someone— whom I now assume was Mr. Eddington—as a mushroom."

Millie sat back, her mouth gaping. "He did?"

Aimee nodded. "He said a wealthy merchant can dress the part and act the part, but he will never succeed in becoming a member of the *ton*."

"Funny, coming from him. I thought Mr. Moreland was the son of a trader," Jennelle hummed.

Millie shook her head. "Grandson. It seems he has a very short memory regarding his ancestry and how the Morelands arrived at their current station in Society."

"Well, he definitely does not want his daughter reversing all of his efforts. The man has spent great energy separating himself from his past and will not be easily persuaded to throw it away on a baseborn person who, as the *ton* say, 'does not keep his place.'" Aimee bristled with personal knowledge about the cruelty of Society's rules. The importance of Society's good opinion may have forever prevented her from having a chance at happiness with Reece.

Millie stood up and put her hands on her hips. "That is ridiculous! Mr. Eddington is not a gate-crasher, and he certainly is not prone to curry favor. Quite the opposite, I assure you. He has a higher opinion of the people who live in the City than those who reside in Mayfair."

Jennelle shrugged. "Well, be that as it may. Mr. Eddington's station is considered beneath Miss Moreland's."

Millie frowned at Jennelle's voice of reason. "So the

real question is how do we persuade a prejudiced father he is wrong?"

"How do you persuade anyone to disregard Society's rules? Especially if they believe in them?" Aimee asked despondently.

Jennelle looked at her blond friend. "You are referring to Reece, Aimee. Are you not?"

"I know he cares for me a great deal, but he refuses to follow his feelings."

"He does it to protect you," Jennelle said in defense. "You are the daughter of an earl. He is the youngest son of a lord. He has no title and lives on a ship. He knows your father would never have approved."

"My father would have approved! He loved Reece as a son."

"Maybe," Jennelle conceded. "Mr. Hamilton has made quite a profit from his trips abroad. You just have to persuade him that his lack of title is meaningless to you."

"Believe me, I have tried. That is why I think you are doomed. You will never change Mr. Moreland's opinion. Why should he change it? He's not the one in love."

Millie suddenly stopped pacing. "That's it! That's the solution!"

"What?" Aimee asked, frowning.

"You just said it. We are appealing to the wrong person. It's the oldest ploy in the book, but it will work."

"What will? Will it work for me?"

Millie pursed her lips and shook her head. "Not exactly, as it is Reece who is your biggest obstacle. In Mr. Eddington's case, Mr. Moreland's prejudice is the key."

"What is your plan?" Jennelle asked pointedly, unable to hide her curiosity.

"I plan to make Lily Moreland jealous."

"How?"

"It is not the how, Jennelle. It is the *who*, and the who is me," Millie answered, grinning.

Aimee clapped her hands together. "Oooh, that is brilliant. *Your* approval of Mr. Eddington will get him accepted by most of Society and . . ."

". . . and if Lily genuinely loves this Mr. Eddington . . ." Jennelle murmured.

Millie took a bite of the apple she had been holding. "She does," she mumbled between chews. "I met with her yesterday."

". . . then she will not take kindly to seeing him with you," Jennelle finished. She stood up and grabbed Millie's hands. "Oh, this is perfect. This may even solve problem number two."

Aimee's brows furrowed. "Yes, what were problems two and three?"

"Problem number two is Charles and Millie. And Millie, do not even try to persuade me that your feelings are those of a sister. I saw your face the day we saw Charles with Mrs. Brinson. You love him."

Aimee jumped up and hugged her friend. "Why, that's wonderful! Jennelle and I had guessed as much the other night when you told us you enjoyed his kisses."

Millie took a couple of steps back and uncharacteristically began wringing her hands. "No, you do not understand. He is going to marry someone else and is planning on announcing the engagement this Saturday!"

Jennelle took in a deep breath and exhaled. "Do you have any idea who?"

"I only know what you do . . . and that it is *not* me. He only mentioned marriage once in my presence, and it was with extreme antipathy toward the idea of our forming a 'permanent commitment.'"

"But you kissed. Charles would not play with your feelings. He just wouldn't. Mother and I would never forgive him."

Millie shrugged her shoulders and sank into a chair by

the hearth. "Those kisses can easily be explained away. One was at Vauxhall when he was trying to hide us from other couples."

"Kisses? As in he has kissed you more than once?" Jennelle asked.

"Did you not just hear what I said? They are *explainable*. If it had been you he caught that night, Jennelle, then you would have been the one he kissed."

Aimee drew a breath. "I don't think so. And by the look on your face, neither do you. There is more than what you are telling us. You, of all people, would not fall in love with the most self-controlled man in England, based on a few 'explainable' kisses."

Tapping her finger on her lips, Jennelle started thinking aloud. "In every book I read, when one lover gets discarded by the other, they try to kill themselves by throwing themselves off a cliff or drinking poison. Remember the play we saw last night, Aimee? You do not plan on doing yourself harm, do you, Millie?"

Millie looked at her friend and scrunched her nose. "Bloody hell, Jennelle. Your books do give you the most strange and bizarre ideas."

"Of course she isn't going to hurt herself," Aimee said definitively. "Our Millie is going to find a way to get her man."

"No, I am not," Millie said, instinctively retreating farther into the chair. "If the dolt wants to marry someone else, then let him. I do not want a man who would even for a moment consider settling down with someone dull and unexciting. No. She may have Charles Wentworth," she finished, wiping away a stray tear.

Aimee got mad. "Millie Aldon, you coward. You want something now more than you have ever wanted anything else in your life. Don't try to deny it."

Jennelle bit her bottom lip. "Aimee is correct. You are crying, and you never do."

Aimee nodded. "That's right. That proves my point. You want my brother, and instead of exhibiting your normal obstinacy when you are told you cannot have something, you are surrendering."

"I am not surrendering. I'm being practical. I cannot win him now that he is . . . wants . . . is going to . . ." Millie stammered.

Aimee went over and clutched her friend's hands in her own. "Millie! Do you not understand? With your plan, you are going to get Charles back at the same time and in the same manner that you are getting Lily for Mr. Eddington. You will make him jealous!"

"Don't be ridiculous!" Millie exclaimed, leaving her chair and heading to the window.

Aimee's hands found a place on her hips. "Now, you may be the ringleader of adventures around here, but I know how to capture a man. I captured Reece, didn't I?"

Jennelle crossed her arms and rolled her eyes. "Well, it all depends on what you mean by capture."

Aimee turned to dress down her friend. "I got him to admit that he cared for me. And let me tell you, that *was* an accomplishment. Don't worry. I will marry the man. I just have to be patient and wait for the right opportunity," she promised and then turned back around. "But yours is now, Millie. And we are going to take it. Lady Castlereagh's ball this Saturday night will go down in history! Have no doubt, by the night's end my brother will be safely in your arms."

At the mention of the word *safe*, Millie's mind raced back to the conversation she overheard in the gardens. "Oh no!"

Jennelle nodded her head knowingly. "You've just remembered problem number three."

Aimee frowned. "Will someone tell me what problem number three is?"

Jennelle leaned back against the bed frame and stared steadily at her petite friend's face across the room. Millie was worried about something. At first, Jennelle thought Millie had concocted some wild adventure just to alleviate her boredom. But Millie's face was an eerie white. Jennelle realized problem number three was much larger than she had originally imagined.

Chapter 13

"Madame Sasha, can you do it?"

"Of course, I can do it. The question is, do I want to do it." Just then a door opened, and the lanky boy they had met during their first visit entered. "Ah, Stuart, finally. Please take Lady Wentworth and Lady Gent to the back room for tea."

"For tea, mum?" the boy replied with his strong cockney accent. "In the back room? There's not a spot for my scrawny arse to sit down in that space, with all your fribble layin' 'bout."

"Stuart, I did not ask for your opinion about my request." Madame Sasha's accent deepened with irritation.

Oblivious to the Russian woman's ire, Stuart pressed. "Well, how's about greasin' me fist for me efforts?"

"There'll be fourpence in it for you if you go now," Madame Sasha said, and then turned her attention to the two ladies preparing to leave. "Beware, Aimee and Jennelle. This one here will turn someone up sweet if he thinks there is any money in it for him. I'll tell you now, Aimee. Stuart was looking forward to such an opportunity as this. I believe he thinks you will 'bleed freely.'"

Aimee looked down at the still growing boy. "He does, does he?"

Stuart shrugged his shoulders unrepentantly. "You three never look like you're purse-pinched. You're all fairly flushed in the pockets from what I can see."

Aimee crossed her arms, trying to fake annoyance at his accurate estimation of her financial status. "Someone so clever at reading his fellow man surely is not as poor as he claims."

Unperturbed, Stuart shot back, "Well, ain't ye a downy one. Yeah, I'm not doomed for dun territory. I's got me dibs."

Jennelle laughed. "And yet a bloke like you could always use more."

Suddenly, as if he could not help it, young Stuart smiled. "No wonder the madame has taken to ye three. She always did avoid those with more hair than wit. Come on. The back room is this-a-way. I hope you aren't lookin' for anything fancy. No one in this part of Town gives a tinker's damn for the frippery of the nobles."

Aimee and Jennelle followed the boy into the back room. It was cluttered and filled with miscellaneous material, threads, and odds and ends from Russia and other countries.

Aimee walked around and lightly touched the beautiful cloth. "How lovely."

Stuart rolled his eyes at her reaction. "Fine then. After being warned, you're obviously no longer easy to part with your blunt. So I'll be off."

In the front parlor, Madame Sasha was grilling Millie. "Well, if that is the whole story . . ."

"It is."

". . . then there is only one plan. Are you sure I cannot tell Cecilia?"

Millie firmly shook her head no. "Normally, I would have done so. But this involves both her late husband and her son. Besides, I only know enough to scare her. Blast it, I only know enough to scare me."

Madame Sasha rose and went to an old cabinet. Millie

watched her search for something in her pocket. She eventually pulled out a strange key. "Do you know how to shoot?"

Caught off guard by the odd question, Millie did not answer immediately. "Ah, um, shoot? Yes, I am actually a fair shot. We all are."

"Good. Cecilia's doing, no doubt," the older woman concluded as she reached into the cabinet and pulled out a small silver pistol. "After all, it was how she caught the late Marquess of Chaselton."

"I thought they met at a ball," Millie murmured in puzzlement.

Sasha turned and waddled back to the chair across from Millie. "Well, yes, I guess you could say they met at a party, but it was Cecilia's ability to shoot him that captured Lord Chaselton's heart at that very ball."

Millie was about to probe further when Sasha held out the beautifully etched pistol. "Here. Keep this with you at all times. It is loaded. And if you want to know more about Cecilia, I suggest you ask her."

Millie took the small object from the wrinkled outstretched hand and held it steadily. "I hope this isn't necessary."

"It is, and you know it. If you did not think it to be so— and soon—you would have refused to carry it."

Millie looked up at the sage woman. "I've never shot a person before."

"Well, if you are lucky, you will not ever have to. But after last Saturday, the men who are after Lord Chaselton think you are involved. You need protection."

"Thank you, Madame Sasha."

"Don't thank me yet. I still have to make something to help you secure the affections of your man. That egg-shell creation you wore was supposed to do that. In fact, I'm not convinced your man does not already consider you his intended. But if he doesn't, he soon will."

Millie could not help it and got up to hug the older woman. "Thank you. Thank you so very much."

"Now go. Go and fetch the others and leave me. I have less than two days to design and produce a masterpiece."

The day before the big event, Millie found herself getting dizzy watching Basil Eddington pace excitedly back and forth in the Hembree Grove drawing room. He didn't even pause to address her. "I must say, meeting you has lightened my heart a great deal. I feared I was soon going to be punting on the River Tick, considering some of my decisions of late. Problems with the heart are dangerous to the pocketbook." He suddenly paused and looked at Millie. "Do you honestly think this will work?"

"I believe so. I hope so," Millie said, rising to put herself in his ever-moving path. Unfortunately, Basil pivoted and changed his pacing pattern. She sighed. "We still have a few more potential obstacles to avoid. The first is getting you approved, which will be more difficult than I expect you know."

"Ah, you refer to the infamous patronesses of Almack's," Basil said mockingly.

"Yes, Lady Castlereagh has no doubt invited them. You would be wise to remove the contempt in your voice when you mention anything that is—in their opinion—above your station. It would take very little to have them turn you away."

"But then why are we going through this act if my station makes their disapproval inevitable?"

"Very simple. They decide the social acceptability of anyone associated with Almack's. And once it is known that a man, or woman, has passed their scrutiny, that person is automatically accepted into Society's highest circles."

Basil stopped his pacing and stared into the fire in the marble fireplace. "Do I have a chance?"

"Lady Chaselton thinks so. You are well mannered—

usually. You're fashionable without going so far as being a jack-a-dandy. I did notice Lady Sefton especially dislikes excessively elaborate clothes and foppish manners. Thankfully, you have neither."

Basil turned and placed his hands behind his back. "But I work for a living."

"*And* you make money. Believe me when I say that some ladies of the *ton* are much more knowledgeable regarding trade than their husbands. They have to be, living on their allowances. No, the patronesses are not easily swayed by social rank or money. I hate to say it, but it is mostly based on their mood that evening. Let us just hope none of them has a headache."

With one hand, Basil began massaging his trendy sideburns. "I cannot believe it. I am placing all my hopes and dreams on whether or not some old harridan has a headache."

Millie walked over to a small writing desk and opened a drawer. She pulled out a sealed piece of paper. "Well, remember, not only do you have to pass their assessment—so does your soon-to-be intended. Right now, my friends are visiting Miss Moreland and extending her an invitation. Yours is right here." Millie handed him the sealed parchment. "You must thank Lady Chaselton for getting Lady Castlereagh to invite you both."

Basil took the extended invitation and lightly tapped it on the palm of his hand. "May I ask you a question, my lady?"

"Of course, Mr. Eddington."

"Why are you doing this?"

Millie smiled. "Are you asking how could I possibly benefit in helping you?"

"Exactly. I am a practical man. A woman, especially one of nobility and beauty, does not just allow someone—a no one, in fact—to pose as her suitor."

Millie casually shrugged her shoulders and moved to sit

down on the settee. "One does if she craves adventure. Something, anything to alleviate the boredom of Society's rituals."

Basil Eddington watched her graceful movements. He knew Millie possessed an adventurous streak, after their conversation at Green Park. But there was definitely something more. A sadness to her eyes. "I can help you, you know. If you would just confide in me."

Millie looked at the gentleman across from her and thought over his words. "My reasons are not exactly honorable. Justifiable, but not what I consider praiseworthy." Millie shifted uncomfortably. "I had an argument with a friend of mine and pride caused me to declare that I had an escort to this week's ball. There is very little more to it than that."

He eyed her uncertainly. "I see. Well, tomorrow then. I shall call for you at nine."

"Excellent. Oh, and please wear knee breeches, a white cravat, and chapeau bras. Countess de Lieven has a particular distaste for trousers, especially at formal events."

Basil walked to the salon doors and opened them. "Good day, Lady Aldon. I look forward to tomorrow night."

Minutes later, Basil was confronted by the reason behind Millie's broken heart. The Marquess of Chaselton.

Chase had been stewing all week, wondering about the man he had seen with Millie. And against his better judgment, Chase had decided to form a better estimation of the so-called gentleman. "Good sir, may I take a moment of your time?"

Basil stopped and turned around. "Certainly, your lordship. How can I be of service?"

Chase quickly evaluated the man. He was neither tall nor short, good-looking, and his clothes were of high quality and well fitted. The man was confident, and most likely sought by many women. He did not appear to be the sort idly sitting by waiting for a dowager to request a favor. "Were you here calling on Lady Jennelle Gent, by chance?"

Basil smiled easily. "No, my lord. My visit was with her friend, Lady Mildred Aldon."

Chase fought his instincts to squelch the man's good humor with a solid punch to the jaw. "I see by your demeanor that it went well."

Unaware of the intensity rising in Chase's eyes, Basil answered with enthusiasm. "Yes, exceedingly. Most encouraging that woman is. Most encouraging. If only more ladies had her demeanor and inclination to men of my position."

Chase's jaw clenched and he flexed his fists. "You remark on her demeanor. Do you think her calm and reserved?"

"Lady Millie? Heavens, no. She has a far more appealing disposition. She's intelligent and has a willingness to seek and experience the unknown. She is . . . a risk taker."

Chase's eyes narrowed perceptively. The man had no idea how near death he was treading. "That is obvious. She is, after all, allowing you to escort her to Lady Castlereagh's."

Suddenly Basil realized just who the Marquess of Chaselton was. He had no idea why the marquess and Millie were apart when they so obviously wanted to be together, but Basil was confident that, with very little effort, he could repay Millie for all she was doing for him. He was going to enact her plan. Once for him, and once for her. He was going to make the marquess jealous. Basil pumped out his chest and broadened his smile. "I'm a very lucky man."

Chase's eyes were now like dark slits, spitting fire. "And why is that?"

"Simple. The most fine-looking lady in London has consented to my escorting her tomorrow night to one of the Season's most influential balls. I realize you see her ladyship often, and your appreciation of her beauty has been dulled, but to others, no one compares. And to think we only just met."

Chase wondered if the man was baiting him intentionally. If so, he was a fool who had very little time left in his short life. "Pardon my intrusion, sir. I am sure I am keeping you from more important matters."

"Not a bother at all, my lord. Hope to see you again tomorrow evening. Good day," Basil replied easily as he entered the hired hack. *Yes, one good deed deserves another*, Basil thought. *By tomorrow's end, I shall have my Lily and Lady Millie shall have her marquess.*

Millie looked out the carriage window again, uncertain exactly why she was nervous. Maybe it was all the advice she received that afternoon. Madame Sasha had come over personally to fit her into her gown and oversee her hair.

"Now, petite one," the modiste began, "the secret to capturing your man's heart is to be coy and untouchable."

"Yes, don't even look in Charles's direction," Aimee had added.

Millie crossed her eyes. "Really? And how am I supposed to avoid looking at him without first determining where he is?"

"We will tell you," Aimee had countered, completely unmoved by Millie's logic.

"Your memory fails you, Aimee. Millie's to be with Mr. Eddington this evening," Jennelle reminded her.

"I forgot nothing, but the way Millie looks tonight, her plan to make Lily jealous will be quickly completed."

Jennelle stood, looking at her friend. "You do look beautiful, Millie. Quite exquisite."

Tears had formed in Millie's eyes. "You do as well, Jennelle. And you, Aimee. Believe me. No one can overshadow either of you."

"Mayhap, but tonight, all eyes will be focused on you."

Madame Sasha had intervened, producing a burgundy

cape. "Wear this when your escort comes to retrieve you. Do not let anyone see your gown until you reach the ball this evening. Promise?"

"I promise."

"Do you have the item?"

Millie had nodded, patting the small pistol. "In my reticule."

That had been almost two hours ago.

Millie instinctively felt for the small purse on the carriage seat, reassuring herself of its contents.

Basil was aware of Millie's apprehension. "You look lovely this evening, my lady."

Millie smiled, welcoming any conversation that would refocus her mind off of what was to come. "Earnestly? How could you tell? We practically ran out of Hembree Grove."

Basil laughed, and Millie could hear that he, too, was nervous. "My pardons, my lady. I must admit I am more anxious in regard to tonight's proceedings than I imagined I would be."

The carriage rolled to a stop. The party exited and headed toward the main entrance. Just before entering, Basil squeezed Millie's hand and whispered, "Do you think this will work?"

Millie removed her cloak and was surprised to find Mr. Willis, the guardian of Almack's, suddenly in front of her, offering assistance. She guessed that this week Lady Castlereagh had him doing double duty.

Mr. Willis collected her cloak and greeted her. "My lady, you look most lovely this evening. Come in and enjoy tonight's events."

"Thank you, Mr. Willis. Please let me introduce you to Mr. Eddington, another of Lady Castlereagh's guests. He has been kind enough to escort me to this evening's ball."

"Good evening to you, sir."

As they entered the main room, Millie noticed Basil's

uncustomary expression of witlessness. "Mr. Eddington, are you well?"

Basil was still trying to collect his thoughts. Never had he seen anything like Lady Mildred Aldon. Her gown was of a white creation overlaid with a sheer silvery material that glittered in the lamplight. The material flowed straight down, allowing the underlying white satin to outline her figure as she moved. Across her shoulders and breasts were several intricate strands of rhinestones. The draped pattern of embroidered jewels continued throughout the sheer overlay.

"Ah, yes, my lady," Basil answered, swallowing. "Very well indeed. My heart is securely taken, but if it were not, it would be in jeopardy this evening. I have a feeling that I will have more than just your marquess to deal with tonight."

Her marquess? But before Millie could covertly inquire as to his meaning, she was whisked inside to the awaiting patroness. Millie wondered if it was her imagination, or did the level of noise in the room suddenly diminish?

Lady Castlereagh approached the couple, but, as expected, the other patronesses of Almack's were right behind her. "Lady Mildred Aldon. How lovely it is to see you again, my dear. Mr. Eddington. Delighted you could escort our newly discovered diamond. Come and let me introduce you to my friends Lady Cowper, Lady Sefton, and Lady Jersey."

"Lady Mildred Aldon. Mr. Eddington," Lady Jersey crisply acknowledged.

Millie curtsied. "Lady Jersey, how are you this evening?"

"Tolerably well. And you, my dear, outshine us all. Are you sure it wise to dress so that you attract every man's attention?"

Basil could feel the tension in Millie rise. He had been warned about Lady Jersey's theatrics and ill-bred manners. Suddenly he felt very protective of the petite beauty standing quietly beside him. Only Lady Sefton's kindness and impeccable timing permitted him to continue with his plan for recapturing Lily Moreland's heart. If Lady Sefton had not intervened, he would have opened his mouth and most likely been summarily kicked out of the stately home.

"Come now, Sarah," Lady Sefton admonished softly. "Lady Aldon is no contest for you. You must realize that most of these men attend for our attentions and not for those of our guests."

"I am in complete agreement," Lady Castlereagh said, winking at Millie. She pointed to the growing crowd. "Lady Aldon, Mr. Eddington, please enjoy yourselves this evening. It looks as if you have time for a quadrille before the meal is served."

Basil took his cue, bowed, and quickly removed Millie and himself from further scrutiny. His thoughts immediately went to Lily, and he wished he could prepare her somehow for the inquisition.

Millie exhaled. Basil smiled. "Well, you did it, my lady. I have been officially accepted. Would you like to celebrate our first achievement with a dance?"

Millie flashed him a dazzling smile. "I would be delighted, Mr. Eddington."

Just as the dance started, Millie spied her friends arriving and knew Lily Moreland was enduring her own interrogation. The dance was almost over when Jennelle signaled her that all was well.

"Good news, Mr. Eddington. Miss Moreland has arrived and has successfully been allowed entrance."

Basil instantly switched his attentions from Millie to surveying the room.

"Calm yourself, Mr. Eddington. Remember the plan. Miss Moreland must look for you, not the other way around."

Basil refocused his gaze back to his partner. "My apologies, my lady. I forgot for a moment that you, too, have a lot riding on our performance."

Millie was just about to ask him for an explanation when

the dance ended and her friends gathered near. Millie smiled. She knew she was about to be somewhat cruel, but silently assured herself that her intentions were good. "Miss Moreland! How lovely it is to see you again. Please let me introduce you to my escort for this evening. Mr. Eddington, Miss Moreland."

Basil inclined his head in greeting. "My lady, Miss Moreland and I are acquainted. We met earlier this Season."

Millie's eyes popped open in innocence, an expression she had perfected on Charlie as a child. "Really? Miss Moreland, how did you ever let him slip through your fingers?"

Lily stood in stunned silence for several moments, digesting the fact that Basil, despite her father's suggestion otherwise, had been accepted by the queens of Society. "I'm not really sure I know, my lady. Mr. Eddington is a very kind gentleman."

Jennelle observed Basil's plight. "Mr. Eddington, would you be so kind as to fetch me something to drink? I find myself quite parched all of a sudden."

Millie watched Basil leave as she continued. "Such a fetching man. Quite a nonesuch. You cannot imagine my surprise, after meeting him, to learn that no lady had captured his attentions." She paused for emphasis. "Miss Moreland, you have known Mr. Eddington longer than I. Tell me, what is it about the man that caused you to reject him as an eligible suitor?"

Lily began staring at her satin slippers. "I truthfully cannot say, my lady. Mr. Eddington has no faults that I am aware of."

Aimee, beginning to feel guilty about the ruse, jumped in. "Let me guess. It was your father. Fathers are always the ones to interfere where love might bloom. Fear of losing their daughters, I presume. Was it Mr. Moreland?"

Lily looked up at Aimee's kind green eyes, her own swimming with unshed tears. "Yes, it was my papa. He believes I can do much better than a merchant."

Millie rolled her eyes for effect. "Well, there are merchants, and there are *highly successful* merchants. And Mr. Eddington falls into the latter category, I assure you. And if you do not believe me, ask the patronesses. My guess is that they would also conclude he is a man without fault."

Aimee elbowed Millie and gave her a threatening stare. "My father also interfered with my choice, Miss Moreland. But despite Society's rules, I am waiting for him, and if ever given the chance, I will be his forever. Despite what anyone might say, I will not marry a man I do not love."

Seeing the crowd move toward the supper tables, Jennelle suggested they relocate to the dining area. As dinner progressed, Basil noticed Lily become more and more agitated as she watched him converse and laugh with Millie. As soon as it was socially acceptable, Lily excused herself.

Millie leaned over and whispered, "Go to her, Mr. Eddington. Tell of her your true feelings."

"What of you?"

Aimee leaned over. "You are losing your chance, Mr. Eddington. Hurry now. We'll stay with Millie."

The Three watched as Basil chased after Lily. Jennelle turned to her friend. "I think we can add this to our list of successful adventures, Millie."

Millie wiped a tear of happiness and nodded.

Knowing Millie's performance tonight was just a sham, Chase had intended to forgo Lady Castlereagh's. Even after meeting the dashing Mr. Eddington and hearing the man praise Millie, Chase was determined to be unaffected. His resolution started to waver upon hearing his mother's indifference to his decision not to attend. But when he received a last-minute reminder of Millie's marriage pact, Chase found himself not only at the ball, but secretly watching her from a distance.

Chase's eyes roved possessively over Millie's every move. The gown sinfully accentuated every graceful movement and each perfect curve, elongating her petite frame to rival that of a statuesque beauty. Suddenly, his father's murder, the Rebuilders, revenge—all were secondary in importance.

Several times, he had to retreat to the cool outside air in order to remain in control. Millie was completely unaware of the attention she was getting. He had never believed the mere sight of a beautiful woman could entice a man into marriage, but over and over again he was hearing exactly that. Men of all ages, rank, and wealth were suddenly considering Millie the most desirable woman on the marriage mart.

With each comment, he reminded himself that none of these men had a chance with his Millie. She had vowed never to get married. Yet even as he convinced himself of her disinterest, he would observe her laughing and engaging a drooling gentleman.

No longer trying to stay out of sight, he made it easy for her to detect his presence. But not once did she look in his direction. His desire to make known to all present that she was his, and only his, steadily intensified.

Chase had never been a jealous person, but he suddenly felt unbearably possessive, and he knew the feeling wouldn't go away anytime soon. He would never be content until she was his. Not just in spirit and in mind, but to the world.

"My lady!" Millie turned to see Basil coming toward her. Behind him was a smiling, blushing Lily Moreland. "My lady, I must extend our gratitude again for making this possible. After tonight's acceptance by the patronesses, Mrs. Moreland believes that her husband will lift his objection. Regardless of her father's decision, though, Lily has agreed to marry me!"

Millie beamed at the jubilant faces before her. "I am so

happy for you both. So very happy. And I happily relinquish your escort responsibilities this evening to Miss Moreland."

Lily reached out to grasp Millie's hand, true happiness shining in her eyes. "I must beg your forgiveness and leave to see to my mother, but I cannot appreciate my gratitude enough, Lady Aldon."

After watching Lily weave her way through the crowd reaching her mother, Basil returned his attention to Millie. "I would like to accept your offer, but how would you get home?"

"Never fear, I will ride home in the Wentworth carriage, leaving you free to accompany Miss Moreland and her mother back to their residence."

Basil grinned with the sheer joy of a man in love. "I knew you would understand."

"Understand? It was part of the plan!"

Basil leaned closer and whispered, "But the whole plan has not gone accordingly, has it?"

"Mr. Eddington, I am afraid you are under the misconception that there was a secondary motive to tonight's events. I assure you there was none."

Unconvinced, Basil asked, "Are you indeed sure, my lady? There is a sadness in your eyes that never leaves, despite your demeanor and smiles."

Millie stared at him, melancholy darkening her eyes. "Mr. Eddington, I promise you I am well. Now go back to your intended."

Basil was aware of the marquess's lurking presence and decided to try one last ploy to help his new friend.

Millie was very surprised when Basil leaned down to give her a hug and a slight peck on the cheek, whispering again his thanks for her help in securing his own happiness. To embrace in public was a highly unorthodox thing to do. They were fairly secluded from the crowd, but not completely hidden. But before Millie could react one way or the other, a fist appeared out of nowhere and Basil Eddington was looking up at her from the floor.

Whirling around to confront his attacker, Millie was shocked to see Chase bellowing at her new friend in full fury. "Unless you want to find yourself on the fields at dawn, Mr. Eddington, I suggest you stay away from my future wife." Chase then turned to Millie, grabbed her hand, and started toward the door.

Basil propped himself on his elbows and used one hand to touch the blood at his lip just as Lily returned to his side. "See that, my dear? That is our debt. Repaid in full."

Millie, unaccustomed to being manhandled, instinctively pivoted, twisting free of Chase's grasp. Massaging her wrist, she looked up and realized her mistake. All of Chase's fury, which had moments ago been focused on Basil Eddington, was now staring at her.

Refusing to show any panic, Millie glared back. "How dare you, sir!"

Chase walked up so that only inches separated them. "How dare I? You haven't seen daring yet, madam. We are leaving."

Outraged, Millie hissed, "I cannot agree more. It is past time for you to leave, my lord. However, I am not as yet inclined to do so."

The words were still hanging in the air when Millie felt a solid thump on her derriere before being thrown over Chase's shoulder.

Acting as if he could not hear or feel any of Millie's attacks, Chase loudly announced, "Excuse me, ladies and gentlemen. My future wife and I have some unfinished business to discuss."

His cool tone infuriated Millie, and she began to pummel his back. She couldn't see where they were going, only the astonished faces of those they passed. "Charlie, put me down!"

"Hush, my dear. I must say good night to Mother before we take our leave."

Millie felt him lean over and was shocked into stillness when she heard Mother Wentworth encourage Chase's behavior. "Do not let Aimee and Jennelle concern you, Charles. I will see them safely home. And remember, son, your father and I had a successful marriage, not by taming the other, but by acceptance."

Millie felt soft hands covering her own as she tried to attain her freedom through poking and pinching. She looked up to see Lady Chaselton lean over and whisper, "You might as well surrender—at least for now. I can tell you with an earnest heart that even shooting him with a pistol would not work. Good night, my dear, and I consider myself extremely fortunate to know that I am soon to have a daughter-in-law like you."

Before Millie could reply and beg for help, she realized Chase was leaving the room. She knew it was pointless to resist, but everything in her refused to give in. She saw Aimee practically running to keep up with Chase's long strides. "Aimee! Help me!"

"Millie, I'm not sure I want to. . . ." But that was all Millie heard as Mr. Willis quickly handed her cloak to Chase as they departed to the Castlereagh manor.

Jennelle caught up to Aimee and stared at the doors through which their best friend had just been carried out. "It was a forgone conclusion that tonight's events were going to be public, but who could have dreamed that Charles would cause the spectacle rather than save Millie from it. Nevertheless, I believe that went well. Not quite as planned, but successful nonetheless."

Hooking her arm with Jennelle's, Aimee began to walk back into the main ballroom. "Oh, Jennelle, I do hope so. I don't think you realize how mad Charles and Millie are at this moment. We may have made things worse between them."

"Fustian nonsense, Aimee. Charles just declared in front of all of Society that he is going to marry Millie."

Aimee stopped and looked at Jennelle. "But did Millie agree to marry him?"

Jennelle exuded confidence and composure. "She will. Our Millie is proud, but she is not a noddy. Her intelligence will overrule her pride." Resuming their walk back to the rear alcove, she added, "And even if I am wrong, I sent Charles some insurance earlier this evening. In fact, I wouldn't be surprised if my note was not the true catalyst for his being here."

Aimee's eyes grew large at the prospect of Jennelle instigating a plan involving subterfuge. "What did you do?"

Jennelle grimaced. "Nothing evil. I love Millie, and believe it or not, I think Charles is the right man for her and that she is the right woman for him. And in that spirit, I sent your brother a small reminder."

"Jennelle, I am close to causing another scene that will make my brother's exit tonight pale in comparison."

"My goodness, Aimee, you are beginning to sound more and more like Millie. It was just a simple note outlining the details of Millie's exception to our pact."

Aimee covered her mouth to hide her pleasure. "Jennelle, you are fiendishly clever. Have I ever told you that?"

"Just wait until I try my charms on you."

"Hah! Please do! I would give anything to have Reece announce I was his intended and carry me off. *Anything.*"

Chapter 14

Millie sat across from Chase, seething. Of all the indignities Chase had ever bestowed on her, this was the worst and by far the most humiliating.

"Care to explain your actions, my lord?" Millie asked, wishing her clipped words had even more bite to them.

Chase regarded her through hooded eyes for several seconds before returning his gaze out the carriage window. "Care to explain yours?" His deep voice was smooth and level, but laced with veiled accusations.

Millie's jaw dropped in outrage. Not wanting to lose the upper hand by exploding, she closed her lips and forced her body to relax. "My actions were above reproach until you started to wallop poor Mr. Eddington and then manhandle me."

Chase gave her a telling glance. "Above reproach? You call crushing your bosom against another man above reproach?"

Millie did not like the edgy new tone in his voice. It was raw, wounded, and very possessive. "Crushing my . . . my . . . How dare you, Charlie Wentworth! It was nothing more than a light hug of gratitude. We barely touched."

"Any man ever demonstrates gratitude with you in such a

manner again, I will kill him. Mr. Eddington has no idea how very close to death he came tonight, thinking he could treat you thus," Chase whispered, his voice dark with solemnity.

He again refocused his attentions outward. His driver was making excellent time, but there seemed to be an inordinate number of carriages on the streets with the sole purpose of getting between them and Hembree Grove. The sooner he distanced himself from Mildred Aldon, the better.

Incensed, Millie exploded. "You really are a horse's arse. Mr. Eddington is *in love with Lily Moreland*. If you took even two seconds to think about what you were seeing, you would have noticed her clutching his arm." Millie leaned forward and gripped the edges of her seat to keep from toppling over. "Tell me one thing: What was the *real* reason behind your horrific actions? Why did you find it necessary to make me the ridicule of every article, gossip, and whisper that will scuttle around Town for the rest of the Season? Did Mrs. Brinson refuse your proposal? Was that what this display was all about? Was this an attempt at retribution? Are you going to drop me off and go running back to your ladylove and threaten her with me?" Millie finished her stream of seemingly endless questions and then sat back, wishing she had kept her mouth shut. The last thing she wanted was an answer to any of them.

Chase looked at her, dumbfounded. "Mrs. Brinson? As in Mrs. Melinda Brinson?"

Millie could not help it. She lashed back. "Do not play coy with me. I saw you with her. She *was crushing her bosom* against you, and you were a more than willing participant! I also know you had planned to announce your banns this week. What happened? Did she say no? Was this a ruse to use jealousy to win back her hand?"

Chase sat still for several minutes, assimilating Millie's words. "I have not asked my future wife for her hand as of yet. And while I had not realized I needed to win her affections, I do now."

Though his reply was cool and calm, Millie was not fooled into believing his strong underlying anger had remotely diminished. She folded her arms as she heard him rap the roof and ask the driver to go to a new destination.

"Where are we going? Are you going to introduce me to your intended? We have already met. She is lovely, kind, and everything a man would want in a wife. I wish you well." Millie knew she was acting somewhat childish, but every insecurity she had ever experienced was bubbling to the surface.

Chase forced himself to unclench his jaw. "Mrs. Brinson is all of which you describe, and I am sure the woman whom I have chosen to marry *will* make an excellent marchioness."

Millie slumped in defeat, taking comfort in the silence that followed. Neither spoke for the rest of the journey.

The carriage stopped and Millie stepped out without waiting for assistance. They were in front of a town house and based on Chase's key to the door, she assumed it had to be Reece's—the place Chase had moved to after leaving Hembree Grove. Moments later, they were inside. The uninhabited rooms were dark and cold. Chase walked over to a large hearth and lit the logs within. He stood up and stared into the flames.

"You may want to keep your cloak on until the room warms."

Millie was startled by the troubled tenor to his voice. It was clear she was going to be staying here for at least a while—wherever *here* was. The tiara headpiece Madame Sasha insisted she wear had gone askew when Chase threw her over his shoulder. It was tearing into her scalp, but pride refused to let her remove it. Millie wrapped her burgundy cape more firmly around her and walked over to the front window to look outside. She refused to stand next to Charles despite the cold.

Minutes passed. Both declined to speak or look at the other. Chase could hear Millie rub her arms for warmth. Millie listened as Chase crouched to stoke the fire.

"It's warmer over here, Millie."

Millie squared her shoulders and jutted her chin. "I am fine right here, thank you."

"Then I shall trouble you no more."

Chase's clipped words reignited Millie's anger, which had only just begun to simmer down. She turned and confronted him. "Trouble me? When have my thoughts and feelings ever affected anything you do? You kiss me at your whim even though you have every intention on marrying someone else." Millie was shaking and emotional and tired. Too much had happened and she could not keep her thoughts bottled up any longer. "Never once did you consider how your such a decision would affect me. You continue your advances, playing with my emotions, knowing full well how you disturb me. But the worst of it all, you are making me crazy. Do you know how hard it has been for me knowing that your life is in danger and not being allowed to even *talk* about it? Will you even discuss it with me? Tell me what those men are planning? What you are planning? And how my amulet is involved? Of course not. And now, for inexplicable reasons, I find myself in a dusty room, without servants or warmth, in the company of a man who loathes me, seeks to make me unhappy, and tries to humiliate me whenever possible. So explain to me, Charlie Wentworth, how *exactly* are you going to trouble me no more?"

For the first time that night, Chase realized Millie's fury with him was very deep and very genuine. In other circumstances, he might have reacted differently, but the memory of seeing another man dare to place his lips against the softness of her skin was still fresh and very vivid. "Excuse me, madam. If you think so little of me, then why were you trying to make me jealous?"

Millie's dainty jaw went rigid. "Jealous? *You*, jealous? First of all, *my lord*, I would have had to know you were in attendance tonight if my goal was to make you jealous. The first time I was aware of your presence was when your fist suddenly appeared over my shoulder and right into poor Mr. Eddington's eye!"

Chase wanted to shake her. "Poor Mr. Eddington! If you say that one more time . . ." He forced himself to take a deep breath. "Poor Mr. Eddington is a very lucky fellow. He should be praising God I did not call him out this evening." Never would she understand the extraordinary act of will it took for him to walk away and not pull the man up by his cravat and hit him again.

Millie tried to adjust the excruciating headdress. The attempt just made the pain worse. "You insufferable . . . egotistical . . . maniacal . . ." she stammered, half in pain, half in anger.

"Would you just get to the insult, Millie? I am getting old waiting to hear it."

"Typical Charlie Wentworth," Millie responded, her voice trembling. "Whenever he is in error, he switches the focus of the argument."

"Unlike you and your childish name-calling." Chase's fingers were clamped so fiercely on the mantel it was a miracle he had not cracked the marble. "Besides, I am not ready to admit I was even slightly in the wrong this evening. Do not try to spin some cork-brained story. Mr. Eddington's eyes never left you. Never has a man made it more obvious that he wanted a woman."

"I guess throwing a lady over your shoulder and marching her out the front door in the middle of a Society ball does not count."

Chase moved so quickly Millie never even saw it coming. One moment he was at the hearth and the next his hand was clamped around her wrist, dragging her to his chest. His eyes glinted with raw possessiveness. "Understand this, Mildred Aldon. You are mine. And no man touches what is mine. If another man dares to kiss you again, he *will* die."

Chase let go and Millie took several steps back. Hot, furious tears burned her eyes. "Well, calm yourself. For while you are correct that jealousy was the topic of tonight's adventure, *you* were not its object. If you could expand your pea-sized view of this evening's events just slightly, you would have realized the only reason Mr. Eddington was staring at me was because I commanded it. The fool almost ruined everything, and would have if he had not finally managed to control his constant need to search for his *true love*, Lily Moreland. Thank goodness the charade is finally over and he and his intended are together."

"You are telling me that everything I saw tonight was to make *Miss Lily Moreland* jealous?"

"Partly, but a good deal more was focused on getting her parents to realize that a successful merchant could be welcomed by higher Society."

Silence filled the room for several seconds before Chase found his voice. "Are you telling me my mother set you up with a *merchant*?"

Chase's voice filled the room, causing Millie to take several more steps back until she bumped into a large settee situated in the middle of the room.

Millie was shocked at his outrage. "Do not claim social superiority above working men. I know you think differently, Charlie Wentworth, especially as you are a working man yourself!" Regaining her confidence, Millie came forward several steps. "Indeed I do! I know you and Reece have started your own specialized shipping company. I also know that you are beginning to turn a tidy profit from your endeavors. So do not expect me to believe you are upset that a man of trade *pretended* to be interested in me."

Chase's eyes narrowed. "Who else have you told, Millie?"

Millie sensed his sudden change and realized her instincts to remain silent had been correct. "No one," she whispered. "I saw the documents one morning when writing regrets to would-be suitors. I moved them to a drawer so as not to disturb them. They were out where anyone could see them, Chase. I did not think them private, but I never spoke of them to Aimee or Jennelle. I thought Aimee might read something into it and get her hopes up regarding Mr. Hamilton."

Chase's eyes softened almost imperceptibly before he turned and roughly raked his fingers through his hair, trying to get his scalp to relax. Nothing tonight was going as planned. "Ah, Millie. How is it that, no matter how hard I try to keep you safe, you come within an arm's length of danger? Please, say nothing of the shipping company. It's very important, love."

His whispered plea affected Millie more than anything else could. She walked over and placed a hand on his back. "Aimee will be vexed when she finds out, but she will not learn about your trade endeavors from me."

Several moments passed, and Millie determined the agony she was enduring mattered more to her than her pride. "Chase, I know you are extremely angry with me, but can you please help me take this blasted headpiece off? I can no longer live with the pain."

Chase turned and inclined his head to look down at the intricate headdress. "Lord, Millie, whatever inspired you to wear such a thing?"

Millie gave him a scathing look. "I was trying to make someone jealous, if you recall."

"Bloody hell, how many pins do you women use to keep your hair in these crazy loops all over your head? I could build a bridge with the amount of wire buried in here."

Minutes later, Millie felt the weight of her mane fall down her back to her waist. "Thank you," she breathed. "I cannot tell you how much better that feels."

Chase watched as Millie shook loose her long, dark locks. He felt his abdomen tighten and all his muscles become tense. He wanted her, but even more, he wanted her to want him. Badly.

The heated look in the depths of Chase's amber eyes rattled Millie's nerves all the way to her toes. There was something mesmerizing about his gaze. It would continue to break her heart if she let it. She closed her eyes and reminded herself he was going to marry another.

"Millie . . ." Chase took a step forward.

Millie's eyes popped open. She quickly avoided his embrace and moved to put the settee between them. "M-my lord, I do not know why you and I affect each other so, or why I cannot stop myself . . . when around you." Millie knew she was babbling. Nerves prompted her to continue. "Jennelle says it is common for a man to physically desire one woman while interested in marrying another."

"She says all that, does she?"

Millie unconsciously bobbed her head up and down. "Ah, yes. Men are often attracted to those they cannot have," she said, frozen and unable to move as she watched Chase go around the velveteen couch.

Chase softly clucked his tongue. "I cannot have you, Millie? Did you not just hear me moments ago vow that you are forever mine?"

Millie gulped. "I just a . . . assumed it was your pride talking. That . . . that you were upset."

Chase gave a single swift shake of his head. "I was not upset, my dear. I was furious. Another man had his lips on your cheek. That is a particular experience only one man shall ever know—me."

The weight of his words suddenly hit her, and a sense of self-worth flooded back into Millie. "And do you honestly expect me to be your *chère amie* while you go off and marry Mrs. Brinson?"

Shock momentarily stopped Chase's advance. His eyes held hers. There was no mistaking their dark look. Every nerve ending immediately responded to their unspoken message. Millie had to force herself to maintain a respectable distance.

"Millie, what the bloody hell are you talking about?"

Indignation rose in Millie and she waved a finger at him. "I told you. We *saw* you. We saw you with Mrs. Brinson. You become highly agitated with a mere peck on my cheek. Well, what do you think I felt, seeing you embrace her on the street!"

Chase's eyes flashed with anger. "You should have realized there was more to what you were seeing! Do you actually think I am so ungentlemanly as to do that to you?"

"But you told Sir Edward you were getting married!"

"Blast it, Millie! What type of man do you take me for? Can you be so naïve as to think that we wouldn't be married after what we shared in Sefton's gardens?"

Tears began to flow freely from Millie's eyes. "But you never said anything. No words of love, no promises, nothing!"

"Bloody hell, Millie. You know I am dealing with some very dangerous people at the moment. Considering a life with you, right now, would be most unconscionable of me. These men would use you to get to me, and it would work. You should have known how much you meant to me!"

Millie thought she could actually hear her heart beating in her chest. Chase was saying words she had secretly longed to hear. Perhaps not the way she had imagined, but nonetheless, the reasons—ones that explained away all the hurt and pain, were suddenly real. Chase wanted to marry her. She was going to get married!

As soon as the idea took hold, Millie knew she would have to let it go. Eight years ago, she had begged her friends to join in a marriage pact. Never had she broken a vow made to them, and she was not going to do so now. She would not leave Jennelle and Aimee alone. That was the whole reason behind the promise in the first place.

Chase watched as tears filled Millie's beautiful lavender eyes. "Millie, whatever is going through that crazy mind of yours?" His voice was deep, husky, caressing.

Millie felt miserable. *Guilt and hurt and anger and uncertainty and just plain misery*, she answered silently. "I cannot marry you, Chase. I made a promise a long time ago. I cannot break it now."

Suddenly Chase understood the full import behind Jennelle's missive. "I understand."

"No, I do not think you do," Millie murmured softly, staring at the carpet. A tear fell and splashed near her feet.

Chase lifted her chin and compelled her to look at him. "At least let me try. You, my sister, and Jennelle made a promise never to get married. However, being wise youthful girls, you each included a single exception to your promise."

"How did you know . . . ?"

Chase placed a gentle finger on her lips. "Your exception was actually a set of prerequisites. Was it not?"

"Yes, but . . ."

"The first set is a little odd, but we must remember your age and unusual inclinations at the time of the pledge. You must be allowed to ride astride, climb trees, and hunt. If I remember correctly, I have never objected to your riding astride; in fact I encouraged it because you have a penchant for riding somewhat aggressively. As for climbing trees and hunting, do so at your pleasure whenever we are at our country estate. I only ask you to refrain while in Town."

Millie narrowed her eyes as she realized one of her friends had obviously disclosed the details of her exception to the pact. "What about your propensity for following rules?"

"You forgot dull and my lack of passion for adventures."

"I do not consider you dull."

Chase gathered her into his arms and looked down into

her eyes. He was drowning, completely lost in Millie's warmth and softness. "Mildred Aldon, I want you more than I have wanted anything or anyone else my entire life."

A tremor went through Millie, and she snuggled against his chest. Chase smelled wonderful, and it felt so good to be this close to him. More than anything, she wanted to be his just as he claimed. "I love you, Charlie."

Chase was not ready for the impact of her whispered words. She was the most beautiful, most desirable woman he had ever seen in his life. And she loved him.

Chase's groin throbbed with a sudden fierce need to possess her. A strange fear gripped him, that if he did not claim her now, he might lose her. He caught Millie's face between his hands, and he kissed her slowly, fighting the desperate urge to yank off her dress and sink himself into her softness. "Marry me, Millie. Marry me and make me the luckiest man ever to live."

As he pulled back, Millie saw the raw need shimmering in his eyes. She swallowed at the enormity of need in those golden pools. Chase genuinely desired her. "Charlie, I . . ."

"Millie . . ." Her name was a soft growl as swiftly mounting desire consumed him. Chase buried his face in the dark waves of sweet-smelling hair, nibbling her neck, trailing his lips to the base of her throat and below.

Millie had never felt more alive, more desired. Tonight it was different from before. Tonight, every mental and emotional barrier between them was gone. Millie heard someone moaning and realized the primal sounds were coming from her. Chase brought his mouth back down on hers in a lingering kiss that scorched her from head to toe.

"Lord, Millie, what you do to me. I must have you, love. I must. I have never needed anything as I need you. I cannot wait. Please forgive me." His forehead came into contact with hers. His breath was ragged and his hands trembled both with need and fear she might say no.

Millie untied his cravat and stood on tiptoe to kiss the small indentation in his neck as she had dreamed of doing every night before she slept. Her tongue swirled against his warm skin, tasting him, loving him. It was far better than she had imagined.

Drowning in her sweet caresses, Chase knew if he didn't have Millie, and soon, Bedlam was soon going to receive a new patient. He reached out and pulled her back to retake her mouth. Just before his lips came down on hers, he vowed, "I love you, Mildred Aldon. Say you will marry me."

Millie stroked his dark hair, realizing that nothing in her life had ever felt so right. "Yes, Charles Wentworth. I will marry you. For you, too, are mine."

Chase looked into Millie's dark violet pools of love and squeezed her tightly before reclaiming her mouth with a deep, tender possessiveness. No longer would he be concerned with her names for him. For no matter what name she used, what emotion was coursing through her veins, her heart beat for him. She loved him.

Chase wanted tonight to last forever and slowed their pace. Before the evening was over, Millie would be undeniably his. He softened the kiss and urged her mouth to open, seeking a response to match his own. Slowly Millie parted her lips and invited him to taste her. A sweet, soft moan erupted from her, and Chase swallowed the beautiful sound. It had been too long since he last enjoyed her sweet lips.

Millie felt the sleeves of the gem-covered material fall from her shoulders. Only the shimmering silver material underneath remained. Strong hands cupped her breasts through the thin cloth, but never once did Chase break from his foray of her heavenly mouth. Millie suddenly wanted to feel him, to actually touch his broad chest and entwine her fingers in his crisp, curling dark hair. She unfastened his waistcoat and tugged on his linen shirt. Emboldened, she pulled her mouth away from his and trailed a line of kisses across his chest. He was so different from her. Hard, powerful, and extremely masculine. She could live a thousand years and never get tired of touching him.

Without warning, Millie stopped and looked at Chase, wide-eyed. Parts of his body were getting very hard. "Charlie, I think something is wrong with you."

When Millie had begun her assault on his senses, it had taken everything in him not to throw her on the floor and attack her. Chase took her fingertips in his hands and kissed them softly. Letting them go, he walked over to a chair, grabbed the large, thick plaid blanket that was strewn haphazardly across it, and laid it on the floor in front of the hearth. Turning, he asked, "Do you trust me, love?"

"With all that I am," she whispered.

Chase stared at the vision walking toward him. She was slim and delicate, incredibly female. He did not think it possible, but he grew even harder as the white satin chemise played over her sweetly curved buttocks. His fingers flexed in anticipation of what was to come. He vowed not to rush anything with her. He wanted her first time to be as powerful and incredible for her as it was going to be for him.

Millie stopped just out of arm's reach and tipped her head back, letting her dark tresses tumble over her shoulders. The look in Chase's golden eyes made her feel sultry, feminine, and unexpectedly powerful. Tonight she would become a woman—Chase's woman.

Chase was so hard, he feared he might burst, but he would endure anything to discover what she was going to do next. He did not have to wait long.

Millie slid one silk slipper off her foot and then the other. Bending over, she inched the white silk up her leg to expose the edge of her stocking. Slowly, she rolled the filmy material down, giving Chase time to view the curve of her lower leg. Then she moved to do the other. Never had Chase imagined the removal of slippers and stockings to be so arousing.

Dropping her second stocking to the floor, Millie stepped forward and finished unbuttoning his shirt. Done, she reached inside and touched him the way she had so often dreamed. It was better than any fantasy. She pressed her lips to the warm indentation in the middle of his chest. Chase trembled and it sent shock waves through her. She smiled and then kissed his nipple, swirling her tongue around its taut tip. Chase moaned. Millie repeated the gesture again and again and again . . . shyly savoring him with her tongue, each time in a different place.

"You taste good," she whispered.

Chase had no idea how a chaste woman who was shocked by his burgeoning manhood could be so unrestrained and free, and he didn't care. He would just be forever grateful she was his.

Unable to stand any more torture, Chase pulled Millie abruptly into his arms and kissed her hard. She did not resist, instead leaning into him and kissing him back with the fervor of a tigress desiring her mate. His tongue thrust into her mouth, then withdrew, then thrust again. His mouth was fierce and demanding. Millie joined the rhythm and felt her knees begin to weaken. A quiver of excitement shook Millie's frame. She clung to him as an anchor in a storm of passion and desire.

Chase found the tapes of her undergarment and undid them in several short, swift motions. Moments later, the silk dream cascaded into a white shimmering pool at her feet. Millie felt no awkwardness for her lack of clothing. She had nothing to hide from this man.

Chase stared at her. Millie stood unashamed and beautiful. When she held out her arms for him, he walked into them knowing that without her in his life, he would never be whole. Chase gently scooped her into his arms and held her. She was the air he breathed. He needed her.

Surprised to be lifted off the floor, Millie instinctively

clutched Chase's shoulders. He was so strong, she thought, yet he shuddered every time she even grazed him with her fingertips. She enjoyed knowing how much she affected him and caressed his arm, then chest.

Her soft touches were killing him. She had no idea the exquisite pain he was enduring. He had not had a woman in over a year. After he saw Millie the night of his return from Spain, no other woman had interested him. Only she could satisfy the burning need in him, and finally she was in his arms.

Chase carried Millie to the hearth as though she were weightless and laid her carefully down on the soft, thick blanket. Millie watched through half-lowered lashes as he shrugged impatiently out of his shirt, yanked off his Hessians and removed his leggings. Millie smiled and trailed a finger along his arm. "You will have to tell me why only you seem to be allowed to wear trousers to Almack's. What's your secret?"

"Someday I will tell you of my first meeting with Countess de Lieven. But right now, I have other things on my mind."

"Other things, my lord?"

Chase chuckled. "Yes, other things, such as this . . ." He lowered his mouth to her breasts and covered a pink bud. ". . . and this . . ." Millie thought she was going to lose consciousness from sensory overload as he moved to the valley between her breasts. ". . . and this." He tasted the second rosy nipple as his hand caressed her other bosom.

Millie felt her whole body respond to the heavy, sensual weight of him. She arched herself against his mouth as his hand moved across her stomach to the curve of her buttocks. Instinctively he pressed his hips closer, letting her feel the long, hard length of his erection. Millie gasped, and he heard himself utter a thick, husky groan.

He retook her mouth hungrily as he lowered himself

alongside her. She was so soft, he thought. So incredibly soft and sweet—and his. He edged his knee upward, spreading her thighs.

Millie felt her blood surge through her veins. Last week at Lady Sefton's, she never imagined she could experience anything as wonderful as what they had shared, but somehow tonight, with all misunderstandings aside, knowing he loved only her, it meant even more. Millie moved restlessly beneath the caress. She wanted more, needed more. Her skin was on fire with need for Chase's touch. Between her thighs, she felt hot and moist and hungry.

Chase felt her writhing and knew Millie's need was building. Her growing desire only heightened his own. His fingers glided over the soft skin of her hip. Slowly he moved his hand down to find the tightly curled hair concealing her damp, secret place. But instead of entering he moved past and slowly stroked her upper thigh, losing himself in the incredible softness of her skin. Up and down his fingers moved, reveling in her heated response.

Millie writhed beneath him, remembering the magic his fingers had evoked before. "Charlie, please," she moaned, begging him to touch her.

Chase smiled against her ear and brought his hand up her leg until he was inches from the hot, damp core of her. He moaned and buried his head in her hair as he slid one finger into her liquid heat. Millie sucked in her breath and closed her teeth carefully around his earlobe.

He felt her body gradually begin to tighten demandingly around his finger. Gently, he eased it slowly out of her tight passage and back in again, lovingly stretching her, preparing her for what was to come. Then he inserted another finger and prayed God would give him the ability to maintain control for just a little bit longer.

Millie gasped. "Oh, Charlie, I . . ." and cried out as he slipped his fingers into her again, then added another. Her hips lifted, and he retook her mouth, his tongue hot and rough and insistent. "Stay with me, Millie. Remember you are a very daring woman, and I promised you many adventures."

The delicious torment seemed to go on forever. Millie arched herself against him again and again, her moans steadily growing louder, more incessant. Suddenly she gasped, arched her neck back, her hands curling into fists. Her muscles clenched and unclenched in small spasms, her entire body trembling.

Chase knew he could hold back his need no longer. He framed her face between his hands. "Millie, trust me. I promise you there is nothing to be afraid of." He bent his head to capture her lips in a searing kiss of love and need.

Chase was on fire, overcome with need. He managed to wrench his mouth from hers long enough to kiss her throat. "Millie, I will do everything I can to be gentle. If you tell me to stop, I will. I don't want to hurt you, but if I wait any longer to be inside you I swear I shall go mad." Millie's lavender eyes caught his golden ones, and he had all the answer he needed.

Millie felt Chase's hard shaft brush against her, probing gently. She gasped as he spread her thighs wider and moved between them. She froze as she realized he was way too big for what he planned to do.

Slowly Chase eased himself into her snug passage. Never, he thought, never would he get enough of her. Chase buried his hands in her hair, twisting his fingers in the silken tresses, hugging her to him and then thrust into her, deep and hard, breaking the barrier that proved he was her first and only.

The pain awakened Millie out of her passion-induced state. She tried not to, but she felt her whole body freeze in reaction to his length buried deep inside her. Tears welled in her eyes and fell down her cheeks.

"Are you all right?" Chase asked, his voice low and raspy, thick with passion and need.

Millie couldn't answer. The initial pain was disappearing and in its place was an irresistible cry for something more. Instinctively she tightened her legs around him and plunged him even deeper inside her.

Chase cried out and his control snapped. Easing himself out of her snug passage, he pushed slowly back into her. "God, Millie, you feel so perfect. You were made for me." Then he drove himself even more deeply, claiming Millie for his own.

With each unhurried thrust, Millie wondered if the slow, intense sensations Chase was creating would cause her to go mad. But she only wanted more, and lifted herself against him, silently demanding he move more quickly. She grabbed his hips and urged him into a faster, passionate rhythm.

Together they strained, instinct driving them to meet each other's rhythmic need. Then suddenly a force—even more powerful than before—exploded within her. Chase plunged one last time and clung to Millie as the heavens enveloped him. He held her for a long time as they both slowly floated back to earth.

As his arms stole protectively around her, Millie curled into Chase's side and gently stroked his arm. He gave her a gentle squeeze. This adventurous, full-of-life woman had just promised, body and soul, to be forever his. He would never be alone again.

Chapter 15

Millie forced herself to walk slowly and calmly into Hembree Grove. In truth, a frenzied panic filled her. A little over two hours ago, she had been so furious with Chase she never expected to talk to him again. An hour ago, she was in his arms promising to be his wife, and thirty minutes later, she realized that she might never get the chance.

She took another step, planning all that she needed to do. Chase was watching her. She smiled, trying to appear like the happy bride-to-be. Anything else and he would realize her intentions and stop her. Another step. The house was dark. The night was still young for most of Society, and she doubted any of the *ton* would release Aimee or Jennelle before the sun rose, several hours from now. As Millie's best friends, the patronesses would drill them both for information.

Millie approached the large covered entry. *This will work*, she told herself and entered the quiet manor. The butler closed the doors, bowed, and silently disappeared, probably to tell Elda Mae she was home. Millie didn't care. She was listening. The second she heard the clopping of horses' hooves and wheels rolling, she glanced out the front window to confirm Chase had left. She sprinted to the servants' quarters and woke Tomas, the young footman sleeping in the hall on a cot.

"Tomas," she said, shaking his shoulder. The young man swung his legs around. Realizing it was not the housekeeper, he jumped up and then momentarily fought for balance as he mumbled a greeting.

Ignoring his sleepy stance, Millie motioned for him to follow her. "Thank the Lord, you are dressed. Come with me, quickly," she said in hushed tones, rushing toward the servants' side entrance.

"Yes, mum," Tomas murmured as he hurried down the narrow corridor in an effort to keep up.

When they reached the side door, Millie stopped and abruptly turned around. She ripped open her reticule and grabbed several coins. "Here are half a dozen sovereigns. It is imperative you find and follow the Wentworth carriage. It just left not more than a minute ago, and I believe it is headed east toward the docks. Be quick and return within the half hour without anyone knowing, and I will double your quarter pay if you can tell me its final destination."

Tomas looked at her as if gauging her sincerity before he snatched the coins and disappeared into the night. Millie watched for several seconds, praying Tomas would quickly find the carriage in the crowded streets. *He will*, she whispered to herself. *He must*.

All the way up the stairs to her room, Millie kept her steps steady and even. Deep down, she knew that tonight, before the sun rose, her future happiness was in jeopardy. With each step, she replayed the conversation with Chase that led her to realize it.

"Millie, I'm taking you back to Hembree Grove."

Millie watched as Chase slipped on his Hessians. Less than an hour ago, she had been in heaven. She had never felt more loved and safe. Now, she had never been more terrified. Chase had never said a word, but she knew what he was about to do. He was preparing to meet the men who threatened to end his life that night Chase had caught her eavesdropping.

"Are you going to meet Lord Marston?"

Hearing Marston's name, Chase hesitated and looked at Millie. It took everything he had not to stop and bed her again. With the firelight behind her, she looked like an angel, tousled hair falling around her shoulders concealing the perfect buds made for his caresses.

"I know you hate him, Charles. Is he the one—the one that you have been after?"

"Millie, do you remember Melinda Brinson?"

Millie looked at Chase and then turned her back to him. He hauled her to his chest. "Listen to me, my jealous little sprite. She was the wife of a good friend of mine. I promised him that if he should die, I would look in on her. When I returned to England a couple of months ago, I found her and her child starving and living off the streets."

Millie gasped and turned around. "What happened? You said she was married!"

"I did, and she was. But her brother-in-law turned her out of her home with a one-time stipend. Most likely she would have been fine, as the sum was not a paltry one. But she was unfortunate to cross paths with Marston." Chase hesitated, wondering how much he should disclose. But there were already too many secrets and he knew Millie would not judge the woman like others of Society would. "He wooed her, lied to her, and left her when she discovered she was carrying his child."

Anger glinted in Millie's eyes. "Marston denied his own son?"

"Only after cleverly draining all Mrs. Brinson's funds. The day you saw us, she was thanking me. Through the clients my mother and you have sent her way, word has spread of her skill, and she is now able to support herself and her child, who will be raised as Brinson's son. I know Geoffrey would have wished it so. They had longed for a child for some time."

"Oh, Charlie. How can life be so cruel?"

"I don't know, love. But I also know it can bestow the greatest gifts of all. Because tonight it gave me you." He bent his head and claimed her lips in a final, possessive kiss. Then he was gone.

She had sat for several minutes numb with fear before she saw it—her pendant—on the floor. Leaning over, she picked it up and fingered the unusual crest. He had been keeping it with him. It must have fallen out of one of his pockets when he had dressed. As the thought entered her mind, so did a dozen others. The two foremost were that Chase still believed he had it and that if he had been carrying it with him, there had been a reason.

Millie closed her eyes to the memory. Opening the door to her room, she leaned against the frame. "Life gave me a gift, too, Charlie, and I refuse to let you go."

She went to her bombé chest and moved the clothes to reveal the items hiding beneath. She quickly shucked her dress and slippers and pulled on the breeches, linen shirt, and coat. The boots were a little large, but they were better than her black half boots. She was buttoning the roomy waistcoat when Elda Mae stepped in.

"My lady, do you need assistance with . . ." As soon as Elda Mae saw Millie dressed in men's clothes she was at a loss for words.

"Elda Mae. Good, I am glad you are here. I need an overcoat. I would prefer it to be black, but it must at least be dark," Millie said, grabbing both the pistol and the brooch from her torn reticule. She looked up and realized Elda Mae was still stunned and unmoving. "Please hurry. I have very little time, and I must be ready when Tomas returns."

"But, my lady . . ."

Exasperated, Millie realized she was about to lose her temper. "I promise to explain later, but I need that coat, Elda Mae, and I need it now. Please hurry and meet me in the salon."

Whether it was Millie's tone of voice or the promise to be fully informed later, Elda Mae turned and hurried down the hall.

It had been almost an hour since Tomas had left in search of the carriage, and Millie was becoming anxious. She was about to go out and look for it herself when from her window she saw a dark figure approach the servants' entrance.

Millie rushed to the back of the manor, arriving just as Tomas entered.

"Tomas, what did you find out?"

"Eh, sir? Do I know you?"

"Tomas, it's me, Lady Aldon. Did you find the Wentworth carriage?"

Astonished by her attire, Tomas stammered, "Uh, yeah . . . I found it. Near the docks, just as my lady said. Practically fell into the Thames, I did, when I saw where we were. My lady, is that really you? You look different."

"Where exactly, Tomas? Can you tell me precisely how to get there?"

"Aye, sir . . . I mean, my lady. He went to Maude's, a real shady place, too, mum. Blokes usually have dipped rather deep before they are tempted by the trollops that work there. And tonight things were too smoky by half. Never thought the lord would be tempted by a place like that."

"If I told a driver to take me to Maude's on the Thames, would he know where to go?"

"Aye, mum, and I don't mean to throw a rub in the way of your . . . plans, but you might want to drop your voice a bit. Throws one, hearin' a lady's voice comin' from a man."

"Thank you, Tomas. I must be going. And Tomas, I must ask that you not say a word."

"My lady, I ain't one to raise a breeze about things I know nothing about. But you didn't forget what you said about my quarter pay?"

"No, Tomas, I didn't forget. Tell Elda Mae not to worry. I will be home soon."

Millie stepped out of the hack and instantly her pulse started pounding. A thin fog was beginning to set in. Getting a hackney carriage had been easy compared to the difficulty she would have finding Chase. Her eyes searched the buildings. He was somewhere hidden in the mist settling around the docks.

"Best take care, lad, and watch yer back," warned the driver. "There's a good deal of gamesters in these parts, willing to part a wee lad from his blunt."

Millie barely nodded a response before the hack disappeared into the haze. She took a deep breath and looked at the rundown building situated on the corner lot across the street. Maude's Place of Pleasure was scrawled in faded red script on a lopsided sign swinging from a corner of the building. The structure was in desperate need of repair; various sized holes in the roof were apparent even in the fog. In the back of the building were several large crates piled in crooked stacks and a narrow staircase providing outside access from a second-story room. Nowhere in sight was the Wentworth carriage.

Millie decided to approach the building from its north side and hide behind the crates as she peered through a window. She was about halfway to her intended destination when she was hauled into the shadows. A sharp, cold blade pressed against her skin.

"Explain your intentions before my knife finds its home in your neck." The voice was low and menacing.

Millie licked her dry lips and tried to respond. "I'm here looking for someone."

Suddenly she was yanked back into the shadows and pushed against the side of the building. Chase swore and then muttered hoarsely, "Mildred, I am going to throttle you!"

Millie sighed in relief. "Shh. I knew coming here would make you mad, but I had to find you. Whether you know it or not, you need me."

"I don't give a tinker's damn what your reasons are. You are going home, and right now."

"But . . ." Before Millie could even begin to argue, Chase's gloved hand reached out and roughly covered her mouth, pulling her deeper within the shadows underneath a wooden staircase built on the side of the building next to the road. Seconds later, she saw the reason why he silenced her. Two men turning off Bridge Street were approaching from the west, heading toward the rear of the building. She recognized them. They were the same men she had followed into the gardens at Lady Sefton's ball.

Concealing Millie behind his greatcoat and the barrels, Chase stepped slightly out of the shadows.

"Interesting place you chose, Chaselton. A frequent haunt of yours?" the taller, younger man sneered as he moved out of the street and entered the area behind the brothel.

The second, older man gave his companion a signal and stepped in front of the light so that his features were masked in the darkness. "We have waited long for this night. Have you brought the items?"

Chase eyed the men carefully, taking his time to reply. "I am afraid I will be unable to have this conversation until your *entire* party arrives."

The younger man scowled and advanced a few steps. "We never agreed to that."

Chase stared at the young fool and then leveled his gaze at the man behind him. "I would advise your friend that if he wishes to live, he should retrace his last steps and quickly." After the impetuous man stepped back, Chase continued. "I want assurance that I will be accepted into your group, and I am wagering neither of you has the ability to grant my request."

Millie could not see, but she heard the approaching footsteps of another man. She felt Chase's body stiffen with recognition and loathing. "I wondered how deep your involvement was. I must admit I did not think you were one to get your hands dirty. Not a *dandy's* line of work we are engaged in," Chase said contemptuously.

"Seeing you grovel makes it all worth it, Chaselton. Where are the items?"

Millie listened to the voice hiss with violence and hatred. She knew instantly who it was: Lord Marston. She swallowed heavily. It now made sense why Marston was so interested first in Aimee, then herself. He was going to use her to get whatever they wanted from Chase.

"Regardless of what your supposed intellect tells you, you are not an important player in this transaction," Chase said, unmoved by Marston's taunts. "I am still waiting, and will continue to wait, for your leader."

Marston eyed Chaselton. "Do you want to know what I think? I think you do not have all the markers, nor do you have a clue as to where they are."

Chase smiled faintly in the moonlight, but the curve of his mouth held no warmth and his shadowed gaze revealed nothing. In truth, Marston was correct. Chase had no idea what the other two items were, let alone their location. Instinctively, his hand slid down to the cloak pocket to find the marker he did have. Alarm went through him. It was gone.

The younger man lost his patience in the silence that fell on the small group. "He knows. Bloody hell, we all know where at least one of the damn things is. It was hanging between the dark-haired wench's bosoms just last week. We all recognized the crest."

Chase's insides clenched, and he felt his control slip at the man's degrading mention of Millie. Never in the past eight years had he had any difficulty keeping his emotions at bay. But since falling in love with Millie, his sensitivity to such slanders had been reborn. Only his need to protect her was keeping him from attacking.

Millie remained hunched between Chase and a crate, listening. She could make out the words, but their conversation made no sense. They mentioned her pendant having a crest. She pulled it out of her pocket and in the dark traced the item. She knew of only two other items that had the same pattern. The same day Chase's father gave her the pendant, he also gave Jennelle and Aimee gifts with the same symbol. Could that be what they mean? It had to be. It was the only thing that made sense. But she could not imagine how any of the three items could be of any value to anyone else.

Marston studied the situation for a moment and then guessed at the truth. "You make my point, Hennessey. He does not possess the markers. He never would have risked Lady Aldon's safety by allowing her to wear one the other night. You are biding your time, Chaselton. Time you no longer have. I think we should kill you now."

Hunched between Chase and the crate, Millie heard a pistol being cocked and became alarmed when Chase did not move to defend himself. She had to do something. Trying to keep out of sight, she slipped the amulet into the pocket of Chase's overcoat, and whispered, "Your father also gave us a key and a chest. They are still in Dorset."

Feeling the heavy item fall, Chase's mouth twisted without humor. "Marston, I shall dicker with you no more." He reached into his pocket and pulled out the amethyst pendant now dangling on its customary chain. "I have the brooch on me for proof of my claims. The other two markers—a key and a chest—are in safe keeping. You want them, and I want to meet your leader."

Marston began laughing. "You think that mere knowledge of the items buys you protection? You have just sealed your fate, Chaselton. If you truly know the markers' location, then you know too much. And do not think you can plead for your life by revealing their location. You will die tonight, screaming, just like your father."

Marston searched Chase's face for some reaction. Finding none, he attacked from a new direction. "I believe your absence will leave several women in your care fairly vulnerable. I wonder whether a certain delectable dark-haired morsel will be more acquiescent without you around. Tell me, Chaselton, is Mildred as tasty as she appears?"

Marston's words were still lingering in the air when the greatcoat Millie was partially crouched behind suddenly disappeared. She looked up to see Chase kick a blow to Marston's chin, spin to miss a knife thrust by the younger man, while dealing a severe side blow to the older man, rendering him unconscious. Marston regained his bearings as Chase quickly disarmed the younger man, who, though he lacked skill at keeping silent, was a very able fighter.

Millie reached for her pistol. She aimed but found it impossible to get a clear shot at Marston. Chase, now fighting both men, secured the younger man's knife before knocking him out cold. Seeing Marston and Chase fight, there was no doubt who the winner would be.

Relieved, Millie lowered her weapon and watched Chase quickly secure Marston in a neck hold with the knife to his throat. She was just about to put the pistol away and step out from the shadows when she heard a door shut above her.

Her heart caught in her throat when she heard the sinister man's voice. She remembered it from the gardens. He must be the leader Chase wanted to meet.

She watched the dark, masked figure slowly descend the creaking stairs with a gun aimed at Chase. It mattered little that Marston, held at knifepoint, blocked most of Chase's body. Only a few feet separated the man from his target, and he was aiming at Chase's eyes.

"Marston, you always were a pompous fool," the deep and heavily accented voice snickered. "Your job was simple, but you could not master it. Charm the girl, get her brooch, and discover if she and her friends were given any other Rebuilder items. You, who woo all women into your bed, couldn't manage to accomplish even that objective."

Chase watched as the masked man stood on the bottom step of the stairs. He felt Marston struggle to answer, and he tightened his grip so only a gargle emerged. Chase felt his facial features harden to an ice-cold veneer as his father's killer approached.

Chase realized his death might be imminent, but before it came he wanted to know the identity of the man who had murdered too many for the ultimate power—the power to control England.

"I take it my request to join your cause has been denied."

The masked man chuckled slightly, but his aim never wavered. "Ah, if you were in truth interested, I would have gladly welcomed you at my side. But I am afraid you are too much like your father, idealistic and far from weak. A combination that made it necessary to hasten his death—and now yours."

The older man coldly watched as Marston struggled again in vain. "I told you to be wary, Marston. But would you listen to me? I've studied Chaselton for years, learned of his skills, and discovered his triumphs. I knew you three were not a match for him. The only way to kill Chaselton is to catch him unawares, but I must admit I thought it would be a tad more difficult than this."

Millie watched as the man shifted his stance, preparing to

shoot. Reacting on instinct, Millie fired. A moment later, she heard a second shot ring out. The leader had fired his pistol before he vanished into the thickening fog.

She came running out of the shadows shouting out "No!" as she stumbled toward Chase, who was falling to the ground with Marston. "Charlie! God, no, not Charlie!"

Chase moved the injured Marston to the side and captured a terrified Millie in his arms. "It's over," he whispered, kissing her hair. "It's all over. I'm fine."

Millie pushed back and looked up, tears brimming in her large eyes. "But I heard him shoot you."

Chase glanced down at Marston and made his decision. Marston would have to die a lingering death, but he would not slit a man's throat in front of Millie. Retrieving the knife, he picked her up and quickly headed into the shadows of the night. Then Chase stopped and placed her between several stacked barrels in a darkened alley.

"Stay here, Millie. Do not make a move or a sound." His words were still in the air when Chase disappeared into the dense fog.

Millie slowly sank down and leaned against the rough wooden barrels. She rubbed her arms, but the cold was pervasive, and she could not stop herself from trembling. She closed her eyes, letting tears slip down her cheeks.

Chase had almost been killed. Marston was part of the group Chase was after. The twisted lord had even helped murder Brumby . . . and all for her brooch, Aimee's chest, and Jennelle's key. Three items that held absolutely no value. It made no sense.

Millie heard men walk by, their footsteps retreating into the darkness. Occasionally she heard a light splash as someone threw something into the Thames. The cold, moist air seeped into her bones, and for the first time in her life, she did exactly what Chase told her to do. She waited.

* * *

Millie felt herself being shaken and forced back to a place that was cold, damp, and full of death. She shook her head.

"Millie, wake up. We must go. I need you to walk. Millie, can you hear me? You need to get up and walk now."

It was the urgency in the voice that finally awoke her. It was half plea, half terror. "Chase, you dropped the pendant."

"Yes. And you bravely brought it to me, remember? But we need to leave, love, and now. It is not safe for either of us here, this time of night."

Millie rose and felt the stinging pain of numb, deadened limbs being awakened. Witnessing her grimace, Chase asked, "Can you walk?"

"Yes, if I must."

Slowly at first and then with increasing speed, Chase led them in silence, south through back alleys and dark streets. They encountered no one. Then they turned and the noise became louder as more and more people wandered the streets. Millie knew where they were. They were near Vauxhall.

Chase moved them again into the shadows. "We can rest here for a bit. I'm afraid we still have a way to go before sunlight. We cannot stay here for long. The Gardens are emptying and the cover of the crowds will soon be gone."

Millie rubbed her hands together. "What's happening? Why are we running on foot?"

Chase looked at her huddled form and reached out for her hands. They were ice-cold. Her face was pale and her eyes were large, making her seem fragile and vulnerable.

He grabbed her hands and rubbed them, blowing his warm breath over her icy fingertips. "I need to get you back to safety."

"That man . . . I shot, is he dead?"

"No, you hit him but not fatally and I was not able to

catch him when he ran away. Unfortunately, whoever he is now knows I did not come alone. I am afraid you have made yourself a target, love. If you are not back at Hembree Grove before morning, he might suspect it was you by my side, despite how unlikely it sounds."

Millie looked around. "There are faster modes of travel, you know." She retrieved her hands. "And warmer ones, as well."

"You chose our mode, love. Not I. Maybe not by choice, but your actions forced my hand." Chase pulled her close. Never had he felt so much fear. The knowledge that at any moment Millie could have been discovered and killed had been nearly paralyzing. "Are you ready? We need the cover of darkness to cross the bridge."

Millie narrowed her eyes at his back as she followed him again into the streets and past the Vauxhall distillery. The man could have acted at least somewhat grateful. It was she who gave him the brooch, told him of the two other items, and saved his life. He had not once expressed any type of gratitude.

After another hour of walking and hiding in the damp streets of London, Millie could no longer keep up. Chase stopped and looked at her. They were still south of St. James's Park in an alley off York Street. They would not make Hembree Grove by daylight at their slowing pace. Chase signaled a hack across the street.

Millie stepped into the small, uncomfortable ride and heard Chase tell the driver, "Leicester Square and be quick," before stepping in.

Chase looked at Millie. Her eyes were haunted, distant, and drained. "We can only travel so far this way, but Hembree Grove is not far from the square."

Millie nodded. "Why can we not just go straight home?"

Chase watched Millie retreat. She had not argued once during this ordeal and had kept up with him despite the hard pace he had set. Still, his racing heart could not be slowed. "Because you put yourself in enormous danger by following me. Right now there are undoubtedly men camped outside of Hembree Grove watching for a carriage. *Waiting for you.*" He paused and saw that his words were only partially registering. She was too cold. He raked his fingers through his hair and tried to explain. "After I dropped you off at Hembree Grove earlier, I realized my chaise was being followed. Most likely it was the man you shot. I had to wait until my driver entered a crowded part of town to sneak a drunk into my carriage as I slipped out. The man will awaken tomorrow very happy to find himself in one of the better London brothels."

"But why?"

"Because whoever you shot wants to know your identity. He will be watching anyone associated with me, and that includes you. Right now, they assume a man fired the shot, but if anyone discovers you have not been safely inside Hembree Grove this evening, they will not take the chance and they will kill you." Chase grabbed her forcefully, just shy of bruising her arms. "And I will *not* let that happen. No one is going to take you away from me." He then released her and sank back into the seat.

His harsh handling brought Millie out of her numb stupor. She fumed in silence until her anger built to where she could hold it in no longer. "Do you not understand I feel the same way? I had to follow you this evening. I love you, Chase. And no one, not even you and your damned pride, is going to take *you* away from *me.*"

Suddenly it was all too much, and she felt herself emotionally crumbling when Chase lifted her and nestled her on his lap. Millie opened her damp lashes and gazed into his golden eyes. There was no mistaking their dark look. Millie shivered at his touch, but this time not from the cold. His lips were so close to hers, she could feel his breath on her upper lip. He leaned down and kissed her mouth hungrily, his tongue softly seeking hers in reassurance, his restraint almost shattered knowing how close he had been, and still was, to losing her.

Millie threaded her fingers through his hair, tightening their grip with the same urgent need. She opened her mouth wider, inviting him to devour her as if this kiss were their last.

Chase ached to be deep inside her and feel her shiver with release. Nothing in his life would ever be this good, this important. "God, Millie, I cannot lose you. Not now, not ever. I need you. Without you I am lost." His voice was deep, husky, and fearful at the thought of life without her.

Millie's eyes were brilliant as she looked up at him through her lashes. Chase felt himself drowning in her gaze. "Never. Never will you be without me," she promised. Feeling an incredible well of peace, she wrapped her arms around his neck and stroked his cheek.

Chase pulled Millie even closer to him and pressed her head to his chest. He would need to hold her for a long while before his fears and memories of this evening subsided.

"We must get you home."

Feeling better, Millie nodded. "Is Marston . . . dead?"

Chase inhaled deeply, recalling how she had saved his life and how he had had to leave Marston dying in order to protect her. "I believe so."

"Who was that man, the man I shot? Why does he want you and my brooch?"

Chase took several deep breaths. It was time, he acknowledged to himself. He had brought no one—not even Reece— totally into his confidence. But for some reason he wanted no secrets between Millie and himself—ever.

"There is a secret group of nobles who call themselves the Rebuilders. Within this group, there is a cluster of corrupt and power-hungry individuals—the man you shot is their leader."

Millie scrunched her nose, trying to recall a group with that name. "The Rebuilders? Rebuilders of what?"

"The British Empire." Chase's voice was without inflection. It precisely conveyed the seriousness of his statement.

"Oh."

Feeling her breath lightly caress his skin, Chase needed to occupy his hands and slowly began to stroke her hair as he continued. "Over a hundred years ago, several noblemen began to meet secretly. They were like-minded individuals who talked politics and government and eventually began calling themselves the Rebuilders. When the American colonies started to thrive, several nobles saw them as a chance to restore England's position of power and wealth in the world."

Millie sighed, loving the feeling of being in Chase's arms and his fingers caressing her hair. "Seems quite improbable, but innocent."

Chase kissed her temple. "For the last two decades, there has been a growing group within the Rebuilders. They were incensed at England's loss of power in the colonial war. Roughly eight years ago, a shift in leadership occurred and key members of the group died and were replaced with power-hungry, self-serving men. During this time of chaos, an anonymous, unscrupulous man became their leader. He and his followers split from the Rebuilders and began calling themselves the Expansionists. They wanted to retake the colonies and continue expanding the British Empire, and their leader was willing to use any means—including the senseless deaths of English soldiers—to attain his goal."

Millie moved so that she could look at him directly. "How are you aware of all this, Chase?"

"I believe an Expansionist leader killed my father."

"But why? Why your father?"

"When I turned two and twenty, the Expansionist faction had grown considerably and several members held positions of power. England began experiencing military losses that perpetuated our country in a state of war when a treaty might have been made—something the Expansionists were unconditionally against. My father believed a traitor was feeding the enemy information and was behind many of the defeats that created the political pressure to put aside thoughts of a truce and continue fighting."

"But how?"

"My father reasoned the traitor was working with someone inside the war department."

"That is why you left for the war."

"Yes, but only after my father's death did I find proof that he was right; England did have a traitor. The evidence, however, did not include a name."

"Good Lord, Chase. What is your proof?"

"Correspondence, most of which indirectly shows the traitor's handiwork, but I have one piece that undeniably proves his existence. Angered by the impending peace treaty to be signed between America and England, the traitor stripped General Sir Pakenham of his more talented advisors and sent him to war—not telling him of the impending treaty. I have a letter from the traitor to an initial *G* outlining the plans that Pakenham unwittingly followed, resulting in the deaths of thousands of English soldiers. His goal was to keep the noblemen's thirst for revenge alive to stop the treaty."

"But that means . . . all those men . . ."

"Yes. We lost over seventy-five hundred men—many experienced veterans—to an unnecessary battle that we were intended to lose."

"But what are you going to do without a name? You cannot go forward with the evidence you have—why, every noble associated with the Rebuilders would be ruined."

"That is why after I drop you off tonight I am going to

retrieve the name and the proof. Then I can find justice for my father."

"But how?"

Chase reached into his pocket and retrieved the amethyst brooch.

"My pendant," Millie whispered.

"You mentioned a key and a chest. Where exactly are they?"

Millie looked up, her eyes glowing. "I can take you right to them."

"No, Millie," Chase said forcefully. "You are going to Hembree Grove, and you are going to remain safe. Tell me where the items are."

Tears filled Millie's eyes as she realized there was no other way. Without the identity of the killer, Chase would never be safe. "They are in the loft, next to all the clothes we used as costumes."

Chase hugged her to him again. "Like the one you were wearing at Vauxhall?" He felt her nod of confirmation and gave himself a mental kick for not thinking to look in the attic. He prayed the others who had searched his home had also made the same mistake.

Millie felt the carriage roll to a stop. She knew in just a few minutes' time, they would be parting, maybe forever. "Promise me you will be careful, Chase. Promise me."

Chase pulled her into his arms, and before he captured her lips in a last, searing kiss, he whispered, "I promise, my love."

Millie slowly entered the salon, staring at the back of the gentleman peeking out the window. He was a nondescript type of man. Neither overly tall nor short. No identifiable characteristics made him stand out. Nonetheless, Millie knew who he was.

This man could easily be a friend and confidant of Chase's, but the stakes were too high to risk discovering she was wrong. *For once in your life*, Millie vowed to herself, *remain composed and say nothing*.

"Sir Edward! How kind of you to visit!"

Edward gradually turned around, slightly stunned at the friendly greeting. "My lady, how gratified I am that you remember me. I must confess I wondered if you would."

Millie donned her most charming smile and reached out her hands in welcome. "Why, of course I remember you. We met earlier this Season at Lady Bassel's ball. You were a most affable gentleman."

Edward feigned embarrassment. "Ah, my lady, you do know how to flatter a man."

Millie indicated a deep cranberry and gold chair nearby. "Please, do take a seat and have some refreshment."

"Thank you, my lady, but I have no need for any beverage. Please, let me apologize for my abrupt appearance. I know I was unexpected."

Millie spooned some sugar in a cup and replied, "No need for apologies, Sir Edward. You are most welcome."

Wincing, he sat in the chair and coughed. "I hear congratulations are in order."

This time it was Millie who feigned embarrassment and elegantly cringed. "The news has spread fast, I see."

Edward chuckled. "Indeed, but that is to be expected. How often does an eligible marquess carry the daughter of an earl out of Lady Castlereagh's ballroom and announce to all that she is to be his wife?"

"Yes, Lord Chaselton and I had quite a lively discussion on the way home regarding that particular method of announcing one's betrothal."

"But I see you have it resolved."

"Yes, and, I confess, I have loved him my whole life. Although not until last night did I discover his feelings for me were remotely similar."

Edward eyed the young, poised woman across from him. "I have a second confession, my lady."

Millie lifted her lashes and widened her eyes. "Oh?"

"While I extend my heartiest best wishes in regard to your upcoming nuptials, I asked to see you today to inquire about Lord Chaselton. Have you seen him, by chance?"

Stay calm and composed, Millie repeated to herself. "Not since last night. However, I do expect him later today. Should I tell him you called?"

"No, it is of no true import. It can wait until I see him later at White's." He paused, staring at her without emotion for several seconds before continuing. "You normally wear an unusual brooch, if I recall?"

Millie sipped some tea, hoping the action would soothe her nerves. Watching him wince with every movement and use his left hand for everything, when he was clearly right-handed, were both signs. The traitor had a foreign accent, but a spy would be adept at imitating another voice to conceal his identity. Knowing that and hearing that simple inquiry, she was certain who sat but a mere three feet from her. Sir Edward was the traitor. Chase's mentor and friend.

She forced herself to smile warmly, as if recalling a fond memory. "Indeed. I feel somewhat odd without it. I do hope Charles returns it soon. He asked for it last night in hopes to have a jeweler create a matching bracelet as a wedding gift."

Edward raised his eyebrows. "I must say, I am surprised by his offer."

Millie put her hand up, pretending she understood his remark. "No, no, it is a most appropriate gift, I assure you. While I know it has a unique and peculiar design, the brooch means a lot to me, and Charles knows how much I treasure it."

"I am surprised, not by your fondness of the item, but of

Chaselton's willingness to have his wife openly wear his crest of the Rebuilders."

This time Millie did not have to act as if she were surprised. "Did you say *his* crest of the *Rebuilders*?"

Edward crinkled his face into an oily smile. "Didn't he tell you, my dear? That he is the leader of a group of nobles intending to rebuild England as a major power in the world."

Millie stared at the man and then laughed aloud. "Sir Edward, you make no sense. My future husband is no leader of a . . . a group of nobles. Up until a few months ago, he was fighting against France. You must be mistaken."

"He did not tell you, then? He did not discuss your amulet? Explain its origins?"

Millie furrowed her brow. "He would not know of its origins for it was his father who gave it to me as a gift. He gave all of us presents and I promise you, they were only trinkets offered to cheer us up."

Millie watched as Edward heaved himself out of the deep chair. She rose as well, mentally rallying herself. If there ever was a time she needed nerves of steel, it was during these next few moments.

"Sir Edward, I feel as if I have been no help to you at all today. Can I deliver a message for you when Charles comes to call? Would you like to wait? I am sure he will be arriving soon. You can discuss my brooch and the other items. . . ."

His reaction was the final proof. "Other items?"

Millie tilted her head and generated what she hoped was a perplexed look. "Yes, the ones I just mentioned. The gifts his father gave Aimee, Jennelle, and me. I gave them to Charles last night along with my brooch. With your knowledge of the crest inscribed on them, I am sure he would like to speak to you after he has finished his errands."

Edward bowed and moved to leave. "Thank you, my lady, for your kind offer, but I must depart." He paused and turned back. "Mayhap I can redirect my route and encounter him on my way through Town. Would he happen to have mentioned what errands he had to accomplish before meeting with you today?"

"Not exactly, no, I am afraid," Millie said, escorting him to the door. "He made some off-handed comment in regard to Hyde Park before meeting my father this morning. Beyond that, I am afraid I cannot be of help."

Edward bowed again. Millie fought to remain composed as she watched him grin with malice. *Take the bait, you cutthroat. Waste your time searching Hyde Park. I know who you are and soon Chase will know as well,* Millie swore to herself as she walked him outside.

"Good day, Sir Edward. Hope to be seeing you again soon." Millie waved and smiled.

Tipping his hat, he said, "Good day, Lady Aldon."

As soon as he disappeared from sight, Millie whirled around and rushed inside. She ran back to the room where she had had her hour-long inquisition. Aimee, Jennelle, and Mother Wentworth had grilled her incessantly about last night's announcement and her future. Seeing them still in the room talking, she sighed in relief. "Thank God you all are still here," she panted. "We have not a moment to lose. Charles is in danger."

Chapter 16

"Run. Run like the wind for me," Millie whispered into Hercules's ear as she urged the stallion into another full gallop. She thanked God for the moonlight and hoped the horse's footing remained sound, as they both were tiring rapidly. She would soon have to stop and rest him again. *Just a little farther*, she thought, praying she would reach Chase in time.

An hour later, they stopped near a river bed. Millie slid off the big animal and led him to the river to drink. "That's it. Good boy. We'll rest here for a bit. We are almost there. One, maybe two more runs."

Millie plopped down on the hard ground and leaned against an old oak. The sun was beginning to rise over a distant grassy knoll. She had been riding hard since the previous morning. In a few hours, she would be at the Wentworth country estate right off the coast between Wareham and Swanage.

She rubbed her eyes and retrieved some dry bread from her pockets to munch on. She would let Hercules rest for about another half hour. Today he was proving the rightness of his name. She was sure Chase had ridden straight to his country estate after dropping her off in yesterday's dawning hours.

With the benefit of being able to switch horses, he could have made the trip in eight hours, placing her almost twenty-four hours behind him. Millie hadn't had that option. Showing up at an inn to get a fresh horse and to let Hercules rest was out of the question. She was already taking a huge risk riding alone. She got up, stretched, and reached for the canteen swinging from her saddle.

Millie grimaced as she swallowed the bitter mixture of water and whatever contents were previously housed in the flagon. Tapping her finger on the container, she calculated how much farther she had to ride.

It had been dark, but Millie was sure she had passed Shaftesbury. The town was the only hilltop settlement in Dorset. Built several hundred feet above the sea, it was hard to miss, even in the dark. That placed her a little more than twenty miles from her true destination—the Wentworth cliffs.

An hour later she could delay no longer. She attempted to swallow another gulp of the disagreeable contents of her flagon and replaced the container on the saddle. She moved Hercules near an exposed root and mounted. She fingered his mane affectionately. "Depending upon the terrain, we have maybe two more hours, boy. Stay with me. I need you, Hercules. Chase needs you."

And with a quick tap of her heels, they were off again.

"I must admit that I am disappointed you are not dead," Chase said in a deadpan tone, seeing the glint of silver from the revolver pointed straight at him. He eyed the rider swinging down from his mount, which was an older mare obviously obtained along the way from London. The man's face was covered, but it mattered little. Chase knew who he was.

Glittering blue eyes full of hatred glared out from

underneath the mask. "I could say the same for you, Chaselton. However, tonight's encounter shall go somewhat differently than the last time we met. It will be *you* who is fatally injured. But, unfortunately, your miraculous recovery will not be as likely as my own."

"And how did you inexplicably heal from a death wound?" Chase asked as he casually leaned against a large cedar. He watched Marston unintentionally wave his pistol as he spoke.

"A superb acting job," Marston replied as he advanced toward Chase, stopping just a few feet away. "I grabbed my stomach so you would believe I was gut shot, when all I received was a mere shoulder wound. And not even my shooting arm."

"I admit you had me fooled," sighed Chase. His demeanor conveyed annoyance at being inconvenienced. "But I wonder if your acting was to fool me or your leader? Your fight with me was clearly one you would lose, but running away was not an option. Your leader would have shot you for being a coward. So you took the only way out; you pretended to be dying. It is not a strategy I would have employed, but then again, I am not you."

Marston knew Chase was taunting him, trying to excite his rage. It was the same tactic he had used to gain an advantage last night. *Not this time*, Marston swore to himself. *This time, it will be your wrath that stirs uncontrollably.* "I pity you, Chaselton. You are so determined to follow in the footsteps of your father. The Rebuilders were once great in their goals and actions. Now they are a dormant group of weak men unable to see the power available to them if they would just—"

Chase yawned before interrupting. "The Rebuilders are interested only in protecting what they have, not empire building. England is still powerful and always will be. It does not need its nobles to employ traitorous ways and send thousands of good young men to their deaths."

Marston's eyes narrowed and he leveled his gun. "It is clear we will never agree. Now, tell me where the items are."

Chase slowly straightened. "At some point in our encounters, I must have misled you, Marston. You mistake me for a fool, and I assure you that I am not. What possible benefit would I receive by telling you their location?"

A sick sneer invaded Marston's face as he removed his mask with his free hand. "Because I am under the impression that Lady Mildred Aldon means something to you. I assure you she means nothing to me, but I will enjoy taking her nonetheless."

Raw fury shot through Chase. He clenched his fingers once and released the pressure. Smiling, Chase replied, "I give you warning, Marston. Lady Aldon is not easily deceived. She will most likely kill you; that is, *if* you leave here alive."

Marston's hand shook with rage. "Tell me, damn you. Tell me where those items . . ."

Suddenly Marston's vision was blocked as Chase threw his cloak over Marston's head. Instinctively Marston pulled the trigger as he was wrenched around. Receiving a blow to his stomach, Marston shot again through the cloak before he was struck on the head and rendered unconscious.

Chase grabbed the man's ankles and arms and tied them with Marston's own clothing. Carefully Chase pivoted, moved to his horse, and retrieved some rawhide. He returned to Marston and expertly retied and secured the unresponsive man's limbs to a tree.

Once finished, Chase looked at the wound beginning to throb painfully in his thigh. Using his last strip of leather, he bound the injury tightly to reduce the blood flow. He hobbled back to his horse and swung into the saddle.

The pain in his leg was increasing. There was no exit wound. Chase knew the bullet was still lodged in his thigh.

Unless removed, he had only a few hours to find and retrieve the items before a fever set in.

Chase awoke to a throbbing headache. The air was damp, it was dark, and the ground beneath him was hard and rocky. He reached up and felt a horse blanket cushioning his head.

He could barely make out his surroundings, but he knew where he was. He was in one of the caves that littered the Wentworth cliffs. Lifting his head, Chase saw a small man hovered over a fire. The man turned, and Millie's face came into focus.

"What the devil!" Chase shouted.

Millie's expression instantly changed from one of concern to exasperation. "Keep your voice down," she hissed, walking over to him with something in her hand. She set the cup down and helped him to a sitting position. "Here, drink this. It's tea. I have some bread if you think you can eat. It's stale, but passable."

Chase took the tin cup. His amber eyes focused on the vision before him, but lost none of their displeasure. "Millie, what in God's name are you doing here? And how did I get *in* here?"

"Why, I brought you here to hide, of course," Millie said matter-of-factly. Retrieving a cup for herself, she sat down and began to sip its contents. "Hmm, this is good. The stuff I was swallowing on the way here was deplorable." She looked at Chase and motioned for him to drink. "Whatever happened to the unexcitable Charles Wentworth I used to know? So indifferent to any emotions such as joy, grief, pleasure, or pain. He would never bellow as you have grown into the habit of doing."

Chase continued to lock eyes with Millie. "He met you and has never been the same."

Millie smiled at his reply. "How fortunate for you, then.

Life is much more pleasurable when you experience it rather than watch it go by."

Chase finally sipped the hot tea and partially relaxed. "Why is it that I have not changed you, as you have me, love?"

Millie moved beside him and stroked his brow. "Why . . . I guess I never realized you wanted someone dull and spiritless. Now that I know, I will see what I can do about turning into the woman of your dreams," she said, smiling impishly.

Chase grasped her arm. He reached with his other hand and pulled her toward him with surprising strength. "Don't you dare, Mildred Aldon. Don't you dare change a thing," he said, his voice barely above a soft whisper. And then he crushed her mouth roughly beneath his own. Millie's soft cry of startled surprise was quickly muffled. Chase's mouth was voracious, his tongue stroking, plunging, beseeching.

Millie groaned deeply. His mouth was like a warm drug on her lips. It soothed her, teased her, and then created a desire within her that only he could satisfy.

Chase could feel his body becoming tight and hard with arousal. His fingers moved slightly on her throat, pushing aside a loose curl of her brown hair. He released her lips and looked into her eyes. This mesmerizing beauty had the power to ignite the blood flowing through his veins.

With his lips almost touching hers, he said, "What I would give to have you in a soft bed right now."

Millie was breathless and anxious and exhilarated all at the same time. She was desperate for sleep, but at the same time completely alive with sensations and needs. Needs that must be put aside, for even if they were in a soft bed, he would not be seeing to them. "Chase, you shouldn't exert yourself right now. You lost a lot of blood before I found you." She sat up and forced herself to back away from him.

For a long moment, Chase thought to argue, but finally acquiesced. "That explains the pounding sensation in my head."

Chase looked down to see his thigh cleaned and bandaged. "But who worked on my leg?" he asked as he watched a lock of Millie's hair fall down her back as she searched for something near the fire. Chase clenched his fingers, fighting an almost overpowering need to see the entire mass of dark brown softness loose about her shoulders. His muscles tensed, and his abdomen tightened.

Millie returned and knelt beside him, offering him bread. Her hands were shaking. "I would appreciate it if you would refrain from getting shot again. I am not too sure which was worse, retrieving the ball from the wound or cleaning it with drink. Your reaction to both was rather intimidating. I'd like to never go through it again."

Chase accepted the bread with a quizzical expression. He didn't remember her doing either. "How did you know to do that? To cleanse the wound with spirits?" Chase knew it was a controversial practice among physicians. Some believed the same whiskey used to make elixirs and poultices could be just poured on the wound; others believed the liquid damaged the exposed tissue. Regardless, Chase had seen firsthand in the field that men who received such painful treatment were more likely to survive.

Millie shrugged her shoulders nonchalantly. Remembering him cry out almost brought her to tears again. "Jennelle read it someplace," she murmured, moving back toward the fire.

The flames illuminated her face and Chase could see the tension and stress in her features. "My God, Millie. How long have I been out?"

Millie wiped away a stray tear and stoked the fire. "Hercules and I found you late in the morning. That was more than twelve hours ago. If you are able, we will need to leave as soon as the sun rises."

Chase calculated that Millie must have ridden Hercules all of yesterday and last night to catch up with him. "Millie, what happened when I left?" He saw her head snap up. "You are impetuous, but you would never risk Hercules by riding him all night unless something or someone drove you here."

Millie lowered her eyes. She had been dreading this very conversation. "I was visited by someone you know, the morning you left. The man came to see me, and while he pretended to be looking for you, he asked about those." She pointed at a small mound covered by a blanket.

Chase lifted the cover and spied a book and a chest. The woman was a miracle. She had not only saved him, but managed to safely retrieve the precious items without getting hurt. Something he had not been able to do.

Chase ignored the burning pain coursing through his thigh. "Did he hurt you?"

"No, no. He never realized I had discerned his identity. I hinted that you and the items were at Hyde Park and encouraged him to leave. You should lie back down."

Ignoring her, his face took on an ominous expression. "Did he believe you?" His low tone spoke volumes.

Millie picked up a nearby stick and threw it on the fire. "I thought he did, but this morning, just after I passed Shaftesbury, I realized I was being followed. I doubled back a few times and lost him, but no doubt he will find Lord Marston in the morning and follow your trail as I did."

Her comment reminded Chase of what had happened right before he blacked out. Millie could read his thoughts, though he gave them no voice. "Don't worry. Lord Marston is still bound quite securely. Though now he is gagged and a much quieter captive. There is a chance he will not be found." Her lack of belief in that possibility was evident in her tone.

Chase stared at her. Millie was trying so hard to spare his feelings. He reached for her and pulled her to his side. "Who is he, Millie? Who visited you?"

Tears filled her eyes, and he could feel them splash on his arm as he attempted to soothe her. "Sir Edward. He told me everything. How your father was a Rebuilder. How you are a part of it now." She moved out of his embrace and again wiped away her tears. "Why didn't you tell me?"

Chase considered forcing her back into his arms but decided against it. "What I told you was the truth, Millie. There is an Expansionist movement, and my father was one of five Rebuilders working against it. At first, it was just a philosophical difference between the two groups. But then more and more signs appeared that England's participation in war, and its actions after war, were being influenced by a shadow leader within the Expansionist movement. Five Rebuilder nobles searched for proof, and for the identity of the Expansionist conspirator. Each conducted his own investigation, very carefully and, even more importantly, privately."

"You went into the war."

"My father was positive that someone inside the war department was a traitor. He needed someone inside to discover who it was."

"Blast it to bloody hell . . . Sir Edward."

Chase smiled and stroked her cheek with his knuckle. "For once, I agree with your . . . coarse expression. Somehow, my father must have found something tying Sir Edward to his traitorous acts. Something irrefutable. Do you have any idea what it is?"

Millie sat back, shocked at the seriousness of the question. "Heavens, no. How could I?"

"Because you, Aimee, and Jennelle have possessed the truth for some time."

Millie's brows furrowed in disbelief. "If you are referring to those," she said, pointing, "then you are mistaken. Your father hid nothing in them, Chase. Believe me. What he bestowed made no sense. He gave Jennelle a large journal with blank pages, and Aimee an old, empty wooden chest."

"I thought you said my father gave you a key."

"'Key' is the name of the book. I assure you there is nothing in the chest or the book. And my amulet, well . . . it is just that. An amulet. The only thing they have in common is the crest. It appears on all three items."

"There must be something there, Millie."

She shook her head. "How can you be so sure?"

"My father wrote of three markers, unmistakable to any Rebuilder who knew to look for them, that when put together, would give undeniable proof of the traitor's deeds."

"Bloody hell," Millie mouthed and rocked back, hugging her knees.

"When Eischel found my father's letter, he immediately reached out to his contacts, Viscount Darlouney and—since my father was dead—me. Darlouney sought Brumby and Edward. Never did anyone realize they were setting off a chain of events that would eventually lead to their deaths."

"That was why you wanted me to ignore Lord Brumby. He knew it was Sir Edward, didn't he?"

"Not at first, but I think by the time I met with him, he suspected Edward. That was why if anyone saw you watching Brumby, they might have wondered why and assumed you knew more than you did."

"But if Brumby knew who the traitor was, why didn't he tell you or anyone else?"

"At first, I think he was unconvinced and didn't want to taint a man's reputation solely upon suspicion. Later, fear drove him to irrational decisions. Three men had already lost their lives. I think he wanted to tell me at Alstar's, but he got spooked. I believe, given time, he would have confided in me. Edward must have suspected my ability to influence Brumby and silenced him before we could meet again. I should have realized who it was then. Only Edward could kill a man in a crowd and disappear without being seen."

"Oh my," was all Millie could whisper. Chase's father, Lord Brumby—all those men. How could anyone be so filled with hate and self-importance? How were they going to find Sir Edward and stop him?

Millie let go of her knees and leaned back against the rock wall. She rested her head against the uncomfortable stone surface and closed her eyes. She was so tired. So much had happened.

She heard a scraping sound from the other side of the cave and stirred. Her brow crinkled in confusion. She was lying where Chase had been sleeping. She sat up and looked around, spotting Chase on the other side of the fire. He was struggling with Aimee's chest.

"Chase, whatever are you doing?" she asked, rubbing the sleep from her eyes.

Chase raised his head, concern filling his expression. "Are you all right, love? You fell fast asleep as you were attempting to complete a thought."

Millie pushed the loose hairs away from her eyes. "When did you move me? *How* did you move me?"

Chase glanced at his watch fob. "Hmm. It's nearly ten in the morning. So I would estimate nine hours ago. And as for moving you, I would not say my leg is completely repaired, but I have survived being shot before, and I will do so again. At least long enough to do what must be done."

His admission jolted her, and she shot to her feet. "You've been shot before! How many times?"

"Twice. You saw the scars on my back," he answered nonchalantly, continuing to examine the chest.

"Those were *gunshot* wounds?" Millie asked in horror.

An inexplicable grin appeared as Chase remembered the shots and the fight following them. "Indeed. An unfortunate misjudgment on my part of exactly when an ambush was to occur."

Millie shook her head. "You knew men were laying a trap for you?"

"Of course."

"Then why the bloody hell did you allow yourself to get shot? Twice?"

"No one *allows* himself to get shot, love. But sometimes it does happen." Chase pointed to his leg to validate his comment and again focused on the chest.

It was obvious Chase was not going to admit any wrongdoing or profess any promises to be more careful in the future, especially when most of his energy was focused on Aimee's lap-size wooden box. Beside him were various odds and ends Aimee, Jennelle, and she had put in the box as their most treasured possessions. One of which was a small handkerchief she recognized as belonging to Reece.

"Why does that chest interest you so?"

"It has a hidden compartment."

Millie bit her bottom lip to keep from laughing. Hidden sections were hard to disguise and the chest, while not small, was about the size of a large hat box. A false bottom or side, even a small one, would be easily recognizable.

Chase grunted and continued playing with the golden crest on the chest. It was embossed, giving one the idea that something might fit into it. Chase was trying unsuccessfully to fit her amulet into the grooves of the crest, just as Aimee, Jennelle, and she had done when they first received the items.

"I interpreted the 'Key' while you were asleep," he continued. "I am now attempting to follow its instructions. Unfortunately, after all these years, the lock must have rusted."

Knowing otherwise, Millie knelt down and looked closer. "You said the Key told you to do this?"

"Read the dedication on the inside."

Millie sat down, picked up the unusually large book, and fingered the hand-sized crest on the cover. It was a bigger version of her amulet. Surrounding the amethyst were two gold stags, one standing on a sword, the other on a rock, with a knotted ring of gold encircling them. She flipped open the book. She had read the words countless times, and still, she could decipher no special meaning.

To Lady Jennelle Gent,

I give you this key and its crest that it may forever be used to turn and bring forth what you seek.

Lord Chaselton

Millie watched Chase fit her pendant into the chest's impression of the crest and try again to turn the item. Suddenly the embossed crest loosened and fell onto the earthen floor.

Chase examined the box, but it remained unchanged. "It cannot be," he mumbled softly, pressing each side again to affirm its solidity. "It has to be here."

Millie reached down and retrieved the fallen crest, turning it over in her hands. "Charles, look here."

He put down the empty box and came closer. Millie showed him the crest that had fallen off and turned it over. On the other side was a jeweled amulet, similar but not the same size as her own.

Chase picked up the book and read its inscription aloud. "'I give you the key *and its crest*.'"

He looked up. As he gazed into her purple pools sparkling with wonder, he marveled at their ability to become more captivating with each hour. Millie read the desire in his eyes and met him halfway as his mouth closed roughly over hers, searing her forever to him.

He released her lips. He wanted so badly to make love to her, but he needed to know she was safe. "Millie, the amulet—the one from the chest."

She handed over the golden item and saw him place it easily into the book's larger version. With a small twist, it popped and then the book's large gold emblem sprung open. Inside were three folded papers.

Chase carefully picked them up one by one and read them. Silence filled the cave as he refolded each item and wrapped it in a piece of protective leather.

"We need to leave, Millie. Collect only what is necessary."

Nodding, Millie gathered the few items, including her amulet and Reece's handkerchief, and put them into her pouch before following Chase farther into the cave. "Chase, I do not think we can get out this way. I used the boulder as an anchor for the rope to lower you in here. Your weight pulled it back over the opening. I tried several times, but it would not budge."

Chase approached and saw a dangling rope wedged between the rock and the jagged lip of the entrance. He handed the makeshift torch to Millie and used his shoulder to try and shove the large barrier.

"Damn," he muttered, reaching back for the torch. "I have no leverage." He brought the torch closer and examined the boulder for several more minutes. He rubbed the thickening stubble on his face. "Well, my dear, if we are not quick we will have to wait until the tide has turned before we can leave."

"But wouldn't that be best? It would give you more time to rest. No one knows we are here."

Chase leaned on the rocky wall for support as he quickly maneuvered down the steep path to the cave's cliffside entrance. The rope Millie had used was exposed on the surface. The sun had risen hours ago. If Edward had followed Millie, at any time he would stumble onto the evidence leading him to their location. "Time is against us, love. The longer we spend here, the more time Edward has to find us," Chase explained, deciding not to expound on all the reasons behind his urgency. "We need to leave immediately. I can hear the tide rising even now. We must reach the entrance before the water enters the cave. The icy currents in the Channel can easily drown a man. Although I do recall one spunky young girl claiming she was a fair swimmer," Chase teased. He knew it would restore her spirits. It did.

"I told you I was an *excellent* swimmer. And I'll have you know that I still am," Millie said, stopping to remove a pebble lodged in her boot.

She watched him disappear around the corner. "Blasted man," she muttered to herself. Even injured, his long legs could move faster than anyone she knew. The least he could do was wait for her.

She took off the overly large boot and shook it. Nothing fell out. Millie reached in and discovered that it was not a rock at all causing her discomfort. Part of the leather on the inside had curled and was now rubbing her foot raw. "Nothing I can do about that," she grumbled.

She looked down the cave and could see a light emanating from around the corner. She sighed and yanked on the boot, murmuring under her breath, "I am no longer a child, Charlie Wentworth, and while I understand your urgency, does it necessitate your leaving me? I think not. I could have fallen. I could be hurt right now, and would you know? No, you would just wait until I finally collected myself and ran obediently to your side."

She smoothed back her loose locks and glared down the cave. Chase had still not returned, but the light was still shining just around the corner. He was waiting for her. "And probably going to give me a good scolding when I arrive. Well, just get your own self prepared, Charlie, because I have a few words I want to share with you as well," Millie fussed as she intentionally took her time walking down the rocky passageway.

Just as she neared the corner, Millie stopped cold. Someone was talking in a foreign accent. The voice was evil, cold, and full of hate. Millie instantly knew who it was—Sir Edward. They were too late.

"Edward," Chase said, opening his eyes. He felt as if his skull had been split in two.

"Chaselton," Edward replied, glad he had been able to bind Chase's hands before he regained consciousness. He stepped back, out of reach, and aimed his gun. "You have no idea how much it pains me to do this, my boy. You were like a son to me, my protégé . . . my mirror image."

Chase heard the soft scuffle of feet behind the stone wall just behind him. He stilled his emotions. Five seconds passed, and Millie did not make an appearance. She must have heard the danger. She was safe, but only for now.

Any moment, Edward could decide to explore the cave for the three items he so doggedly sought. Chase needed to buy time. He needed to persuade Edward to leave without searching the cave. But how? "It will never work, Edward. I have already sent word to Reece. Even if I am dead, he will see that you are brought to justice."

"I doubt that very much. Would you risk the reputation of every Rebuilder? Your father wouldn't, and neither will you, nor will Reece. Can you imagine what it was like when your father told me of his plans to catch the traitor? How easy it was to circumvent your efforts to find any evidence?"

"But I did find it," Chase grated.

"I let you find those letters in Spain, my boy. And I made sure none of it could be linked to me directly," Edward scoffed. "I just wish I had been as clever two years ago. It turned out I was thwarting your efforts too well. Charles became suspicious when you never found a single hint of the Expansionists. He was so distrusting of everyone that he guarded his fears and began keeping only himself as counsel. He lured me into believing he was of a different mind and no longer considered the Expansionists a threat. Oh, slowly . . . very slowly. And nothing overt, nothing I would suspect. He was very clever. He made only one mistake. He forgot to tell you. You were still hunting for the traitor. When I discovered your father had not changed your mission to find evidence of the Expansionists' activities, I knew he had played me false. It pained me to kill him; he was a good friend. One I regretted losing. It will pain me to kill you, as well, dear boy, but how you die is completely in your hands. Shall it be quick and reasonably painless? Or shall it be long and full of agony?"

Chase considered him briefly. "You will not get what you seek: the proof, the Rebuilders, power, nor the respect of the *ton*."

Edward's laughter sounded like a sick hiss. "Think not, eh? I *want* the proof your father cleverly hid away, but I do not *need* it. Only you are aware of its importance, let alone its contents and location. With the recent mysterious deaths, the Rebuilders are experiencing an unexpected leadership void. As your father's faithful friend and your trusted mentor, it should be effortless to step in and guide the floundering group. And as for Society's respect, if I do not have it now, I soon will have. Do you remember the dark-haired virgin of whom I spoke so fondly? Of course you do. I believe you recently claimed her for your own quite publicly, if rumors are correct. Pity your engagement will be so short-lived."

Chase's eyes glinted as he longed for something other than useless words with which to shelter and safeguard Millie from harm. "Stay away from her."

Edward inclined his head and clicked his tongue, but the revolver never once wavered. "Respect, Chaselton. You are correct that I covet it above all else—perhaps more than power. And Lady Mildred Aldon, the daughter of a wealthy earl, is a quick way to acquire it. She is intelligent, graceful, and though not conventional, she is a stunning beauty. With her as my wife, no one will remember my father was a trader. And those who do will no longer care."

"She will not have you. Think, Edward. If Marston and his handsome features could not tempt her, how will you?"

"Marston was a fool. A fool who no longer lives to plague me. I probably should thank you for making it so easy for me to find and dispose of him. Of course, I made sure the evidence points to *you* and not me."

"Millie will know," Chase countered, trying in vain to free himself from his bonds. "And there is nothing you could do to entice her to accept you. She is intelligent and will quickly realize what you are."

Edward watched Chase's struggles and laughed. "And what am I, Chaselton? An Englishman who loves his country? A man who is tired of seeing British lands that Englishmen died for be handed back to the enemy?"

"How many good men did you send to their deaths in New Orleans? You murdered them, Edward, just as you murdered my father, Darlouney, Eischel, and Brumby. Lady Aldon will never accept your hand—never."

Edward's face flushed a dull red. "Maybe not for love, but she will be mine if she desires to protect those your father loved. Aimee. Your mother. If she refuses, the House of Lords will receive falsified evidence indicting most of your fellow Rebuilders. It is a bit drastic, but it is well within my abilities—and my inclination. I am a determined man, you see."

Millie swallowed heavily and began biting her lower lip. *Think, Mildred. Think*, she silently cried. Chase was obviously trying to buy time and warn her off, but to where? Edward was blocking the only exit. If she waited too much longer, Edward would get tired of verbally sparring with Chase, do the unthinkable, and then find her when he searched the cave. She looked around. There was no place to hide. No boulder—nothing.

Millie brusquely rubbed her cheeks. She needed to find a way to get the upper hand with Edward. She scrunched down and peered around the corner, trying at the same time to remain out of view. Her pulse raced.

Fifteen feet away, down a steep incline, was the mouth of the cave, and the tidewaters were already lapping into the entrance. Edward was standing just inside the lip, and she could just make out Chase's Hessians outstretched. Then she saw the rope and realized his hands and feet were bound. Millie turned back quickly and took a deep breath. She had only two things to use to her advantage.

Millie tiptoed out of earshot and then ran as fast as she could back to where they had camped. She grabbed the chest and started loading rocks into it. She picked it up and set it back down, taking out two of the larger stones. She closed the chest and placed the book, and then her amulet, on top. She smashed the chest's amulet against a rock, shattering the amethyst. Then Millie selected the sharpest shard, grabbed everything, and headed back to the mouth of the cave.

Millie paused at the corner and sighed in relief. They were barely audible, but she could hear Chase respond as Edward taunted him. She took a deep breath and began speaking as she turned the corner.

"Chase, why did you leave so quickly? You left me to grab these things all by myself. Do you realize how heavy . . . they are . . . ?" Millie let the last few words die as she feigned shock at the scene.

"An excellent question. Lord Chaselton, do you have an answer for the good lady?" Edward asked, his voice full of mockery.

Chase just stared at the man standing just out of reach.

Millie bent over to set the chest down beside Chase and released the sharp stone from her hand. She gathered her courage and stood to look at the evil man who held their lives captive. "Sir Edward."

Edward shifted his focus, but the pistol he carried never

moved from its target. At any moment he could fire. At this range, Chase would not survive the wound.

"My dearest lady, I must say you are amazing. Even clad as a man, with your hair tousled and dirt smudged across your cheek, you are indeed desirable."

"And you seemed to have acquired an accent."

"Actually, after so many years abroad, I consider the English form of speaking an accent as it requires more thought." He paused and spoke again, this time in the voice she recognized as Sir Edward. "Would you prefer, my dear, to tell you of my plans for us in this dialect?"

Possessive fury roared through Chase. "Stay where you are, Millie."

"I think not," Edward sneered. "Lady Aldon, would you please join me at my side? And bring with you the items you just set down. Do not worry, my dear. I shall shortly assume their weight."

Millie stared, wide-eyed. She knew that if she responded too fast to obey Edward's order, it could be just as lethal for Chase as a complete refusal.

Millie took a single step forward. She eyed the water filling the cave. Soon it would seal them in. "What do you want, Sir Edward?"

"Besides yourself? That chest and that book. Tell me, my dear, what were its contents?"

Millie slowly knelt down and picked up the book and the amulet along with the chest. "I would appreciate it, Sir Edward, if you would refrain from such familiarities. Especially under the circumstances."

"Come now, my dear. A husband would be lucky indeed if you were to bring even half the passion to your marriage bed that you exert when riding your monster of a horse."

"Millie, do not take one step!" Chase shouted. His eyes shifted and he vowed, "I swear, Edward, I will not wait for your trial. I fully intend to kill you."

A sick smile invaded Edward's bland features. "Really? And will your ghost be able to manage that feat before or after I bed the succulent Lady Aldon?"

Every muscle in Chase's body flinched as he watched Millie begin to walk toward his nemesis. Every protective instinct wanted to stop her. But he had to stay alive if he had a prayer of saving her.

Keep Edward talking, Millie said to herself. Chase had better be right about the temperature of the Channel, she thought as she stopped just a few feet from Edward's reach.

"Do not play games with me, Lady Aldon. I will only remove my aim from his chest if he is dead."

Millie swallowed heavily. Edward was on a steep incline and his view of the cave's mouth was hampered. The tide was rising. In a few minutes the entrance would be completely filled. Millie had a narrow window to make her move. One jump and Edward would realize his folly.

"I am not playing games," Millie countered. "But I must ask, what makes you think I will marry you?"

"To keep me quiet, of course."

"And how is that persuasion?"

"Did Chaselton neglect to disclose exactly what is in those items you now hold in your hand?"

Millie nodded her head.

Edward smiled at Chase. "Clever, dear boy. My lady, somewhere in those items are several letters between Charles's father and me. The man ingeniously gained my trust and claimed to support my ideals and plans. You see, my dear, even if you had escaped before my arrival, those documents would have done you no good. For those letters implicate not only me, but Chaselton's father as well. Are you willing to sully the Chaselton name?"

Millie stared, pretending to mull over Edward's assessment. She glanced over her shoulder. The pain she saw in

Chase's eyes ripped at her heart. "Charlie, remember how you found me so long ago—alone, with only one option? I must leave now that same way."

And then she dived into the cold water lapping into the cave's tunnel. She aimed down and kicked as hard as she could. The chest was helping drag her farther into the sea's depths. Millie could feel the current swirling around her and thought her lungs would soon burst. Only when she saw Edward almost on top of her did she drop the chest. He grabbed it with both hands and she smashed his jaw with her boot. He faltered and began to sink, still holding on to the chest. Millie headed toward the surface as fast as her legs and arms could take her. It was hard to know if she was going in the right direction. The frigid water was murky and all one color. Frantically, she searched for the lighter shades of the surface.

Using the stone shard Millie had dropped beside him, Chase finally cut through the ropes binding his wrists. Fear ripped through his heart as he rushed down and plunged into the sea. Pain lashed through his leg as salt water soaked his wound. Chase ignored it. His only focus was on finding Millie. Adrenaline surged through his veins as he breached the surface. Where was she? He dived again. He came back up. A stiff breeze was making the sea choppy. It was impossible to see across the water for any distance.

Millie was kicking. She was sure of it, though she could no longer feel her legs. She had been swimming up, fighting the current, for what seemed like forever. Just as she knew her lungs could hold out no longer, her face felt the slap of cold wind and she gasped for breath. Millie told her arms to move and swim to shore, but they would not respond. She felt herself slipping beneath the surface of the cold water. She glanced around and did not see Edward. *You are safe, Chase,* she thought as she felt the waves sweep her under.

Her mind was just accepting the inevitable when strong hands grasped her and shoved her up and into the icy air. She inhaled. From far away, she heard Chase yelling at her. It rankled her. She had saved his life and still he would not give her peace.

"Please stop ordering me around, Charlie. I cannot abide being told what to do. I want to sleep now. I am so cold, so t-tired . . ." Millie stammered, her last words trailing off as she went limp again.

"Stay with me, Millie. God, don't leave me now. I need you. I cannot live without you. Do you hear me?" Chase yelled at her, fighting the pounding waves. Dragging her limp body, he swam along the cliff wall until there was an opening.

Chase lifted Millie onto the grassy shore and started rubbing her limbs. She was breathing, but she was a frightening shade of white. "Come on now, love. Wake up. I know you are cold, but I need you to open your eyes and speak to me. I thought you said you were an excellent swimmer."

Chase stripped off her one remaining boot and her breeches and began to furiously massage her legs and feet. He moved to her arms. There was no response. Chase smoothed her hair away from her face. She was so pale, and her lips were an unnatural bluish gray. Tears began to fall. He leaned over and kissed her. It was soft, full of longing and love not yet realized. "Please, Millie. Please don't leave me."

Millie felt so cold and so tired. She didn't want to wake. She wanted to be left alone in her misery. But the voice was pleading with her, and something inside her knew she had to respond. "I am an excellent swimmer, Charlie. It was the damn chest. It dragged me down, and I couldn't let go until I knew he would go for it."

Chase sat back, pulling her with him. She was going to make it. Millie had more fight in her than any man he had ever met. Sheer pride would see her through. "Indeed, my love. You are an excellent swimmer . . . without a chest."

"I killed him."

"No, the waters killed Edward. That and his greed."

Millie shook her head against Chase's chest. "No. I kicked him. I saw blood."

Chase kissed her hair and replied, "You did the right thing, Millie. There is no way he could have survived these cold waters this long without help. It's done. It's over, my love."

Millie coughed against his neck. She was still cold, but Chase's brisk rubbing was helping to thaw her frozen limbs. She sniffed. "Aimee and Jennelle will be quite miffed about missing all the excitement. Never was there an adventure to compare with today."

Glad she was alive, Chase could not find it in himself to be angry with her. "And never shall you experience an adventure like this again, my love. Not if I have anything to say about it."

"I know you will not believe me when I say this . . . but I think I have had enough excitement for a while."

He chuckled and kissed her wet hair. "I pray you are incorrect. I was hoping the adventure of becoming the next Marchioness of Chaselton might be of interest."

Millie could not believe it. She was wet, cold, and shivering, and still she found herself physically drawn to this man. Suddenly she wanted nothing more than to strip naked, tear his clothes off, and make love to him. Too bad her limbs were too numb to agree. "I don't know," she drawled out in an obvious and mischievous manner. "Will it be interesting?"

Chase grinned and whispered into her ear, "I cannot guarantee the excitement of your days, but I promise you the evenings will forever be full of pleasure."

"How about stimulating?"

"Very," Chase said roughly, his pulse quickening.

"And thrilling?"

"Positively breathtaking."

"Promise?" she asked, lifting her face to favor him with a blindingly bright smile.

"Yes, love. I promise," he whispered as his lips closed roughly over hers, claiming them for his very own.

Epilogue

Chase stepped through the door into the dimly lit room. Despite the lack of light, he knew Millie was not there. His eyes darted toward the bedroom door. It was still locked. He tied his robe and went to the large glass doors that opened onto the balcony.

Chase caught his breath as he stepped through. He never thought he would ever again see anything more lovely than Millie when she had walked to his side earlier that day. The ceremony had been small, with just close friends and family, and she had looked breathtaking. But as his gaze took in the ethereal creature before him, he knew he had been wrong.

Millie's hair hung down past her waist in waves of curls freed from their earlier constraints. The moonlight caught her face, highlighting the delicate cheekbones and perfectly shaped lips. He could barely think as he took in the tempting outline of her breasts, the pink erect nipples, and the dark triangle of black curls. He wondered if she knew how transparent her nightdress was and quickly decided never to tell her.

Unaware of Chase's presence, Millie leaned against the column as she looked out at the Chaselton lands. Then she heard the click of the balcony doors and twisted slightly to watch Chase approach. Her deep lavender eyes were big and questioning in the shadows. She turned away, giving Chase a view of her vulnerable nape and her shapely figure.

He stepped in and hugged her from behind, nibbling at the inviting earlobe. "Why are you out here, love?"

Millie closed her eyes and bit her lower lip. She had thought to deal with her unease alone, but she had made promises today. Promises she believed in and would forever uphold. "I don't think I can do this, Chase."

"Do what?" His question was casual as he continued kissing her neck and then her shoulders. Her scent was like the lavender of her eyes. Intoxicating.

Millie twisted in Chase's arms, and her eyes clung to his, imploring him to understand. "I cannot sleep in there. And I certainly cannot sleep with *you* in there," she said, pointing at the wall concealing her bedroom.

Chase frowned, not comprehending.

Millie pursed her lips and tried again to explain. "That is your mother's room. I have known your mother all my life. She befriended, believed in, and guided me. *She* is Lady Chaselton. That is her room, not mine. How can I possibly fill her shoes?" Tears started spilling. "There is no way I can sleep in there, Chase. Please do not ask it of me. I cannot do it."

Chase released a soft chuckle and hugged her gently to him. "Then you shall not."

Millie pulled back and wiped away her tears. Her eyes were very wide as she searched his face. "I won't?"

Chase smiled and brushed her lips with his own. "No, you won't," he whispered as he cradled the nape of her neck in his large hand and deliberately deepened the kiss.

Millie shivered in response. She wanted to know where she would sleep, but she couldn't find her voice as Chase began to expand his assault on her throat.

A deep satisfaction swelled in Chase as he felt an undeniable wave of desire flare within her. Chase's eyes burned with need. He caught Millie's face between his palms and kissed her brow and the tip of her nose before capturing her mouth for a tender but possessive kiss.

Instinctively Millie curled her arms around his neck and pressed in close as his tongue probed the warmth of her mouth. A moan escaped her lips as she met his passion with her own.

His fingers closed around her in a crushing grip that spoke volumes about the fierce emotion coursing through him. Millie's gasp only fueled the wave of desire exploding in his veins. Tonight he would make Millie his wife in every way.

Chase's lips never left hers as he scooped her up in his arms and carried her through the balcony doors. Millie tensed, but whatever she was going to say was lost forever as Chase continued to seduce her mouth in a slow, seductive, and mind-numbing kiss.

He kicked open the door between their rooms and walked into his adjoining chambers. By the time he laid her down, crushing her into the soft bedding, Millie was barely aware of anything but him. She clutched his shoulders, her nails biting through his robe, and arched her back, pressing her breasts against him. Her body was eager to experience the incredible pleasure they had shared before.

His hands began to shake as they found and massaged her breasts through the fabric of her chemise. He brushed his thumb across her nipples, teasing them until they hardened into taut nubs. Millie shivered and moaned aloud.

"Chase, my God, what you do to me."

Chuckling, he whispered, "Millie, it is you who has no idea what you do to me. I am going to know every morsel of you before this night is through." He leaned in and framed her face with his hands. "Tomorrow morning, you will no longer wonder whether you are truly Lady Chaselton."

Millie sighed, welcoming the gleaming possessiveness

of his gaze. "I am not so sure, Chase. But I have no doubt whatsoever that I am yours."

Chase looked into her lavender eyes and swallowed. He was drowning in the love swimming in those purple pools. "I love you, Mildred Aldon Wentworth," he whispered, and bent his head and kissed her with a slow, inviting passion that prevented either of them from further discussion.

Slowly he exposed her bare skin as he began removing the delicate undergarment. His mouth was amazingly gentle as his tongue caressed every inch of skin he uncovered. She was so soft, so willing, and so responsive.

He trailed kisses along her jaw and neck, working his way down. He cupped her soft, perfect breast in his hand and sucked on the nipple. It hardened instantly. "Millie . . ." Her name was a soft growl as he gently eased her gown completely off, dropping tender kisses across her silken abdomen.

He removed his robe and forced himself to slow down. It had been a difficult feat to refrain from making love to her again until they were married. He was not going to rush things now that Millie was finally in his arms. The past few weeks had been hell—seeing her, knowing what it was like to touch her, but never being able to.

Eager to further inflame her passion, Chase brushed his teeth lightly across the taut nipples. Millie arched her back as a pleasant tension began to build deep inside her. She reached for him with a hunger only he could satisfy. She ached to touch him and have him touch her.

Chase could feel the curve of her hips press into his thigh and thought he would go out of his mind. He responded by moving his palm over the inside of her leg until he touched her damp softness. His hand possessively closed over her mound. Slowly he began stroking her in ways he knew would give her pleasure, teasing the areas where she was extra sensitive.

Millie flinched in response, but she did not pull away. She

stretched and writhed under his light caress. Chase was barely touching her, and at the same time tormenting her, creating a rising need within her.

Chase let out a low, husky groan and entered her slowly with his finger. He could feel the heat of her, and he knew he would never have enough of this woman. Millie cried out softly when he at last eased a second finger gently inside her. He almost lost what was left of his self-control. She was tight, hot, and damp, and vibrating with liquid fire.

"Millie . . ." His voice was heavy with passion as he moved his fingers within her snug channel. "My lovely little Millie, how I need you." He slid his finger back out of the tight passage and used her own dampness to lubricate her small, swelling button of desire. Again he slowly eased his fingers into her and then out, pausing to leisurely tease her female flesh. He did it again. And again.

Millie lifted herself against his hand, silently begging for more. Chase continued to stroke and tantalize her, riveted by her response. The delicious torment seemed to go on forever. Millie thought she would go mad. "Charlie, please. Oh, please . . ." she cried, clinging to him, pleading for more.

Chase's manhood ached with pent-up need. Each time she arched her back, her breasts rubbed against his chest, and it throbbed even more. The desire he had worked so hard to conceal on the days leading up to their wedding had created a sense of urgency and aching hunger in him that only Millie could relieve.

He was shaking as his fingers urged her legs apart and he lowered himself over her. Straddling her hips, Chase stared down at her body, watching her chest rise and fall with her deep breaths. He had never experienced anything more rewarding in his life. "Millie, you are perfect."

Millie felt the hard heat of Chase's shaft against her leg. She gasped and instinctively opened her thighs farther. She wrapped her legs around him, pulling him toward her, urging him to make her his in every way.

His desire had become painful, and he could no longer restrain his release. Positioning his hips above hers, he eased himself slowly and deeply into her warm softness. Millie met him with an upward thrust of her hips. They were finally one.

He intended to go slow, but the sudden sensation of heat and tightness surrounding him was overwhelming. He plunged even deeper, sinking blissfully into the snug, wet channel of her body.

Millie felt him retreat slightly and then drive back into her. Her hands trembled as she gripped his shoulders. She had never felt this way before. Last time, Chase had held back. But tonight he demanded all, and Millie responded by giving her body and soul to him. She rocked against him, taking him deeper and deeper inside her.

Chase tried to control the depth of his steady thrusts, but Millie's arms and legs gripped him. Her scent filled him, overwhelming his awareness. He plunged again, burying himself in her core, knowing that nothing in life would ever compare to making love with this woman.

He reached between her parted thighs, found the point where his body joined hers, and touched the sensitive female flesh. Millie's body clenched in reaction. She twisted beneath him as Chase doubled his sensual attack with kisses. Pulled into a vortex of sensation and passion, she started quivering uncontrollably, her muscles clenching and unclenching in small spasms. And then, with a soft exclamation, Millie surrendered to the convulsions as her body pulsated with much needed release.

Hearing Millie call his name, Chase surged, climbing higher and higher. Suddenly the world exploded, and he felt himself shatter into a million pieces. Every muscle, every nerve, every part of his body exploded with spasms of sexual release. He knew he could never lose her. Ever. Only when he was with her did he feel whole. He sagged against her, releasing a triumphant sigh.

For several minutes, only the sounds of deep breaths could be heard in the room. Both lay limp in each other's arms, awed by what they had just shared.

Gently Chase moved onto his elbows and looked down at Millie. Her dark hair was fanned out on the pillow, and the embers of their shared passion still kindled in her beautiful eyes. Her smile was soft and inviting, telling him in that timeless, feminine way she was his.

"I will never be able to get enough of you." His voice was thick and raw.

"You promise?"

And as he took her again to the heavens, Millie knew that indeed his promise to her was the same as hers to him. Love, now and forever.

Please turn the page for an
exciting sneak peek of
Michele Sinclair's next
McTiernay historical romance,
coming soon from Zebra Books!

Caireoch Castle, 1316

He was caught.

And not just in any trap. It was one that held no escape.

That he had not seen the blatant plot as it gradually ensnared him was humiliating enough, but that he was a *McTiernay* caught by a *Schellden* would be cause for derision he would suffer for several years—if not decades.

Craig's heated blue gaze darted to the curvaceous figure across from him. Far from apologetic, two large hazel eyes glared at him, finding no joy in the situation. Instead, the dark green depths flickered with accusations as the melted gold surrounding them shined with fury. Meriel correctly believed herself to be just as caught as he.

Looking at her lightly clasped hands and slightly arched eyebrow, she appeared to be in a seemingly composed state. Most of the crowd surrounding them no doubt believed Meriel indifferent to their situation, for Laird Schellden's daughter had always been a difficult person to read. People's attention was usually focused on her twin sister—who never left a question in anyone's mind as to her emotional state. It was just one of a myriad of characteristics that proved that while they looked alike, their personalities certainly were not.

Meriel exhibited a limited number of emotions, but that did not mean those were the only ones she felt. She was a master at hiding her thoughts behind a facade of naïveté borne from genuine sweetness and reserve, but Craig McTiernay knew exactly what angry thoughts his best friend was thinking. In her mind, *he* was the dolt behind their current predicament.

She had just warned him to be careful less than two days ago, but it was when everyone was preparing for the feast and visiting neighbors were creating chaos in the household. While most of the Schellden clan had given up trying to prove the feelings Craig and Meriel had for each another went far beyond that of friendship, a select few had not. Craig knew Meriel had been correct, but never had he dreamed that his sisters-in-law would resort to such subterfuge to support their false beliefs.

Needing to look his accusers in the eyes, Craig turned his head slightly to the left and glared at the two women standing at the Great Hall's head table. Raelynd was practically beaming with satisfaction. At least his brother Crevan, who was standing next to her, had the decency to look somewhat apologetic about his wife's obvious handiwork. Laurel's expression on the other hand was more reserved, but he knew she was involved. Too much finesse had been required to ensnare him and Meriel so publicly.

For years, the sword dance had been a commonly held event at celebrations, but the simple dance had turned into something of a unique rivalry for the Schellden and McTiernay clans. Craig remembered the night the fun pastime evolved into a game of endurance. The music had started and several of both clans' finest soldiers pounded the floor, deftly hopping between the quarters made by crossed broadswords, to the quick beat of the music. By the end of the lively song, only one McTiernay and one Schellden remained and both had refused to stop. After that night, the sword dance continued until someone was proclaimed the champion.

That was until Craig's eldest brother married Laurel.

One year she actually challenged the men, stating that Highland women played the game of endurance every day with cooking, cleaning, and raising their young. And that night, the tradition evolved once again. Now the battle was between men and women. A custom that made its way to the Schellden clan after last year, when Raelynd and Meriel spent several weeks visiting the McTiernay home.

So tonight, when Craig entered the Schellden Great Hall after successfully winning a game of horseshoes, he was not surprised to see the broadswords being laid out and eagerly joined the large number of people participating. Having been part of the humiliation created by Laurel's first and surprisingly successful attempt at the dance, Craig had vowed never to be outlasted by a woman again. And he hadn't. When the song ended, he was always among the few men who were still on their feet.

Tonight, however, the goal had changed slightly, unbeknownst to him.

"Just do it already," Meriel hissed, recapturing his attention. She had somehow moved to be right in front of him. She was far from short, but she still had to crane her neck to look at him when standing this close. "And make it good, so that when it doesn't work it will end all questions tonight and forever."

Craig's eyes widened at the notion for he had originally planned to give her just a quick brotherly peck. But Meriel's idea was a rather brilliant one. And what could it hurt? It was not as if they really *did* like each other and feared the emotional sparks a genuine kiss might cause. They were just friends! Sure, he had thought about it over the past year. Slim and delicate-looking, Meriel was exceptionally beautiful. But he had always known that the moment their relationship became anything more, the things he cherished the most— the qualities that made her so important to him—would be in jeopardy.

Besides, desire was not prompting their current dilemma. Maybe he wasn't caught in a trap. Perhaps he and Meriel had just been handed an opportunity to finally put persistent rumors to rest. Besides, he had heard from more than one source that Meriel, while not free with her body, was an *excellent* kisser. As her best friend, it was time he found out.

Meriel had felt her jaw drop when she heard her sister Raelynd announce that the last woman and man standing would be rewarded with a kiss—*from each other*. Now that she was married, Raelynd had a penchant for seeing love everywhere. Their father, who had indulged them as children, continued to allow her sister's whims today.

Meriel *knew* she should have deserted the dance right then, but she had still believed Craig to be in the courtyard playing horseshoes. Besides, it had been some time since she had been kissed and the idea of possibly meeting someone new to pass the time with was appealing. That was until she saw both women and men drop out, feigning exhaustion, at an alarming rate. The reason why dawned on her just as the second-to-last woman ended her supposed attempt. Meriel halted immediately, but it was too late. She was already the last woman standing.

Her eyes scanned the few men still competing and spotted Craig near the back, smiling at the crowd—and clueless.

Mentally she implored him to look her way so that she could give him a hint to stop and thereby prevent her sister's attempt at matchmaking. But to no avail. Everyone else in the room was practically staring in her direction, but Craig? No. He was too busy applauding himself for his stamina. Only when the song ended and people clapped him on his back with congratulations, explaining once again the nature of tonight's sword dance, did his expression reflect one of true understanding.

Meriel watched as he briefly studied her and then shifted his gaze to the real culprit—her sister. However, Meriel suspected that Laurel might also have been involved. Raelynd was capable of an idea such as this, but its execution? That needed a more experienced hand. Only Lady McTiernay could imperceptibly move throughout tonight's crowd, giving instructions without Meriel or Craig wising up that *something* was being planned.

And now she was stuck, being forced to do the one thing she had promised herself *never* to do—kiss her best friend. Oh, she could refuse, but in her sister's and most of the clans' minds it would only prove that Craig and she *did* feel something more for each other than they claimed. And it would be not just difficult, but near impossible to change their minds again. No, they were destined to kiss this evening, but fate in the form of her meddlesome sister had not dictated what kind. Would the crowd see a sweet, brief touch upon the lips? Or something that would shock all?

Having decided a few years ago that while marriage was not something she was interested in, for many reasons, Meriel was not about to periodically forsake the pleasant diversions men offered. She knew Craig to be of a similar opinion about marriage, but because he was tall, dark-haired, and had bright blue eyes that sparkled with enormous charm, she also suspected that the rumors of his experience with the ladies were based more on fact than fiction. It was therefore not an unnatural leap to assume he was a good kisser. Besides, she had entered tonight's competition with a certain goal and, as the winner, she was entitled to a kiss. Fortunately for her, Craig understood her cryptic message and seemed to agree.

What she wanted was some passion, something to remind her that she was a woman, and an attractive one. She should have realized the moment Craig's fingers buried themselves in the softness of her hair, that no number of encounters she had had with other men had prepared her for what was about to happen.

True to her request that he embrace her in a way that would end all rumors, Craig pulled her close and then twirled her in his arms so that she was practically lying in his hands, depending solely on his strength to keep her from falling. Determined to be just as dramatic in her pursuit to end speculation about them, Meriel let her arms steal around his neck and returned the embrace with a surge of exasperation and enthusiasm.

His tongue began to trace her lips and instinctively she opened her mouth to welcome him in, glad to realize she had been right—Craig *was* a good kisser. A *very* good one.

He invaded the sweet, vulnerable warmth behind her lips with an intimate aggression that seared her senses. Her fingers clenched his shoulders, and then one of them groaned. While Meriel would have sworn it was Craig, her body was starting to respond as if it had a mind of its own. She felt as if she were melting, hot clay in his hands as they slid slowly up her spine while his mouth drank heavily from her lips.

And then, just as suddenly as the sensual onslaught began, it changed. Craig's voracious mouth became tender, inquisitive, almost reverent. One hand moved to cup her cheek as he kissed her long and soft and deep. The gentle embrace, if possible, was even more consuming and passionate, as his teeth lightly bit at her bottom lip before capturing her tongue and drawing it into his own mouth. It wrenched her soul.

Meriel could only clutch at him, overwhelmed and aroused and unable to understand what was happening. This was *Craig*. Her friend, her *best* friend, but he was kissing her with a low, inviting passion that took her breath away. It was getting harder and harder to remember that the sparks igniting between them were part of an act to end the baseless suspicion people had of their mutual attraction.

She reminded herself that she had received many kisses, but in most of those circumstances she had been the aggressor. It had been natural, as the men too often became timid the moment they realized they were alone with Laird Schellden's daughter. But this was different. Craig was dictating the speed and intensity of their kiss and all she could do, all she *wanted* to do, was get closer to him and follow his lead.

Returning his bold strokes inside her mouth, Meriel knew she should signal to end the embrace, but she could not muster the will to stop the passionate assault upon her senses. At least not yet. Until now, she had not known what was missing, but this—being with Craig, touching, kissing—for the first time it felt *right*.

The hot, tantalizing kiss suffused her body with an aching need for more. With a soft, low groan, Craig increased the urgency, and their embrace became darker, more demanding, and far more blatantly erotic. No longer could she pretend she was enjoying a pleasurable activity with a friend. This was something far more meaningful. Meriel was sharing a piece of herself, as he was with her, proved by the mutual ripple of need running through them.

Suddenly she was back on her feet and the cool air on her lips shocked her into remembering that they were not alone but in the midst of a crowd. A crowd buzzing with half whispers.

"Now all in this room *must* agree that the kiss you just witnessed would ignite a spark of passion—*if there was one*," Craig's voice boomed, capturing her attention. He stretched his arms out wide and grinned infectiously, winning over the stunned mass. Then, with a pompous show of male superiority, he threw one arm over her shoulders and hugged Meriel against him. "And that, good women and lads, should end all doubt about what Meriel and I are to each other. We are *friends* and nothing more."

Feeling physically trapped, Meriel elbowed his side and gave him a forceful, angry shove. Craig immediately let her go and playfully doubled over in an exaggerated bow. The throng of people surrounding them laughed and began to return to whatever they had been doing before the sword dance had been called. Only then did Meriel realize Craig's overbearing actions had been designed to elicit such a violent response from her. She was the one who had made his speech believable. A woman in love typically did not assault the man who had just kissed her with incredible tenderness and passion.

Unable to keep her eyes from following him, Meriel watched as Craig casually sauntered away from her, laughing and romping across the floor with his fellow soldiers as they headed toward the hall's exit. Meriel should have been filled with relief. Didn't her reaction prove that she was *not* in love with Craig? Didn't his?

"I must admit to being surprised. I really thought you two cared for each other."

Meriel briefly glanced back as her sister walked up to her side before returning her gaze to Craig. "We do care for each other."

"You know how I mean. The first time Crevan kissed me like that I wanted to tear his clothes off, and I can assure you the feeling was mutual." Raelynd waved her hand at Craig's departing figure. "That man is not acting like someone who just experienced an incredibly sensual kiss. But then, neither are you," she finished, looking both perplexed and disappointed.

Meriel swallowed at the implication. Fact was, she wasn't *acting* like it, but inwardly her senses were reeling. Outwardly she forced herself to appear calm, but she felt as if she had been ravaged, and worse—she craved more. Maybe Craig was also hiding his reaction to what happened. His overly jocular departure was atypically dramatic, even for him. The more she thought about it the more Meriel was convinced. Craig McTiernay was definitely covering up some kind of emotional response to what had occurred between them. But what? Then again, what was her response?

Meriel bit the inside of her cheek and made a decision. Until she was able to comprehend her own emotional state, she was not going to tackle the onerous work of guessing at Craig's. Usually the man paraded his feelings for all to see and hear. He kept them private only when they were raw, undefined, extremely personal, and involved someone he loved. During those rare times, to keep people from detecting his true thoughts, Craig tended to become excessively cheerful, just like he had tonight.

Raelynd grasped her arm and swung her around to head back to the main table. "Tomorrow you can admonish me severely, but tonight we are celebrating Marymass, and soon Father will be offering the first bread. Come and think on nothing else but this year's harvest and all the good things that are to follow."

Meriel let her sister direct her back to the main table. Tonight she would enjoy the upcoming activities to honor the Assumption of the Blessed Virgin Mary. Tomorrow, however, she would give earnest thought about what had just happened between her and Craig.

"Don't deny it. You were part of that display of lust we just witnessed," Conor McTiernay growled at his wife.

Laurel licked her lips and refused to look into her husband's accusing silver eyes. "Perhaps marginally."

She was doing it again. Flicking her pale gold hair behind

her shoulder to catch his eye. Moistening her lips with her tongue. Taking a deep breath so that her chest swelled, giving him a delicious view—all in an effort to distract him from knowing her true focus. And it was working.

As the eldest of the McTiernay brothers, Conor had spent years studying the behavior of his clansmen in an effort to become a better chieftain. He prided himself on being able to predict most of his people's needs, anticipate their reactions to certain events, and prevent problems before they arose. But no matter how hard he tried, he could not transfer such knowledge and power to better his understanding of his own wife. He was just glad that he was starting to be able to tell when she was in the middle of a plan so he could carefully extricate himself from it.

He let himself enjoy the sights for a few more seconds before pushing for more information—an absolute requirement for knowing just how to duck and avoid getting caught in whatever trap she was weaving. "And did you get the outcome you were looking for?"

Laurel was not sure how to answer as she studied the scene. Craig was cleverly making his exit while Raelynd was talking to Meriel absent-mindedly.

When Raelynd revealed her plan to have the two winners of the sword dance kiss, Laurel had been quick to realize that the idea was rather ingenious, but highly improbable. Aye, both Craig and Meriel were competitive and likely to win, but not if they suspected a setup. And despite Laurel's quick intervention—persuading the other participating men and women to voluntarily lose—it almost did not happen. Meriel had quickly grasped the situation and almost quit before the last woman could drop out. But it had worked, and Craig and Meriel had definitely kissed as planned. But if that kiss had changed anything in their attitudes toward each other, Laurel could not discern it.

The fact that the two of them were in love was not in question. Most were not sure, but Laurel had no doubts. It came down to whether the long and passionate kiss that all had witnessed tonight would prompt two of the most stubborn people in Scotland to admit it. Not to the their family and clansmen . . . but to themselves.

"You should feel ashamed, forcing them to prove their friendship in such a way," Conor admonished halfheartedly.

"Why? Either way it serves their purpose. If there *was* more between them, they would have been thankful for the act of kindness. If not, then Raelynd and I gave them the opportunity to end all rumors otherwise."

"I give up." Conor sighed, grabbing a mug of ale and downing it. "Just make sure that your efforts to find and foster a love match for my brother don't affect me."

"They shouldn't," Laurel said and then added under her breath, "but no promises."

The kiss Craig and Meriel shared had practically heated up the room, confirming what she knew to be true. Raelynd had believed her sister might be falling for Craig and that Meriel was too afraid to admit her feelings. But Raelynd had been wrong. Meriel and Craig had fallen in love long before, soon after they had first met. Unfortunately, both of them were so savvy to the ways of love and how to avoid it, they had been able to avoid it with each other. Laurel abhorred the idea of an arranged marriage or forcing two people together, but Craig and Meriel had already been together a year, and she felt she had no choice but to agree to help Raelynd execute her plan.

But Conor's question troubled her. Had she secured the outcome she was looking for? With any normal couple, a kiss like that would have resulted in a wedding. But getting a Schellden, let alone a McTiernay, to admit their feelings? That took patience.

It had happened once, between their siblings Raelynd

and Crevan, but both Craig and Meriel were unbelievably strong willed and stubborn. And for some reason they each felt incredibly resolute about keeping their friendship *only* as a friendship. If what transpired tonight did not convince either of them otherwise, Laurel was not sure any outside influence could. It would take far more than patience to change their minds.

It would take a miracle.